Black & White

R. B. CARIAD

NUMBER 21
R.B. CARIAD

Connect With R. B. Cariad

Join R. B. Cariad and The Cascade of Lies by signing up for her newsletter and giveaways at

Home – R. B. CARIAD author (rbcariadauthor.com)

Follow RB on Facebook
R. B. Cariad

Instagram
@rbcariadauthor

Tik-Tok
@rbcariadauthor

Acknowledgments

To my beautiful family, thank you for the love and support.

To my dad, who read more than anyone I know. The man I miss every day and inspired me to be myself always, no matter the cost.

To Kay, my wonderful editor who continues to teach me with every book. Your knowledge and expertise has been a Godsend.

To all the crazy Celt's out there, and to everyone who's ever been told they can't,
You can!

And to everyone who loves to get lost in a world of dark and handsome bikers.
This one's for you!

CHAPTER ONE

My Time to Shine!

"For fuck's sake! Can't a guy get a minute's peace?" Noah cussed as he climbed out of the pool to retrieve his ringing phone.

After drying his hands in the soft towel that B had laid out for him, he picked up his flashing phone to discover that he didn't recognize the number. Angered by the disturbance, he grimaced, tapping the green icon to answer.

"Yeah!" he said, expecting to be greeted by a voice at the other end of the line, yet silence met him.

"Right, who the fuck is this? I've got no time for bullshit today!" he bellowed as his eyes tracked water droplets running along the indents of his black, rash guard that clung to his chiseled torso.

"Hello, boy!" snarled the familiar voice.

Noah's eyes widened, and his heart slammed into his sternum, forcing him to drag in deep breaths as he tried to comprehend the greeting.

"What do you want, old man?" Noah asked.

"You know what I want, boy! I want my club back! I want the fucking life you and that Irish prick stole from me!"

Noah laughed. "Are you for fucking real? You have the audacity to call me after the shit you and Uncle Mauler pulled. You must have fucking rocks in your head! I suggest you run, Blaze and keep fucking running! Because when we catch you, I'm gonna let Zander finish you off properly next time."

"I'm not going anywhere, nephew! I'm taking the club and your precious Dragon, and I'm gonna gut Mack and the prick who shot me."

"Goodbye, Blaze. You're a dead man walking. I'll see you soon!" Noah said, ready to hang up.

"Well, from where I'm standing, Dragon is the one ready to meet her maker. Oh, and she looks real fine in that pink bikini. Maybe I'll end her, here and now, to remind you who you're dealing with!" Blaze said to the sound of a rifle being loaded.

Panic washed over Noah's face as he turned to see B emerge from the house. His head snapped around as he glanced about the garden trying to locate Blaze. "If you touch her, I'll fucking kill you!"

"Oh, judging by the panic on your face, I now have your attention."

"Where are you?"

"That's not the question you should be asking."

"What the fuck do you want?"

"I want what's mine, and if you don't want the dragon's brains splattered across her pool, I suggest you meet me at the Old Mill Coffee House in twenty minutes."

"What, and leave Dragon for your taking? I don't think so."

"Dragon can live for now if you meet me. I just wanna talk. It's a public place, and I don't want that kind of heat on me. I have bigger fish to fry."

"Funny, that's never stopped you before."

"My patience is wearing thin, boy. Last chance, because I won't hesitate to pull the trigger here."

Noah continued to survey the area, but there was no sign of anyone.

"Fine! Twenty minutes, but if you try anything, I'll have the whole of Uskiville hunt your ass down," Noah said, gritting his teeth in frustration.

"Don't keep me waiting!" Blaze growled before hanging up.

Noah stood, rubbing his beard. His nostrils flared as his eyes continued to dart around the garden as B approached.

"Beer, my lovely!" she said, flashing him a smile and handing him the brown bottle.

"Cheers! Where's Mack? I need to talk to him."

"He's at the bar with the boys. Is everything alright? You're as white as a sheet!"

Noah cleared his throat. "Uh, yeah! Jimmy wants to talk to him about ordering more cuts. I'll head over now to sort it. Jimmy won't quit until I call him back."

"No worries! I'll head to the office and finish up some paperwork, then. Mackie's been slipping since Ari arrived on the scene. I'll drown in it if I don't catch up soon."

"Cool. I'll come find you once I'm done?"

"Great!" she said as she headed back inside.

Noah gathered his towel and followed her inside, pausing briefly at the door to check over his shoulder. Then he stepped through and locked the door behind him.

After what seemed like the longest ride of his life. Noah arrived at the Old Mill Coffee House. He inhaled a deep breath of the clean air before pulling on the chrome door handle to enter the bustling café. Scanning the room, he shuddered at the sight of the menacing looking Red Pitbull cut he was previously accustomed to. His body trembled with anxiety, a definitive reminder of his past pain and trauma.

Blaze appeared to be alone as he sat at the counter with his back to Noah. Nonetheless, Noah didn't trust his uncle and felt the need to check the Glock in his waistband, ensuring its state of readiness.

Noah could hardly look at Blaze as he approached the brown marble counter. His body fueled with rage as he seethed, "Right, I'm here, now start talking asshole!"

"Slow your roll, boy. Let's not make a scene here."

The waitress approached, flashing Noah a seductive smile. "Can I help you fellas?"

"Two coffees, black," Blaze snapped, causing the woman's smile to vanish.

Noah smiled at the waitress. "Don't mind his tone, darling. He's a little feral. He doesn't understand how to talk to folks."

The waitress turned back to face Noah, her smile returning to her plump face. "At least one of you has manners."

"My mother taught me well," he teased, throwing her a smile and a wink as she wandered to the coffee machine.

Noah sat on the stool next to Blaze. "Well? Do you need something? Because I haven't got all day."

"What's up? Late for the Sultry Slalom, are we?"

Noah glared at him.

"Oh, I know everything, boy. I've been keeping a close eye for months now."

Noah's patience grew thin. "Stop with the games and tell me what you want, or I walk out that door."

Blaze glowered at the waitress as she delivered their drinks, then he turned to Noah. "Easy boy. I have eyes on Dragon. No. We're going to enjoy a nice coffee together, and you're going to tell me how you plan on signing the club over to me. I am aware you've assumed ownership already."

"And why would I give you my club?"

"To stop me using this on your precious Dragon," he said, placing the rusty claw on the counter.

"Where did you get that? That should've stayed buried with the monster who wielded it!"

"Things don't stay buried for long. This claw is my birth right too, my legacy."

"Legacy. Ha! You're as crazy as your brother, old man."

Blaze poured sugar into his coffee. "That's the thing about legacies, boy, they live on. I once wished you would continue in my honor. Not anymore. It's my time to shine now!"

"You're deluded!"

"No, boy! I've ascended and you've got seventy-two hours until Dragon dies, but not before I torture her. I'm finishing The Mauler's assignment! Now I want the club, so sign it over, fetch Dragon. Mack and Zander, too while you're at it!"

"Good luck with that. She has an army behind her, and I'll never give up my brothers."

"Is that a fact?"

"Yeah, it fucking is!"

"Then I'll kill you and everyone in this coffee shop instead," he announced, pushing a gun into Noah's ribs.

Noah stared in shock. He recognized the sadistic sparkle in Blaze's eyes. He'd seen it countless times before, just seconds before Blaze wiped out his enemies. There was no bluff here.

"You wouldn't?" he questioned, already knowing the answer, but stalling for time.

"Well, I'll just start with the waitress. It's clear she likes you," he said as he called to her. "Excuse me, sugar—"

"Wait, wait! I'll get the papers together, but I'll need a week."

The waitress approached. "Can I get you anything else?"

"No thanks, darling," Noah said, shooting daggers at Blaze with his stare.

A slick grin slid over Blaze's face. "Bring the papers to the Bacon Shack in Telles Creek in one week at twenty hundred hours. I'll deal with Dragon and your brothers in my own way. It's beautiful when a predator catches its prey unexpectedly."

"You're a sick man, Blaze."

"As my brother once said; revenge is a dish best served cold. You got your week, boy. But I will kill everyone if you try to fuck with me. If you think I'm here alone, you're very wrong. I have an army of my own," he said standing to leave.

Noah glanced around to see at least twelve men stand from tables around the café, to follow Blaze.

Blaze turned, grinning back at him. "My little spies are everywhere, boy. Fuck me on this and everyone will die before you take your next breath!"

Noah couldn't help but gulp. Blaze was back, and he was coming for everyone Noah loved.

CHAPTER TWO

The Dragon's Charm

B stared hard at Noah, not quite questioning his loyalty.

"Jeez, Baby Face. I know you're keen to sort things, but is this cloak and dagger shit necessary so late at night? Are you sure you want to do this? Mackie will become your enemy once I sign this contract."

Noah grinned, his teeth showing like white sheets of snow. "Hell, yes! Mack promised you'd help, and that's what you're doing. It was the only time my guy could fit us in. Otherwise, it's another month's wait.

"You could have told me on the weekend. I mean, you were at my house a few days ago. I've had to make another excuse to escape, and Mackie is getting suspicious."

"Dragon, my club needs this and so do you. No more begging for scraps or caging Dragon! You'll have your freedom, and together we'll rule Sunnyville," he laughed maniacally, as the real estate agent shifted uncomfortably in his leather chair.

"Don't you mean me and Jimmy? You know, I'm still not comfortable working with someone I don't know or trust."

Noah stepped forward, clasping his hands around each of her biceps, reinforcing his words. "Dragon, Jimmy is sound. You can trust him."

B shirked from his grasp, taking a seat adjacent to the real estate agent and tapping the tips of her fingers together. Her uncomfortable tone high-lighted her distaste for his decision making. "I just don't understand why you're stepping down. We've spent months working together and look what we've achieved. We're one hell of a team, Noah, and what if I don't click with Jimmy?"

Noah knelt beside her. "Look, I'm remaining Prez until everything's done, and you're working with the club like a well-oiled machine. Besides, I'm staying on as VP after the vote goes through, so I'll always have your back and keep things right between you and the wolves."

"You bloody better, Boyoh."

"I will! So can you just sign the God damn contract, so you own my club already?"

"Okay, let's do this!" B said, reaching for the contract laid upon the walnut coffee table. Removing her expensive fountain pen from her shirt pocket, B sighed and signed on the dotted line, knowing her life would never be the same again.

"Congratulations Ms. Jones. Lovely doing business with you. Noah, thanks for the business." The suited real estate owner collected the contracts and then escorted them out of the building.

B rested her hand on the hood of her Humvee, grinning at a happy Noah.

"Step one in our long and illustrious plan is complete, my lovely. No going back now!"

Noah raised his hands into the high ten position, baring his teeth in his cheeky boy smile. "Thanks, Dragon. For everything! My pack is finally going to provide for their families. Hell! Some of the wolf cubs may make it to college because of you."

B reciprocated, clapping her hands against his. "Because of us, lovely boy," she corrected wanting to pinch herself now that their business venture was finally coming into fruition.

"And next week, you promise you will meet Zander?"

B rolled her eyes as she climbed into her Humvee. "For the love of Christ! Yes, I will meet the crazy Scot, but let's get one thing straight. I'm meeting him, that's it. Nothing else!"

"Dragon, he has a huge crush on you. The Scottish hamper you sent him at Christmas drove him wild, and you were flirting with him on the phone."

B's face flushed scorching hot. "I did not flirt with him. I was just being nice. In the festive spirit and all."

Noah shoved her playfully. "You're full of it! You loved it! Especially when he gave you that pet name. He adores you."

"Noah, it's never going to happen, and I'll tell you what I told him on the phone. I don't settle down; I won't be an old lady or controlled. I'm not submissive."

"That's what he loves about you. Your take-no-shit attitude makes him hard. He says he wants to be the one to break in the beautiful, fiery dragon," Noah teased.

"Fuck off!"

"Dragon, his heart pounds every time your name flashes across my phone. That's why he keeps stealing my phone when we talk, and I've never seen him like that before."

"He wants his end away to tick off the bucket list, nothing else."

"No, he wants beautiful Celtic babies with his Welsh Cake, and I want my Godson, Noah Jr!"

B rolled her eyes, starting her truck. "You're bloody dreaming, good boy. And why do you keep pushing this, anyway? You've been trying to push us together since the day we grappled. Why?"

"Because despite what Mack says, I think you two would be great together. You're like fire and ice, yin and yang, and it would be a shame for you guys not to try."

"Shit, you honestly believe that we're meant to be together, don't you?" B said, shaking her head in disbelief.

"Yeah, I do, Dragon." With a tender smile, he gave her a knowing nod. "You're two broken souls who can fix each other. Twin flames even, and I think you need each other."

"Jeez, I need a bloody drink after all this sissy talk. Bring it in so we can leave," B insisted, opening her arms for his embrace.

Noah stepped up into the truck and embraced B, taking a little longer than he normally would. "Hey Dragon, I have something real special for you. I want to give you a gift, to thank you for everything you've done for me and the club."

Noah reached into his pocket to retrieve a white handstitched handkerchief. Handing it to B, he gazed at her.

B's eyes stared at the delicate cloth in confusion.

"This was my mother's. She gave it to me just before she passed away. She told me, when the time was right, I'd know what to do with it."

B unfolded the handkerchief to reveal a beautiful silver charm bracelet with several charms attached to it.

"Noah, this is beautiful! But I can't accept something so precious to you. You should keep this," she said, trying to place it back in his hands.

Noah stepped down from the truck, raising his hands with urgency. "No, Dragon, please? It's not meant for me. I think my mother must have known I'd meet you because she told me I'd know who it belonged to someday and to keep it safe until then. Look at the charms, Dragon, please?"

B studied the beautifully hand-crafted charm bracelet. A unique collection of charms hung from the piece of jewelry: a baby boy, a house, two entwined lovers, a motorcycle, a wolf, and a dragon.

B gasped. "There's a dragon and a wolf here."

Noah laughed, "I know! I added them!"

B stared at Noah, "I don't understand!"

"Well, the house represents our family. I mean, we are family now, right?"

B nodded.

"The bike represents the club; the boy is our club's future. This wolf represents the MC members, and you are the dragon," he said, smiling at her, showing off his baby-faced dimples.

"And the lovers?"

"Well, I think it's you and Zander, but that's up to you. This is your bracelet now."

B flushed again. "I'm speechless, Noah. Thank you!"

"You're welcome! Hey, let's see what it looks like on you."

B smiled as Noah took the bracelet and placed it on her wrist. "Beautiful. It's a perfect fit!"

"Thank you. I love it!" she said, giving him a peck on the cheek. "You are a wonderful friend Noah, and I'm glad I've had the pleasure of getting to know you these past eight months."

"Me too, Dragon. Listen, I need you to promise me one more thing.... just promise me, if anything ever happens to me, you'll look after Zander. He's not like Jimmy. Jimmy's weathered and built for anything. Zander, he needs an anchor. He needs you, Dragon."

B's brow furrowed. "What the fuck are you talking about? Why would you say that?"

"Well, I could get hit by a bus tomorrow," he joked with a laugh that didn't quite ring true.

"Don't mess with me! Why, Noah?"

"Don't worry, I'm not planning on going anywhere. I just want to know you have our backs, no matter what."

B's concern didn't falter. "Promise me Noah. Promise me, there's nothing you're hiding,"

Noah laughed again. "Jesus, Dragon, I'm just trying to give you a gift and making sure we will always have each other's backs. Now calm the fuck down and enjoy your bracelet."

B's tension eased as she shook her head, flashing Noah a smile. "Fine, thank you for the bracelet."

"Right, shall we get food before your fiery dragon eyes come out? I know what you're like when you're hangry," he teased.

"You know where I can get decent loaded fries at 11 o'clock at night?"

"You're damn right I do!"

Noah returned to the MC a little after 2 a.m. to find Jimmy and Zander sitting in the church.

"Well, where the fuck have you been? You said a couple of hours," Zander snapped.

Noah glanced at Jimmy, who sat across the table, sipping his whiskey.

"Has he been like this all night?" Noah asked.

"Ever since you left," Jimmy said.

Noah eyed Zander tapping nervously on the table, his war face raging with anger. It wasn't much different from his usual serious face, but Noah knew he'd ruffled some feathers by meeting B tonight.

Taking a seat in his Prez seat, he poured himself a whiskey. "I haven't slept with Dragon, if that's what you're thinking, Zand. You're my best friend. I wouldn't do that to you."

"Then why all the sneaking around? Who does business this late at night?"

"I do. I didn't want to wait another minute, so I locked things down. Mack might've discovered the plan and put the brakes on everything if I'd waited much longer. Look around, brothers, he's left us high and dry. If Dragon didn't agree to help, we would be screwed right now."

Jimmy knocked back another shot of whiskey as Zander fell silent.

"You know, he's going to go fucking mental when he finds out you poached his dragon. He worships her, man. Do you think he's going to let her just walk away?" Jimmy asked.

"He doesn't have a choice anymore. Besides, no one has poached anyone. When I met Dragon, I could tell she was angry, frustrated, fucking hurt, even. She's not happy in Uskiville. Her home is no longer her home, and what do you think will happen if she finds out he loves her, when he's been grappling with her, his hands all over her body, violating her on the daily without her knowledge?"

"Aye, but what if she finds out you knew all along?" Zander asked.

"I'll just explain to her that it wasn't my lie to tell, and he's the club's founder."

"But you're about to screw Mack by taking away the love of his life," Jimmy said.

Noah slammed his hands onto the table, face crumpled in anger. "He's using her. They both are. Ari sloughs around all day and expects everyone to wait on her. As soon as Dragon comes home from work, Ari offloads the baby and sits on her ass whilst Dragon does everything, and in the dragon's fucking house. Mack is just fucked in the head. In love with the two of them. He's just keeping Dragon where he wants her.

Jimmy's and Zander's eyes widened in shock. Noah had always been the calm one until now.

Now he sat fueled with frustration and rage as he continued. "We need help, and she needs to be freed from her cage before she loses her shit and fucks us all off. Besides, she's my friend, so end of discussion!"

Zander looked up from his glass, his glare stern and serious. "Aye, I get you, brother, but you have to see things from our perspective. You've been up there alone every other weekend. You leave us on the border of Portland on Friday and meet us on Sunday. We're no' comfortable with our Prez going off on his own. It's no' right. We're no' comfortable no' knowing anything anymore. It's been eight months since you met her, and this club is struggling. We need a face-to-face with Dragon! We demand to know what's going on. This is the end of the lone Prez antics."

"You're just worried I'm fucking Dragon!" he said, casting him a devious grin.

Zander got up from his seat, spitting in frustration. "Fuck you! If you're gonnae act like a petty prick, I'm off."

"I'm joking, Zand, please sit down. Look, you're meeting her next weekend. You both are. Now sit down."

Zander's smile grew until he was beaming. "You better no' be screwing with me."

"I'm not! Look, I gave her my mom's bracelet today, and I told her it's her destiny to be with a wolf. I told her you're meant to be together. I've never, ever slept with her, Zander. You have my word. She doesn't like pretty boys like me. She likes the rough-and-ready type, trust me."

Zander sat scratching his cheek. "You said that? That she's meant to be with me, I mean."

"Of course, I did. Look, man, we've never seen you like this with anyone before. All it took was you catching sight of her picture, and you were hooked. Over a year on, you're still craving her, and as your brother, I'm doing my best to make that happen. I've had to play the long game with Dragon. Mack was right. She's so intense and doesn't trust anyone! It's taken me months to build that and now next week you'll meet her and know everything."

"What did she say? When you told her, I mean."

"She blushed, man, and I've never seen her blush. But she's unlike any other woman you've met, Zand. I've seen her make men crumble with one kiss, and she'll push you away for sure, but you have to keep trying if you want her."

"Aye. Did she take you to the Sultry Slalom again last weekend?"

Noah's head jerked in laughter. "Of course, she did. She's a sex mad Celt just like you."

"Hmm…"

Noah shot a look to Jimmy, who was smirking at his sulky brother.

"Zand, you can't be pissed at her for getting laid. She hardly knows you, and you have your end away whenever it suits you," Noah said in a humorous tone.

"Aye, I know. I just hate the thought of anyone being inside her. She may no' know it yet, but she's mine! She needs a real Celt, and Mack doesn't have the right tools for the job. I'll tame Welsh Cake, and when she's mine, I'll kill anyone who looks at her!"

"Okay, I gotta ask. How can you feel so much for a woman you've met once over video chat?" Jimmy asked, trying not to laugh.

Zander smirked as he became lost in his memory of her. "I saw her, and I couldn't breathe, and truth be told, I still can't. Talking to her at Christmas, my heart raced, smashing against my chest with every word that left her lips. I dinnae care if she's hard work. I dinnae care if she pushes me away a million times. Every fiber of my being tells me she's mine!"

Noah and Jimmy exchanged grins. "Okay Casanova, you'll get your meet. Just promise me you won't act like an obsessed psychopath when you do. She doesn't do crazy."

"Get to fuck!"

"I'm just saying you got it bad for her! If you don't want to screw things up, go slow. Trust me!" Noah pressed his point home.

Jimmy interrupted. "Well, now that we've established Mr. Serious here is jonesing for a Dragon, can we talk business?"

Zander punched his arm, almost knocking him out of his chair.

"What? You are! Now. Tell us, has she given you any green for us?" Jimmy asked.

Noah shook his head. "I turned down the green, fellas."

"Why the fuck would you do that?" Jimmy snapped.

"It's a trust thing. Dragon damn near threw the green in my face, but I didn't want her thinking we were using her. We gotta have trust, brothers, and show her we're in this for the long haul."

"That's great, but you realize we're going to struggle to keep the lights on this month?" Jimmy sighed.

Noah laughed, lighting up a cigarette. "We're not struggling ever again! Dragon is the club's new owner. Period!"

Jimmies stared at him with surprise. "She isn't!"

"Hell, yeah, she is! She owns the club, the big ass building next door that she's been fixing up for months, and in ten months she'll own the old factory behind us. Dragon and I have been setting up our empire for months."

"I don't understand. Why would you give away the club?" Jimmy asked.

"To keep her safe. If Blaze ever comes back, he'll not harm her if she owns the club. That club means everything to him. He's been waiting for ownership to pass to him for years."

Zander took the half-smoked cigarette from in between Noah's fingers. "Aye, but we've not seen hide or hair of him since that night. He'll no' be stupid to come back now, and if he does, his ass is mine!"

"I know. It's just, I wanted to give something back. She's become family to me, and she is investing big. We have big plans, and you know what they say: 'go big or go home,' and we're going big brothers. The bunnies are the only thing left to go!"

"Jeez! What's she got against the bunnies?"

Noah ran his fingers through his tight curls. He knew that Jimmy wouldn't like the bunnies leaving.

"Bad for business, Jimmy. They gotta go."

"What the fuck is her problem? How am I supposed to get laid? I wasn't blessed with your baby face or Zander's hot mess psycho charm," he seethed.

"You'll get plenty of pussy when we rebrand. Besides, nothing's changing until the building work is done."

Zander leaned into his brother, blowing cigarette smoke into the air. "You mean to tell me that enormous complex getting fixed up is hers?"

"Well, it'll be all of ours if we behave and play our cards right. But she won't sign off on that until she's settled here and trusts everyone."

Zander raised his eyebrows and Jimmy blinked rapidly, their brains working vigorously to digest Noah's information. They couldn't speak as Noah bellowed. "Are you alright, brothers?"

Zander shook his head, snapping himself out of his shock. "We're going legit?"

"Yes, we are! I promised you no more scraps, and I meant it. Dragon and I have discussed pensions and private medical insurance for everyone. She even wants the club to have its own food bank and on-site doctor."

Jimmy and Zander beamed at one another. Their wide-mouthed frog expressions humoring Noah who burst into a fit of laughter.

"I told you; Dragon is big on family, and like Mack says, 'if you're lucky enough to be welcomed by her, then she'll fight to the death for you.' Times are changing, brothers, and we need to embrace it. Now let's toast to new beginnings, and whatever happens, this stays between us until I say so. Mack stays in the dark until Dragon tells him."

"Aye!" Zander cheered.

"Agreed," Jimmy said, looking a little less convinced.

"There's something else. Promise me you will look after Dragon, no matter what. I mean to the death! She's smart, so what she says goes, and I know you're not used to having a woman tell you what to do, but this one's different, fellas. She's special and can lead this club to greatness if we give her the chance. So, promise me, give me your word that Dragon will remain protected until the day you die."

"Of course," Jimmy answered quickly.

"She's my future old lady, I'll no' let anything happen to her, Noah. I want to fill her with beautiful Celt babies."

"Yeah, we know!" Noah and Jimmy shouted in unison.

CHAPTER THREE
Best Friends

B woke to the clatter of dishes. Remembering her boys were at their dad's, she rushed to the kitchen.

"Morning," Mack greeted as he flipped pancakes.

"Morning," B said, plonking herself at the dining table where a fresh pot of tea sat. "To what do I owe the pleasure? I've not seen you in my house this early since before you got with Ari."

Mack placed an enormous stack of cinnamon pancakes in the center of the table and poured her tea before sitting next to her. "I just thought it would be nice to have breakfast with my best friend. Nice bracelet, by the way."

B covered her bracelet with her sleeve. "Cut the bullshit and tell me what's going on, Mackie boy."

Mack almost choked on his pancake. "What?"

B shot him a firm stare, raising her eyebrows.

Mack's face softened. "Okay, I'm worried about you. You're running yourself into the ground between the business and coaching, and Noah is here every other weekend. I know you're helping him, and I appreciate that, Dragon, I do. It's just, I don't want you getting in too deep with Sunnyville. They're still one-percenters, and they've pissed off many people. I just don't want you caught up in their chaos."

B helped herself to three large pancakes, drowning them in maple syrup. "So, you're jealous of Noah?"

"What? No Dragon. That's not it at all!"

She speared a bite with her fork. "Whatever you say, Mackie boy." She popped the forkful of pancake into her mouth and chewed.

"I'm worried you're going to get hurt. You two are getting too close, and I don't like it."

"Stop being a sissy and just ask me, Mackie. You clearly have something to say, so get everything off your chest."

Mack dropped his fork onto his plate and wiped his mouth with a napkin. "Fine, I don't want you to see Noah anymore! There, I said it and I don't care if you're fucking him, or he's given you his mom's bracelet. It needs to end because he's not good enough for you."

B raised her eyebrows, pushing her lips together into a wry smile. "How long have we known each other, Mackie?"

Mack stared at her, confused. "Years. Why?"

"And in all our years have you ever seen me take a baby-faced, blond-haired, blue-eyed pretty boy to bed?"

Mack looked at her, puzzled. "Er... No."

"Exactly. I'm not fucking Baby Face. He's not my type. Yes, we've become great friends and yes, I'm helping him because you told him I would."

"Yeah, but I worry he hasn't got the best intentions for you at heart, and as for that Scottish prick, if he ever steps a foot on this land, I will tear his fucking head off. I'm sick of Noah telling you how much he wants you. You deserve the best. Not a one-percenter ex-con."

B stared at Mack. His chest pumped as he worked himself up. She took his hand. "Mackie, let me live. I'm feeling like a caged animal here in Uskiville. Noah is my friend, and it's nice to do the things that we used to do together. Yes, we're close, but no one will replace you as my best friend, okay?"

Mack placed his hand over hers, squeezing it. "Dragon, I don't trust him anymore. He turns up when he wants and wants you all to himself. I hate it, and Frankie isn't keen on him either."

"Mackie, Am I stupid? Do I do anything I don't want to do?"

Mack's eyes narrowed, chest still pumping. "No!"

"Then you know I'm fine and you have nothing to worry about. I do what I want. He's not using me. We have mutual interests. Oh, and leave the Scot alone. He's not done anything to you."

"He wants you, and that's bad enough."

B laughed. "And what if I met him and wanted him? That would be my choice, Mackie, not yours. Now you know me. I don't do relationships, I'm not a submissive, I'll never be an old lady, and I certainly don't do handsome Scots. So, you have nothing to worry about."

Mack leaned into B, placing his head on hers for the first time since they'd reconciled over Ari. "Dragon, please be careful. My heart hurts every time you leave with him."

"Mackie, I'm always careful. Now please let me live my life. I'm suffocating, and I don't like it. It's bad enough with Ari setting me up with random guys all the time, and now I have you stressing. So please just breathe and let me live again."

"You're right. I'm sorry. I've no right to ask this of you. I'll get back in my lane." He pulled away like a hurt puppy.

B took his hand again and brushed her thumb over his knuckles. "I appreciate how much you care, I do Mackie, but sometimes it feels like I'm married to the two of you and nobody told me. I love you, but I need my space, okay?"

Mack nodded and broke away from her then took his plate to the kitchen.

As he walked away, she angled her head and studied him. "Are we okay, Mackie?"

"Yeah," he said without turning. "I'm just having a hard time adjusting to losing my best friend again."

"For fuck's sake, Mackie, how do you think I felt when you brought Ari into our lives? This is hard for me too. You can't expect me to stay home, cook and run around after you all every day. I'm fucking exhausted."

Mack threw his plate in the sink. "Oh, I'm sorry. I didn't know being a family was an inconvenience to you. You used to enjoy having us around. What is it? You have your new BFF and we're not good enough anymore?"

B's dragon eyes emerged. Her temper boiled, and she screamed in frustration. "Fuck you, Mackie! All I've asked is for you to give me a break. Where do you get off telling me who I can be friends with? You may be the founder of the Gray Wolves. You may own your biker buddies and you may own Ari, but this is my business, my life, and you'll never fucking own me, good boy!"

"I'm not trying to fecking own you, Dragon, I'm trying to keep you safe! You don't understand the dangers out there!"

"What fucking dangers? Because the only danger I see is you suffocating me, and it ends now!"

Mack dropped his head in despair as he white knuckled the countertop. His face appeared red and fit to burst as he opened his mouth. "You are in..."

Just then, Ari entered the house. She stopped dead in her tracks and regarded the sight before her: B's dragon eyes glowering at Mack like fire and Mack ready to explode behind the counter.

"What the hell is going on here? The whole retreat can hear you arguing," she said.

"Ask that bloody control freak. I'm going for a bloody shower. Thanks for breakfast, asshole," she hollered as she left.

"Oh, real mature Dragon. You're fecking welcome, by the way!" he snapped before hammering his hands onto the counter repeatedly.

"Hey, hey! What the hell happened? You said you were coming over to bond with her. Not fight. Because you'll lose. I mean, you know you'll lose, right?" she said with a laugh, only half joking.

Mack couldn't help but let a chuckle escape his throat. Turning to her, he scooped her up in his arms. "Yeah, I know. She would snap me in seconds. Would you like to chop my balls off to make me feel more insecure in my time of need or is teasing me about my best friend's ability to kick my ass enough for you?"

"I'm sorry, honey. I hate seeing you both argue. It reminds me of the big fallout you had when we first moved here. It broke you, and I never want to see you like that again."

"I have a feeling we're breaking again, sweetheart, and I don't know how to fix things." He sighed and kissed her cheek.

Ari pulled away to look at him. "What have you done, Mack?"

"Me? Why does it have to be me? Miss Perfect could be in the wrong, you know."

Ari studied him, tilting her head slightly. "Mack, tell me!"

Mack walked over to the sofa, dropping himself down onto it in a huff. Ari approached as he dragged his hands down his face. Kneeling down before him, she pulled his hands away.

"Not again, Mack. Don't do this to yourself. Just tell me what it is, and we'll fix it."

Mack's eyes looked troubled and full of hurt. "I told her I didn't want her seeing Noah anymore."

Ari glared at him. "You did what? How dare you, Mack? You don't get to do that. You don't get to tell B who she's allowed to be friends with. Why would you even do that? What possessed you to come out with that?"

Mack checked over his shoulder to ensure they were alone. "Because she's in fecking danger, hanging around with him. If Blaze comes back, Noah is the first person he'll seek revenge on, and what if my dragon is with him? Blaze wants her. I know he does."

"Oh, not this again Mack, Blaze is gone. It's been over a year. If he was going to try anything, he would have already."

"No, sweetheart. I know him from old. He'll bide his time until he's ready to execute whatever fecked up plan he has, and I promise you: he's coming for her!"

"Mack, stop obsessing over this. It's making you paranoid, and you're going to drive Dragon away at this rate."

"And what about you trying to force her on dates? Because that's going to drive her away too."

Ari sat next to him, biting her fingernail. "Okay, so maybe we're both being overbearing toward her. Now, let's make it right, okay?"

"Ari, I don't care what you say. I know I'm right, and I'll lock her up to keep her safe if I have to."

Ari's jaw dropped in horror. "Mack, get your head right. Go to the cabin for a few days, do some fishing, anything. This isn't healthy."

He released a long sigh, rubbing the back of his neck. "Maybe you're right. I'll go talk to Frankie. Just promise me you'll let me know if she leaves Uskiville again."

Ari kissed his head. "Okay, honey, and listen, I'll talk to her, okay? Smooth things over."

Mack stood, taking Ari by the hand. "I don't know what I'd do without you keeping me right, baby."

"Me neither, now go on, I need to have a talk with my BFF."

A knock came on B's bedroom door before Ari pushed it open. "B it's Ari, I'm coming in."

"Hey," B said as she threw on her vest top. "Did he send you in to smooth things over?"

Ari sat on the bed next to her. "No, I thought I'd come check on my friend."

"There's no need. I'm fine," clipped B.

"Don't do that, B. Don't shut me out. You're shutting everyone out again, and it's making Mack crazy."

"Me making him crazy. Ari, he's trying to tell me who I can and can't be friends with."

"He's just worried about you."

"He needs to stop, Ari, because I can't take any more. God, I can't wait until I mo—"

"You what?"

B grew lightheaded as the blood drained from her face. "Nothing, it doesn't matter."

"You can't wait until you *what*, B?"

"Ari, just drop it, okay?" B exited her bedroom and headed to the kitchen to make some tea, with Ari hot on her trails.

"B, what's going on? You've been distant toward me for months now. It's like I don't know who you are anymore."

B let out an enormous sigh. "Fine, I'll tell you, Ari, but if you say one word to Mackie, I'll kill you, you hear?"

"Fine, spill!"

"No. Promise me, Ari. You wanted to be BFFs. You wanted me to confide in you. Well, I need to know you won't tell Mackie shit."

Concern flashed over Ari's face; her eyes fixed on B. "This is serious, isn't it?"

B couldn't look Ari in the eye. "Life-changing."

"I think I'm gonna need something stronger than tea for this, then."

"It's 10:15!"

Ari retrieved a bottle of whiskey from the cupboard. "Well, it's late somewhere."

B took a seat at her dining table where the remnants of this morning's breakfast still sat. Pushing the plate of now cold pancakes away from her, she rested her elbows on the table and looked Ari dead in the eyes. "I'm leaving Uskiville."

Ari clasped her hand to her throat as if she was struggling to breathe. Her voice strained as she forced out her words. "You're what?"

B didn't break her stare. "Ari, I'm moving to Sunnyville once my contract ends this summer. I own Noah's club, and my old complex dream is underway next door. The high school has offered me a deal of a lifetime, Ari, and now that you and Mack are settled, it's time for me to move on."

"Why?" Ari whispered, her eyes stricken.

"Because Uskiville isn't home to me anymore, and the boys want to attend the high school in Sunnyville. They asked me last summer, and the timing coincided with a new contract. Spencer told them I would be a free agent, and they made me a ridiculous offer. The team isn't great, but the boys haven't asked for anything since we came stateside, so I have to do this for them."

"So let me get this straight. You and the boys are unhappy, and you are taking a job with a shitty soccer team to *keep* them happy." She shook her head in disbelief. "And what's going to happen when you're on your own and life gets tough?"

B placed her tea down on the coaster. "Ari, life is already tough for me. I can't breathe here anymore. My life hasn't been my own since you moved here. I mean no offence, but things have changed. I don't want to be a third wheel in your relationship, and I feel like I am, and you and Mack are far from self-sufficient. Mackie does less now than he ever has. It's about time you both learned to stand on your own two feet. You can't do that with me around."

Ari held her hand to her chest, unable to speak. Tears fell from her eyes as B dropped her head in despair.

"Ari, I will always be there for you, but can you honestly say I have a life here? You play dress-up with me trying to force me into finding a suitor, and Mackie won't let me out of his sight. Did you know he has me followed whenever I leave now? I see Scamper tail me every time."

"B, you don't understand."

"I think I do, and it has to stop. I'm leaving for all our benefits. But don't worry, I'm keeping the cabin and I'll be up once a month to do the books."

Ari slammed her glass down onto the table. "Once a month? Are you kidding me? What do you think is going to happen when Mack finds out you're ditching him for Noah? He's going to kill him, B, and anyone else who gets in his way. He worships you, and you're just going to up and leave without telling him. What's wrong with you?"

B's eyes flickered at Ari's response, her rage building in her stomach as she swallowed down the air to calm herself.

"I'm going to tell him, Ari, as soon as the contract is signed. I'm not doing it before because he sabotaged my last one when he found out I was thinking of moving to Telles Creek. Ari, open your eyes. You must see, we have the most dysfunctional family. I want more for me, the boys, you, Mackie and baby Alex. That's why I want Mackie to take my role as head honcho here. Uskiville will be his to run, whilst I'm starting fresh in Sunnyville."

"B, this isn't you talking." Ari gave a sad shake of her head. "Noah has corrupted your mind."

Releasing an exasperated huff, B glared at Ari. "Bloody hell, Ari. Listen to yourself. You're talking about the man who saved your life. You know Noah, and you know he wouldn't hurt a fly. Now my decision is final."

"B, how will I explain this to Junior? He worships you!"

"I've secured him a contract with the Uskiville Storm Academy for fall. I was going to talk to you about it next week. They're offering him a scholarship, Ari, and it's a once in a lifetime opportunity."

Ari gasped. "Jesus Christ! You've thought of everything, haven't you?"

"I'm trying to make this as painless as possible."

"B, you're going to rip out Mack's heart, and I don't know if he can cope with that."

B swallowed down the bile that burned her throat. The stress was making her ill. She didn't want to break her bond with Mack, but she was desperate to be free.

Grasping the ends of the table to control her rage, she tried to make Ari understand her pain.

"Ari, I love Mackie, but I can't take it anymore. I don't know what's made him act the way he does toward me, but ever since we made up, he's changed, and I can't be a prisoner anymore."

Ari sobbed. "Please B, let me talk to him. I can make him change. This will ruin all of us. Please?"

B scooped her friend into her arms and absorbed Ari's trembling. "Ari, please. I don't want to hurt you guys, but I need to live my life, and I can't do it here. The boys and I need a fresh start. Please tell me you understand that!"

After a few moments, Ari nodded. "I do, but I'm scared of what this will do to our family. The club. The ramifications will be huge. Who else have you told?"

"Nobody. Just you and Noah. That's it."

"What about Frankie?"

"No. He'll want to join me. Mackie needs him, just like he's going to need you, Ari."

"Oh, God. I hate this. This is all my fault, isn't it? I should never have pushed Mack into making me move here. I shouldn't have tried to force you on dates and—"

"Ari, stop lovely girl. You've become my BFF, and I never thought I'd have a girlfriend. Nothing is going to change, and you and Mackie can visit. You won't even recognize the place when I'm done." She gave Ari a light squeeze. "Now please tell me you have my back!"

Ari pulled away from B's grasp. "I can't change your mind?"

B shook her head. "Not this time, lovely girl. I'm going house hunting next weekend, and I need you to cover for me so Scamper doesn't follow me."

"You're asking me to keep this from the man I love, B."

"Yes. Just until after next weekend. Please do this for me."

"Okay, just promise me you'll be careful with Noah. Mack thinks he's up to something."

"He's a good boy, Ari."

"Promise me, B."

"Okay, and you promise to keep this quiet until I'm ready to tell Mackie?"

Ari wiped her tears. "Promise."

"Well, I sure as hell don't!" Remy said, standing in the doorway.

The women gasped and Ari approached Remy as B put her hands on her hips and cursed at the ceiling. "Jesus!"

"Remy. How long have you been here?" Ari asked.

"Long enough to hear Aunt B is breaking up our family and moving away. Mack is going to break again, isn't he?"

"Mack will be fine, Remy, and we can't expect B to put her career on hold for us. And as for the boys, they have dreams, just like you. You want to go to Stanford after high school. Do you think I would discourage you from that?"

Remy huffed. "No, Mom, of course not!"

"Exactly, so you can't expect B and the boys to put their dreams on hold. Now, promise your Aunt B you'll keep her secret. It can't leave this room."

"Fine, but I want my curfew moved to eleven on the weekends."

"10:30."

"11 p.m., Mom."

"10:30 and that's final."

"Fine, but don't expect Mack and Junior to be this reasonable. They're going to lose their sh—"

"Language, Boyoh!" B snapped.

"Sorry, Aunt B. I do want you and the boys to be happy, you know."

"I know, thanks, buddy!"

CHAPTER FOUR

The Return of The Claw

Blaze sat polishing his brother's old claw, waiting patiently for his little spies to return to his office. He had sent them to make sure that his latest spy was in place, ready for his next mission.

After fleeing his home in fear of being captured by the Gray Wolves, Blaze spent over a year waiting for revenge. He had recently instructed his spies to retrieve the claw and exhume The Mauler's body from Uskiville, desperate to lay him to rest alongside his predecessors. Perched in his old armchair, and reminiscing about the night of his brother's demise, his anger consumed him. The desperate and frightened look in The Mauler's eyes was the last thing Blaze saw before Zander prevented him from saving his twin. The same image had haunted him since he'd escaped with his own life, and Blaze woke every night as the guilt coursed through his veins like venom. Blaze wanted to make things right by finishing what he had started.

Slipping his fingers into the glove-like claw was like ascension to Blaze. He believed he was leveling up to his higher calling, continuing from The Mauler and his ancestors before him. The rusty metal claw had been handed down through the generations, wreaking havoc upon its victims, and now it belonged to Blaze.

Marveling over the sharp tips of the claw, he declared he would finish what his brother had started by killing Mack and taking his dragon.

Mack and Zander will die horrible deaths, and I'll make Dragon beg for mercy before I slice her throat and take everything she owns!

Shaking his head, he removed the claw, the pain and torment too much as he rubbed his scarred shoulder, scarred by a gunshot wound left by a man he despised. Blaze reeked of revenge. Zander had prevented him from saving his brother, and Blaze had a score to settle.

A knock at the door interrupted his thoughts.

"Come in," he barked.

A skinny-legged, rough-looking man in his thirties entered the room. His beady eyes fixed on Blaze.

"Everything's ready, Prez." he said, too fearful to make eye contact with his leader.

"Good! Make sure he keeps me informed. I want to know everything! Now get out."

The terrified spy scarpered out of the office, closing the rickety door behind him.

Blaze guzzled his beer as he stared out the window, lost in his thoughts as he tried to look beyond the miles and miles of nothingness stretched over acres of picturesque farmland. He had been hiding at his sister's old ranch since his escape. The idyllic plot of land had been left to rot by The Mauler, after retrieving Noah from there when he was just a teenager. No one would find him there. The Mauler told Noah the man who killed his mother had claimed it. All lies, of course, crafted to stop Noah from ever searching for the truth about his mother's death.

Blaze loved remembering the yester-years, visiting Courtney and Noah; they had all been so close until The Mauler got her tangled up with his heroin supplier. After failing his supplier for the last time on another botched drug run, Courtney had paid the price for his brother's indiscretions, leaving Noah without a mother.

Blaze had arrived in town for Noah's sixteenth birthday and bought him his first motorcycle. Upon their return from the dealership, they were confronted with a horror scene so awful that Blaze couldn't allow Noah to see his mother's body. It destroyed Blaze, knowing his brother was responsible, only forgiving him after checking in on Noah two years later. Blaze knew Noah had never forgiven him for abandoning him for so long after he had already lost his mother, and as years passed, Noah became distant, acknowledging Blaze as no more than an old acquaintance whenever he arrived in Sunnyville.

Courtney's house had always been decorated with family portraits depicting the happy times, but now, the quiet and dusty house appeared haunted by the chilling nightmares of that horrid night.

Tonight did not differ from any other night for Blaze in Noah's former home. His all too consuming grief becoming too much for him. Plagued by the deaths of his siblings, he questioned whether The Mauler's death was karma for the fate his twin brother bestowed upon his sister. He questioned whether karma was calling in old debts for the life they'd lived. Wondering whether his sister's spirit had somehow empowered Noah to make different life choices, like divine intervention, forcing him to step away from his destiny. It was all too much for him.

Fueled by cheap whiskey and rage, Blaze left the office, dragging his beer bottle along the wall as he walked the short hallway to Noah's room. It had been left untouched since Noah had left his family home. Posters of motorcycles and heavy metal bands lined the walls of the dusty, box-shaped room. The time capsule-like bedroom mirrored the untidiness of the teenager who once lived there with an unmade bed and candy wrappers littering the floor. The pile of folded clothes, still sitting on Noah's desk, suggested a mother's touch had been present: no doubt the handy work of Courtney before her untimely death. Blaze stroked the folded pale blue T-shirt, thinking of his sister and the good old days, until his eyes met with a photograph of Noah and his school friends. The mischievous grin staring back at him from the 6x9 photograph frame, prompted a knee-jerk reaction from Blaze.

Slamming the frame down onto the desk, he watched the crystal-like shards of glass scatter. Grimacing, he launched his beer bottle at the wall, his all too consuming rage ripping through him like the claw through flesh. Crying out in anguish, like The Mauler's victims once had, he lashed out, clearing the dusty bookshelf of Noah's precious motorcycle models. Still searching for relief, Blaze growled with frustration, picking up the desk and throwing it to the floor like a smackdown wrestling move.

The neat pile of clothing was now strung across the floor, disrespecting the final act of Courtney's love. But none of that mattered anymore. Noah had betrayed him and his family, and after all Blaze had done to keep him fed, warm and clothed, paying for his upkeep when The

Mauler spent his money on beer and drugs. Blaze had deposited everything he could spare, so his nephew wouldn't suffer after his brother insisted on taking custody of him as penance for Courtney's death. Blaze had wanted to raise Noah as his own, but he knew his brother needed to do right by Noah for his past sins, choosing to support him from afar instead.

His nostrils flared at the thought of Noah, a family tell that revealed disturbed emotions, passed down through generations. Noah's betrayal was unforgiveable, and now he too would pay the price for his part in The Mauler's death. Noah had aided in the loss of Blaze's last remaining sibling, betrayed the family, and stole the family MC that by rights belonged to Blaze. His father had purchased the Sunnyville MC fifty years earlier, and Blaze believed it to be his birth right, and now the time for revenge had come for those who betrayed him.

CHAPTER FIVE

Noah, Zander, and Jimmy

Zander picked up a new face from the bar to entertain him. But even as he dragged her off to his room, he couldn't stop thinking about the woman who had invaded his dreams this past year. He wanted B and had been waiting months to meet her, but Noah hadn't come through, though he promised that Saturday it was going to happen.

Brimming with frustration, Zander was fit to burst and had enough of using his hand to relieve his pressure. So, a half-drunk bar girl from downtown Sunnyville would do tonight and once he had Welsh Cake, he would forgo any other women, as he only needed her. The crush on B was over a year old. She made him feel for the first time, and one Christmas hamper and a five-minute video call was all it took to thaw his icy heart.

Tossing the wafer-thin blonde woman onto his bed, he ripped off his clothes, desperate for release before meeting the woman of his dreams in person. He couldn't risk being a one and done guy after waiting so long for her company. Noah told him B was a man-eater, having her wicked way with men before tossing them away, and Zander was determined to hold his own with her.

Tearing off the woman's skirt, his heart raced with desperation as he entered her. He wasn't interested in foreplay anymore. He had one aim: to release before his big day with B, and she was all he could think about as he settled into his stride.

Sex had become trivial to Zander, something to pass the time in his miserable existence, until he laid eyes on the picture of B in Uskiville. She changed the narrative of his life, and in a matter of days, he would make her his.

The nameless woman he pinned to his bed didn't please him. She didn't mean enough to him to ask her name. She was a sex toy he played with, as he cheated her of her orgasm. He was close to his own climax when Noah tapped on the door.

"Busy," he growled.

"I'll be back in a bit brother, I gotta nip out."

"Give me five minutes, we're almost done here," he said breathlessly, as he continued to rattle the headboard with his lusty stride.

"We're all good, Zand. I won't be long. Give the lady a good time."

"Aye, right then," he panted.

"Love you, man," Noah said before leaving.

CHAPTER SIX

Traitor!

Noah took a deep breath as he stepped off his bike outside the Bacon Shack. Removing his helmet, he scanned the area. It was eerily quiet for a Tuesday evening. The place was normally crawling with high school kids.

Adjusting his cut, he headed up the steps to the popular diner to be met by a grizzly looking, bald man who proceeded to rough handle him.

"Who the fuck do you think you are? Get the fuck off me, you bald prick!" he said as he shook off the man's grasp and headed inside.

The atmosphere was deadly as the heater buzzed, catching its latest prey with its orange glow, giving off vibes that death was looming.

Noah caught sight of the owner, Lenny. The happy-go-lucky chap was a far cry from his usual self as he slumped unconscious against the under-counter fridge, blood dripping from a head wound, no doubt inflicted by Blaze or one of his spies.

Noah's nostrils flared. The telltale sign he was furious, along with a deep vein bulging from his temple. Turning to the bald spy, Noah grimaced, head-butting the man, feeling the crack as his nose broke beneath his forehead.

The man's nose gushed a sea of red as he gasped in response, and Noah delivered a fist to his temple, sending him crashing to the floor.

"He better be breathing, asshole, or I'm coming back to slice your throat!" Noah spat, before being dragged off by two spies.

Noah green-eyed the spies in contempt as they released him at the booth.

"Well, somebody sure has his panties in a twist," Blaze teased.

"What the fuck is this, uncle?" Noah slammed, throwing his arms up in the air in frustration.

"I'm simply taking precautions to look after my own interests. Blaze said, wiping his mouth with a napkin before tossing it onto his empty plate."

"Precautions? This diner is normally bouncing, and you've cleared out the place. Are you trying to attract unwanted attention?"

"Oh, I figured tonight should be an intimate affair."

"And what the fuck is that supposed to mean?"

"Do you think I'm stupid, boy? Did you think I wouldn't know you signed my club over to your whore of a dragon? You've screwed me over for the last time!"

Noah couldn't help but smirk. "I thought you'd be proud, uncle. Doesn't it make me more like you?"

"You're nothing like me, boy. You are a disease that needs to be eradicated."

Noah glared at Blaze. "You won't kill me. We're family, and you need me to get your hands on my club."

"Don't fuck with me boy, that club is mine, not yours!"

"Fuck you! I earned it after everything you and your sick and twisted brother did to me and my mother!"

Blaze gripped him by his throat, lifting him off the ground. "I loved your fucking mother. Hell, I even loved you until you became a traitor to your own kind, and for what? Some Irish prick and a wannabe ball-buster of a dragon. You're no family to me anymore!" he said, tossing him onto the ground."

Noah, winded by the fall, gasped for breath. "Fuck you! Dragon owns everything now. She is building a fucking empire! Something you and Uncle Mauler could never achieve! You fucking lost, Blaze. She's untouchable, and my brothers will die for her if they have to."

"Just like you, then."

Noah's face screamed with confusion. "What? My mother's death wasn't enough for you and Uncle Mauler? You have to kill her son, too? I know he was responsible, but you could have prevented it, you sick fuck! She'd be so disappointed. She's probably turning in her fucking grave."

Blaze shot him a sinister grin. "Well, why don't you ask her? You'll be seeing her soon!"

"Fuck you!" Noah spat in disgust.

"I tell you what, let's make this interesting. You remember the cat-and-mouse game you loved as a kid? Well let's play. I'll give you a chance to get to your bike before I pump you with bullets, but I want you to know something before you meet your maker."

"Is it that you're going to die by my brothers' hands?"

Blaze took his boot to Noah's face, sending blood splatter across the floor like a masterpiece.

Noah laughed. "What? You thought I'd beg for mercy? I knew I'd meet my maker tonight, uncle. Why do you think I came alone? Why do you think I got Dragon to sign that contract? The wheels are in motion, and you ain't never getting your hands on my club or Dragon. It's over!"

Blaze picked him up with one hand, with Noah wrestling to break free.

"Oh, it's not over, boy! It's only just begun, but you won't be around to see what I do to your brothers or your precious Dragon. Mark my words, you'll see them soon enough. Now, I'll play fair and give you to the count of three to get out of here," he said, releasing his grip on Noah's jacket.

Noah looked at him, confused. "Just do it, you sick fuck. I won't play your games anymore."

"Turn around," Blaze demanded.

"Why? Not man enough to face me when you kill me? You fucking pussy!"

Blaze glared at his two spies, who jumped in response, grabbing Noah's arms to turn him away from Blaze.

Noah laughed, almost hysterically, until he closed his eyes and took a deep breath, waiting for it to be over. He would meet his maker tonight knowing he had kept Dragon safe and given his family a chance to prepare for the war coming their way.

"Goodbye, boy." Blaze pulled the trigger, unleashing a round into Noah's back.

Noah let out a guttural gasp. His lifeless body dropping to the ground before Blaze reloaded and fired again and again.

Letting out an enormous sigh, Blaze turned to his spies. Make sure you wipe the cameras, and empty the cash register. Make it look like a robbery gone wrong. I want the element of surprise with these pricks. I'm in the wind as far as they're concerned, and I want to see the looks on their faces when they learn how much I've fucked with their lives.

"Prez?" the bloody-nosed bald guy questioned.

"We're playing the long game, Sully. It's smart! It'll ruin them from the inside out. There's going to be nothing left of Dragon and the Gray Wolves by the time I'm finished with them. Now call my little spy. We got work to do!"

A couple of hours later, after taking Noah's advice, Zander escorted the woman out of the club and headed back to the bar to Jimmy. Tiny and Tyr had returned from their Sabbatical earlier in the day, so the MC was booming as the bunnies serviced the unattached MC members and the old ladies serviced their biker husbands in full view of the bar.

"Beer," Zander said to the new bartender.

A young ratty-looking thing seeming eager to please, handed him a beer. Zander didn't like the young man who Noah had taken off the streets recently. He didn't trust him.

Zander snatched the beer and turned his attention to Jimmy. "Where has he gone now?"

Jimmy shrugged, adjusting himself on his rickety bar stool. "Dunno. He's been gone a while, though, and he made Gnarler come back inside. Insisted he had to go alone. He took a call and said it was urgent."

Zander planted his hands on his hips. "For fuck's sake, what's he playing at? I said I'd go with him."

"Nah. Knocking on your door was just for your benefit. He knows you're getting ready for your big moment with Dragon."

"Aye, well, I dinnae want to disappoint her. I've no' been with many lassies since she got in my head. I want to be fresh if I take her to bed."

"Wow, you really have it bad for this woman, don't you? For as long as I've known you, you've fucked and got rid, yet you see one dragon and you're whipped."

Zander moved to the other side of Jimmy, resting his forearms on the bar. "I'm no' whipped pal. I just like what I see. I've never looked at a lassie and thought she could me my old lady until I laid eyes on Welsh Cake."

"Why do you call her that?"

"'Cause Dragon is not a way to describe someone as beautiful as her. When I was in the army, I had a Welsh pal. His mother would always send him Welsh cakes and they tasted like heaven. To me, that lassie is a Welsh cake and I bet she tastes as good as one, too," he grinned.

"But you don't know her, and she seems a bit of a hard-faced bitch."

Zander laughed into his beer bottle. "Good, if she's gonnae be my old lady, she'll have to hold her own."

Jimmy finished his beer, waving his hand he instructed the bar boy to fetch another.

"What if she doesn't like you? Noah has already told you she doesn't date."

"She'll date me pal, I know she will. I can feel it."

"Whatever, Romeo. I just don't want my best friend getting hurt."

Zander laughed. "Nothing can hurt me Jimmy, I'm made of steel remember."

"You got that right," Jimmy scoffed as he caught sight of the sheriff entering the bar.

"What's he want?" Jimmy asked as the Sheriff approached.

Zander slammed his beer onto the counter, glaring at the Sheriff approaching him. "We've not done anything wrong, sheriff, just having a wee quiet one in our club."

The Sheriff loosened his top button and removed his cap. "I'm afraid I have some bad news, fellas. I've just come from the Bacon Shack, and I'm afraid your associate, Noah Wilson was killed in what looks like an armed robbery an hour ago. He took three rounds to the back. I'm so sorry fellas. Noah was a good man."

Zander's heart stopped, feeling like a dagger had pierced him there. His breath rattled so loud in his chest; he could hear the thumps hammering in his ears.

"What?" he asked in confusion.

"I'm sorry, Zander, he's gone. He was dead before he hit the ground. Now, I need to—"

Zander launched his beer bottle at the window, and bent over in agony as the pain tore through him like a riptide. Jimmy clambered to the bar, knees buckling as he stepped from his stool, in tears over the loss of his best friend.

The rest of the MC rushed to their aid, sharing sobs of their own as the quiet bartender stood shaking like a leaf. Noah had brought him into the club and now he was dead.

Zander shook his head in disbelief. "Where is he?" he asked through gritted teeth.

"The coroner has him. When he's done, you'll need to identify the body."

"I wanna see him now!"

"I'll take you down after you answer my questions. Now why was he in Telles Creek?"

Zander saw red, greeting the Sheriff with a demonic stare. "I swear to God if you dinnae take me to him right now, I'll slit your fucking throat."

"I know you're mad, son, but why was he alone in the first place? Tell me why he was the only guy in the diner, cameras knocked out. Owner knocked out and cash register empty. Yet Noah was shot multiple times. Was this a robbery gone wrong or a gang war? Because this is my town, and I plan to get to the bottom of this incident."

Zander puffed out his chest and stared down at the sheriff. "I ain't telling you shit, cop. Whatever it is, it's club business and we'll finish it. Now take me to my brother."

CHAPTER SEVEN
Distraught

It was around three a.m. when Mack's phone rang, waking the entire house. Desolation rumbled through him as he heard the news. Noah was dead! Dropping the phone, he sat up in bed, numb as Zander's trembling voice called out to him from the phone now lying on the bedroom floor.

Fumbling, Mack steadied his hand as he picked up the phone.

"Mack, we're on lockdown until we find out what the hell happened here, but I need to talk to Welsh Cake. I want to tell her. She deserves to hear it from me, and... I need some answers."

"No! You're not going near my Dragon. None of you are. You'll not get a sympathy feck out of her either. Now stay put, and I'll bring a team down. That's an order from the founder. And Zander, I want to know what's fecking happening," Mack said shrugging into his T-shirt.

"Fuck you, you Irish prick. Noah was my best fucking friend, my brother. You may be the fucking founder, but dinnae ever bark orders at me, pal. Noah might have put up with it, but I won't. To me, you're the same Irish prick you were when we met. Maybe if you stuck to your word and helped us out, Noah would still be alive right now," Zander barked into the phone. His raw emotion sent shivers down Mack's spine. Zander was terrifying when angered. His roar placed the fear of God in most people. Despite Mack's distaste for Noah's relationship with B, Noah was Mack's friend, too. He didn't have to imagine the pain Zander was experiencing. That same pain tore through his soul, creating a hole that could never be filled.

"You're hurting, brother, so I'm going to let that one slide for now, but let's be clear, the only reason Noah is dead is because you failed him as his VP. I want to know why he wasn't protected. Why have you been letting him fly solo? Yes, we agreed on an exchange at the border when he came to me, but that was it. No Prez rides solo, ever!"

The phone went quiet. Zander said nothing. He had no answers for the club's founder.

"You better have answers for me when I arrive, and don't worry about my dragon. I'll take care of her; The South won't be involved with her anymore. Now get your club in order. I arrive at oh eight hundred hours."

Mack seethed before hanging up, turning to Ari, who was in floods of tears. She'd heard everything. One of her knights in shining armor had been killed.

Mack held Ari whilst calling a code red, an instant lockdown of the retreat. They had never had one in the club's brief history, so everyone panicked. Every entrance and exit would be heavily armed, and no club members could leave without permission from Mack or Frankie.

Mack called a meeting, demanding everyone join him in church. Tired and confused faces gathered until Mack entered the room. The news rocked the club to its core. Everyone loved Noah. He had become a well-respected family member to everyone in the Uskiville chapter.

Sullen faces now decorated the room as Frankie posed the question in everyone's minds.

"Have you told B?"

Mack scratched his beard, clawing his hand down his face. "Not yet! I have five prospects surrounding the two cabins, as well as Scamper and Bamfa, who I filled in earlier. This is going to hurt her, and we all know how unpredictable Dragon gets when she's hurting or angry."

Frankie leaned forward in his chair, placing a hand on Mack's shoulder. "Do you want me there when you tell her? I'd like to be there for her," Frankie said quietly.

"Uh, yeah, pal, and I'm going to need you to stay with her whilst I go to Sunnyville. She won't have anyone else parading around the house, you know what she's like."

"Understood. Are we clear on what's happened down there yet?" Frankie asked.

Mack poured himself another whiskey, passing the bottle around the table. "No, but we have to take this as a threat to our organization. Noah was our brother and I want blood for what happened to him."

"B won't like that, Mackie boy," Frankie said, his disapproving yet sympathetic stare evident to a quick-tempered Mack.

"I'm done with what she wants, Frankie. My only concern right now is her safety and everyone else's. Now you all have your orders, so lock and load, we ride out in an hour." he said, smashing the gavel onto the solid mahogany table.

Everyone left the room, pale-faced, and shaken by the news. The MC was a quiet club, and now they were preparing for a war.

Mack remained seated with Frankie, drinking whiskey like it was water after the others left. Frankie glared at Mack, "Are we going to address the elephant in the room or are you going to pretend this isn't happening?"

Mack pursed his lips. "We know nothing yet."

Frankie slammed his hands onto the table. "Oh, wake up, Mackie boy, execution a town over, no witnesses who can talk, no cameras and why the fuck was he alone? It sounds to me like he was set up or lured there. Now I know I wasn't keen on him, but we have a duty to find out what's happened, and we need to know if Blaze has returned. B could be in danger."

Mack shook his head, rising from his chair to pace the small rectangular room. "He wasn't set up. Sunnyville would die for him, and if it was Blaze, why now and why not take out the whole club? It would make sense he wants his brother's club."

Frankie stood, stopping Mack in his tracks. "Mackie, Noah drafted in seven new members in six months, four of them seasoned Nomads. He said they did checks, Mackie, but you can't say trust has been built there this soon. Maybe someone wanted the Prez spot, and as for Blaze, I don't know brother, I just want B safe."

"That's what we all want. She can't know the truth about anything,

Frankie. We tell her it was a robbery gone wrong, that's it. We know nothing more than that right now, but you need to stay close to her. Just make sure she understands the risks without pushing her dragon buttons. She won't listen to me right now."

"You got it." Frankie said ushering Mack towards the exit.

"I mean it Frankie. I can't lose her!"

Frankie gripped his brother's hand tight, demonstrating solidarity. "Never going to happen, Mackie boy. Now come on, let's get this over with."

Mack used the spare key to let himself and Frankie into B's house. He positioned Bamfa at the front door with two prospects around back, communicating via high tec security equipment to ensure B's safety.

Mack and Frankie entered B's room with Frankie sitting in B's rocking chair opposite her bed and Mack sitting on the bed next to where she slept. Turning on the bedside lamp, Mack removed a stray hair from her face, his own face strained, knowing he was about to break her heart. He had witnessed B getting close to Noah these past eight months. They had become inseparable after hitting it off at their first encounter, and breaking the news to her was going to be hard for him. But it was a necessary evil that needed to be done.

When he shook her gently, B woke, and her eyes jolted open as soon as she saw Mack and Frankie. Jumping up in bed, clutching her blanket to her naked body, she gasped. "What's happened? Where's Ari and the boys?"

"Hey, they're fine," Mack whispered.

A puzzled expression flashed across her face. "Then why are you both here?"

Mack took her hand as B followed him with her eyes. "Something has happened in Sunnyville."

B's sleep-filled eyes bulged in shock. "Tell me."

Mack dropped his head, tears coursing down his cheeks, as Frankie stood up to approach his struggling brother. Kneeling before B, he brushed her cheek. "Noah was shot dead in an armed robbery tonight. We don't have a lot of details, but Mackie locked Sunnyville down and we must do the same. I'm sorry B, I know how close you guys were."

B's face hardened. Her jaw line tightened as she slammed her lips together. Her eyes lit up like flames burning in a forest fire, pulling her hand away from Mack, glaring at him. "Tell me this wasn't you."

Mack's jaw dropped in disbelief. "What? You think I did this? What the feck Dragon?"

"You didn't want me seeing him. You said you didn't trust him, and a few days later, he's bloody dead. He was my friend, Mackie!"

"Jeez, Dragon. Is that who you think I am? The guy who kills his friends in a jealous rage. I've been here. I woke to a phone call from Zander. The cops found Noah a few hours ago. Seriously, Dragon, how can you *think* that of me? I may have wanted him to stay away from *you*, but he was my fecking brother. I fecking loved him!"

B nodded. "Promise me, when I find out what happened, it won't lead back to you."

Mack dropped his shoulders, more tears escaping his tired eyes. He moved close to her, grabbing the back of her neck to pull her head to his. "Dragon, I promise you, this isn't on me. Please believe me. I love all of my family, especially you, and it breaks my heart that you would think this of me."

B gripped his shirt, pulling him in tight as he hugged her back. "I'm sorry!" she whispered. "You just get so possessive, Mackie, and I don't understand why this happened. He was a good boy with a big heart. Why? Mackie, why?"

Mack held her tight as Frankie rose to sit on the other side of her, placing a hand on her back. B was shaking in anger; rage consuming her as they tried to comfort her. Mack could feel her fury ripple through her body as she dug into his back with her rage, trying to control herself.

Frankie leaned in to whisper in her ear. "Listen B, we'll find the bastards who did this! They will pay for what they did. It's club business now, and this needs to be handled to ensure the safety of the club."

B turned to Frankie. "No! You find them and you hand them over to the police. You stay white. This club, our family, stays white!"

Frankie's face softened as he cupped her cheek once more. "We have to do this B. If we don't, we're opening the floodgates for every one-percenter to take what's ours. The news will spread like wildfire.

Sunnyville was one of the biggest one-percenters in the states, and their Prez has been killed. People will expect ramifications, all-out war. We have to set a precedent here!"

"No! I didn't work my ass off building this for us to turn black. Not now, not ever!"

Mack placed her head between his hands, grabbing her attention and staring into her eyes. "We have to do this, Dragon. We need justice for our fallen brother. Noah would want this. He would want us to avenge him, and with all due respect, I'm the founder of this club. You may own it, but it's mine and I am calling the shots for the safety of our family. I'm leaving for Sunnyville now, and I'm making this shit right."

"You go black again, Mackie, and I pull out of everything. I will not go black, and you're wrong. Noah *wouldn't* want this; I know he wouldn't. He wanted Sunnyville to go straight like us. That's why I agreed to help him."

"It doesn't matter what he wants now. He's dead, and the bastards who did this will pay. With or without your support!"

"Then I've lost two people tonight."

"Dragon, I love you and all your crazy black and white shit, but if it means keeping you and our family safe, then I'll have to live with that. Now I have to go, okay?" he said, kissing her on the forehead.

"I won't go black, Mackie, but I'm going with you," she said, diving out of bed, naked then taking a moment to throw on her dressing gown.

"The hell you are! It's not safe for you there."

"Fuck off, Mackie, I'm going to pay my respects." B said pulling clothes from her closet.

"Over my fecking dead body, Dragon!"

"That could be arranged, good boy. Now I'm getting dressed, and I'm going."

Frankie and Mack glared at one another as Frankie became adamant. "B, you're staying put, and that's an order."

"I don't take orders, good boy. I give them. Now don't test me," she said, hauling on her jeans and zipping them.

"Not fucking happening, B," Frankie said.

B stopped in her tracks; her fiery dragon eyes fixed on her brothers. "And you're both going to stop me?"

"Abso-fecking-lutely, darling. I'm not losing anyone else tonight,"

Mack said, before talking into his microphone. "Bamfa, slash Dragon's tires."

"You wouldn't bloody dare!"

"You fecking heard me right, Bamfa. Dragon doesn't leave this fecking retreat unless I fecking say so. Now do it or I'll chop your fecking balls off."

B threw on her woolie sweater and darted to the door as Frankie dived in front of her.

"This is for your own good B," he said, picking her up and pinning her to the bed.

"Go!" he said to Mack, who hesitated until it dawned on Frankie what had to be done.

"Forgive me, B. I can't let you get hurt," he whispered into her ears before slapping a set of cuffs around her wrist then attaching her to the bedpost.

"What the fuck? Frankie. Why would you do this to me? Noah's my friend."

"And you're mine. My family even. I'm not letting anything happen to you. You're too precious to me."

B ripped her hand away from the bedpost, rattling the cuffs as she tried to break free. "Let me go, Frankie or I swear I'll..."

"I'll let you out when you've calmed down and Mackie is on the road. It hurts me to do this to you, B, but sometimes you're your own worst enemy."

"Someone has killed my friend, and instead of going to help his family, I am cuffed to my fucking bed. What's wrong with you?" she said, tugging at the cuff.

Frankie sat next to her, placing his hand on her shoulder. "Stop, please! You'll hurt yourself. They're military grade and you're not breaking free. I have guards placed everywhere to keep you safe, so you're not leaving until Mack finds out what happened tonight. If you want to help, I'll get you VP's bank details and you can pay for the funeral. Give Noah a good send off."

B ran her free hand through her hair, tussling it as Frankie watched her seethe. "You don't understand Frankie. I have to help them. I promised Noah I'd look after them. Now please, unlock these cuffs."

Frankie kissed her cheek, knowing he was the one person B would never attack. They had an unspoken bond. Very different from her bond with Mack. Their bond was more like a sibling bond, with Frankie being the over-protective big brother. B would understand why this was necessary when she calmed down.

"I'll go get the good stuff," he said, leaving the room with B cradling her head in her hand.

CHAPTER EIGHT
Return to Sunnyville

Mack arrived in Sunnyville with a strong team of ten men, all of whom were ex-military friends of Frankie. Frankie and Mack had stepped up security in the wake of The Mauler's attack on their home.

A wave of nostalgia struck Mack as he approached the MC. It hadn't changed in his absence, looking like the same old MC apart from the Gray Wolves MC patch draped above the entrance. At Mack's side was Rubble, his Sergeant of Arms, Breaker the club's enforcer, and Dirt the Roadie, who walked just behind as they headed toward Zander and Jimmy, who were emerging from the club.

Mack watched an evil-eyed Zander stroll in confidence toward him, his gun tucked into his waistband, looking like he was ready to kill. Tiny, Sunnyville's club enforcer, and Jimmy walked beside him.

Mack embraced his Celtic brother with a firm clasp on his back, feeling the raw emotion in his tense chest.

"I'm sorry we're meeting like this, brother. Noah was one of the greats in his short time as Prez," Mack said.

"Aye, thank you!" Zander said in a low growl.

"Frankie sends his regards. You must understand, I've had to take some precautions for everyone's safety back home."

"Aye. Is she alright?"

Mack grimaced. "Fine, now let's get everyone inside, shall we?"

The rest of the brothers exchanged grappling hugs before Zander led them to church. The bunnies rushed around with urgency, handing out cheap beers to the guests.

No one sat in the Prez's chair, and a glass of whiskey sat in place as a sign of respect for the fallen Prez.

Discussion got underway regarding what happened to Noah, with Mack demanding answers.

"Why did he send Gnarler away?" he asked.

"We don't know, Mack. He had been acting strange lately, disappearing. We tried to talk to him a couple of days ago. We told him 'no more,' but you know Noah. Stubborn son of a bitch," Jimmy said.

"Police reports? What're they saying?" Mack said, rubbing his temples.

"Armed Robbery. Noah was in the wrong place at the wrong time. Nobody saw anything."

"Why was he there?"

"No fucking idea?" Zander sighed.

"Feck, then what do we know?"

"That our brother was murdered, and someone has to die!" Zander said in a cold growl as he stared into his glass of whiskey.

"You'll have your revenge, brother, but first we need to discuss the possibility that a bigger plot is at play here."

Zander glared at Mack.

"You know it's possible, brothers. We never found him."

"Aye, because he knows better than to return. Besides, he would have hit the club and taken his time with Noah. Sent him back in pieces. Blaze wouldn't execute him like that. He needs more than that to feed his desires, his revenge." Zander said, shaking his head.

"What makes you so sure?"

"Because it's exactly what I would do. It takes one to know one, brother. Trust me, this ain't his MO."

"Right! Then we go on a scavenger hunt. I wanna know who killed Noah by the end of the day. We need to make this right."

"Understood," Jimmy said.

"You also need to vote in a new Prez. I know it's hard, but we need to display strength to our enemies. Now the obvious patch is Zander, so let's get this vote done."

"No!" Zander growled.

A stir of echoes ricocheted around the room, gasping at Zander's refusal.

"Excuse me?" Mack growled.

"I said No! I'm no' your Prez. Noah wanted Jimmy to take his place, no' me, and I'm no' wanting it. I'm no Prez. I'll stay VP."

"This is your club, Zander. You were made for this." Jimmy pleaded.

"No, brother, you were, and I'll hear no more about it. Now let's vote that shit in."

"I'll leave you to your vote, and when it's done, we mourn our fallen Prez and welcome our new Prez," Mack said, slamming his hand on the table, refusing to handle the gavel.

The Uskiville MC members headed into the bar, leaving Sunnyville to cast their vote. Zander's shaking hand took hold of the gavel, his voice trembling as he spoke. "All in favor of Jimmy taking the gavel?"

The room echoed in agreement. Jimmy was the new Prez at Sunnyville. Zander struck the gravel in confirmation. "Congratulations brother, it's what Noah and I wanted," he said as he embraced Jimmy and handed him the gavel.

Jimmy's mouth slackened in disbelief, and he was still lost for words as Eddie, the club's chaplain, handed him the Prez flesh. Running his finger over the patch, he turned to his brothers.

"First order of business, vengeance!" he said before slamming the gavel onto the sound block.

The other members left the church after congratulating their brother, leaving Zander and Jimmy to talk.

Jimmy looked at Zander's grief-stricken face. "Are you alright, Zand? Are you sure you want this? It doesn't feel right."

Zander's voice was low and sincere. "Yeah, brother, this was Noah's dream for you. I was supposed to be happy with Welsh Cake, and you got the club."

"And Noah?"

"He was going to become VP and I was dropping down the ranks, too. We were going to be free. I guess he is now, though," Zander said, staring into his glass again.

"What the hell are we supposed to do now? He's built a wall around Dragon from what he said on the phone, and we can't keep the club in the dark forever."

"We wait. Welsh Cake will show Jimmy, with or without Mack's permission. Noah told me how desperate she was for freedom. She still owns everything here, and I have a lot of fucking questions for her."

"But will she continue with their plan now that Noah is gone? He said she had trust issues."

"Then we better show her how trustworthy we are, but first we're getting some fucking answers. I want to know what the hell happened between them, and I won't rest until I do."

The old ladies and the bunnies put on a fine spread for the northern wolves, and everyone fueled themselves with food and alcohol. Mixed emotions were cast over the bar like a rainbow in a gray sky. It had been a hard day for all, as no further clues emerged regarding Noah's murder. MC members cried and laughed, reminiscing about the fallen Prez. There was the usual orgy taking place in the bar's corner, with the new Prez having his pick of the bunnies.

Zander sat at the bar, alone and isolated. Seething and drowning his sorrows, he glowered at Mack, returning from his call to Frankie, watching his every move until he perched himself on the opposing bar stool.

"All quiet in Uskiville," he said as he perched himself next to Zander.

Zander nodded, uninterested.

"Look, Frankie has informed me Dragon made a large deposit into your account this morning. She wants to pay for Noah's funeral, and if there's anything else you need, just ask," Mack said.

"Funny, we needed help months ago. Where were you then? And as for Welsh Cake, you should have allowed her to pay her respects. I know she would be here now; I know how fond she was of Noah. She told me so at Christmas. Besides, I want to talk to her."

Mack shook his head in firm disagreement. "It's not safe for her, Zander. I'm not letting anything happen to her."

"Nothing will happen to her here. I will protect her!"

"Like you protected Noah?" he said through gritted teeth.

"Get to fuck, you Irish prick! You can't keep her caged forever, and if she's a fraction of the Dragon, you make her out to be. She'll break free from her shackles and fucking ruin you." Zander snatched the bottle of whiskey off the table before stumbling away, leaving Mack shaking his head at the grieving VP.

Zander locked himself in his room, spending the following two days in a beer-fueled slumber as his unanswered questions bounced around his brain. He didn't bid farewell to Mack and his Uskiville brothers when they left for home. He couldn't stomach it, only leaving his room to retrieve another bottle of whiskey. After waking from another booze-filled night, the rage and unanswered questions still poisoned his soul. Zander needed to know what happened to his brother, and he believed B had the answers. His alcohol-induced rage and anxiety became too much for him as he believed she was responsible for Noah's death. Clambering to his feet, he grabbed his keys: the potent stench of sweat, whiskey and cigarettes following him out of his room as he strolled through the bar.

"Hey, where are you going, VP?" Eddie shouted across the bar, only for his words to fall on deaf ears as Zander continued out the door.

Zander climbed onto his bike, bringing it to life.

"Where the fuck is he going? He's in no fit state to ride anywhere," Jimmy shouted as Zander sped off.

"No idea!" Eddie said.

"Shit!" Jimmy snapped, realizing where Zander was going. "Get everyone and follow me! He's heading to Uskiville, and it won't be pretty."

CHAPTER NINE

Zander's Rage

B parked in her driveway following another team win that she couldn't bring herself to celebrate because she was still mourning the loss of her friend. She hoped the team understood. Noah's death puzzled her, and she couldn't put her finger on what it was she didn't quite grasp. Casting her mind back to the night he gifted her with the bracelet, his words sending shivers down her spine:

If anything ever happens to me, look after Zander.

She trembled at the thought of Noah knowing his fate, making B shake her head as if to cast the thoughts out of her mind. It was all too much for her. If Noah had been in danger, why couldn't he confide in her? Their friendship had been built on trust, and now B began to doubt even that. Her thoughts crashed over her like waves trying to drown her; she couldn't fight them, she couldn't breathe.

The roaring sound of a motorcycle distracted her perilous thoughts as she rested against her fixed-up Humvee, rescuing her from the waves and back to reality.

She didn't recognize the bike, or who was riding it, and B knew everyone who stepped foot on her land.

The old bike pulled into her drive, and her hackles went up.

Who the bloody hell is this?

As the rider parked and began to unbuckle his brain bucket, B witnessed an entourage of bikers riding up the street toward her, making her feel uneasy. The biker's helmet came off to reveal a thick mop of black hair, and as the rider raised his head, it became clear to B who it was.

The breath in her lungs escaped as her eyes tracked his movements. *But why is he here?*

"Scottie," she murmured as he approached with tired eyes and a furrowed brow. He looked exhausted and menacing, as if he hadn't slept.

Stopping dead in front of her, he towered over her, grabbing her arm by force, and pulling her toward her house.

"We need to fucking talk, Welsh Cake!"

B, alarmed and confused by his demeanor, yanked her arm out of his grasp.

"Take your bloody hands off me, Scottie, and what the fuck is your problem?"

Zander's agitated demeanor panicked her as he stood a breath away from her, grabbing at her shirt, reeking of tobacco and cheap whiskey.

"I'll tell you what my fucking problem is, darling! You getting my best friend fucking killed."

B's eyes tempered up like wildfire, anger coursing through her veins like a snake's venom. It was bad enough that Frankie had cuffed her to a bed and now the Sunnyville chapter believed she was responsible for her friend's death. B's self-destruct button had been pushed, enraging her with Zander in the firing line. Without a moment's thought, she gripped onto his precious cut and head-butted him in the mouth, watching as blood poured from his lips.

"How bloody dare you! Noah was my fucking friend. I trusted him. You're the psychopathic criminals, not me good boy!"

"You bitch! I'll fucking—"

Just then, Jimmy came from nowhere, taking hold of the Scotsman. Three other members of the Sunnyville chapter raced to help their Prez wrestle with the infuriated Scot.

B watched as an angry Zander tried to push them off: "You think I'm responsible? Why the bloody hell would I want him dead, Scottie?"

Zander lunged at her, but his brothers held him off.

"I wanna know what the fuck went on between you and Noah."

"Fuck you, Scottie. Who do you think you are?"

"Why have all those midnight meetings? The weekends not enough for you? You were seducing my brother for your own gains, Welsh Cake, and I wanna know what happened to him."

B stopped dead in her tracks, almost hyperventilating with confusion. "Wait, what? I met him the Saturday night before he died, Scottie, that's it. The weekends, yes, but I only met Noah at night once, at his request."

"Liar!" Zander said, breaking free of his brothers to lunge at her, pushing her onto the wooden, porch steps behind her.

B's head hit the solid, oak handrail as she fell upon the steps, grazing her temple. A little disorientated, she heard a familiar voice coming from behind her.

"What the feck are you doing to my dragon?" Mack bellowed, landing a punch on Zander's jaw.

Zander didn't flinch, returning the favor as the two men brawled with the rest of the wolves, trying to pull them apart.

B sat on the steps trying to get her bearings as Frankie raced to her, dropping to his knees to cradle her head in his hands.

"Let me look at you B," he said, retrieving a clean handkerchief from his jeans pocket.

"I'm fine. We need to help Mackie," she said, pulling herself up onto her feet.

Frankie wrapped his arms around her waist. "No, B! You're staying put. VP needs to be put in his place. He needs a good slap for turning up and causing trouble."

"Then let me bloody do it!" she snapped as she tried to break free of his grasp.

"No! You're staying put!"

Anger burned inside her soul as she witnessed Mack and Zander rain heavy blows down on one another until the sound of a gunshot halted everyone and Ari emerged with a shotgun.

"Stop it! Are you all animals? This is a quiet retreat!"

Mack and Zander stood, dusting themselves off before Mack took the gun from Ari, reloaded, and pointed it at Zander's head. "You better have a good explanation for this."

"Oh, aye brother. How about my brother is dead after spending all his time with that bitch you call Dragon?"

Before Mack could respond, B spat back. "Fuck you, Scottie! Noah was my friend. I was helping him."

Zander wiped his mouth with the back of his hand and glared at her. "Then what happened to him?"

"How the bloody hell should I know? You're the bloody one-percenters, good boy! Killing is part of your repertoire, not mine! And Noah thought you could change? Hah! Once a one-percenter, always a one-percenter." She pointed a finger at him. "Now fuck off! My boys will be home now, in a minute, and you're not scaring them, you bloody bully."

"I'm not going nowhere until I get some answers about you and Noah."

B's lips stretched into a sinister smile.

"Paranoid I was riding your friend and not you, Scottie? Is that it? I'm not telling you shit!"

"Then I'll just have to drag the answers out of you."

Gasps echoed around the drive as Frankie and Mack stepped in front of B to protect her, only for B to push past them.

"When you're big enough, good boy!" B snapped.

Zander growled, but he gave a startled jump back, surprised by a car pulling up out front.

B quickly wiped the excess blood off her head and pushed past Zander with Mack and Frankie in tow.

Mack handed the gun to Ari, who hid it under B's Humvee, whilst the rest of the wolves looked on.

"Hello, my lovelies, I missed you!" B said as Rhys and Madoc emerged from their father's car before it sped off in haste.

"Aye, we missed you, too. Hey, what happened to your head?" Rhys asked as he hugged his mother.

"Just me and Uncle Mack grappling again."

"Be careful, Uncle Mack. You know my mom can kick your ass." Madoc said as he too greeted his mother with a hug and a kiss on the cheek.

"Hey! Language sunshine, or your phone is mine for a week."

"Sorry, Mum, sorry Uncle Mack."

"Good! Now, my purse is in my office. Why don't you order a load of pizzas for tea tonight?" B said as Mack tussled Madoc's hair in passing.

"Oh, sweet!" Madoc said as the two boys headed inside.

B watched them close the door before turning to face Jimmy.

"Right! I need to talk to Jimmy alone, but you better put your bloody wolf on a leash because he's not stepping foot inside my house."

"No! You talk to me, Dragon!" Zander snarled.

"Fuck you!" B said to Zander before turning back to Jimmy. "Take it or leave it, Prez. I got shit to do!"

Jimmy glared at Zander, shaking his head at him.

"Stay put Zand. That's an order from your Prez!"

"What?"

"You heard! It's bad enough we had to come up here after you. Now let me sort this shit!"

Zander huffed, running his fingers through his hair as he stormed down the drive.

B headed up the wooden steps, giving Frankie and Jimmy a nod. "Take them to the bar and make sure they stay out of trouble, please?" before heading inside with Jimmy.

B welcomed Jimmy into her office.

"Drink?" she said, offering him a whiskey from the cabinet in the office's corner.

"Sure!"

B poured two enormous glasses of the good stuff and headed over to the chocolate leather sofa in her office. "Sit, please?" she gestured as she handed him the glass and watched as he settled into his seat next to her.

B took a sip of her whiskey. "Did Noah ever explain our plans to you, Jimmy?"

"Not really. He told us you own everything around us, including our home, and he was going to introduce us at long last, right before he died."

"I had nothing to do with Noah's death, Jimmy. Why would I want to kill the man who was helping me escape Uskiville? It makes no sense."

"Nothing makes sense to me, Dragon, so enlighten me, Please?"

B stared at him for a second as if to figure out if he could be trusted. "I need you to promise our conversation does not reach the ears of Mackie and Frankie."

"Fair enough! Noah said you want to tell Mack yourself."

"That's right! When the time comes, I need to be the one to tell him. This all goes away if he knows before."

"I don't know what this is."

"Did you trust, Noah?" she asked.

"With my life!"

"Then let's not let his dream die by fucking it up and telling Mackie and Frankie, okay?"

Jimmy clinked his glass to hers. "Agreed. Now start talking."

"Noah knew from the moment he met me that I was lost. I needed a fresh start and when we got talking, I knew my future was no longer in Uskiville."

"So, what? You and Noah just hatched a plan to help you escape?"

B curled her lips into a reminiscent smile "Well, it didn't quite happen like that. I needed an out, and Noah wanted Sunnyville to become white. He wanted more for the club. We both did."

"I'm listening."

B set her glass down onto the coffee table. "I own everything, but I have a coaching job. Right now, I need people I can trust to build my business. Noah gave me the club as part of a deal to ensure the future of the Sunnyville chapter. If I gave you stability as a chapter, he would help me run my business. He wanted you to take over as he was going to step down as Prez. You were the one to lead, he said."

"Yeah, Zander said."

B retrieved her glass once more, nervousness and hurt cascaded through her body as she knocked back her whiskey. "It's true. Noah wanted the club to have a future, but he didn't want to lead."

"What about Zander. He was supposed to be happy, too, right?"

B laughed. "Oh, he had plans for him to run off and have Celt babies with me. He honestly thought we could be together. Can you believe that shit?"

"Dragon, Zander has been pining for you for a long time."

"Funny way of showing it. Besides, I don't do relationships!" she shrugged.

"Look, he's besotted with you. He's just messed up with grief. He's always been merciless, but Noah kept him grounded just enough to function and now he's lost his anchor."

B shot Jimmy a look of surprise as her promise to Noah came to mind.

"Are you alright? Did I say something wrong?"

B shook her head, taken aback by it all. "It's just Noah said the same thing. He made me promise to look after him."

"What do you mean?"

"The last time I saw him, he asked me to meet him late to sign the club over to me. To show me that Sunnyville could be trusted. He made me promise to look after Scottie if anything happened to him, saying he needed an anchor."

Jimmy narrowed his eyes at her. "What?"

"Jimmy, I swear, I questioned him about talking like that, and he promised nothing was up and now I can't think about anything else. I should have pressed him, but he insisted he was going nowhere. I trusted him, and now I have to live with that. So maybe Scottie is right, maybe I am responsible, because something was up Jimmy. I just know it, and I'll never forgive myself for that," B said as she hung her head in shame.

Jimmy edged toward her, placing his arm around her and startling her. "Listen, Doll Face, this ain't on you! Noah told us the same thing. For whatever reason, he chose his path. So don't waste another minute feeling guilty. He wouldn't want that. Now tell me, did you tell anyone about this?"

B shook her head. "No."

"Good. We need to keep this between us until we know what's happened."

"Okay."

"Good! Now what happens next?"

"I have business in Sunnyville to seal the deal in a few weeks. Once the deal is done, I can get the ball rolling with you, but you need to control your wolf. I can't have him terrifying my boys. They're not used to being around one-percenters. We live a peaceful life here."

"I'll talk to him."

"Good luck. He wanted to take my head off."

Jimmy tilted his head in a humorous smile. "You did headbutt him."

"I don't enjoy being manhandled."

"No shit!" Jimmy chuckled before returning the same question. "What about you? Can you control your wolf?"

"Consider him handled," she said, giving him a wink.

"Jeez. You're a right ball-buster, aren't you?" Jimmy smirked.

B grinned, pouring another shot into Jimmy's glass. "I didn't get where I was today by being a sissy, Jimmy, but I'm sorry I lost my shit out there! I really want this to work."

"Me too! We're screwed without you. Our club is hanging on by a thread. I have brothers who are considering going back to the old ways if they don't see any green soon. They have families, bills to pay, and they're struggling. So, we would appreciate it if we could earn some green now."

B knocked back her shot. Rising, she approached her safe and removed multiple bricks of cash and a manilla envelope. Returning to her seat, she poured another shot and slid the cash across the table.

"Here, this will tide you over until I sort your contracts. I tried to give it to Noah months ago."

Jimmy's eyes widened, his jaw slack in shock as he stared at the cash.

"There must be about twenty grand there."

"Thirty! I don't want anyone struggling anymore. No more temptations back to black. If we work together, you stay white. You got that?"

"Absolutely! And we'll pay you back every cent."

"Consider it a signing on bonus, and that's your contract. As you can see, it's signed by our boy, but I'm willing to consider some adjustments seeing as though there's a new Prez. Read it over and let me know if you're in. You can confirm in a few weeks when I visit, and if you're not interested, then no hard feelings. Oh, and Mackie has my details, so let him know if you need anything."

"I'd appreciate that, Dragon. Like I said, we're broke."

"No problem. Now look at the contract."

Jimmy picked up the manilla envelope and removed the contract. Taking his time, he explored the brief as B retrieved some pizza that had arrived moments earlier.

"You and Noah came up with this?"

"We did!"

"It's a genius idea. There's nothing like this there."

"I know," B said dangling a slice of pizza into her mouth.

"And this is what you want in Sunnyville?" he said, raising an eyebrow and grinning like a Cheshire cat.

"It is!"

"And you think you can convince the townsfolk to trust a bunch of ex-cons?"

"Well, I did here, didn't I? Look Jimmy, I got this. But do you all have me? I need confirmation that my boys and I have a future there. I need to know they'll be safe."

"Dragon, I've read the brief and yeah, they'll be safe. However, this needs to be voted in."

"Do what you must, but your wolves need to keep it shut when it comes to Mackie and Frankie. Especially that loose cannon of a VP."

"He won't say shit! I told you; he likes you."

"I saw the look in his eyes. The man wanted to tear me apart."

"He thinks you and Noah had a history."

B burst into a fit of laughter. "Me and Baby Face? That's the most ridiculous thing I've heard. I don't screw pretty boys."

Jimmy sighed. "Yeah, but Zand is pretty screwed up right now. He's lost his best friend right before he was due to be introduced the woman of his dreams. His world has fallen apart, and he likes and needs you. See Zand don't get up close and personal with no one. Never has, but he wants to with you. It's always been the three of us and now he's lost. Just like he was when he joined the MC."

"I'm sorry, Jimmy, and I feel for the guy, but I don't do loose cannon Scotsmen. I've had my fill of them!"

"I noticed your boys' accents. You clearly have a soft spot for other Celts."

"I'm a very proud Celt, good boy! But I have no interest in settling down. Now do me a favor, take that pizza to the wolves, then go home and vote. I don't want Mackie any more suspicious than he already is."

"I hear you! Just one more question... Mackie would die for you. So, why leave him?"

B stood and opened the office door.

"Mackie doesn't love me, Prez. He needs me. There's a difference. I used to think he did, and I love him like a brother. I would die for him, but he betrayed me, broke my trust. This past year he's been different, secretive and agitated, and I can't live like that. The time has come for a fresh start. So, hide that contract, take the pizza, and go talk to your brothers."

"Right, then." Jimmy said as he wedged the contract in his inside pocket and buttoned up his cut.

"You'll come to the funeral?" Jimmy asked.

"I'll try, Jimmy, but that won't be a straightforward task."

"Noah would want you there."

"I know!" she sighed. "Come on, get going. We don't want hangry bikers."

Jimmy laughed as B led him back to the kitchen and handed him a stack of pizza boxes. She opened the door where Bamfa was waiting.

"Take him to the club, please."

"Mackie wants me on you?" Bamfa said.

B's hackles went up, startling the young brother.

"You pissed me off by slashing my tires, good boy. Do you want another shiner to match the last one I gave you? Escort Jimmy to the bloody club and tell Mackie if I see a patch on my door again, I'll choke him. Understood?"

"Understood," he muttered.

Jimmy's eyes widened as Bamfa gulped in fear.

B gave him a cheeky wink. "Chap my door when you're on your way, Prez." she said, before heading inside, still troubled by the onslaught that occurred on her drive.

B had a splitting headache and figured a shower might help her feel better. As the water soaked her skin, she tried to fathom Zander's reason for believing she was behind Noah's murder, but she couldn't understand it. Her head pricked like a bee sting as she washed the dried blood from her grazed temple and her mind spun back to him, Zander, the man who had invaded her dreams since their video call last Christmas. She was unnerved by him. This perfectly chiseled, tattooed man, who had begged to visit Uskiville had lashed out in a grief-stricken rage this evening, unlike her fantasies where he seduced her.

B had been secretly looking forward to meeting him, the only man to catch her eye since her ex-husband. She had slept with plenty of Sultry boys for the sake of scratching an itch, but nobody had gotten under her skin like Zander. He'd plagued her thoughts and dreams, and now that Noah was gone, he wasn't the flirtatious and fun-loving guy she thought he was. He was a crazed predator hunting his prey, and B was just that.

B felt bad about head-butting him and as much as she wouldn't admit it to anyone, he'd scared her on the driveway when he took hold of her, resulting in her lashing out. B was a hard-faced woman. She would allow no one to see her insecure or unconfident. That was the old B; the new B couldn't tolerate that.

Heading out of the shower, she wrapped her hair in a towel and got into her red silk night shirt and dressing gown before heading back into her office. Sitting at her desk, she stared at the blank note pad in front of her with a plan to write Zander a note apologizing for her actions. She knew Noah would not want them to become enemies. B believed his actions were confirmation that her fantasies were just that, and there was no chance of her pursuing him further after witnessing his true nature. Besides, they were going to be working together, and B never mixed business with pleasure.

B rolled her eyes, huffing at the thought of an apology letter. She didn't apologize. People often needed to apologize to her, yet here she was putting pen to paper.

Dear Scottie,

I want to apologize for my actions today.

You startled me with your angry demeanor, and I should have seen how much you were hurting.

I know you think I'm to blame for what happened, but I promise you, hand on heart, I had nothing to do with Baby Face's death.

Baby Face had become my friend and confidante. He talked about you often, and if he'd had his way, we would have been married by now; ridiculous, I know!

He loved you and his pack.

It shouldn't have been his time, and I'll find out what happened to him. That, I can promise you.

We planned to do something special in Sunnyville, and I would like to pursue it. I don't want to be your enemy, Scottie, so I offer you this olive branch.

Baby Face gifted this to me the last time I saw him. He told me what each charm meant, and although it's precious to me, I think you need it more right now.

Just promise to keep it safe and maybe one day you'll let me tell you about it.

Enjoy the good stuff and toast your fallen brother for me as you drink it.

From one heartfelt Celt to another, I am so sorry for your loss.

Welsh Cake

xxx

B placed the bracelet Noah had gifted her along with the letter in a small white envelope and retrieved two new bottles of the good stuff before placing it by the front door, ready for Jimmy's arrival.

CHAPTER TEN

Watch Your Fucking Tone VP

Zander waited in church for Jimmy's return. He sat staring into his drink until Jimmy entered a while later, dumping a load of pizzas on the table.

As soon as he took a seat, Zander pounced. "Well. What she tell you?"

Eager eyes laced the room awaiting Jimmy's reply whilst they stuffed their faces with cold pizza.

"The truth! She had nothing to do with Noah's death!"

"Of course, she didn't. She's white! Now I'll ask you again, what have you boys gotten yourselves into?" Mack said.

"Fuck all!" Zander spat, staring at Jimmy and getting up from his seat. "You've had your shot, Prez. Now let me have mine. I'll drag it out of her!"

Jimmy rose to meet his gaze, taking hold of his cut from across the table. "You made a promise to Noah, just as I did. Now I'm asking you to show me the same fucking courtesy. Now listen when I tell you, Dragon didn't do it. She's a hard woman, but even I can see she's hurting. Grieving, for fuck's sake, and you're trying to slap her silly."

"You're lucky she didn't kill you," Mack spat.

Zander brushed Jimmy off, pulling away from him and scoffing at Mack's remark.

"Oh, you think I'm fecking joking? You just made an enemy of my Dragon. You're fecking done, pal!" Mack snapped.

"Your bitch of a Dragon dinnae scare me! I'll snap her pretty little neck!"

Frankie rose from his seat. Chest puffed out as he met Zander's gaze. "Watch your fucking tone VP. Otherwise, the only neck getting snapped is yours. B's like a sister to me and she's no fucking killer!"

"Enough! We have a funeral to sort!" Mack snapped, banging his gavel to call order.

"No! *We* do, and we're leaving now!" Jimmy said.

"I still want answers!" Zander said.

"I don't fucking care what you want! I'm the Prez, and I'm telling you we're leaving now! We don't know who took out Noah, and our club could be vulnerable. Now move your ass, the lot of you!"

Zander glared at Jimmy's stern expression. He knew Jimmy had discovered something. Something he didn't want the Uskiville pack to hear. Zander was impeccable at reading the room, and despite wanting answers, he knew he had to dance to Jimmy's tune. Jimmy was Prez now. That had been Noah's wish, and Zander would respect it.

Zander, Jimmy, and the rest of the wolves walked back to B's drive, ready to head home. Zander was unhappy about leaving, but he respected Jimmy enough to know when to quit. He also knew B must have confided in Jimmy to make him want to leave. Approaching his bike, Zander climbed on and watched as Jimmy headed up the steps to B's cabin again.

"Where are you going?"

His question fell on deaf ears as he watched B open the door in nothing but a silk dressing gown. Zander's body trembled as if his heart wanted to lurch into her presence. Take hold of her, make her his. However, his head was screaming at him, telling him to stay put. He watched as B embraced Jimmy with a warm smile as she wrapped her hands around him, making Zander's blood boil.

Jimmy left with a smile on his face, making his way to his bike with two bottles of Welsh whiskey as an infuriated Zander glared at him.

"What? I suppose I'm fucking Dragon too now?" he said, shaking his head in disgust before placing the whiskey in his bag and climbing onto his bike. The stream of bikers' engines roared in chorus, and Zander let out a huge sigh as he revved his engine in harmony with his brothers before taking one last look at B's house and speeding off into the sunset.

On arrival at the Sunnyville MC, everyone gathered at church, eagerly awaiting on what Jimmy had to say. Hopeful faces sat around the table, except for Zander, who grimaced impatiently. He wanted answers, and he knew Jimmy had them. Jimmy entered the room holding a manilla envelope and two bottles of Welsh whiskey, placing them on the table, he sat in the President's chair. Zander studied him as he retrieved a larger envelope and several bricks of cash from inside his cut, placing them on the table too.

"Right! First order of business. Dragon isn't responsible for Noah's murder, and if anyone wants to say otherwise, step up and say it to my face. Understood?" Jimmy barked.

"Ayes" echoed around the room as Zander grunted in acknowledgement.

Jimmy continued. "You need to understand a few things. Noah and Dragon were working on something big for Sunnyville, and because of that, Dragon now owns our club, the land it sits on, and everything around us."

Gasps and confused stares flooded the room.

"Yeah, and tonight, I read the contract Dragon and Noah put together, and I have to be honest. It's fucking genius."

Zander's eyes widened as he waited for Jimmy to continue. "Don't keep us in suspense. Tell us what's happening."

"All right, Jeez! Well, we have a choice. We go back to the old ways and let Noah's dream die with him, or work with Dragon and go legit like Noah wanted. Now hear me out. If we go back to the old ways, I'm pretty sure she'll cut all ties with the club, but if we stay white, as she calls it, this is what we get," he said, pushing the large envelope and cash in the middle of the table, whilst his brothers looked on with slack jaws.

"What the fuck is this, Prez?" Zander asked.

"It's thirty large to tie us over and a contract securing the club's future. It's bold and beautiful fellas and I'm talking pensions, a livable wage, an onsite doctor- a future! Noah and Dragon were working on something special, but don't take my word for it. Look yourselves.

Skeptical eyes darted around the room as Zander snatched the envelope and studied the contract. Everyone watched as his eyes widened before he stared at Jimmy.

"This is for real?" he asked, raising an eyebrow at him.

"As real as you and me, brother. Noah came through for us. All those promises, they're right there and that Dragon you want to kill is the one making it happen," Jimmy said as he rose to gather a set of whiskey glasses. Pouring equal measures into the glasses, he distributed them across the table.

"Dragon has promised to help the club and turn this place into a money-making pit. She wants to build a live lounge bar that attaches to the club and all that crashing and banging we've been putting up with, well that's her gym, sauna, steam room, bistro, shake shack, and food bank. She owns it all, and she wants us to run it with her, legit like. We're talking serious green in wages. Or we go back to fighting for scraps," he said, shrugging his shoulders.

Each member took their time to study the contract whilst Jimmy gave everyone an equal share of the cash B had given them.

"There are three big ones for each of us and the rest goes into the club. There are no conditions for this cash. This is a gift and Dragon is paying for the funeral, so we need to plan the perfect send off. Agreed?"

"Ayes" echoed throughout the square-shaped room before Jimmy continued.

"There's one more thing you need to know, and this doesn't leave the room," Jimmy said as he glanced at Zander.

Zander nodded in approval before Jimmy continued.

"A few days before Noah died, he made Zander and I promise to keep Dragon safe, and I mean take a bullet for her if necessary. He trusted her, and I know we don't know her yet, but I need you all to make the same promise. And not because she's Ms. Moneybags, but because she was special to him. Special enough for him to gift her with his mom's bracelet, and we all know he never took it off."

"So, she was his old lady?" Tiny asked.

Zander stood in a fit of rage. "No! She was never his! He was setting me up with her. Keep your filthy hands off. She's off limits!"

"No offense, VP. I don't think you two are exactly a match made in heaven. You wanted to kill each other a few hours ago!" Eddie chortled.

Zander growled. "A misunderstanding is all! She'll still be mine soon enough, and once she learns her place, we'll be good."

"I wouldn't be so sure. I think she hates you. But don't worry, I'll show her a good time for you," Tiny teased.

Zander slammed his hands down on the table. "Touch her and you die! Clear?"

"She's fair game, VP. Club rules! You've not claimed her, so we get to see who she takes an interest in. I got fifty on me," Tiny teased again.

"I'll fucking kill you!" Zander spat, diving across the table at the club's enforcer.

"That's enough! Tiny! I'm not finished! If you want to continue breathing, I suggest you pipe down." Jimmy slammed, pushing Zander back to his seat.

"Sorry, Prez," Tiny said.

Zander's blood pressure soared. Lost for words, he stared at his president, waiting for him to finish.

Jimmy straightened his cut. "Right then. We need to vote on this, but whatever happens, Uskiville doesn't hear a word. Mack doesn't know Dragon and Noah have been cooking this up and if he finds out before Dragon has everything in place, we're all fucked. Now I want your word, fellas!"

"Shit! The founder doesn't know. I'm not sure about this, Prez," Tiny said.

"Then fucking get sure, because if anything happens to Welsh Cake because somebody in this room opened their mouths, they're done!" Zander snapped.

"VP is right! This is Noah's last hurrah. It was his club, his dream, and I know he's not here to see it through, but we are. Now you know everything, so let's vote. Those in favor of reverting to the old ways raise your hands.

All hands remained around their whiskey glasses, so Jimmy continued. "All those in favor of working with Dragon and continuing Noah's legacy, raise your hand."

The room filled with raised hands.

"Nine out of nine. Welcome to the future, fellas! Everyone get cleaned up. We meet back in an hour to discuss the funeral," Jimmy said, smashing the gavel down to seal the deal and watching the pack disperse.

"Uh, not you, VP. Close the door. We need to talk."

Zander closed the door and turned to Jimmy. "Look, I know I fucked up..."

"It's nothing to do with that. Here, Dragon asked me to give you these," Jimmy said, handing him a small white envelope and a bottle of her good stuff.

Zander peered down at the envelope. "What's this?"

"I don't fucking know. I'm just the messenger!" Jimmy said before leaving Zander alone with his gifts.

Zander sat on his bed, staring down at the envelope in his hand, with *"Scottie"* scrawled across the front. It felt a little heavy to be just a letter, and the nerves ripped through him as he contemplated opening it. His heart pounding, desperate yet frightened to open it. He knew he'd' messed up today, and the worst part was, he didn't really believe B was responsible for Noah's death. The thought of them being entwined enraged him, and he was desperate to find out if Noah had, in fact, betrayed him. It would be easier to grieve if he had. Zander's heart was breaking. He needed to take the pain away, and if Noah turned out to have betrayed him, it would be easier to get over his death. He never imagined the onslaught that occurred at B's house afterwards. In his head, she would cry on his shoulder and then he'd make her his. Everything was crystal clear in his head, only things didn't pan out the way he'd planned.

Taking the cap off the whiskey, Zander took a huge glug before opening the envelope.

Inside was a handwritten note and the bracelet Noah had gifted her. Reading through the note, Zander's heart ached. He could tell she was hurting by the tone of the letter, and it wracked him with guilt. He'd made her feel responsible and less deserving of the bracelet she had enclosed in the envelope. Reading the words, he could sense the purity of her heart and became angry about the way he'd treated her. Zander struggled with his emotions. He couldn't breathe as his chest became tight. Catching his breath, he headed to the office where Jimmy was looking at a casket catalog.

Zander stared hard at him, losing control as his body shook. He hated the thought of burying his best friend.

"You alright, VP?" Jimmy asked, placing the catalog in the desk drawer.

Snapping himself out of his dread-filled consciousness, Zander adjusted himself where he stood. "Uh, aye! I'm needing Welsh Cake's number."

"Why?"

"Why do you think? To talk to her."

Jimmy rose from his chair with flailing arms. "Oh, no. No fucking way! You've done enough. Just let the dust settle for a bit, yeah?"

"Jimmy, I need to talk to her. I want to apologize. Please pal? She gave me this and this is no' meant for me. Noah wanted her to have it." he said, holding up Noah's mother's bracelet.

"Then return it to her if she makes it to the funeral. Besides, I don't have her number. She never gave it to me."

"Wait, what do you mean, *if* she makes it?"

"You really think Mack will let her go now, after your antics today? He was bad enough before you pulled that shit."

"He better, Jimmy, or I'll kill him."

"How about we sign the contract first and— Aww, crap! Did you lift the contract from church?"

"No, you're the fucking Prez. It's your job to keep it safe!"

"Fuck! It better still be there!" Jimmy said in a panic as he left his office.

Zander shouted after him. "And who's gonna steal it. It benefits all of us, you numpty!"

CHAPTER ELEVEN

Little Spy

"Where the fuck is my update?" Blaze snapped as he paced his office.

A tall, slim, middle-aged man with no teeth stood in the office doorway, trembling. "Uh, he's not checked in yet, Prez. I've tried calling him, but he's not responded."

"If he's double-crossed me, I'll christen my claw on his flesh and gut him like a fish."

"H-he is undercover, boss. Maybe he's just busy blending in?"

Blaze stopped in his tracks, rubbing his chin with his cigarette-stained fingers. "You're right! Why didn't I think of that?"

"Uh, I dunno boss."

"Come here, I want to commend you for your intelligence."

The man approached Blaze, appearing rather pleased with himself as Blaze placed a caring arm around his shoulder.

"You're a clever guy, Duck. You really are. Sometimes too clever for your own good," he said, punching him in the face.

The man struggled to catch his breath as Blaze gripped him by the throat. "Now, the next time you run that smart mouth, I'll cut your fucking tongue out. Comprehend?"

"Yes, boss. Sorry, boss!"

Blaze dropped the man to the floor, turning to his desk to light up a cigarette.

"If I don't hear from him within the hour, he's done. Now get out of my sight and clean yourself up, you piece of shit!"

Blaze watched his little spy drag himself out of the office, closing the door behind him. His breathing grew heavy, and his patience was wearing thin. The reformed Red-Pitbulls MC was struggling, and he knew he was running out of time. If his undercover spy had failed his mission, he would have no choice but to move in on Dragon to coerce her into signing Sunnyville over to him.

Deep in thought, he began jotting down his options on a scrap of paper from his desk when his phone rang.

His heart raced in anticipation as he answered the call. "Where the fuck have you been?"

"Sorry Prez, the shit has hit the fan here, and I had to wait until I gathered all my intel before giving you feedback."

"Fucking spit it out then."

"Shit's unravelling here. Mack is furious with Sunnyville, and I'll be honest. The feeling seems to be mutual here after Zander lost his shit and tried to attack Dragon. He's blaming her for Noah's death somehow."

"Oh, this is fucking priceless. Tell me more."

"He rode up to Uskiville demanding answers, and the feisty bitch head butted him. You can only imagine his reaction..."

"Ha ha! I'm liking this Dragon. Maybe we can use her, change her mind. Make her see that she's picked the wrong MC?"

"I dunno, Prez. The club is buzzing tonight after she's decided to work with Sunnyville, leaving Mack in the cold. She's done with him and plans to shaft him when the time's right. I studied the contract and Sunnyville is going to be huge."

"Oh, the gods are in my favor at last. What else?"

"She's coming to Sunnyville to seal the deal in a few weeks. I doubt she'll make the funeral. Mack has her locked down."

Blaze pinched his chin between his thumb and forefinger. "Couldn't risk it, anyway. They'll have too many allies in town for Noah's send off. It'll have to be later. Anything else?"

"Yeah, her pockets seem to be way deeper than we thought. She's building an empire here. I've sent you a photograph of the contract she offered. She's loaded."

"Great work. I knew I could always trust you! You're loyal to the cause."

"Absolutely! Long live the Red Pitbulls!"

"That's the attitude! Now make me proud and let me know when she's in town."

"Will do, Prez!"

Blaze hung up the phone, punching the air with glee. His little spy had come through, and he was going to take Sunnyville by force.

CHAPTER TWELVE
Mourning

Mack rushed around the cabin, tossing his clothes into his bag, ready to attend Noah's funeral. His team were assembled and readying themselves, and even Frankie would make the trip.

B had refused to talk to Mack since his arrival home from Sunnyville, despite his efforts to defend her on the driveway. Instead, she chose to lock herself in her office, barely speaking to anyone. Frankie informed him how he'd freed her from her cuffs a few hours after he'd left for Sunnyville, only for B to lose it after seeing the state of her Humvee, punching a frightened Bamfa in the face and insisting on having her car fixed by morning. Frankie watched over her, and she didn't attempt to escape, instead she remained mute until her boys returned home on the Sunday evening.

Mack made it his first stop to check in on B, heading to the school office on Monday morning to talk, only to be told that B was unavailable. He tried again, waiting for her and the boys to arrive home after school, but B pushed past him as if he wasn't there. She was acting like he no longer existed. In fact, she shunned all the MC members who had aided Mack in her captivity that night. She was done with them.

Ari was the only person to get through to her after Mack became withdrawn, unable to cope with his dragon, ignoring him. She had spent hours over at B's as Mack waited with Frankie for her to bring B over so they could make peace, only for Ari to return and lose it with them for handcuffing her. Ari explained how unforgivable it was for them to stop her from conveying her condolences and suggesting they allow her to attend Noah's funeral and protect her themselves. This was to no avail, leaving Mack in Ari's bad books and taking baby Alex and the boys to stay with B. Both the women Mack loved had shut him out with a week passing without a word from either of them, making Mack frantic. He was about to leave for Sunnyville when Ari showed up with the baby.

"Hey," he said shrugging into his cut.

"Hey, I figured today is going to be hard for you, so I wanted to bring Alex over to see her daddy before you left," she said, handing him his daughter.

Mack kissed Alex on her button nose and played with her. "Thank you. I've missed you all. The cabin isn't right without you."

"Well, whose fault is that?"

"Don't start this today, Ari. I'm hanging on by a thread as it is. Now I've apologized a million times to both of you. What more do you want? Blood? Is that it?"

"Mack, you locked up your best friend and kept her from grieving. Yes, you defended her when Zander lost his shit, but you won't even let her go to Noah's funeral, and there's plenty of you there to protect her. She can look after herself, so let her go."

Mack threw his head to the ceiling. "God dammit! No Ari! If Blaze—"

"Oh, stop it, Mack. Blaze is gone. Noah's death was an unfortunate shooting. You said so yourself, so stop imprisoning your friend before you lose her for good."

"Ari, I know you'll never understand my logic, so let's just leave it, sweetheart, please?"

"Fine, then don't expect us to be home when you return. I don't want to be around someone who is hell bent on hurting the ones he loves."

Mack placed Alex in her portable crib after she had fallen asleep in his arms and took Ari by the wrists, pinning her against the wall. His eyes like daggers as he stared into hers, "You will fecking be waiting when I get back, and you'll be wearing something that pleases me. You're mine, remember, not Dragon's, mine, and while I appreciate the solidarity that you have for one another. You're my old lady! You agreed to stand by me the night Junior went missing and I made you mine. Filled you with myself as part of our union. You don't support my dragon, you support me, and I don't care how much she's hurting because at least she's still breathing. You got that, woman?"

Ari nodded, remembering the vow she had taken that night. She remembered how Mack took her and made her his, taking her as part of the club charter requirements when acquiring an old lady as property. Ari knew her loyalty had to be to Mack and the MC, so she softened at his orders.

"You're right, honey. I'm sorry! Let me make it up to you," she said as she leaned in to kiss him.

Mack allowed her to part his lips with her tongue, releasing her hands as Ari unzipped his jeans.

Dropping to her knees, she released him from his boxer shorts and ran her fingers down the length of his shaft, taking the base of his cock in her hands.

"Good girl! Now take me in your mouth whilst I consider forgiving you for your insubordination!" he demanded.

Ari did as she was told, wrapping her moist lips around his erect cock, delivering soft and repetitive blows to his eager tip, and tugging on his shaft.

Mack moaned, fisting her hair, inviting Ari to indulge in every inch of him. His rough, low growls arousing her as he thrust his hard cock into the back of her throat.

"Oh Ari, you suck my cock so well. I'll forgive you once you make me come baby."

Ari continued devouring him, gripping his shaft. She knew just how to please her man, and she knew he needed it. She hadn't been near Mack since before he left for Sunnyville, and she knew his release would be imminent as she became relentless on the end of his cock. His whole body became rigid, and Mack exploded, flooding the back of Ari's throat with his climax, crying out in relief.

When she was sure he was done, she released his cock and headed to the sink to get a glass of water without saying a word. Mack pulled up his boxers and jeans and approached Ari from behind, wrapping his hands around her waist and kissing her neck.

"Thank you for remembering your place, sweetheart. It means every-thing to me right now."

Ari turned. Finished drinking her water, she placed the glass in the sink and wiped her mouth on the back of her hand.

"You know, Alex is still sleeping, we could—"

"No! You don't get pleased until you've learned your lesson, sweetheart. You can have me when I return. God knows I'll need it then, too."

Ari sulked in frustration.

"Tell me you love me, Ari. I need to hear it," he said as he bit down on her ear lobe.

Ari gasped and squeezed out, "I love you!"

"Thank you, now look after Dragon. Frankie is coming with me, leaving Bamfa, Scamper, and the prospects to keep an eye on things here. They will look after you all, so stay at Dragon's until I return."

"Okay, Mack. But B headed out early for work. She has a huge game tonight, remember? So you won't catch her before you go."

"Did Bamfa go with her?"

"Yeah. The prospects are eating breakfast, and don't worry, Bamfa has them versed."

"Good. I don't have time to stop there. Now you just be ready for my return, baby. I'm going to need your love and tender care when I get back," he said, kissing her cheek.

"You got it, Prez."

He pulled away, kissing his sleeping daughter, then grabbing his bag to leave. Turning to her, he said: "Tell the boys I love them and tell Dragon she'll thank me one day for keeping her safe."

"Okay, baby. Love you!"

Ari watched Mack and the other riders hit the road before retrieving her phone from her back pocket and hitting the call button.

"Hey, where are you? He's just heading out."

"I'm about fifteen minutes away. I'm going to park in the multi-story car park across the road until it's time. Where's Bamfa?"

"He's still sleeping with the prospects on your sofa."

"Jesus, Ari, how much did you give them?"

"Enough to buy you until after the ceremony. They're fine! Now, you sneak in and get back before they return, and don't worry about Bamfa and the boys. They won't want their precious Prez knowing that two old ladies did them in."

"I'm no old lady, Ari."

"Girl, you're my old lady and don't you forget it."

B chuckled. "Ari, I can't thank you enough for this. I know the risk you're taking here."

"You're my BFF and don't worry about Mack. He may like to be rough in the bedroom, but he wouldn't hit me. He loves me. Now get off the phone, and I'll speak to you later."

"Thanks, lovely girl."

Ari hung up the phone and scooped up Alex, nestling her into her bosom before heading back to Bs to look after the sleeping wolves.

Mack, Frankie, and the Uskiville MC members arrived in time to pay tribute to the open casket at the club before the funeral. All the club members, old ladies and bunnies attended; the place was packed. Zander didn't greet Mack at the door like Jimmy did. He hadn't moved since Noah's casket had arrived the night before, remaining by his side and only leaving to get showered for the funeral.

Mack approached Zander, whose head was resting on the casket, wearing Noah's mother's bracelet. He looked exhausted, as if he hadn't slept for a week, and he hadn't. Mack placed his hand on Zander's shoulder before placing a bottle of Welsh whiskey and an old photograph that Junior had given him in the casket. Kissing Noah's head, he said to him: "Sleep tight brother, have a drink on me and Dragon."

Zander lifted his head to scowl at Mack.

"You didn't bring her, then? You selfish prick! That lassie has every right to be here. What the fuck have you done to her? If you've hurt my Welsh Cake, I'll—"

"You'll what, brother? Because you couldn't fight your way out of a paper bag in the state you're in. It's not me that went for her outside her house, and why the feck would I hurt MY dragon? I'm keeping her safe, away from you and this chapter."

"And she's happy with that?"

Mack shrugged. "I don't give a monkey's ass, whether she's happy. I'm the founder and she'll do what she's told."

Zander laughed, mocking Mack. "Oh, brother, you've done it this time.

You think she's going to love or trust you again after this? You've kept her away from someone she called a friend, a confidante. What would Noah think? He'd be fucking ashamed of you!"

Mack clenched his fists, leaning into Zander. Zander rose to his feet, towering over Mack. Both men scowled at one another, ready to brawl. Frankie and Jimmy stepped between them as a nervous and packed MC stared with terrified eyes. If Mack and Zander fought each other again, the club would be destroyed.

"Right. That's enough! It's not the time to be playing who has the biggest dick. Today is about Noah, so put your dicks away and stay clear of each other. You've got the entire club pissing their pants."

Mack glanced around the club to be met with a sea of scared members. He didn't want to make trouble today, so he broke away first, leaving Zander growling at him as Frankie led him away.

Jimmy took hold of Zander's chin, stepping up in his role as Prez.

"Hey, hey. Look at me. You need to fucking snap out of this shit. Now we're all grieving, and I know you hate to feel Zand, but I need you now. I can't do this without you, brother."

CHAPTER THIRTEEN

I Got You!

B arrived in Sunnyville, parking her car out of sight in a nearby parking lot. She wasn't used to Mack treating her this way and whilst she understood his concerns, she never understood why he was being so protective. Normally, she would respect his wishes, but something deep down in her soul told her not to stay away from the funeral and Ari had helped her hatch a plan to make sure she didn't miss her chance to say goodbye to her friend.

Ari had drugged Bamfa and the prospects' coffees with leftover sleeping pills from her doctor after The Mauler had attacked her. Ari was always out like a light, minutes after taking them.

B knew nothing of the plan until she saw Bamfa lying on the sofa, out cold and after a brief discussion with Ari about morals, B realized it would be her only chance to escape. B rushed to pack her bags, while Ari drugged the naïve prospects, only requiring Bs strength to get them on the sofa when the job was done.

After a quick embrace, B slipped into the garage and crept off her drive. Her only obstacle was Scamper on the gates. Knowing he was desperate for money for his gambling addiction, B offered him five grand to look the other way and promised to deal with the ramifications if Mack ever found out.

Relief washed over her as she sat in her black dress and switched out of her comfy driving trainers to her black heels. Fixing her make up and checking herself in the mirror one last time, she inhaled a deep breath and stepped out of her truck. She knew Mack and Frankie would be infuriated with her and she wasn't sure how Zander, Jimmy, and the other MC members would react, but she didn't care. She was determined to pay her respects to Noah.

B watched from afar as droves of biker families poured into the church. It made her smile, knowing how loved her friend was. Motorcycles lined the church grounds, with a variety of patches making their way to say their last goodbyes to Noah. The hearse pulled up, and she watched as Mack, Frankie, Zander, Jimmy and two other men she didn't recognize placed the casket on their shoulders and made their way into the church. B hurried along the path, hoping to slip in behind them and hide in the rear pews just before the door closed, but she wasn't quick enough.

Shit, she cursed as she continued to make her way to the door.

Hoping to slip inside unnoticed, she pushed the black, heavy church doors open, to be met with seas of bikers staring at her. Her cheeks went scarlet as she slipped into the vacant pews to her right, watching as Mack and Frankie's faces turn sour with rage. The two men stood to address her but before they could move, Zander rushed to her.

Staring into his doe-like eyes, she watched as he relieved himself of an enormous sigh, his big chest heaving as he did so.

"You shouldn't be here, Welsh Cake," he said to her in a rough tone with hurt in his voice.

"I'm sorry, Scottie. I just want to pay my respects."

Zander gazed at her before looking over his shoulders. "I know, but you should be up front with me darling, no' back here on your own," he said, holding out his hand to her.

"Is that an apology, Scottie?"

"It's what Noah would've wanted."

B shook her head, frustrated that she had apologized for her actions, yet Zander hadn't. Not to mention, he was wearing the bracelet Noah gifted her and then she had passed to him.

"Then, fuck you, Scottie! I'll stay put!"

Zander pursed his lips. Stepping forward, taking her hand, and, to her surprise, he pulled her into his warm embrace. Kissing her on the cheek, he whispered into her ear, "I'm sorry Welsh Cake. I'm just so broken right now. Forgive me, please?"

B saw desperation in his eyes as she gazed upon the bearded biker. He was hurting like a wounded lion, and she hurt for him.

"Apology accepted," she whispered.

"I knew you'd come! Thank you. Noah would want you here, darling. Now let me put this back where it belongs," he said, showing her Noah's bracelet. He unclasped it and removed it from his wrist before taking her wrist and refastening the bracelet on her. "Thank you, but this is no' meant for me, darling. Noah gifted it to you for a reason. You keep it. Please?"

B nodded as she embraced him, holding him tight, not wanting to let him go as his enormous frame cradled her, intoxicating her with his scent of lavender, vanilla, and chestnut. Zander pulled away first, smiling at her and taking her hand to lead her to the front pews.

Heads turned as he walked down the aisle holding her hand. Nobody had ever seen Zander do anything so sincere. He didn't embrace people other than a five second hug of his brothers, and he didn't embrace women or hold their hands. Drag them off to his room by the neck, yes, but put a loving hand around a woman or hold a hand in a display of public affection? Never!

B watched as Zander walked tall, head held high and led her to her seat. There were seas of shocked expressions displayed around the church. Some sneered, giving B a look of disgust until her eyes glanced across the second row where Mack and Frankie's faces raged at her. Zander squeezed her hand, giving B enough confidence to fire her fiery dragon eyes at them, staring them down.

They reached the front pews, where Zander pulled her down to sit next to him, making his brothers shuffle along.

He draped his arm over her shoulder. "And dinnae worry about that Irish prick. If he starts, I'll no' hesitate to put him back in his box. I know he tried to stop you from coming here, and I'll no' have it darling."

B smiled at him and kissed his cheek, making a normally icy Zander blush, as shocked gasps echoed around the church in an acoustic tone. Nobody knew who the mysterious woman was, but they knew Zander and they knew Mack. Mack's growl echoed, displaying the church's fine acoustics as B sat up straight, her eyes like wildfire. She didn't care about Mack in that moment. Noah and B had become so close these past months, and now he lay still in a casket.

The chaplain delivered a beautiful service with tears flowing from everyone as they all mourned Noah. B and Zander kept a stiff upper lip, jaw clenched, shutting down all emotion. Zander's arm remained tight around B's shoulders and his other hand in hers, squeezing it tight throughout, and as the service ended, the opposite row of pews emptied.

B turned to Zander and whispered in his ear. "I can't leave yet, Scottie. Please let me say goodbye to him."

Zander nodded and squeezed her hand. "I got you, Welsh Cake." And as the front row left, B remained seated.

Jimmy and his brothers glanced at B as they wiped away their tears.

"She needs a minute!" Zander said, staring them down as if he was protecting her from his pack of wolves.

Jimmy nodded and walked on by, ensuring the pack followed with a nod of his head. The church emptied, leaving a chill in the air and B motionless in her pew.

B exhaled as she approached Noah's casket, unaware of Zander's presence behind her.

Looking down at Noah, she touched his icy hand.

"Oh, Baby Face, what the fuck did you get yourself into?"

Shaking her head, she continued. "What kind of trouble were you in? You could have told me. I could have helped. We stuck together. You were meant to be there when we created our new world, and now you've left me alone with your pack of fucking wolves who will never trust me. What the fuck am I supposed to do now, lovely boy?"

"You're no' alone darling, and you never will be. I got you!" Zander interrupted, as she felt his fingers entwine with hers.

B shook her head. "This is such a fucking mess. It wasn't supposed to be like this."

"Aye, I know," he said, brushing her cheek with his free hand. "You can cry, you know. There's no shame in crying."

B smirked, shaking her head at him, remaining silent.

"Yeah, I haven't cried yet either. I thought I would, Noah is.... *was* my brother, my best friend, and I thought if anything could make me cry, it would be his death. But I guess we're both just numb."

B looked at him. *Finally, someone who gets it.*

Zander continued. "I get it, you know, locking all that shit up, so your heart doesn't get shredded up, putting up wall after wall because you've been stung before. Not allowing yersel' to feel because if you feel one thing then the flood gates will open and you'll feel too much, you'll feel everything until you feel weak and break again."

"Yeah," she said in shock at the words coming out of her mouth. She'd never admitted that to anyone. Not even Mack.

"So, what was it that broke you? Before, I mean."

She shook her head; she didn't want to answer.

"Ah betrayal, me too! Only mine wasn't a lover, mine was a friend, my brother in arms. I told myself I wouldn't feel anything again because that ruined my life. That was, until I met Noah. But you, I'm guessing it was the laddies' dad."

B tilted her head as if she was trying to read him further.

Zander winked at her. "It takes one to know one, darling, trust me. Noah knew it was a man, too. He said he could tell as you took your prey to bed at the Sultry Slalom. He said you would just pick up a guy, dominate him, and when you were done, you would toss him out like trash in a display of dominance and control.

"They didn't seem to mind," she joked as she retrieved her hip flask from her handbag and sipped her whiskey.

Zander smirked. "A beautiful Welsh Cake like you, I bet they didn't. So, is that what you need, to feel in control?"

B said nothing.

Zander grinned at her silence. "Me too, darling and dinnae worry, your secret is safe with me. We can be numb together," he said, nudging her arm and lifting her hip flask out of her hands.

Taking a sip, he let out a sound of satisfaction. "Ah, that's superb shit."

"Yep, I call it the good stuff."

Zander leaned in closer again as B studied his every movement. "Hey, can I ask you something? Why didn't you meet me sooner? Do you hate Scots now or something?"

Stealing back her hip flask from him, she turned away so he couldn't see her face. "No, it's because Scots are my kryptonite. They weaken my defenses," she said with a strained face.

Scottie's eyes widened. He was lost for words.

"But Scottie, if you tell anyone that, I'll choke you to death and put you in that casket with your brother," she said, dead serious, turning to him with fire in her eyes.

Scottie smirked, taking the flask again. "Like I said, Welsh Cake, your secrets are safe with me."

B flashed him half a smile before looking down at Noah.

"Scottie, we had a plan, and we were so bloody close to the finish line."

"You wanna talk about it?"

"Not tonight. I just want to get off my tits."

Zander choked on his whiskey, laughing. "That I can help you with."

"Sorry. I need to leave after this. I don't think I'm welcome here, and I don't want trouble. It's Noah's day."

Zander took hold of her waist, pulling her tight to his firm body.

"You're more than welcome here Welsh Cake, and I want you to stay. I need you to stay, please?"

B narrowed her eyes at him, pursing her lips. "I'll come back for one drink."

"Two, and see how you feel?"

"Fine, but then I'm off. I'm not really speaking to Mackie or Frankie."

"You dinnae have to talk to them."

"Well, I think we better lay the pretty boy to rest first."

"Aye," he said, kissing Noah's head and squeezing B's hand for support.

B kissed Noah's head too. "Sleep tight Baby Face," she said, before Scottie led her outside.

Meanwhile, outside, a frantic Mack ordered a search for B's truck, to check for explosives. Unable to find it, he readied his pack as the other guests became uneasy. Hordes of people flocked toward Jimmy, raising concerns regarding their well-being.

"Look, everything is fine. Zander just needs a minute. Now get yourselves along to the burial site. We'll be along soon," he said, ushering them away and turning his attention to Mack, who was acting like a commander sending his soldiers into battle.

"Mack, what the fuck, man? You're making everyone nervous."

"I don't give a shite, Jimmy. I need to make sure my Dragon is safe."

"And she is. Look around. No one would be stupid enough to strike today. There's too many of us, so fucking calm down."

"I'll be calm when I find her truck and ship her ass back to Uskiville. Heads will fecking roll for this calamitous mistake. People will fecking die upon my return."

"Have you heard yourself lately, man? You're like a crazed psychopath. I know you love the woman but she's not a fucking Queen, brother, she's a piece of ass."

Mack's eyes narrowed as he threw Jimmy against the hearse. "What the feck did you call her?"

Jimmy pushed back at him, shrugging him off. "I'm warning you, brother, Founder or not, you ruin this day and you're fucking dead to me."

"Come on, Mackie, not here. B is here, and all we can do is protect her," Frankie said, putting an arm around him.

Mack jerked away, running his hands through his hair as he walked off.

Frankie turned to Jimmy, "I got him man, just keep an eye on Romeo and Juliette, will you?"

"We have plenty of eyes on them, don't worry,"

The burial service ran smoothly with only club members and close friends of Noah's in attendance. Once again, B sat next to Zander, who squeezed her hand throughout, until they walked back to his bike with Frankie and Mack observing from afar.

"Where's your car?" he asked.

"My truck is in the parking lot across the street."

"Well, jump on my bike and I'll take you across."

B pressed her lips together. "I don't like bikes, Scottie."

Amusement flashed across his face. "And why not?"

"Because I value my life too much. The proximity between my body and the road is an issue for me."

Zander beamed. "The mighty Dragon fears two wheels."

"No! I think they're bloody reckless, and please don't call me that. I bloody hate it."

Zander leaned in and whispered in her ear, glimpsing Mack scowling at him in the distance. "Well, if you're no' scared, get on my fucking bike and let me take you for a ride."

B's body burned with desire, making her breathless. "Fine, but if you kill me, I'm coming back to bloody haunt you."

"I told you; I got you Welsh Cake," he said, taking his helmet and placing it on her head.

B hitched her dress up and gripped his bulging biceps as she straddled the bike. Wrapping her arms around his waist, she pressed her chest to his back, as Zander raised his eyebrows, revealing his big, dimpled smile.

Glancing over to Jimmy and the other patched members who appeared wide-eyed, he shouted, "I'm taking Welsh Cake to fetch her truck in the parking lot across the street."

"Right, man. We're coming with you," Jimmy shouted back.

"Aye, well c'mon then," he said before glancing over his shoulder to B. "You ready, darling?"

"Ready as I'll ever be."

Zander revved his bike, waiting for Jimmy to take the lead, before he sped off with his pack, leaving the founder seething.

B waited by Zander's bike while Zander and the pack checked her vehicle for potential explosives, ensuring B that they had upped security in the wake of Noah's death. B thought it was all a bit much and wondered if Zander was laying it on thick to impress her. She knew she was on his bucket list yet couldn't help but marvel over his muscular physique as he clambered around beneath her vehicle. They were just finishing their checks when Mack and his pack appeared at the side of B's truck.

Zander escorted B to her truck, as Mack approached, stopping her from opening the door.

"Dragon, we need to talk."

Glowering at Mack, Zander said to her: "Do you want me to stay put?"

Mack growled at him.

B placed her hand on Zander's oversized chest, shaking her head. "Give us a minute, Scottie, please?"

Zander nodded, strolling back to his bike where Jimmy stood, keeping a watchful eye.

Mack tried to take her hand and B stepped back, ripping it away.

"Dragon, I just want to talk."

"Then make it quick. My patience is wearing thin."

"Look, I didn't want you here because it's not safe for you."

B turned on her heels. She'd heard enough, and Mack grabbed her wrist, making Zander step forward but Jimmy held him back.

"Take your fucking hand off me, Mackie, or I promise you I'll show you up in front of your pack."

Mack removed his grip. "Can we just talk like adults, please?"

B pushed past him to reach for her door, making Mack bellow.

"Just fecking talk to me, Dragon. I can't take any more!"

B didn't turn back, "We're done! I'm done with you, with Uskiville. With all of you. I never thought I'd say this, but Ari is the only one in Uskiville who gives a damn about me. I don't even know who you are anymore, Mackie."

B opened the car door, only for Mack to slam it shut again.

"We're not done Dragon; we'll never be done. You can be mad at me, but we all know you can't cope without your support system. We'll be fine, I know it. You're just too broken to cope without us. You won't stand a chance anywhere else."

B turned to face him, sneering at him. "You forget who you're talking to, lovely boy. I put you on that power-crazed throne you sit on, and I can easily throw you off! So don't fucking push me. Now I'm going for a drink at the club and you, Mackie, will stay away from me."

"And if I don't?"

"I'll snap those arms so you never ride again, and we all know what happens to a Prez who can't ride, Boyoh."

Mack stepped back away from her, putting his hand on his hip, and shaking his head as he watched her climb into her truck.

B's hands trembled as she started the engine. Checking her rearview mirror, she saw a face she didn't recognize staring back at her. She couldn't take being around Mack anymore. She hated who she'd become in his presence. Her knee-jerk reaction to his constant control made her unrecognizable to herself, and she'd had enough. As she pulled away from Mack, she had a moment of clarity. B would leave Uskiville at the end of her contract.

CHAPTER FOURTEEN

My Nephews Funeral

Blaze received a call from his little spy informing him of the Dragon's presence in Sunnyville.

"Do you want to initiate the plan?" the voice at the end of the phone asked.

"No. I told you. It's too risky. They'll be watching her like a hawk. Keep your ear to the ground. I want as much information as I can on her before we move.

"You got it, boss. Anything else?"

"Yeah, don't get too cozy in Sunnyville. Their time is ending, so be ready and always remember what side you're on."

"Absolutely. I'll be in touch."

The line went dead, and Blaze reached for another bottle of cheap whiskey. His funds were getting low, and he had no contacts left since The Mauler had burned them during his reign of terror, wanting nothing to do with the troubled family anymore. Too complacent, they told him when he reached out to them after his brother's death. He had the odd stolen property gig, and his little spies committed enough robberies and petty crimes to keep the lights on, yet Blaze yearned for the family club in Sunnyville. It was his club, his birth right, and he wouldn't rest until he took ownership again and snagged himself a wealthy dragon.

While he was brooding in his thoughts, a knock at the door interrupted him.

"Enter," he snapped.

In strolled one of his little spies with a young-looking woman dressed to impress in a short, blue dress and knee-high boots.

"Uh, sorry, boss. Candy here just wanted to convey her condolences. I asked her to stop by to cheer you up. I hope that's cool?"

Blaze looked the woman up and down. "That's mighty thoughtful of you, boy," he said, reaching out to take the woman's hand and pulling her onto his lap.

"Leave us," he said, waving to the little spy standing in the doorway, before turning to the redhead.

"You know, it was my nephew's funeral today, and he was like a son to me. Can you make an old man forget his troubles for a while?"

The young woman stood up, extending her hand to him, and Blaze took it, allowing her to lead him to the sofa behind them.

CHAPTER FIFTEEN

Tension Rising!

The MC was booming by the time B arrived, with bikers filling every crevice of the parking lot.

B parked near Zander after following the pack, who had raced ahead of her after her spat with Mack. After locking up her truck, she turned to see Zander waiting to escort her into the club. Taking her hand once more, he led her toward the entrance as the crowds parted, making a clear path for them. Up ahead, Zander called to Tiny, who was just finishing up a call by the club's entrance.

"Hey, where did you disappear to? The pack stays together, remember, asshole?"

"Sorry man, my mother needed me to sort something for her. You know, my dad's stuff."

"Aye, well, keep us in the loop next time. No more patches going solo, you got it?"

"Absolutely," Tiny said before getting the door for them.

Approaching the bar, Zander asked Glen for two beers, with Glen fumbling once again as he handed over the drinks.

"You make him nervous," B said.

"He should be. I don't trust people I know nothing about."

"Smart, but you don't know me, lovely boy, and yet you had me on the back of your bike. Kind of dangerous, don't you think?"

Zander laughed. "Welsh Cake, I know more than you realize darling."

"Oh?"

"Noah told me everything."

"Oh, I doubt that, Boyoh."

"Well, almost everything. I'm hoping you can fill in some gaps for me, though."

B's eyes lit up as she knocked back her bottle and signaled to the bar boy to fetch her two more beers. He scurried along, handing them to her, and B handed him a wad of notes.

"There's five grand there. Let me know when it runs out. Nobody buys a drink tonight and here, put this in your pocket. You would have earned it by the end of tonight," she said, handing him an extra few hundred bucks.

"Gee, thanks, lady."

B nodded, turning to Zander, and handing him a beer.

"You dinnae have to do that."

"I wanted to. I promised Noah I'd look after you and the club and that's what I'm doing."

"Funny, he made Jimmy, and I promise to look after you, too."

"Figures, but I don't need looking after, big guy." she said, giving him a cheeky wink.

"Too bad darling. You're stuck with me now."

"No offense, Scottie, but I've had my fill of overprotective bikers. They're all full of shit and lie through their teeth. I'm done with that."

Zander stroked her cheek. "You dinnae have to be hard-faced in front of me, darling. I see you. I know you're hurting."

B laughed. "I hate to break it to you, good boy, but I'm no damsel in distress. I can take care of myself."

"That, I dinnae doubt for a second Welsh Cake. I'm just saying, if you want to talk or someone to hold you, I'll be there."

"Oh, that bucket list must be eating away at you now, Scottie for you to be getting all sensitive on me, but I don't need a man to make me feel good about myself. I'm the composer of my orchestra and my music is my happy melody."

Zander whipped his head back in a fit of roaring laughter. "Shit, he told you about that?"

"Oh yeah, and the bit about the Celtic babies. A little desperate, talking like that about a woman you don't know, isn't it?"

Zander's face went scarlet as he choked on his drink again.

"Are you alright there, Scottie?".

"That mother fucker. Is there anything he hasn't told you?"

"No, I pretty much know everything, even your social security number and your bank details."

Zander's eyes sparkled and his dimples showed off the ruggedness of his handsome face. "Dinnae worry darling, Noah told me plenty about you too, and to answer your earlier question, yes, you're on my bucket list. It's my dream to bed a beautiful Welsh dragon, and I think the Welsh and Scots make a beautiful combination."

B tugged on his shirt, pulling him close to her. She could feel his heart racing in his chest, making her bite her lip with pleasure. "Scottie, you couldn't handle me, sunshine. I'm too much woman for you," she said, before releasing his shirt and flattening the creases down again.

Zander's grin was unbearable to her. She wanted him, and she knew he wanted her.

"How about a wager?" he asked.

A flash of amusement flashed on her face as she licked her lips.

"Play me at pool and if I win, I get to take you to my room and cross you off my bucket list."

"And if I win?"

"If you win, darling, nobody has ever beaten me at pool. But if you win, you can have whatever you want from me. Just name it."

"It's funny that you think I want something from you, Scottie."

"Oh, I'm no fool darling. I see what's behind that devilish grin and those fiery dragon eyes. Noah told me Mack only let you sleep with small guys, and I can feel your pulse rate quicken with every stroke. Face it, Welsh Cake, you want to be in control of a big guy like me tonight. That fiery Celtic passion burns through my soul, too, darling. The desire to take me, to relieve the pressures of the day, is becoming too much for you. So cut the crap and accept the challenge."

B bit down hard on her bottom lip. She hated that he was right. She wanted him, her body screamed to be entwined with his, she wanted to ride his rock-hard body until she exploded.

"You're on, lovely boy. Rack them up and I'll get the beers in."

"That's my girl. Go easy on those beers though unless you're planning to spend all night in my bed."

"Dream on, lover boy, I don't sleep with anyone."

Scottie racked up and swapped B a pool cue for a beer.

"Cheers! May the best man or woman win," he said.

"Oh, don't worry, Boyoh, I plan too. Now break."

Scottie broke and landed on the yellow balls, potting a few and becoming cocky as he did.

"You're looking worried Welsh Cake. Dinnae worry, I'll go easy on you. You're probably no' used to having a real man inside you," he teased.

"Slow your roll, tough guy. I'm just warming up," she joked as she potted half her red balls off the table.

Scottie's grin cascaded into a jaw drop.

"Who's looking worried now, Scottie? Don't worry, I'll go easy on you. You're probably not used to having a real woman ride you," she teased back.

Momentum around the pool table picked up as the surrounding tables listened to the flirtatious banter while Mack and Frankie sat at the far table, oblivious to their surroundings.

The score was tied. Both Zander and B had one color, and the black left to pot. Zander puffed out his chest, confident of his victory, taunting B. "Oh, I cannae wait to tear that dress off you. It's going to look fucking amazing on my floor."

The bar cheered, already accepting their VP's victory.

"You gotta pot the bloody balls first, sunshine."

"Darling, dinnae Noah ever tell you, I dinnae miss?"

"There's a first time for everything, especially for cocky Scots!"

"No' tonight, darling. I'm crossing you off my bucket list," he said, undressing her with his eyes, before he bent over to take the shot with B in his eyeline.

B fluttered her eyelashes, tracing her tongue over her top lip as she waited for him to take the shot.

Zander shook his head, grinning as he potted the yellow ball. He strutted around the table, planting a kiss on her cheek as he passed her and set up for the black ball. Indicating the pocket where the ball would go, he took the shot, sending the black ball ricocheting off the pocket and bouncing back out, missing his shot.

B burst out with laughter, almost crying in hysterics, whilst the bar erupted in shock that he'd missed. Zander hung his head in shame, shaking it in embarrassment at his first ever miss as B hunched over, unable to contain her laughter.

"Aye, aye. I fucking missed, but you still have to make your shots darling."

B composed herself. She couldn't help but grin, showing Zander a rare glimpse of her own dimples. Approaching the table, she looked at Scottie.

"How about we end it here and get a drink, good boy? I don't want to embarrass you any more than you've embarrassed yourself."

"Why? What's up? Scared I'm gonnae take you on my next shot?"

"Have it your way, big guy. But you better get yourself a stiff drink because this dress is walking out the door," she said with a laugh then bent over to take her first shot.

The red ball crashed into the corner pocket, before B made her way toward the black ball.

Zander, now looking a little nervous, intercepted her path. "Okay, maybe we should end it now and let me get you that drink. I'm no' done with you tonight."

B bit her tongue, beaming at him. "You had your chance, lovely boy. Now step aside and let me end this."

Scottie glowered at her before extending his arm to let her pass, allowing B to set herself up for the shot. The bar went quiet so she could nominate her pocket and take the shot, and as she did so, she gave Zander a cheeky wink.

Zander watched as she potted the black in the center pocket to win the game and the bar erupted into cheers. He put his hand to his mouth as he cast her a look of sheer disbelief, watching her face flush as she reigned victorious over him. Approaching her once more, he took her hand, punching it into the air to acknowledge her win.

"Go on, tell me I'm an arrogant prick," he said to her.

"Why would I say that?"

"Because I made a dick out of myself and lost."

B grinned at him, taking him by the hand. "Did you, though?"

"Oh, Christ. You're serious?"

"Yeah, but we play by my rules or not at all."

Zander raised an eyebrow. "And what rules are they?"

"I have full control over you. I take what I want, and you cross me off your list."

Zander stared in disbelief. "If that's what you want…"

"It is, Scottie. It is."

"Aye, okay, deal."

"Wait!" she said, palming his chest. "Are you clean? I don't wanna catch anything you've caught from these filthy bunnies."

Zander laughed, leaning in, and whispered into her ear. "Never tried a bunny, never want to. I've always eaten out and wrapped up. Regular check-ups too, darling. I'm no' stupid and I'll no' give you anything."

"Scottie, there is one more thing. After tonight, it doesn't happen again."

Scottie's eyes narrowed, his face stern. "Why no'?"

"Because I don't date. I don't have boyfriends. I fuck for one night only and that's it. Take it or leave it."

Zander curled his upper lip, running his index finger down her arm. "How about you see how you feel after tonight, and if you feel nothing, I'll back off?"

"Fine. Now lead the way. And Scottie? Your sheets better be clean, lovely boy."

"Fresh on today. Only the best for you," he teased, ushering her toward the back corridor.

B's heart pounded with excitement. She was going to ride her big-chested Scot. Two of her guilty pleasures in one handsome package. They'd just reached the corridor when B felt a tug on her arm. She turned to find Frankie pulling her toward him.

"Frankie, what the fuck?"

"Just answer me one thing before you take him to bed."

"What?" B snapped.

"Are you doing this to get back at Mack? Because that's not fair on VP or the club."

Zander and Frankie stared at B, waiting for an answer.

"Frankie, it's none of your fucking business, but if you must know, I'm going to ride this handsome Scot because I'm attracted to him. It's high time, I got to enjoy myself for a change, and if you want any chance of being part of my family after tonight, I suggest you keep Mackie from coming anywhere near me."

Frankie shrugged. "Fair enough! Go have fun."

"Thank you!" she said, turning to leave.

"Oh, and B, try not to kill him. He's one hell of a VP," Frankie said, giving Zander a nod.

B smiled, "Thanks, Frankie."

"I'll give you as long as I can," he said before vanishing into the crowd.

B turned to Zander, who picked her up and carried her the rest of the way. Her legs wrapped around him; he pinned her against the door to retrieve his keys from his pocket. Their chests pounding into one another in excitement as Zander opened the door, walked through, then kicked it closed behind them. Pinning her against his bedroom wall, a breathless Zander panted. "You're fucking beautiful. I cannae wait to see you naked and riding my cock."

B didn't answer, she was too busy tearing off his shirt.

Zander slipped his hands under her dress, gliding it off her body before covering her mouth with his.

B reciprocated by massaging his tongue with hers, pulling away long enough to bite his lip.

Zander growled as he reached to unclasp her bra, watching in amazement as he freed her breasts and began feasting on them.

Growling and moaning, Zander snapped off her black thong, uncovering her entrance as the pair clawed at each other, desperate for every kiss and touch. Zander freed himself from his pants with one hand, keeping the other grasping B's firm ass. B could feel how big and hard he was as he approached her opening.

Sucking on her neck, B realized she wasn't in total control, but tonight she didn't care. She wanted him. Running her hands through his hair, B bit down on Zander's ear lobe, sucking it before moving onto his neck and becoming intoxicated by his rugged essence again.

B felt Zander's breathing change at an alarming rate, his chest smashing against hers as if he struggled to breathe, so she stopped to look at him. His face strained as he gasped, trying to remain upright. B jumped down to steady him as he staggered, struggling for air. "What the fuck is happening to me?" he gasped as she directed him to his bed. Boots still done up and pants around his ankles, as he tried to drag in his next breath.

Zander was having a panic attack. B had seen plenty of them to know what they were.

She kneeled before him, placing one hand on his chest and one on his cheek. "Scottie, you're having a panic attack, my lovely. Now I got you, okay? But I need you to listen to me. Can you do that for me?"

Zander nodded, hyperventilating.

"Good, listen to my voice. Just concentrate on that and nothing else. I want you to look around for me and tell me five things you can see. Five things Scottie, look around the room, handsome and try to slow your breaths, okay?"

Zander nodded as he scanned the room, "Door... chair... cup... pen... Welsh Cake," he managed through jagged breaths.

"Good, keep dragging in those slow breaths, in through the nose and out through the mouth and just focus on my voice. You're doing great."

Zander kept his eyes fixed on her, and B could feel him tremble in fear, his heart still banging against her palm.

"Okay, lovely boy, now I want you to tell me four things you can feel."

"Legs, I feel weak, my blanket, your hand on my chest, and your hand in my hair," he managed. His breaths came a little easier than before.

"That's it, Scottie, keep going. I got you. Just keep taking those breaths and when you're ready, tell me three things you can hear."

Scottie's breathing slowed as he opened his eyes. "My heartbeat, music, and your voice."

Meeting his gaze, B smiled at him, nodding, "I got you, just keep going and tell me two things you can smell."

Zander managed a large inhalation, bringing his heart rate back down to normal ranges with B's hand still placed on his chest.

"Your perfume, summer and berries," he said, now realizing that his body had calmed again.

"Good, now one thing you can taste, handsome. You got this!"

Zander gazed at her, his eyes full of emotion, exhausted by the last nine days, and answered her. "You," he said as a flood of tears left his eyes.

B got up and sat on the bed next to him, pulling him against her chest as Zander broke down. Not only did the panic attack shake him up, but the exhaustion and trauma of Noah's death had caught up to him as he clung to her, sobbing like a baby. B held him tight, stroking and kissing his head, "I got you Scottie," she told him over and over, until he ran out of sobs.

After a while, he pulled away, unable to look at her. Embarrassed by his moment of weakness, Zander sat with his head in his hands, and B sat in silence beside him until he spoke to her.

"I'm sorry Welsh Cake. Tonight, you wanted a man, not a fucking pussy who can't breathe and sobs in your arms."

B clasped her hands to his cheeks. "No, lovely boy. Tonight, I wanted you and that's what I got and there's no fucking shame in having a panic attack. I've had them, and Mackie used to suffer terribly when he first came to me, so don't go beating yourself up over it. You'll only make things worse."

"I thought I was dying."

"That's because they're fucking scary, but I got you, and you're alright. Now let me help you out of these boots, because that can't be comfortable," she said, reaching to untie them.

Smiling at him, B removed his boots and socks and slipped off his pants and boxers before ordering him back into bed. "Come on, lie back and relax."

Zander brushed her cheek with his knuckles. "Can I tell you something?"

"Of course."

"I panicked because the last time I was with a woman, Noah died. I was fucking some nameless woman when he told me he was heading out. He was dead after he insisted I stay, even though I offered to go with him."

"Oh, Scottie," she whispered.

"Welsh Cake, I've waited forever for this moment with you, and I fucked it up because all I could think about was that night. My friend got blown away while I fucked some random woman I dinnae care about," he said as his voice trembled.

B caressed his face, running her hand through his rugged beard. "Listen, lovely boy. Noah's death wasn't on you. If you had gone with him that night, you would be dead too. It wasn't your time, Scottie, and as much as it hurts to lose someone you love; you have to keep fucking going. You'll get through this, I promise you. It will hurt forever, but each day gets a little easier, and in time, you'll remember all the good times as they flood your veins like a drug, filling you with ecstasy. You will see brighter skies again, handsome."

Tears fell from his eyes, and B wiped them away with the pads of her thumb. "I made a promise to Noah that I'd look after you, so tonight you get one free pass. You get a cwtch or whatever you want from me for one night only, okay?"

"Thank you, Welsh Cake. I want you. Look at you, you're perfect. I just dinnae know if I can ever become intimate again after what's etched in my brain. I fucking hate it."

B smiled at him; "I can help you, Scottie, but you have to trust me. I can get you over this mind fuck of yours, but only if you want me to."

Zander pulled her in, holding her tight. "Please Welsh Cake, take my pain away."

"All I can do is try. If that's what you want?"

"God yes!" he moaned with uneven breaths as he met her stare.

"Okay, lay back and relax."

Zander did just that, trembling a little.

"Don't be nervous, Scottie, I got you. Now close your eyes, and I don't want you to open your eyes again until you feel comfortable to do so."

Scottie closed his eyes and took a deep breath.

"Your safe word is Black. Tell me your safe word Scottie."

"Black."

"Good. Now if you want to stop, you just say that and I'll stop, okay?"

"Okay," he whispered.

B looked down at Zander's body, stroking his head. She ran her fingers through his hair and down the side of his neck.

"Breathe, Scottie, just focus on my touch and breathe. Every time your mind wanders, you bring it back to my touch, okay?"

"Okay, beautiful."

B stroked his body using the pads of her soft fingers. Starting at his chest, she traced her fingers along his chiseled body. Her fingers traced over every scar and tattoo, covering every inch of his chest with her soft touch. Zander's breathing changed, allowing a soft moan to escape him as he welcomed her seductive strokes. As she witnessed him relax, B kissed his lips, taking it slow as she parted his lips with her tongue, stroking the inside of his mouth with delicate blows. Traveling south, her lips caressed his neck before trailing along his pecs, stroking them with her tongue as they hardened with every touch.

"Is this okay, lovely boy?"

Zander moaned, "Oh, I love your lips on my body, darling."

Acknowledging his enjoyment, B used her lips and tongue to travel down his torso, making her way to Scottie's enormous, hard cock. It stood up to attention as B licked its length, making Zander gasp, his heart rate skyrocketing: he was panting again.

"Breathe Scottie. Listen to my voice, feel my lips around you," she said as she took him in her mouth, sucking and massaging him with her tongue and lips.

Zander moaned, gritting his teeth, as B removed her mouth. "Say the word and I'll stop."

"No, please? I want this," he moaned, eyes shut tight.

B continued to devour him with her gentle touch, clasping her hand around him to explore his length. Feeling his arousal, she kneeled to straddle him. Placing one hand on his chest as she whispered in his ear, "Are you sure you want me, Scottie?"

"Fuck, yes! Dinnae stop for anything!"

B lowered herself onto him, struggling to take his size as he stretched her channel. She moaned as she invited him in, inch by inch, until he filled her. Peering down at him, she smiled as she found him staring back at her, eyes glazed over in delight, and looking at her with wonderment. She leaned down to kiss his lips, feeling his hands rake through her long hair, fisting it, as his hips thrust, driving into her, to match her rhythm.

Soaking him with her juices, B rode him at a steady pace as he grabbed her breasts, bringing his mouth to meet them. Rugged gasps and delicate cries engulfed their ears as B increased the tempo, riding him hard and fast as Zander's hands fondled every inch of her.

The Scot mesmerized B. She loved how big he was. His chiseled concrete chest drove her crazy. Mack had always forbidden her from having sex with anyone bigger than him and yet here she was breaking the rules of engagement with a man at least twice her stature. She couldn't get enough of his big and strong hands all over her body. His strength as he picked her up and lowered her onto himself early on.

B increased her tempo as he stiffened inside her, pressing against the walls of her sex. Lowering herself down, she kissed him passionately as her body pressed against his. His skin glistened with his essence as he became drenched in sweat and B lusted after his touch. She wanted him, and not like the guys she took in the Sultry Slalom: they were just child's play to her. Toys that she would use and get fed up with after five minutes. No, Zander was different. Her body screamed for his kiss, his touch, his everything, and it scared the hell out of her.

"Oh darling, yes," he cried as she took in all his glory. Her sleekness aroused him to greater heights as he reached his impending climax.

"Fuck, Scottie, you're driving me wild," she moaned. Astonished that anyone could make her say such a thing as he grabbed her ass to aid his thrusts.

Sensing his urgency, B grabbed hold of his headboard to gather momentum and rode him as fast as lightning, clenching around his hard cock as he threatened to release.

"Oh, fuck!" he cried. His body trembling as he reached his climax. "Oh, darling please come for me, I want to release with you."

"I'm close Scottie," she cried, his hard cock pulsating through her like electrical energy threatening to short circuit.

"Shit darling, I need to feel you, please?" he gasped in desperation and at his request B screamed as her orgasm gushed through her body like a river bursting its banks, making her buck and writhe as she clenched around him.

Scottie unleashed a guttural cry, incapable of holding back as he pulled her down onto him, grabbing her around the waist and thrusting hard to match her writhing body.

"Oh, Christ," he cried, unleashing himself inside her.

Continuing to writhe as one, they slowed to a stop as Zander swept the stray hairs away from B's face.

"Christ, Welsh Cake. You're incredible. Thank you," he said as he sucked her tongue.

"You know, you weren't so bad yourself."

"Darling, I've not met anyone who could make my heart stop and my cock sing. I want to fill you all night. I know you have to be in control, but please let me climb on top of you and give you everything I have."

B smiled, "You have me for one night, lovely boy. I suggest you make the most of it. Just don't try to restrain me."

"One night isn't enough. Fuck, a lifetime isn't enough," he said as he gazed at her breathlessly.

"Then you better get to work, because tonight I want to feel everything!"

CHAPTER SIXTEEN

Macks Rage

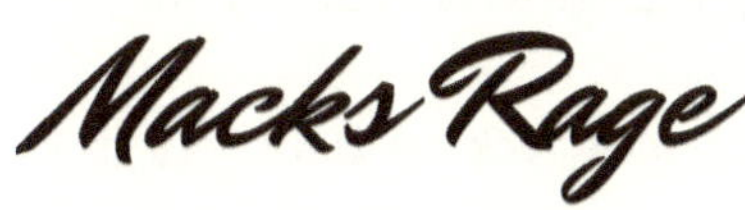

Meanwhile, out front, Mack had just finished his phone call with Ari, explaining he wasn't happy about his Dragon being in Sunnyville. B had already prepped her on her way back to the MC, telling her to tell Mack she found Bamfa and the prospects on the couch when she returned to B's house, to make out B went rogue. Mack wasn't sure what to believe. On one hand, he knew all about his dragon's moral compass, but on the other, he knew she hadn't been herself of late, thinking Noah had rubbed off on her before his untimely demise. Either way, he would punish Ari with everything he had on his return. He was desperate to release that night, but there was only one person he'd ever consider cheating on Ari with and she was inside flirting with a Scotsman. It made Mack's blood boil, seeing how close his Dragon let Zander get to her, allowing him to take her hand and kiss her cheek.

Feck, maybe she would have turned to me if I hadn't been such a hard bastard and tried to keep her safe.

He despised how close they were and how comfortable B was with Zander. They hadn't even met in person before today, to his knowledge.

Was that another thing she kept from me?

It devastated him. She betrayed him by turning up today, and he could feel her slipping away as each moment passed. Putting his phone in his back pocket, he raised his head to the night sky in despair, inhaling a large drag of cold air.

"Here, boss, get this in you. It'll calm your mind."

Mack turned to see Tiny offering him a smoke. He could smell how potent it was as it wafted up his nose.

"Cheers, Tiny," he said taking a long drag, allowing the buzz to hit him.

"Feck, I forgot how good your shit is, Tiny. Still growing your own?"

"You know it! What's it like in Uskiville?"

Mack laughed. "My dragon would chop my fecking balls off if I brought anything onto the retreat."

Tiny laughed. "Can I ask you something? Serious like?"

"Sure man, go ahead."

"This dragon of yours. Is she the real deal? I mean, you used to be a one-percenter, you didn't take any shit from women. Why is she so special?"

Mack took another drag of the joint, feeling the ever-growing buzz spiral through his body in a euphoric dance, relieving his mind of its tension. "Because I owe her my life. I would be dead right now if it wasn't for her. She's made me the man I am today. A better man. Don't get me wrong, I'm still a sick son of a bitch. He's still lurking deep inside, but that woman has me by the balls. She has my heart in a vise and my dick suffocating for her."

"But what about Ari?"

Mack sighed, leaning against the club's wall. "Oh, Ari is my Queen. But I'm telling you, brother, if I brought Dragon to bed with me, she'd welcome her. She loves her as much as I do. The only problem is, I know my dick would only want my dragon in the end, and I'd eventually hurt Ari. Besides, Dragon doesn't want me. It's besties or nothing."

"Is that why she's let Zander take her to bed tonight?"

Mack let the joint fall from his mouth. He gulped, finding it hard to swallow as the pang in his chest felt like he was being stabbed. "What?"

"Didn't you just hear the commotion? The club is dancing in there now, brothers fucking in every corner after witnessing the pair of them play for sex. Zander made a bet with her. If he beat her at pool, he'd cross her off his bucket list once and for all, and if she won, she could have whatever she wanted from him tonight. The club went nuts when he lost, but she took him to bed, anyway. Seriously, boss, the whole fucking bar witnessed it. How the fuck did you not see it?"

Mack's face turned purple as if he was being choked. His eyes went black as he grimaced, rage ripping through him, fueling his body with adrenaline.

"Fuck, boss, I thought you knew. I'm sorry!"

Mack screamed in anger, picking up a stray beer bottle and launching it against the wall, before storming off, leaving Tiny puffing away at his joint and shaking his head.

Ripping open the cast iron door, Mack stormed through seas of drunken club members, scanning the room. He was desperate to see B in the bar. He didn't want to believe she was with Zander.

The Scot, of all people. I knew she once had a thing for Scots, but I thought that would make her stay away from them, considering a Scot made her see the world as she does. Why the fuck is she with him? But then again, that big-chested bastard is like a forbidden fruit to her, and she's pissed. What better way to get back to at the ones she loves? Petty bitch, I should drag her out of his room and bend her over in front of the entire MC, make her take it, make her mine, so that Scottish prick backs the hell off. She's my dragon, mine!

He thought the words over and over as he pushed people out of the way, making his way to the members' private quarters.

Mack had almost reached the corridor's entrance when Frankie and Jimmy stood in his way. He gave them a menacing stare as he barked at them. "Step aside. I know where she is. Why didn't you stop him from taking her? She's mine!"

"No, Mackie boy," said Frankie. "Tonight, and for however long, she wants, she's his. Now walk away, brother."

"Remember your place, VP. I want her out of there now and that Scottish prick is going to lose his cock for this."

"No, Mackie, I'm not and he's not! You've not laid claim to Dragon. As per *your* charter, a patch can only claim one woman, and you have claimed Ari. You don't have the right to stop VP from claiming her."

Mack lunged at Frankie, and Frankie used his momentum to pin him against the wall.

Mack was no match for Frankie's strength, and he knew it. "You insubordinate fecker. You're done at this club."

"I don't give a shit about the club when it comes to her, brother. Now B and VP want this. She doesn't want you, and maybe he's the one to tame her, so leave them be."

Mack continued to spit through his teeth as Frankie held him with one hand by his throat. Jimmy stood by as club members and their wives witnessed in horror.

"Take your God damn hands off me, brother, or I swear I'll..."

"You'll what, Mackie boy? I've told you before, my loyalty lies with B, and if that means forsaking a club I live and breathe for, just so she can free herself from her torment, then so be it. I should have never cuffed her to that bed. She has a right to be here. She is meant to be here. You understand me?"

Mack dragged in some deep breaths, raising his hands to Frankie. "Fine, she has tonight, but we're dragging her ass out of here first thing."

Frankie released his throat, and Mack shrugged him off, straightening his shirt, pushing past Frankie. He turned back, calling out at him. "Hey, VP."

Shaking his head in frustration, Frankie turned to his brother once more, only to meet the end of Mack's fist as it connected with his jaw. He didn't flinch as the blood dripped down his chin. Straightening his head, an evil-eyed Mack met him.

"You ever lay a hand on me again. I'll strip you of your patch," Mack snarled.

Frankie looked back at him, unfazed. "Don't interfere with B's happiness, and I won't have to."

Mack shook his head. He knew he had no right to act, and he knew Frankie had every right to stop him, but his heart was breaking. It was tearing him apart, and he knew he couldn't live like it anymore.

Frankie approached him at the bar, and Glen, the bartender, fetched a bottle of whiskey and two glasses.

Frankie poured them both a drink. "Mackie, start owning your shit. It's getting too much, and I hate to tell you this, but if Zander claims her tonight, you have to stand down. Otherwise, you won't just lose your dragon, you'll lose your home and your club. I'm telling you, something is happening with her and the way she was around VP tonight, so natural and comfortable in his presence. You gotta ask yourself if it's fair to stop that shit from evolving."

"She will never let him claim her. If she was capable of that, I would have claimed her myself, a long time ago."

"Mackie, she was smiling tonight. Despite all the shit that's happened, that big-chested fucker made her smile. A real fucking smile, and this. It didn't fucking bother her one bit," he said, gesturing to the busy club, filled with bikers taking advantage of their old ladies in the bar's corners, and wayward activities entangling everywhere.

Mack's eyes scanned the room with discontent as Frankie continued. "She's home Mackie. She may not see it yet, but I do. Are you really going to stand in her way if she decides this is what she wants?"

"She won't survive without us Frankie."

"No. You mean *you* won't survive without *her*. You know, she's tougher than anyone and if anyone can survive on their own here, it's her."

"And what if Blaze returns?"

"Then I look forward to watching her tear him apart. If he's out there, he will die by her hands, Mackie. We just need to ensure she survives the aftermath with blood on her hands."

Mack topped up his whiskey, filling the glass. "I'm going to lose my best friend, aren't I?"

Frankie knocked back his whiskey and wiped the excess blood from his chin.

"That, my friend, is up to you!"

CHAPTER SEVENTEEN

Cwtch

Zander stroked B's back as she slept soundly on his chest. Peering down at her silken skin, he couldn't believe what had happened between them tonight. To him he had landed himself a goddess, an Amazonian queen, as he gazed upon her tattooed body in amazement. He loved how her curvy body snaked around his. Her perfect backside in full view as she wrapped her legs around him, breasts pinned against him as she breathed into his chest. He didn't care that he hadn't laid claim to her tonight. They'd become intimate beyond his comprehension. That was enough for him, and as much as he wanted to claim B, the timing didn't seem right to take her like that tonight. It had been perfect, despite his panic attack early on, and he couldn't believe her special skillset of calming him during the worst night of his life. It all seemed surreal. He was supposed to meet B and still have his best friend.

It wasn't supposed to be like this; he told himself as he played with the bracelet on her wrist. Running his finger across the precious charms, he couldn't help but chuckle to himself, imagining what Noah's face would be like if he could see him right now. What he would say to the pair of them. Smiling, he raised her wrist and laid a soft kiss on her bracelet.

I got her now Noah, dinnae worry, I'll keep her and the club safe.

Placing her hand back onto his chest and holding it there, Zander couldn't take his eyes off her. She looked so calm and still. Her gentle breaths pushed against his solid chest.

"What the fuck happened, to make you so God damn strong, beautiful?" he whispered as he kissed her forehead.

She'd told him she didn't trust anyone, that she had to be in control, and he'd let her be at first. But she didn't stop him as he ripped through her body like wildfire, demanding her orgasms, one after another, as he gave her everything tonight. She had given herself to him for one night and slept on his chest despite promising him it would never happen, and as Zander gazed upon the sleeping dragon, he knew he had a fight on his hands if he wanted to keep her there.

Morning came and the early birds sang on the club's tin roof, informing the world of daybreak. It was a little past dawn when Frankie slipped into Zander's room to wake B who appeared content, nestled into Zander's chest. He'd never seen her looking so peaceful, but he'd told Mack they would leave at dawn, and he didn't want Mack and Zander to confront each other this morning. He was too tired for that today.

He tapped her shoulder, and B's eyes opened in an instant. Frankie handed over her dress. "Sorry B, we need to leave and clean up the shit you left back home," he whispered, smiling at her.

Frankie watched as she gazed at Zander sleeping. A flash of both humor and confusion crossed her lips before she turned to him, sliding out of bed and modestly covering her nakedness with her dress.

Frankie couldn't help but grin at her. He was happy for her. Zander was a good man, and he'd put a smile on his best friend's face, a smile that Frankie hadn't seen before. Of course, he'd seen her smile, but not like this. It was a bashful, smitten smile. Her cheeks were rosy, and her grin revealed dimples he didn't know she had.

He waited for her to slip out of the bedroom, carrying her shoes, being careful not to wake the big Scot she left lying in bed. Frankie watched her take one last glance at the sleeping Scot before she closed the door quietly and he knew she wasn't ready to leave.

"I'm sorry B. I didn't want to disturb you."

B slipped on her heels. "It's fine. I need to make things right with Bamfa, Scamper, and the prospects anyway."

"Did you get what you needed from VP?"

B flushed. "I did, and he got what he needed."

"I bet he did! It's nice to see you smile like that."

"How was your night?" she asked, changing the subject.

"Uneventful."

"Really?" she asked clasping his bruised chin. "Is he alright or is he still sulking like a sissy?"

"What do you think?"

"For fuck's sake."

"Just do me a favor and be nice, please? My head is throbbing from babysitting all night," Frankie asked holding the door open for her.

"Shit, sorry. Why didn't you come and get me?"

"And ruin all our nights? No, I handled it."

"I thought you'd have your end in a bunny," she teased.

"Ugh, fuck off. They're riddled with disease. I could catch herpes just by looking at them."

B laughed. "I saw what some of them were doing last night and it was unsanitary. I mean, I'm no prude, but they're downright nasty."

"Well, they don't float my boat either. I'll get myself a nice honey for breakfast."

"You want me to give Tiffany a call for you? To make up for you taking one for the team last night?"

"B, if you can make that happen for me, I'll babysit whilst you ride VP any day of the week."

B's eyes danced with laughter, proceeding to her truck, she pulled out her phone, texting as they headed outside. Her phone buzzed back in a heartbeat, making B grin at Frankie. "She's heading over to warm your bed for you."

Frankie grinned as his heart pumped with excitement. He scooped her up, throwing her over his shoulder. "Oh, my days, I fucking love you!" he said before placing her back down and kissing her cheek.

Beaming, he watched as she stopped to talk to Glen, who was picking up the stray bottles that lined the walls of the MC.

"Hey, can you tell Jimmy I'll be in touch?"

"Sure, and thanks for the tip last night."

"No worries, you earned it, good boy," she said before turning back to Frankie.

"What's that all about? Why are you going to contact him?"

"I need to help them, Frankie. I made a promise to Noah."

"Well just be careful, he's Team Mack and always will be."

"Gotcha."

Heading toward B's truck, Frankie gave Mack a nod as the other patches checked over the truck before B could head out.

Mack rested his head against B's driver's side door, looking like a lost boy as he waited for them.

Frankie put his arm around B and whispered in her ear. "Please play nice. I don't want to referee this morning now that there's a honey in my bed waiting for me to play."

"Okay. I'll be nice Frankie, for you though, not him."

"Thank you. I appreciate that B," he said, releasing her from his grasp.

"Ready?" he asked Mack.

Mack stood and zipped up his cut. "Yeah," he said, giving Frankie a wink.

Frankie squeezed B's biceps, giving her a grin. "I'll see you soon."

"Sure," she nodded and turned her attentions to Mack as he stood looking at her.

"What's he grinning about?" Mack asked in a miserable tone.

"Tiffany is waiting in his bed for him."

"Shit. How did he manage that?"

"I called in a favor."

Mack grinned. "Of course, you did."

Turning away, he kicked a stray stone. "Did you feck him?"

"Why are you asking me that when you know the answer already?"

Mack pursed his lips and nodded. "Just tell me, why him?"

"I don't know, Mack. Why do I fuck anyone? Grief, relief, his big, fuck off chest and his come to bed eyes. What would you like to hear?"

"But Zander? Dragon, as much as I love him and he's my brother, you promised me no big guys and no wolves. You *promised* me, Dragon."

"And you promised me no bunny boilers, yet Ari is your old lady now."

"I thought she was your BFF?"

"She is. I'm just saying, we both gave into our desires and that's okay?"

"Is it?"

B narrowed her gaze. "What do you mean?"

"Did you let him claim you?"

B raised her eyebrows, a glint of humor flashing across her face. "Mackie, how many times do I have to tell you I don't belong to anyone? I am not an old lady, and I never will be. Ari may be alright in relinquishing control, but I'm not. Now please, can we get home so I can get out of this bloody dress?"

Mack breathed out a sigh of relief, flashing her a smile. "Thank God for that."

B smirked, unlocking her truck. She was about to dive in when he called out to her. "Hey Dragon. You look fecking smoking in that dress. You should wear it more often."

B shook her head and laughed at him before getting in her truck.

Strutting toward his bike, Frankie eyed Mack's big grin. "What's changed your face?"

Mack climbed on his bike, placing his lid on his head. "She didn't let him claim her."

"Of course, she didn't. This is B we're talking about. That doesn't mean he won't though."

"Oh, there not crossing paths again brother, I'll make sure of it. Besides, it's clear that he's just another Sultry boy to her."

"I wouldn't be so sure, Mackie boy. I found her cradled in his arms this morning, sleeping like a baby. So, if she goes down that road, you need to back off."

"We'll see. If she can sleep with *him*, who knows what the future holds?" Mack said, giving him a wink and signaling to the others to ride out.

Frankie shook his head, revving his engine. "You're delusional, asshole."

"No. I'm an optimist," he said before roaring out of the parking lot.

CHAPTER EIGHTEEN

She's Mine!

Zander stirred to the sound of roaring engines and reached across the bed, hoping to find B. Opening his eyes, he frowned and sat up to scan the room, checking the bathroom until he revealed B had gone, devastating him.

Crashing down onto the corner of his bed, he rubbed the back of his neck and sighed. He couldn't understand why B had left without saying goodbye. She had allowed them their night of passion, and now she was gone. Her lace thong lying underneath his jeans, the only reminder of her presence.

Zander picked up the thong as he thought about B's body against his and how their night had woken his senses. He hadn't felt like this about a woman before and it angered him she left without saying goodbye.

Frustrated, he hoped he would find her at the bar waiting for him, but deep down he knew she had gone.

Stumbling into the bar in nothing but his jeans and his boots, he approached Jimmy, who was nursing his head with black coffee as Glen rushed to fix him one up too.

"Morning," he groaned, taking the coffee from a terrified Glen.

Jimmy looked him up and down. "Well, somebody had a good night at least." He nodded to the bite marks on Zander's chest and shoulder.

Zander looked down, realizing they were there, and grinned.

"So, come on then. Was the fearless dragon worth it? Did she meet your high expectations?"

Taking a sip of his coffee, Zander nodded. "She surpassed them. She was beyond incredible and took me places I dinnae know existed."

"Yeah?"

"Yeah, right after I thought I'd blown it too."

"What do you mean? You two were all over each other last night. You were the talk of the bar, anyone could see the sexual chemistry between you."

"Aye, and it was like that until we got to my room. We were crazy, but then when I had her pinned against the wall, naked and looking fucking perfect, I panicked and all I could think of was fucking that bar girl whilst Noah was being pumped with bullets, and I couldn't breathe brother."

"Shit man, I'm sorry. So, what happened?"

"Well, I thought I was having a heart attack until she put her hand on my chest and made me breathe, but I tell you Jimmy, it scared the shit of me and when I calmed, I dinnae know what happened. I just started crying. I broke, Jimmy, and I broke hard."

Jimmy's face grew strained. He'd never seen Zander cry before. "That's grief for you, man. It fucks you up when you least expect it."

"Aye, but Welsh Cake was amazing. She held me, and afterwards I was raging, thinking I blew it. I was so angry, and I thought she would think I was a pussy. Only for her to straddle me and blow my fucking mind."

"She was good, then?"

Zander huffed air from his cheeks.

"Jimmy, that was just a warm-up. I have met no one who could make me feel so vulnerable, yet so fucking exhilarating. Honestly, brother, she was like a relentless goddess, and I lost count of how many times I came. It was like one big climax that lasted all night. We connected. She gifted me one night with her and I made the most of it."

"I bet you did, you dirty bastard. Did you claim her?"

Zander laughed. "What do you expect? I waited long enough. and no, I dinnae want to push her or rush her. The only thing that's pissed me off is she didn't say goodbye."

"You're kidding. Did she leave a number?"

Zander investigated his coffee, jaw tightening so much that the cup struggled to take the strain. "No."

"So, you're not seeing her again, then?"

"Oh, I'm seeing her, brother. I'm gonnae ride up there later and talk to her. She cannae leave me like this."

Jimmy placed his empty coffee cup on the bar.

"That won't work, Zand."

Zander glared at him. "Why no'?"

"Because whilst you were having the ride of your life, Mackie found out his precious dragon had disappeared and attempted to find you and chop your fucking balls off. He lost his shit, man."

Zander slammed his cup on the bar, smashing it to pieces, sending coffee everywhere and frightening Glen, who rushed to clean up. "What the fuck is his problem?"

"You are! He loves her, man. He always has, and you God damn know it. Yet you and Noah still went on a dragon quest, and I kept my mouth shut because I never thought it would happen between the two of you. But last night, you took something that didn't belong to you and broke Mack's trust. What the hell do you think it means for this club? He'll never help us now and we're fucked if Dragon doesn't come through for us."

Zander's chest was heaving in anger. "Welsh Cake is mine, no' his! He never claimed her. He's got Ari and I'm having Welsh Cake. Noah was right, he's fucked up, Jimmy. Welsh Cake doesnae belong to him, never has. She wanted me last night, no' him, and she let me please her, no' him. He's no' having her brother. I am, she's mine! And as for his help, we dinnae need it. Welsh Cake will come through for us."

"And what if she doesn't?"

Glen approached the bar with a nervous expression written all over his face. "Sorry to interrupt, but B said she would be in touch. She told me before I left, and I've been so busy, I forgot to tell you," he quivered.

Jimmy's puzzled expression stared back at him.

"Did she leave a message for me?" Zander asked.

"N-no sir. They headed out shortly after I saw Frankie enter your room. She just said to tell the Prez she would be in touch. Then she joked with Mack before they left."

Zander clenched his teeth and fists. He was livid hearing Jimmy had a message, and her leaving without saying goodbye was the icing on the cake.

He smashed his hands down on the bar, just missing the broken cup.

"Calm down!" Jimmy shouted, taking hold of him.

"No! I'm riding up there. I want to see her. I know something happened between us last night. Frankie had no right to take her."

"Well, maybe he did! He took a punch for you last night. In front of everyone, he refused an order to stand aside from his Prez. He ensured you both had a night together but promised to leave first thing. Mack was like a man possessed last night and you will start a war by going to Uskiville. I'm not having it!"

"Jimmy, I have to see her. I need to understand why she left."

"You know why. She fucks and runs, remember? Now get this shit out of your head. It's not doing you any good."

"You're wrong brother. I wasn't a Sultry boy last night, and she no' a one-night fuck for me, either. Something incredible happened and I'm no' giving up on that."

"At what expense? Are you willing to tear this club apart when you don't even know if she wants another piece of you? She's dangerous brother. Dangerous to you and to this club. Now, we need her, but I hate what she's doing to you both."

Zander's face became contorted with rage as he picked up the bar stool and launched it across the bar. His chest pounded as the rage burned through his body. He waited so long to meet her and so many barriers prevented their relationship from blooming. Barriers he had no time for. He wanted his Welsh Cake, and he wanted her now. Turning to Jimmy, he threw him a hostile glare. "If she's so bloody wrong for me and this club brother, then why no' mention that when Noah was alive? Why no' challenge him when he explained his plan of working with her or decline her offer when she gave you that contract?"

"Because I never believed he could pull it off. Zander, she owns this club and Mack has no fucking idea she wants out. Who do you think is going to get it when he finds out? Because it won't be Noah. We need to be smart here and you mixing business and pleasure will not end well, so leave it alone so I can protect the club."

Zander shook his head with his hands grasping his hips. "We made a promise to Noah that we would look after her. Are you breaking a promise, Jimmy?"

Jimmy pointed to the whiskey and Glen the prospect handed it to him along with two shot glasses. Pouring the amber liquid into two glasses, he handed one to Zander. "I won't break my promise, but I won't watch you, or this club, get hurt."

Zander snatched the shot, hurling it down his throat and hunching over the bar. "Then help me, please Jimmy. I am so tormented right now. Please, help me come good on Noah's wishes."

Jimmy poured himself another shot and handed Zander the bottle. "You think he was right about her? You know, taking the club into greatness?"

Zander drank straight from the bottle. "Yeah, I do. Jimmy, I saw a glimpse of who she is, and I'm fucking mesmerized. You know she paid for everyone's drinks last night. She doesnae know anyone, and she just handed the prospect the cash."

"I thought Mack did that."

"No, I watched her do it. She gave the prospect a good wedge too, didn't she Prospect?" he said, looking at Glen.

Glen stepped forward. "It's true boss. She gave me three-hundred bucks as a tip. She seems real nice too."

Jimmy remained silent.

"See, even the prospect likes her," Zander teased.

"Bollocks! Fine, but you're not fucking going up there today. We wait until she calls, and I do the fucking talking. I'm the Prez of this club, and I don't want you fucking things up by thinking about what your dick wants."

"It's no' just my dick that wants her, Jimmy. She cracked me wide open yesterday. She thawed this right out and it's hurting for her," he said, beating on his chest.

"All the more reason to let me handle shit."

"Jimmy, do what you want, as long as I get to see her again."

CHAPTER NINETEEN

Punishing My Dragon!

The sound of roaring engines echoed throughout the quiet retreat as the pack arrived home. Mack got off his bike and headed to Scamper, who was guarding the gate. He took one look at Mack and his face dropped. He knew what was coming.

Mack floored him in an instant.

"Next time I give you an order, you fecking listen. You're lucky I don't kick you to death," Mack said.

B parked up her truck and rushed to grab him.

"What the fuck is wrong with you? He didn't have a choice."

"There's always a choice, Dragon and he made the wrong one,"

B grabbed Mack's head to make him look at her. Grimacing as he glared into her eyes, his chest puffing until one look from her made his heart melt, calming his stormy body and mind.

"Mackie, no more violence, please? Let's be done with this shit now. It's driving me mad."

"You could have been hurt," he said, unable to take his eyes off her.

"But I wasn't and we're home now, Mackie, please?"

Mack nodded, placing his head on hers. His heart pounding, so close to her, but yet so far. His urges were getting stronger. He wanted to pull her into him, drive his tongue down her throat, and hitch up her dress. He thought about taking her right there and then in front of everyone. Struggling to control himself, he was about to pull her into him so she could feel the effect she had on him all this time, when she pulled away to pick up Scamper.

"You okay, my lovely?" she asked, dusting him down.

Mack's eyes refueled with rage as he got back on his bike, watching as she looked after Scamper.

"She should be looking after me, tending to my needs," he muttered as he sped up the road to his house.

An angered Mack was hard, and ready to explode. Scrambling off his bike, he marched through his front door, slamming it behind him.

"Oh, hey honey."

He didn't give Ari a chance to breathe as he forced his tongue down her throat.

Releasing her, he stared at her with pleading eyes. "Please tell me the house is quiet and Alex is asleep."

"Nadia has taken them all out for the—"

"Good, because I need to blow," he said, taking her by the wrist and dragging her upstairs.

Reaching the bedroom, he pulled Ari into him, slamming her into his chest.

"I'm ready to punish you, baby. I'm going to take you as if I'm making you mine again, to remind you who you belong to."

Ari moaned as he tore off her housecoat and discovered her revealing underwear.

"These better be crotchless, baby. I need you now!"

"Then you better take me, Prez,"

Mack pushed her down on the bed, unbuckling his jeans and kicking off his boots, before pinning Ari down.

"You're keeping your cut on?"

"Yes baby, now stop talking so I can turn you over and take you like I'm making you mine all over again."

"Yes, sir," she teased as he kissed her breasts and flipped her over.

Dragging her up onto her knees, he pushed his hard cock inside her, making her yelp.

"I'm going to make you scream baby and you're going to take it, to please me, aren't you?"

"Yes," she cried.

"Bite down baby, because I'm taking you hard, so you can remember who you belong to."

"Oh, God, Mack."

"Call me Mackie as I take you. I want to hear you scream it as I punish you for betraying me."

Mack knew Ari's release was imminent; it always was. He couldn't wait for his release as he thought about his dragon in her cute black dress. How it clung to her body. It was a rare sight to see her in anything other than work clothes, and Mack couldn't shake the image out of his head.

"Fuck," he said as Ari clenched around him, screaming into her orgasm, and now he could take her, ravage her. It was only fair he pleased her first after what he was about to do to her. Feeling himself harden, stretching her as she continued to moan for him. Mack took her by force. He was relentless as he took her with everything he had for the first time since they met. Fisting her hair, Mack was oblivious to her needs, his thoughts crystal clear as he thrust his rage through her.

"Oh yes, take it!" he said, pushing himself deeper inside as he felt Ari clench around his hard cock.

His thoughts still fixated on his dragon, fantasizing about ripping off her dress in front of the patched members. In front of the Scot she had taken to bed.

"I'm punishing you, baby, and you're going to take it," he said, whilst thinking about punishing B for breaking his promise.

Pulling her hair like reins, he quickened his lusty thrusts, growling and still oblivious to Ari's cries. She was close once more, but Mack was unaware as he took her as if his life depended on it.

Ari came hard again, tensing around him as he drove into her, the pressure on his cock waking him out of his fantasy.

"Fuck!" he gasped, fucking her through her orgasm.

Her cries rattled in his brain as he exploded inside her, thrusting uncontrollably. He couldn't stop. So much pressure had built up inside him, his relief was too much. It felt like a thousand volts of electricity had shot through him as he released. Pouring himself into her, he screamed in ecstasy, and it had never felt so good. He had fantasized about his dragon and finished with his queen. It made him feel like a God at first. The thought of having both women blew his mind, but as he removed himself and turned his old lady over, heartbreak swept through him.

Ari pulled him in to kiss her, ecstatic with their lusty reunion, as Mack closed his eyes in disgust. He had betrayed his queen, and it sickened him to his stomach. Mack had been desperate for B for years, but the realization hit him now that he had his own perfect queen. Ari didn't deserve this, and he didn't need anyone else. The guilt consumed him as she continued to shower him with her lips.

"God, Mack, that was incredible. I'll misbehave all the time if you're going to please me like that. It felt like the first time, all over again."

"Oh sweetheart, I'm so fecking sorry. I took you like a man possessed when I should have made love to you."

Ari's brow furrowed in confusion. "I loved it honey, it was fantastic, so please don't apologize."

Mack felt bile burn the back of his throat in disgust. He had done the unthinkable. He should be worshipping Ari as his old lady and giving her whatever she desired. He had to make things right, only he couldn't break her heart by telling her. Climbing on top of her, he kissed her, staring into her eyes.

"If I could give you anything right now, what would you ask for?"

Ari stared at him, nervously, "There is something, but I'm scared to ask."

Mack stared at her in desperation. Whatever it was, he would give it to her. He had to. "Tell me."

She whispered, "I want you to put another baby inside me. I want to grow our family and give you the pack you've always wanted."

His heart banged in his chest. "Oh baby, I'll fill you with however many babies you want. I'll fuck you all day, every day, until I plant my seed inside you."

"Really?"

"Yeah, baby. No more birth control. Let's grow our family."

Ari burst into tears, and he kissed her lips. Tears fled down his face too as he thought about what he'd done to her. He was going to do everything he could to make her happy. He was going to learn to stop feeling for his dragon to save his marriage and his family.

Everyone saw a relaxed Mack two weeks later. He had stopped the tail on B and tended to his wife's every need. They went for evening strolls, and he showered her with flowers and kisses every day since his bedroom betrayal.

They were on another evening stroll when Ari turned to him. "Mack, we need to talk."

"Oh."

"Be honest with me."

"Okay."

Ari blurted out her sentence. "Did you fuck B at Noah's funeral?"

Mack stopped to glare at her. "Are you fecking crazy? No. I didn't. What the feck, Ari?"

"You came home so frantic."

"Yeah, because I was mad about her turning up."

"She's been distant toward me; she's avoided me for two weeks now, Mack. Why would she do that?"

"I'm guessing it's because she doesn't want to tell you about spending the night in Zander's bed."

"Shut the front door!"

Mack grimaced, walking ahead. "Yeah."

Ari rushed to his side. "Oh my, so that's why you were so mad when you got home?"

"Yeah, baby, and I want to forget about that if you don't mind."

"She spent all night in his bed?"

"Grrr."

"Shit, no wonder you came home and took me like that."

Mack shot her a guilty expression.

"Mack, I'm not fucking stupid. I've always accepted there's a part of you that will always love her, and I made peace with it because she's not into you. That was until you came home all hot and heavy and she started avoiding me. I panicked because if I was going to lose you to anyone, it would be her."

Mack stopped to face her, taking her hands in his. "Baby, you'll never lose me. I want you, always and forever. I just got so mad when she went with him. What makes him so special? I don't want to lose her, Ari. She's my best friend."

"Mine too, honey, but you need to accept that one day she will meet someone, and if you ever come into our bed thinking about her like that again, I'll kill you."

Mack went white. "Shit, Ari baby, I'm sorry. I had one slip, that's all.

Just for a split second until I looked into your eyes and realized what a horrible prick I was. I felt sick, like I betrayed you."

"Mack, you came home to me and fucked me senseless. You didn't fuck one of those nasty little bunnies, and you're going to fill me with as many babies as I want, to make up for it."

Mack pulled her in close and stared into her eyes. "I'm so sorry, baby. Please, please forgive me. Feck, I'm a horrible prick, and I don't deserve you. I promise you; I am trying to let her go. She is still my best friend, but I cut that shit out. Please believe me."

"I do. I've seen the effort you're making, letting her live a little and now you have to keep building on that. B will always be there for you Mack, but now you have to let her grow."

"Forgive me, Ari, please? Let me hear the words, and I promise you I'll never hurt you again."

Ari smiled and kissed his nose. "Mack, I forgive you, but when will you realize no one will love you like I do? When will I be enough for you?"

"Baby, I realized it the moment I opened my eyes after I took you that day. The thought of what I'd done and thinking I might lose you scared the shit out of me. Now you have my heart, baby, all of it. I won't make you share it anymore. Dragon is and will always be my best friend and nothing more. I'm done hurting the two of you."

"Well, it's about time."

Mack drew her in, kissing her hard, relieved that everything was out in the open. He meant what he said. He didn't want to hurt Ari anymore, wanting to be a better man for both Ari and B.

Ari squeezed his hand and led him down the dusty path toward home.

"Why do you think she's avoiding me, Mack?"

"Because you're the one she opens up to around here. My guess is, she's struggling with spending the night with him. Frankie found her sleeping in his arms. When have you ever known Dragon to be like that with anyone?"

"Do you think she has feelings for him?"

Mack let out an enormous sigh. "I hope not, baby. Sunnyville isn't safe for her."

Ari gulped, trying to hide her nervous expression. "Yeah, right?"

CHAPTER TWENTY

Selfish Dragon?

Ari hovered on B's front porch, waiting to catch her coming home from the school run. It had been two and a half weeks and B had hardly said a word to her, and Ari was missing her friend. She was tapping her fingers on the porch swing when Mack came looking for her. Gliding baby Alex through the air like a superhero, he danced up the steps.

"So, this is where Mommy is hiding," he said, planting a kiss on her lips.

"Hey, honey."

"She still not back then."

"No."

Mack put his arm around her. "She loves you, baby. She is just figuring shit out. I'll talk to her."

"No, Mack, I'm going to talk to her. I want to know what I've done."

"You haven't done anything."

Ari said nothing, staring at the forestry beyond the cabins. She couldn't understand why B was ignoring her. The last time they spoke was when B left for Noah's funeral and since B's arrival back in Uskiville, she avoided Ari. Every time Ari tried to talk, B headed off in a rush.

"I'm going to call her. She told me when we grappled this morning, she would talk to you. She promised me."

"You spoke to her?"

"Yeah, I don't like how she's making you feel, baby."

"Great! No wonder she hasn't returned from the school run. Why didn't you stay out of it like I asked you? I won't see her for another week now."

"I wouldn't be so sure of that," Mack said, nodding toward B's truck approaching the drive, before escorting Alex back down the steps to greet B, who was parking.

B climbed out of the truck, kissing Alex on the head.

"Hey, everything alright?"

"She's hurting, B. She doesn't know what she's done wrong. Please talk to my baby. I can't take seeing her like this."

B pursed her lips. "Sorry Mackie, I'll talk to her," she said, giving him a kiss on the cheek before heading up the steps and plonking herself on the swing next to Ari.

They watched Mack head home with Alex, and then Ari launched her attack.

"What the hell, B? I helped you get to the funeral and then you ignored me. What did I do to deserve that?"

"Nothing. You have done nothing to deserve it. I've just been a little confused, and I needed time to digest before I spoke to you. My head's so messed up, and I knew if I spoke to you sooner, I would have snapped and taken my frustration out on you. I'm sorry, Ari, you're the last person I want to upset."

Ari reeled back. "Whoa, did the fiery dragon just apologize? What the hell happened? Did you bang your head?"

"Piss off!"

"Oh, come on! You deserved that! Now spill."

B put her head in her hands, much to Ari's shock, and she automatically stroked her back to provide comfort.

"Shit, B, what's happened? Did he hurt you?"

B sprung up in her seat. "What? Who?"

"Zander?"

B looked at her in disgust. "Jesus Ari. Of course, he didn't. He was fucking perfect."

Ari choked on the fresh air. "Did you just call a man perfect?"

B laughed, the hurt still on her face.

"I guess I did."

"Oh, my God. You like him!"

B stood, tilting her head to the sky in frustration. "It was just sex, Ari. Two people getting over their grief."

"But you slept in his bed."

"I was tired."

"I bet you were with the size of him. Tell me, is he you know...?"

"What?"

"You know?" Ari gestured to his size. "As big as he looks."

B grinned, raising an eyebrow at Ari.

"Whoa, did he exhaust the mighty dragon?"

"A dragon doesn't kiss and tell,

"You better give me something because you have ignored me for two weeks."

B sighed, biting down onto her bottom lip. "I connected with him, Ari. I didn't expect to, and it shook the hell out of me. Something happened, and I can't explain it. We were just so natural together. He seeped into my mind, and it wasn't my usual fuck and run. For the first time since I met the boy's dad, I didn't want to run."

"B, this is mental and a little scary, if I'm being honest."

B's Jaw tightened. "Ari. I gave him one night to cross me off his bucket list. So, we could both get everything out of our systems, but that's it. I can't go back to him."

"B, he fancies the pants off you, but maybe it's for the best. Tell me you won't see him again."

B sat down again, her disappointment obvious to Ari. "He's a one-percenter, Ari. It started and ended with one night."

"Promise me it's done and out of your system."

"Ari, he's not white, he's black as night. Not to mention, I am incapable of having a normal relationship, and I'll never become property like you."

Ari's face became stern, "It's not like that, B. Mack worships me. Being his old lady is an honor. I'm worshipped by the man I love, and it's an incredible feeling."

"I don't believe that shit. Nothing lasts, Ari, and you're a fool to think it does."

"That's just fear talking."

"No, I just won't bow down to anyone. Besides, Mackie is already pissed with me. I broke the two rules. Could you imagine if I saw Scottie again?"

"Scottie?"

B flushed. "Yeah, that's what I call him, and he calls me Welsh Cake."

"Pet names?" Alarm colored her words. "B, tell me you won't see him again. I love him and all, but you're supposed to end up with a nice, respectable guy."

"Someone you and Mackie approve of, you mean?"

"Yes, and I'll find you one!"

B slammed her palms into her thighs. "Ari, stop, please? This is why I've been avoiding you. I knew you'd go all gooey, and I'm not going down this road. Just because I stayed the night, it doesn't mean I'm looking for a relationship. I'll do business with Scottie and that's it. I don't need any more complications. I have to sign my contract this weekend as I'm going to New York on Monday for a week to clear my head. When I return, I'm going to tell Mackie about the move."

Ari stood up and backed away from B. "What? You're still going through with it, after everything that's happened with Noah? Are you mad?"

"No Ari, I'm not! Nothing has changed. I made a promise, and I'm seeing it through. I own the club and lots of land down there. My gym is half-finished, for crying out loud."

Ari paced up and down the porch. "I thought you were just mad and would change your mind after what happened there. Mackie has called off the wolves. B, everything is wonderful now. Please stop this and stay. It's safer here!"

"God, not you as well. Mackie's paranoia is catching, I see."

"Yeah, but who will protect you down there with Noah gone?"

"Ari, I don't need protecting. I want to live like a normal person, so please can you just tell Mackie I'm at a conference?"

Ari huffed. "B, you're going away for over a week and not telling him. He's already pissed about you going back to the UK in a few weeks. How do you think he will react?"

B lost it. She had eyes of fury. "For fuck's sake, Ari! I'm sick to the back teeth of worrying about what Mackie thinks! I'm sick of being caged, and I'm sick of you and everyone else trying to control me. Now I'm heading out soon and I'm staying at The Crest Hotel for the weekend. So, will you please just cover for me one last time?"

"B, please? What will everyone think if you abandon us? How will it look for the club?"

"I don't give a shit how it looks or what anyone thinks, Ari. Now, for the love of God, let me live my life!"

Ari stood motionless, stunned at the spot.

B rose from the swing, frustration clear across her tanned face. Approaching Ari, she put her hand on her shoulder. "I'm sorry Ari, I didn't mean—"

"No, you're not. You're a selfish bitch! I'll do this for you, and then you're on your own. All we've ever done is love you B and you're so fucked up; you won't let us do that. Well fine, see if I care. Oh. and you're right. You're not ready for a relationship because you'll just hurt the poor schmuck that comes into your life, like you hurt the rest of the people who love you," Ari said and ran off into her house, leaving B standing there.

CHAPTER TWENTY-ONE

Once a One-Percenter, Always A One-Percenter

Two weeks had passed, and Zander still hadn't heard from B. That, coupled with the loss of his best friend, was killing him. He couldn't sleep. He'd lost his appetite and found himself exhausted. But it wasn't just Zander who looked depressed. The entire club had a glumness about them. It still broke everyone up about Noah's death, and they wondered what the future held for the MC after hearing nothing from B.

Jimmy had explained to Zander that if he didn't hear from B by the weekend, he would call Mack to explain their financial situation, requesting aid. Despite the cash gift from B, the club was still struggling. The thirty-thousand dollars divided amongst them didn't even begin to cover the members' debts. Most of the members had been in financial turmoil since the beginning of Noah's reign, the debt stacked against them even threatened the foreclosure on some members homes. Some members were considering going back into crime. Carjacking had been big business to them until Noah ordered them to go straight. The money had put food on the table, and they had children to feed. They relied on the MC business for everything and with Noah refusing to accept financial aid to build the Dragon's trust; the club had fallen deeper into despair.

They had a scrap metal yard bringing in a steady income, but since Noah ordered them to go legit, business had slowed. The members would have previously stolen cars, stripped them bare, and sold the parts to the highest bidder, but not since Noah promised a legit business. All the members put their faith in Noah's legacy, voting to go straight, but now they were in disarray and considering a vote on overturning their original vote to become one-percenters again, looking at potential drug-run deals. The uncertainty around their future, because of B's absence, was making them miserable.

In the last church meeting, Jimmy promised he would have answers by the following Monday. and Monday was three days away. Jimmy had to give them something or the vote to go back into crime would move forward.

He was ready to out B and Noah's plans to Mack. Noah was gone, and he didn't care for B. In the grand scheme of things, the club was his priority. The only thing stopping him from informing Mack was his promise to Noah regarding B's safety.

Jimmy and Zander had worked the books, attempting to see where they could claw back some revenue or bide their time until B came through for them. They hoped she would do it soon. She promised she would be in touch, but two weeks was too long for a struggling MC. They needed a resolution to their problems, and fast. It was early afternoon when Zander stepped out for a drink at the bar. It was all he seemed to do of late, and the entire club was talking about it. They dared not confront him about it, though; they valued their lives too much.

Glen had just poured Zander a scotch when the phone rang, and amusement shot across Zander's face as he heard Glen address a woman on the phone.

"Yes, ma'am, I'll hand you over now."

"Welsh Cake?"

"I don't know, VP. She just asked for you," Glen said, handing him the phone.

Zander's heart was trying to claw out of his chest. His hands shook as he took the phone.

"Welsh Cake?"

"Sorry Zander, it's me, Ari?"

"Oh, hey, what's up? Is Mack okay?" he said, waving Glen away from the bar.

"Mack's fine. I took your number from his phone while he's in the shower. I need your help."

"Ari, I'm not getting involved in anything behind the Prez's back."

"Please, Zander, I'm desperate. She needs your help."

Zander swallowed hard against his Adam's apple that felt like it was lodged in his throat. "Why? What's happened?"

"Nothing yet, but I'm worried about her. B left for Sunnyville a couple of hours ago on her own, and she has no idea how dangerous this move is. She's staying at The Crown Hotel, and I need you to talk to her and tell her what a mistake she's making. Tell her Sunnyville isn't for her and make her come home. Mack's only just called off the pack and if he finds out she's in Sunnyville, he'll lock her up and throw away the key. Oh, and don't tell Jimmy. He'll be on the phone to Mack in an instant."

Zander's eyes narrowed, and he made his voice stern. "Ari, If Welsh Cake wants to start fresh down here, then I'm no' gonnae stop her. She's a grown woman who can hold her own. Now I'll go check on her because you're right. It's too dangerous for her to be alone when we still don't know what happened to Noah, but I'll no' try to stop her. Mack has caged her for too long."

"Now's not the time to be selfish, Zander. I know you like her, but with Noah gone, she needs to forget this deal and come home, for all our sakes."

"*Me* selfish? That's the pot calling the kettle black, right there. Let's be honest, here, Welsh Cake is the money in Uskiville, with your live-in fucking babysitter and chef, and as for Mack, well, we all fucking know what he thinks of her. No wonder you want her to stay." He concentrated on unclenching his fists then finished. "Look, Welsh Cake wants a life, so let her live it."

"How dare you? I love my best friend."

"Then why aren't you supporting her? Why call me to help you?"

"Because you don't know her, what she's like. How her mind works. You and her aren't a good fit. She's more woman than you can handle."

Zander scoffed. "Excuse me?"

"Look, I know you like her. God knows Noah rammed it down Mack's throat every time he visited, and yes, she showed a moment of weakness with you, but it won't last! B is incapable of being in a relationship. She's broken. Damaged goods."

"Well, if she's so broken, why are you desperate to keep her locked away? Why no' offload your problems?"

"We love her and want to look after her."

"No, you want to control her. Well, sorry, but the Dragon is free and if she wants to come here, then I'll welcome her with open arms."

"Zander, please!"

"Sorry, Ari, I won't do it. I like her, and this wasn't just a moment of weakness for either of us."

"Okay, look. Your night together messed up her head. She didn't expect to connect with you in the way she did, and it threw her. A confused Dragon is dangerous to everyone, and I want you to do the right thing here."

Zander closed his eyes and drew a deep breath. *I knew we connected.* He forced his attention back to the phone call. "And I am, Ari. I'm gonnae talk to her, offer her a hand and support her in whatever she wants to do here. Maybe you should try that too, by keeping Mack occupied until she's ready for him to know and dinnae worry, I'll keep her safe."

"Wait! Just answer me one question."

"What?" he snapped.

"Just tell me where she slept the night you had sex with her?"

"Um, nestled into my chest in my bed. What kind of fucking question is that?"

Ari's gasp rattled down the line. "Shit, shit. This is bad."

"Excuse me."

"Zander, B doesn't sleep with anyone, she fu—"

"Fucks and runs. So, everyone keeps telling me. Well let me tell you, she dinnae with me. She slept soundly all night, and I'm positive she would have stayed if she wasn't dragged away at first light."

Ari cackled. "I think you're getting a little ahead of yourself, there, Zander, I mean, I know she said you guys connected, but sleeping in your bed. I mean, she actually closed her eyes and slept?"

"Why is that so hard to believe? Tell me something Ari, did it ever cross your mind that she met someone she wanted to spend the night with? Or am I that much of a monster that you think I'm incapable of making someone feel like that?"

"Shit, sorry. I didn't mean it like that. It's just that she locks her heart away. She has nothing real with anyone."

Zander sighed, almost crushing the phone in anger. "Well, she fucking did with me. I felt it and I know she did."

"That's what I'm afraid of."

"Why? What's so bad about it?"

Ari's sharp tone threatened to pierce Zander's ear drums. "Look, I've only known B a short time, but she opens up to me more than anyone and after she slept with you, she avoided me until this morning. She didn't want to talk to me about it and B spills all about her Sultry boys, but with you she shut me out, which tells me she's struggling. B isn't your regular piece of ass, Zand. She is one big bundle of hurt and fuck you! So, if you're planning on using her for sex, you'll get more than you bargained for. Somebody will get hurt. And Zand? It won't be B."

"And what if I want her to be my old lady?"

Another harsh cackle wailed down the line. "Have you got rocks in your head? It's never going to happen. You may have caused a stir in her head, but her heart is encased in iron. She will never open it to you or anyone else. B is forever broken, so do us all a favor, forget about her and do right by the club."

Zander reached out and grabbed a bottle of beer then deftly twisted the cap off. "Oh, now we are getting to the root of the problem. Like I said earlier, you are just worried your cash cow and babysitter is going to go rogue and compromise your perfect world." He took a sip of cold beer. "Well, newsflash woman, I ain't backing down and Uskiville isn't my concern. You didn't give a damn about us after we helped you with Uncle Mauler, so dinnae talk to me about the good of the club. It's only for the good of the club when it suits Uskiville. Now, if you dinnae mind, I need to shower if I want to look good when I find my future old lady. See you 'round, Ari. Don't call me, I'll call you."

"Well, if war breaks out, it's on you, because Mack will not let her go."

"Fine by me. But be careful what you wish for because I dinnae think Uskiville will bode too well without their precious dragon," he said before hanging up.

Heading out from behind the bar, he saw Glen standing by the doorway. Zander raged, gripping him by the scruff of the neck.

"Were you eavesdropping?"

Glen trembled. "No, VP, I wasn't. I promise."

"You breathe a word of this to anyone, and I'll snap you like a fucking twig, chuck you on a fire and watch you burn." He shook the bartender like a rag. "You understand me?"

"Yes, VP."

"Good," he said, releasing him from his grasp.

Zander headed back to his room, his body fueled by a combination of lust and adrenaline. Desperate to see her again, he showered, changed, and put on his favorite aftershave. Then, he set off on his motorcycle to find her.

CHAPTER TWENTY-TWO

Mack entered the kitchen, sweeping Ari off her feet and planting a kiss on her lips.

"Hello, baby. I've missed you." he said as he sat on the breakfast stool at their gleaming white marble kitchen countertop.

"Hmm, what's gotten into you today?" Ari laughed as he continued to nuzzle into her neck.

"Nothing. I wanted to continue where we left off this morning. We are trying to make another baby, you know."

With that, a gangly teen walked into the kitchen. "Oh sick! C'mon! That's my mom, for heaven's sake."

Mack released Ari from his grasp with an enormous sigh.

"Sorry kiddo! I didn't realize anyone else was home," he said, tussling his hair as he left the room. "Oh! Has anyone seen Dragon today? I didn't get a chance to talk to her after you this morning, baby and her truck hasn't been there all afternoon?"

Remy glared at his mom as Ari replied with haste. "She's at another conference this weekend. Didn't she tell you?"

"Jesus! Where is she this week? That's the third one this month! I know she loves her job, but she has a business to run here. I am gonna have words. She can't keep ditching her responsibilities!"

Ari approached Mack, wrapping her arms around him.

"Listen, I know you're missing your best friend, but B has a life away from the club, too. These conferences make her happy and you know how passionate she is about her job, so just give her some space, okay? Besides, she is the owner. She doesn't have to answer to you, Mack. It's a polite courtesy she extends because of your friendship!"

"Well, the last time I checked, I run this fucking retreat, too! She only had to let me know. You know, maybe extend me a polite courtesy. We're supposed to be partners, best friends and she's never not told me where she's going before."

"It was last minute," Remy added as he plonked himself in front of the tv with a bowl of cereal. "It was school-related this time. I think it's in her contract she has to attend so many per year or something, she was saying to Madoc about it."

"Look! You know she'd do nothing to upset you. She loves you and I get she hasn't been around to grapple with you much of late, hell she has spent no time with me and I'm her best friend too. But let her have this, please? We have each other. B isn't as fortunate because she doesn't approve of me hand picking her dates. She needs this after you kept her under lock and key for so long," Ari said.

Mack softened. "She told you this?"

"She doesn't have to. This is B we are talking about, remember? She doesn't talk about anything that involves feelings. Just call it a woman's intuition!"

Mack placed his travel mug under the coffee maker, striking the start button. "I just wish that she'd said something. I would have sent Bamfa with her to keep her safe. I hate the idea of her traveling around the country on her own. Blaze is still out there, and she could get hurt if someone recognizes her," he whispered out of Remy's earshot.

"Mack! She is the most successful soccer coach on the west coast. Everyone recognizes her, and she's not exactly fragile. She hands you your ass every time you grapple. She needs her freedom, and if you keep treating her like a prisoner, it won't end well."

"I'm not treating her like a fecking prisoner! She does what she wants. I'm just asking to be kept in the loop! Is that too much to ask?"

Ari began emptying the dishwasher. "So, talk to her when she gets back. Just remain calm and explain to her how you feel. But don't lose your shit with her. It won't end well, and we have a good thing here. I just don't want it ruined; besides, all this anger won't help us grow our family. You know what the doctor said."

Mack sighed, retrieving his mug of fresh coffee from the machine. "You're right, my queen, I'm sorry! I'll make it up to you later, I promise," he said as he kissed her softly.

"Ugh, get a room!" Remy shouted from the couch.

"Fine! I'm going!" Mack Slammed.

"I love you!" he whispered as he left the house via the back door.

Ari let out a sigh of relief.

"Nice save mom!" Remy said without taking his eye off the tv. "When is she going to tell him? We can't keep this up."

"Well, if you hadn't been eaves dropping on my conversation, you wouldn't have to keep anything up."

"And you would have blown Aunt Bs cover already. You're a rubbish liar, mom and that's a good thing, but Mack will lose it when he discovers the truth."

"Aunt B should tie everything up this weekend so she can tell him, and we can relax."

"You think? Jeez mom, he is gonna go berserk! His best friend is moving as far away from him as possible, and you think he'll be okay with that?"

"Well, he doesn't have a choice." Ari said, placing clean plates in the cupboard.

"Why are you calm about it? She's your best friend too and you don't seem to care! I don't want her or the boys to leave and you're not trying to stop her. Why?"

Ari shrugged. "Because I want her to be happy, and she's not happy here anymore."

"Maybe if you stopped trying to set her up with the town idiots every weekend, she'd want to stay."

"I do not! I just want her to be settled like me and Mack."

Remy got up to leave the room, slamming his cereal bowl and spoon onto the counter.

"Newsflash mom, she was happy, thrilled even, until you started sending blind dates to her door every week. Mack knows she doesn't like it, and it infuriates him, too. You say he's suffocating her, but you are both doing it and have been since we moved here."

"Remy, that's unfair!"

"No mom, she cooks all week long. You guys are never out of her house. It's no wonder she can't breathe and wants to leave! Junior and I will suffer now that our family is leaving, and Junior will be heartbroken. You know how close he is to Aunt B. So, please stop trying to fix things because you are making it worse," he yelled as he left the house too.

Ari called after him, to no avail. He had gone to blow off some steam, leaving Ari wondering if she was doing the best thing by helping her friend.

CHAPTER TWENTY-THREE
Frustration

B arrived in Sunnyville a little after lunch, meeting Spencer in the Sunnyville High school parking lot prior to signing her new contract. She was excited, being one step closer to freedom, and couldn't wait to sign her name on the dotted line.

Spencer, B's oldest friend and the first friend she met after moving to the states, was a big-time lawyer. He was just five foot two inches in stature but so fierce he'd become the best in the business. He lived on a vineyard with his husband David and their dog Bruno, a bulldog who B and the boys adored. B hadn't seen Spencer in person for a couple of months, but they always spoke on the phone to sort B's contracts, so when he saw her step out of her truck, he threw himself at her.

"There she is. I missed you, sweet pea," he said, embracing her.

"Missed you too, short stuff."

"Hey, less of the short stuff. I make up for my lack of height in other ways."

"I don't want to know about your bedroom escapades with David, thank you!" she teased.

"Always a joker you. At least I have a healthy relationship, better than those Sultry boys of yours."

"I'll take your word for it, lovely boy. Now come on, let's get this done."

The pair headed toward the school entrance, with B laughing at the size of Spencer's briefcase.

"Couldn't get a smaller briefcase, then?"

"Piss off!"

They were just about to head inside when Spencer stopped her in her tracks.

"B, I just want to say how sorry I am about Noah. I know you were close, but now he's passed, you're not obliged to do this anymore. You could stay where Mack can look after you. I think you'll be lost without him."

B rolled her eyes. "For fuck's sake. Not you as well. I am doing this, Spencer. I made a promise! This is for my family. It's beautiful here and being away from Mack is more appealing by the day. So, let's sign this contract, shall we?"

Spencer stopped in his tracks, taking her hand. "B, hold up. I want to make sure you are making the right decision. Mack and Frankie have been your rocks for years now. You're a team and I know Ari has altered the dynamics a little, but are things so bad you have to leave your home?"

"Spencer, they cuffed me to my bloody bed to stop me from going to see Noah after he died and made me feel like a prisoner in my own home. Mack has changed. Something has tripped a switch in his brain. The only thing the boys have ever asked for is for me to move here and I no longer feel comfortable in Uskiville."

"Sweet Jesus. But is Sunnyville the right choice for you?"

"Yes! Please, I want this. Help me create a better life for myself and the boys."

Spencer released her, raising his palm. "Okay, but if Mack tries to kill me, you better save me. He still scares the shit out of me."

B laughed. "He's a bloody teddy bear! Now come on already."

Heading into the reception area, the receptionist studied them curiously before greeting them.

"Good afternoon. Blethen Jones and Spencer Smith, we are meeting with Principal Beckett," B said.

"Oh, I'm sorry. The principal left for the weekend."

B raised her eyebrows. "How is that possible when he confirmed this meeting last week?"

The receptionist looked sheepish as she fumbled with the keyboard on her desk.

"Oh, uh, let me just check the system," she replied.

B tapped her fingers on the desk, nostrils flaring and blood pressure rising as Spencer's face displayed his nervousness about the whole situation.

The receptionist stared at them with apologetic eyes. "Uh, I'm sorry, there seems to have been a mistake. My associate should have contacted you last Tuesday to rearrange."

"Well, she bloody didn't, good girl. So, I suggest you get the principal back here pronto!"

The color drained from the short haired woman's face, with Spencer stepping in front of B to handle the situation. Smiling at her as he hovered over the desk and giving her a wink.

"I apologize for Ms. Jones. She is very busy and only available this weekend. If you could inform the principal that if the deal isn't honored today, then my client will be accepting a deal in New York on Monday morning and I'm sure he doesn't want to lose the most decorated coach on the west coast now does he?"

"Uh, no. I will try to contact him."

"Thank you," he said to her, before turning to B, who had stepped away from the desk.

"Hey, unclench your fists, you look like a psychopath, and this is a school, remember."

B spat through gritted teeth. "What the fuck, Spence? I don't have time for this. This deal needs to be signed today or I'm screwed. Ari won't cover for me anymore and I don't fancy being a prisoner for the rest of my life. I'll end up killing Mack."

"Don't worry. I'll sort this!"

"Yeah, how? He's not here?"

"B please. I got this. Leave it to me and get some fresh air, will you? You're scaring the receptionist."

"Fine," she huffed as she headed outside, scowling, and propping herself up against the bike rack. B was close to breaking point; she just wanted the deal done so she could confront Mack and leave Uskiville. She was becoming desperate.

Spencer came out moments later, displaying a scowl of his own.

"She is going to keep trying him and call us back. He's at a doctor's appointment."

"He'll need more than a doctor if he doesn't call back this afternoon. Spencer, I need this!"

"B, I promise you will have it signed before the day is done. Trust me, you are hot property right now. I have his mobile number, too. He won't want to cock this up. He knows the clubs are lining up to snap you up."

B raised her arms, gesturing to her surroundings. "So, what now? You have appointments elsewhere. Can you even fit another meeting in if he sorts something?"

"I'll make it work. I have another meeting at four in the next town over. It'll take a couple of hours and I'll keep trying Beckett. You visit the town and get some food. Relax. If you remember how to do that?"

B scowled at him. "I'll relax when I've signed the contract."

"And you will. Now, allow me to do my job."

"Fine! Bring it in, good boy."

Spencer embraced her once more. Looking up at her, he sighed. "I'll sort this, okay?"

"I trust you," she said with half a smile.

"Tell your face that, then."

B chuckled. "Right! Yeah, sorry, I'll go drop my bag off and see you in a bit," she said, pulling away from him and getting into her truck.

CHAPTER TWENTY-FOUR

Secret Spy

"Boss, is that you?"

"Of course, it is numb nuts?" Blaze said.

"Oh, right yeah."

"So, what have you got for me?"

"A lot. Dragon showed up at the church and boy, did she turn heads."

"She made it to Sunnyville?" Blaze asked.

"Affirmative. Hey, Zander and Dragon had something going on. You never told me. I could use that."

"What are you talking about?"

"I am guessing they already knew each other by the way he greeted her. Their embrace shocked the hell out of me. Zander is a cold bastard. Yet they sat hand in hand. They had a cozy chat over Noah's casket, too. What's that all about?"

"I don't know, but you'll find out. Anything else?"

"Yeah, they made a bit of a statement. Zander took her on the back of his bike to collect her truck and Mack was pissed. He hated seeing them together. Mack and Jimmy were even at loggerheads when they got outside. Mack freaked when she arrived unguarded, and his face was a picture when Zander held her hand throughout the service."

"You're shitting me? This is priceless! What else?"

"You were right about her being loaded. She put thousands over the bar. She also spent the night in Zander's bed."

"Oh, this just keeps getting better. I get to torture three Celts at once. The Irishman shunned now, is he? And that Scottish son of a bitch will pay for shooting me. They can both watch whilst I devour their Dragon."

"There's more boss."

"Spit it out then," Blaze said, walking to his favorite window, allowing the fresh air to wash over his face.

"There're some mixed loyalties within the ranks. Frankie, the marine, stopped Mack from disturbing the love birds, blocking his path. I haven't deciphered the dynamics yet, but Mack laid one on his jaw for insubordination."

"They are unravelling. Keep spinning your webs and keep me informed. I will let you know when it is time to strike. Until then, play the game and keep your head down."

"Absolutely boss."

"Good work! When this is over, you can take your place as my VP."

"I appreciate that. Over and out!"

CHAPTER TWENTY-FIVE

Ducks In a Row

"So, I guess that's it then? I will be stuck there forever, suffocating in that bloody town. Spencer, I can't breathe anymore. I just feel trapped! I love them so much, but they have changed. Nothing has been the same since Ari walked into our lives. This was my one chance to escape, be free and live my life again."

"Now, hold on, nothing's over yet. I told you I would seal this deal and I will! I have explained to the principal that it's now or never. He knows that half of the country wants you, so he'll come through. Just head down to the bar and chill out and I'll ring you as soon as I hear something."

B climbed off the bed and slipped on her shoes. "And what if you don't? I can't keep making excuses every weekend. There are only so many conferences and public speaking engagements someone can attend. I am running out of excuses and Mack's not stupid; he will clock on and then I am well and truly screwed!"

"B! I am the best God damn lawyer in the country, and I know I can seal this deal. Have a little faith in me, please?"

"Fine! I'll get a drink then," she hissed.

"Good! And B, get yourself laid. It'll do us all some good."

"Piss off! Get my deal done and dusted!"

Spencer chuckled. "Will do! Speak to you soon."

B put down the phone and ran her fingers through her hair in despair. She needed this deal to work, she needed her freedom, and her life back.

She opened a bottle of whiskey that she brought from home and took a huge glug before setting it down on the bedside table of her over expensive hotel room. B couldn't risk her preferred choice: a cheap motel, for fear of being recognized by anyone. She also figured she would be safe there during her Sunnyville visits and didn't imagine the hotel to be hospitable to rough and ready one-percenters.

B picked up her phone and purse and headed to the bar, praying Spencer would call to tell her the deal was in play. A deal that would free her from her shackles and allow her to breathe again.

The bar was vibrant as she walked in. Neil the bar boy saw her approaching and instantly fixed her a white wine and placed it at the bar, as well as turning the soccer channel on the bar tv. He had met B a few times during her previous stays and loved to chat about soccer.

"White wine?" he said as she approached the bar.

"Yes please. I'm also going to need a scotch and an order of dirty fries."

"Coming right up," Neil said, fixing her drink.

"Grab a drink for yourself as well."

"Great! Thanks B."

B faked a smile as she climbed onto the bar stool, only to see Zander sitting at the bar opposite her with a devilish smile on his face.

"For Christ's sake," she said as she sucked in a deep breath, trying not to roll her eyes. It was the last thing she needed. Zander was a huge complication for her, even if the sight of him made her breathless.

B's attention turned to Neil, who had brought her a scotch and her dirty fries. Placing the crystal whiskey glass to her lips, she expected the smooth, amber liquid to engulf her palate with its satisfying taste, only to find that her drink tasted like vile fire water.

"Jeez! What the hell is that?" she said as she coughed violently.

"Neat scotch," Neil laughed.

"That's not scotch, my lovely, that tastes like bloody turps or something."

"Turps?" Neil quizzed, and before B could respond, Zander had taken up the stool next to her and let out a huge chuckle.

"Paint stripper, laddie. Here, try this one," he said, ushering Neil to pour B a shot of his choosing.

Neil handed B the glass, and she raised an eyebrow at the Scot.

"Please tell me this is scotch?"

Zander grinned. "Well, it's the closest thing to scotch here, Welsh Cake. Unless you happen to have a bottle of the good stuff up your shirt."

B ignored him, knocking back the shot in one.

"It's certainly not the good stuff, but it'll do. Two more please, my lovely," she said to Neil before turning to Zander. "What are you doing here, Scottie? Who sent you?"

"Karaoke."

B shook her head and rose from the seat. "I don't like liars. In truth, we have trust and lying to me tells me I can't trust you. So, I'll take my food up to my room. See you around."

Zander narrowed his eyes as he blocked her path, palming her waist. "Okay, okay. Ari is worried about you."

B shook her head, sitting back on her seat and knocking back a second shot before taking a mouthful of fries, chomping on them with a scowl on her face.

"Keep the scotch coming, good boy," she said to Neil, who topped them up again, before she turned to Zander.

"I don't need a babysitter, Scottie. It's funny though, I didn't peg you as a lap dog."

"I'm nobody's fucking lap dog," Zander growled.

"Then why are you here trying to cage me? Let me guess, Ari told you to change my mind and send me on my way, right?"

"Aye, she did."

B shook her head, pouring her shot of whiskey into her wine, bringing it to her lips. Zander took hold of the glass, placing it back down on the bar.

"Slow down with that and tell me why you're being so hostile. I can see your dragon eyes are baying for blood."

B stared into her plate of loaded fries, ignoring him. She couldn't look at him.

"Do you let anyone into that fiery head of yours?"

"Not if I can help it."

Zander tutted. "It must drive you mad, knowing you let me in that night. That you let me get close to you and see you vulnerable. Ari said I got under your skin. Is that why you're pissed at me and left without saying goodbye?"

B pursed her lips and dropped her fork, wiping her mouth on her napkin.

"Ari needs to learn to keep her mouth shut and no, me being pissed has nothing to do with you. We spent a night together to relieve grief, that's all. I mean, what the fuck do you want from me Scottie? One minute you wanna kill me and the next you wanna fuck me. Split personality much?"

"Takes one to fucking know one, darling. But I think you want me, too. Just like you did that night."

"We had a grief fuck, nothing more!"

Zander leaned in, whispering in her ear. His warm breath sweeping across her cheek. "You keep telling yersel' that, but remember, I know what makes you quiver, writhe, and explode. You cannae lie to me when your body screams, fuck me!"

"And you think I don't know how hard you are right now? Go fuck yourself, Scottie. You'll have to use your hand tonight, lovely boy."

"Why avoid the inevitable? Let me take you upstairs so I can taste you, make you scream."

B rolled her eyes. "Dream on Captain Crazy. It ain't happening!"

"Just tell me why no'."

B picked up her whiskey-wine, sipping it. "Because I don't trust you after you and Ari have been conspiring against me."

"I wasn't conspiring. I told her to step off, and for the record, trust is earned darling."

"Isn't it just?"

Zander sat back on the bar stool, sipping his drink. "Look, you're clearly pissed. At least tell me how I can make you feel better."

"Nothing will make me feel better now. Everything is just so fucked up. Things were supposed to be different. I came here to get my ducks in a row and..." she said, allowing her words to slip away.

"What?"

"It doesn't matter."

Zander shook his head in disbelief. "If you keep bottling that shit up, you're gonnae explode. So, let's head up to your room and talk about it. Or at the very least, let me ease your tension."

"You'd like that, wouldn't you?"

"As would you, judging by how I made you scream that night."

B flushed, making Zander laugh as he placed the back of his hand on her cheek.

"You seem a little rosy in the cheeks. Oh my God, is the fiery Dragon, embarrassed?"

"Please don't fucking call me that. I told you, I hate it," she spat, her face like a thunderstorm.

Zander's eyes narrowed. "But everyone calls you that."

"No, Mackie calls me that. I have a name, you know."

"Sorry, I should have asked what it was when I met you. I apologize. How about we start again? Alexander McGovan, but everyone calls me Zander. Pleased to meet you," he said, extending his hand.

B's lips curled into a seductive smile. Extending her hand, she placed it inside his, shaking it. "Blethen Jones, but everyone calls me B."

Zander brought her hand to his lips, kissing it, sending shivers down her spine.

"Blethen is a beautiful name. Welsh, I take it?"

"Yeah, it means wolf cub."

Zander's wide mouth curled into an enormous smile. "No way!"

"Look it up if you don't believe me."

"A beautiful name for a beautiful woman, but I prefer Welsh Cake myself."

"Good, because I'm not calling you Zander. It's Scottie or nothing."

Zander leaned into her once more. "You can call me whatever you like, looking like that Welsh Cake, but mark my words, I'll make you scream my name one day."

"You keep telling yourself that, good boy."

"Welsh Cake, you should know that once I set my sights on something, I'm relentless and dinnae stop until I have it."

B pushed her plate away. "Great! Another bloody stalker. I think the founder has filled that position, sunshine."

"I'll no' stalk you, darling. I just want you to know that one day you will be my property. Mine. No' Mack's or those Sultry boys you like to play with, all mine."

"Wow, another archaic and misogynistic asshole. Keep digging, Scottie, you're doing great," she teased, sipping her whiskey-wine mix.

"Ooh, I do like a bit of sass, but you've got that all wrong."

"I don't think so, good boy. I helped Mackie build the Wolves Chapter, and I watched him draw up the rules and regulations. I know you claim your women to demonstrate control. It may be natural to a lot of folks, but I'll never be controlled, Scottie. Not by you or anyone!"

Zander laughed. "You're mistaken. Control isn't what it's about. It's about loyalty and being an old lady is an honor. Giving yersel' to one person, trusting them and telling them it's them and only them is what it's all about. MC patches worship their woman fiercely and protect them with their lives."

"Until you hit the road and then it's a woman in every state."

"No darling. If you love someone, it's only them, no cheating. Well, for me anyway."

"Forgive me, Scottie, but you're full of shit. People can't help themselves, it's human nature. People suck you in, lie, chew you up and spit you out and anyone who believes anything else is a bloody idiot!"

Zander stopped in his tracks, shaking his head. "Just because you had your heart broken Welsh Cake, it doesnae mean you have to lock it away. That's no' living darling. That's a life sentence."

"No, I'm just saving myself from more lies and bullshit."

"Pain, you mean. Being frightened and scared is part of living, just like finding someone that makes you feel like you've won the fucking lottery does."

"That doesn't exist. Everyone lies, everyone looks out for number one and the sooner you get that in that beautiful brain of yours, the better."

Zander smirked. "It does. You just cannae see it because you won't remove the shackles from your heart and let it beat again. Do you know something, Welsh Cake? The night I spent with you was beyond amazing. You made me feel. The sex was euphoric and by far the best I've had."

B whipped her head back in a burst of laughter. "You poor, poor man."

"Stop it! Please just cut the crap for a minute and let me talk."

B composed herself, sitting up straight, her eyes fixated on him.

"Cards on the table. I see you underneath all that fire and attitude. You're attentive and loving and everything felt exhilarating that night. Your touch, your kiss, your calming effect on me when I couldn't breathe. Even your sexy accent, but do you know what made it perfect?"

B looked at him, pursing her lips and shaking her head.

"How you, wait, how do you Welsh say it? How you cwtched into me. Experiencing you, calm and peaceful, as you breathed into my chest. The smell of your hair and perfume intoxicating me as you slept. That was fucking special to me, darling. Thing is, I cannae figure out what I did wrong. Why did you leave without saying goodbye?"

B's words evaded her. This experience was alien to her, frightening even, as fight or flight kicked in. B was devoid of feelings until Zander took her breath away. He wasn't like Mack or the other bikers, as she expected. Sat before her was a vulnerable man, asking why she had left him after what he believed was a divine union. It was most unexpected to B, who fidgeted uncomfortably on her bar stool. She had just mustered up the courage to answer his question when the DJ called out to him from the stage before them.

"Zander, you're up in five."

B raised an eyebrow, her mood changing as she smiled at him, curious.

"You really sing karaoke?"

"Aye, I'll no' lie to you darling. You shouldn't tar me with the same brush as Ari and Mack. I just wanted to see you."

"And you can sing?"

Zander shrugged. A hint of embarrassment flushed on his cheeks. "I have a go, yeah! The hotel slums it on Friday nights to bring the locals in. I sing here every Friday, except for Noah's funeral and last week where I was licking my wounds, after you left without saying goodbye."

"Scottie."

Zander stood, taking a step back. "Look, I am gonnae sing one song and I would appreciate it if you're still here once I'm done."

B's bashful smile radiated as she spoke to him. "I've got nowhere to be, Scottie."

"Thank you," Zander said, planting a kiss on her cheek before turning to the stage.

"Scottie," B called, almost mad that the words came out of her mouth.

"Yeah," he said glancing over his shoulder.

"You didn't do anything."

He looked at her, curious.

"Wrong, I mean."

Zander pursed his lips into a bashful smile as he nodded in acknowledgement and headed on stage.

B observed him, stunned that he was about to sing.

Zander approached the microphone, glancing over at B, giving her a cheeky wink and a smile.

"I just want to dedicate this song to Welsh Cake. I wish you could see yersel' through my eyes, darling. Anyway, this one's for you."

B's face went scarlet as she picked up her phone to record him. She wanted to capture him in this moment and as she hit the record button, Scottie burst into his own rendition of her favorite love song, as if he knew what it was.

Goose pimples rode across her body, and her hair stood on end as his voice tantalized her ears. He was pitch perfect as B became lost in his song.

Zander grinned as he stared at her, as if he could sense what she was feeling. He encapsulated her. His rugged voice echoed inside her heart, as it tried to free itself from the shackles, she bound it in for so many years. Her breath was shallow and uneven as she tried to comprehend what was happening to her until a phone call from Spencer interrupted her thoughts.

Not wanting to be rude and desperate to feel lost in Zander's voice again, she ignored it, thinking she would call him back, but he rang again.

"A minute more won't hurt," she said to herself as she hit the end call button, bringing her attention back to Zander.

B stepped closer to the stage, mesmerized by the unconventional biker until she felt a firm hand on her bicep. Spinning around, she saw Spencer staring her down.

"Answer your phone, will you? We got twenty minutes to sign this contract. Now move your butt and get in my car. It's parked down the street," he said, dragging her away.

"Wait," she said, pulling away and heading to the bar.

"Tell Scottie I'm getting my ducks in a row and won't be long. Charge all his drinks to my room too and here's your tip," she said to Neil, handing him a bunch of twenty-dollar bills.

Neil nodded as Spencer yanked her arm again.

"Come on already, we can't miss this B," Spencer said, dragging her toward the exit.

"Okay," she said, glancing at Zander with a strained look on her face and watching his face fall with disappointment as his eyes tracked hers.

Outside, it was still warm as they headed to Spencer's car. The night sky was looming and despite feeling guilty about leaving Zander, B was excited to be sealing her deal. A fresh start meant so much to her, and B fantasized about seeing Zander more regularly as Spencer hurried her along. They were a stone's throw from his car when B heard Zander call out to her.

"Welsh Cake!" he bellowed as he ran up to her.

B's heart raced, watching him run after her in all of his stature, his hair swishing as he ran at a pace of knots, leaving B wondering how someone so big could run so fast. Stopping inches from her face, he panted and glared at her in confusion until he saw Spencer's hand on her arm. Anger filled his face, and he gripped Spencer by his suit collar.

"Take your fucking hand off her!"

B grabbed his chin to get his attention.

"Scottie, stop. He's my lawyer."

Zander's chest heaved as he turned to her, releasing a terrified looking Spencer from his grasp.

"I thought..."

"I'm fine. I need to sort something."

"Getting your ducks in a row?"

B nodded. "Yeah, I'll not be long."

"Let me come with you."

"No. I have to do this on my own. Now, give me your keys."

Zander's eyes widened. "I'll no' follow you darling."

"That's not why I'm asking for them. Now hand them over."

Zander's tone softened. "Nobody has my keys but me, darling. My bike is my life."

"If you can't trust me with your keys, I can't trust you with my body," B said, her dragon eyes reigniting as she shook her head.

"Welsh Cake—"

"Once a one-percenter, always a one-percenter, right Scottie?" she said, leaving Zander stunned, watching Spencer open the car door for her.

"Tell Jimmy I'll be in touch tomorrow. See you around."

"Welsh Cake."

B turned, scowling at him as he tossed her his motorcycle keys.

Snatching them out of the warm air, she gazed down at the keys and back at Zander, stunned by his actions. Her lips curled into a wry smile as she nodded in acceptance before entering the mustard, yellow Lamborghini. As Spencer sped away, B glanced over her shoulder at a sullen Zander standing alone on the sidewalk.

CHAPTER TWENTY-SIX

Mack's Going to Sunnyville!

Mack was heading to the club to blow off some steam when his phone rang. Retrieving it from his pocket, his eyes narrowed.

What does Jimmy want now?

"Hey Jimmy! How you keeping?" he said upon answering the call.

"Hey boss, I'm sorry to ring out of the blue, but I need your help. We didn't get to talk much at Noah's funeral, and you took off so soon. I didn't get a chance to talk club business with you."

"Sorry Jimmy, I wasn't in the best of moods. What can I help you with?"

"The club is in serious financial trouble, man. With Noah pulling us out of the criminal world, we have lost our primary source of income and our savings are gone. Noah and Dragon had plans for the club, but nobody knows the details, and we got mouths to feed."

"Jimmy... Dragon would tell me if contracts were on the table. I'm the Founder and her business partner for feck's sake, and what do you mean about money trouble? I thought Dragon bailed you out?"

"Noah turned it down to build up trust with her. Mack, I hate to be the bearer of bad news, but they were up to something big and a week before he died, he told us that Dragon owns everything now. The club, the building work next door, the lot. She confirmed it herself when we spoke at her house that day. She said she was going to explain everything to you," Jimmy said, providing Mack with the bare skeleton of what he knew. He didn't trust Mack enough to explain about the contract with Dragon.

The line went quiet.

"Mack, you still there, man?"

"I'm here," he growled.

"I'm sorry. When all is said and done, you are the Founder and Dragon is the money. As the new Prez, I have to do something, and fast."

"I hear you, Jimmy. Tell me. What did Noah say about plans with Dragon? Were they brought up in church?"

"No. Noah didn't give details and asked us to trust him, and we did. Now, this has been months in the planning, but now, without Noah, we're screwed."

"Jimmy, what were you all thinking? Everything goes through church. You know that."

"Come on Mack. Who were we to question the Prez?"

"It's in the fecking charter! Zander should have questioned him or come to me for guidance."

"Well, hindsight is a wonderful thing. Look, boss, I wouldn't ask if we weren't in the shit. We have patches behind on their mortgage and they're considering going back to crime or going Nomad. Their kids gotta eat. Now, I've been honest with you, and you need to help me. We need you and Dragon to come through for us!"

"I hear you, brother. I tell you what, why don't I come down tomorrow afternoon? We'll sit down, look at your books and I can speak to Dragon when she comes home later and find out what the feck's going on. She's on a work conference and probably fecking some Sultry boy as we speak."

Jimmy kicked the bar. "I'm sorry, boss, but that grinds my fucking gears."

"What does?"

"Dragon out fucking whilst Zander has done nothing but sulk these past two weeks. He's fucking pining for her."

"Zander can feck off. He's messed with her head, too. She hasn't said two words to us, except when I grapple with her. Only she chokes me out whenever I mention him. I'm so fecking angry he fucked her. She's too good for him."

"I beg to differ. Besides, you're just jealous he fucked the woman you love."

Mack raised his voice. "I am! I just don't get it. What does he have that I haven't?"

"Uh, he's handsome and has a massive cock."

"Feck you! Are you trying to piss me off? I thought you wanted my help."

"I do, but I won't lie to you to make you feel better, man. You have Ari, the kids and everything you could want, so why not let Zand have her?"

"Pigs will fecking fly and he will die before I let that happen. Now, where is the Scottish prick? He's on my shit list, and I want to warn him to stay away from her."

Jimmy couldn't help but chuckle at Mack's choice of words. "It's Friday night. Where do you think he is?"

"He's still doing that karaoke shit?"

"Every week, besides Noah's funeral and last week because he was too cut up about Dragon. Has she really gone to fuck those Sultry boys because I've never seen Zand like this?"

"I don't know. Maybe not. She doesn't mix business and pleasure and I've let her off the lead a little these past weeks. She doesn't have a tail tonight, and I didn't even know she'd left, to be honest with you."

"Is that wise when we don't know what happened to Noah?"

"Had I known she was going, she would have had a tail, but she's shut me out since Noah died. I'm gonna have to put a leash around that neck of hers for good. And Jimmy, I don't know what she's up to down there or what she had planned with Noah, but whatever happens, she will remain in Uskiville where she is safe. Do I make myself clear?"

"Alright, don't get your knickers in a twist. You can keep her as long as you talk to her and find out what's fucking happening?" Jimmy said tidying the whiskey shelf.

"Yeah, I'll talk to her. Look, I'll let you know when I leave tomorrow."

"Thanks boss."

"No worries, brother. I gotta go. See you tomorrow."

CHAPTER TWENTY-SEVEN
Celtic Fire!

Zander sat at the bar grimacing and tapping his glass with his fingers. He normally belted out a few songs at karaoke, only tonight he hadn't returned to the stage after his last song. He wasn't in the mood. He couldn't shake the image of his Welsh Cake being dragged out of the bar, not to mention handing over his motorcycle keys.

What the fuck was that all about?

He was giving up hope of seeing her again tonight, her absence feeling like an eternity to Zander, who did nothing but watch the clock and knock back whiskey.

Staring into the glass, he huffed, fed up with waiting and frustrated with the man who stole her away after he thought he was getting somewhere with her.

"Another round, please? My lovely," B said to Neil as she approached the bar, making Zander spin around in his seat to gaze upon her.

Zander's heart pounded as she sat on the stool next to him, smiling as she placed his keys down on the bar.

"Sorry, I was so long. I had to get my contract signed."

Zander picked up his keys and stuffed them in his jean pocket.

"I was wondering if you had taken it out for a spin."

"Not likely, lovely boy. I value my life too much," she said as she knocked back her whiskey.

Zander smirked, "You know that you're supposed to sip and appreciate a good Scotch, darling?"

"I tell you what, my lovely, pop a bottle of the good stuff in front of me and I will quite happily sip away! But that's cheap rubbish, and I have had a crappy day, so I will bash on if that's alright?" she said, giving him a cheeky wink.

B fascinated Zander. Unable to hide his excited eyes and huge smile, he leaned in, to whisper in her ear: "Well, if I had a bottle of good stuff in my room, I wouldn't be down here drinking this stuff!"

"Maybe I like the company," she teased, waving to Neil to pour her another.

Zander's eyes grew like wildfire, "Well, you may want to sip this one darling, it's much stronger than the good stuff. Otherwise, I'll be carrying you back to your room."

B laughed. "I thought you'd like that, Scottie."

Fuck! I want her so bad.

His thoughts running wild as he gazed upon her, admiring how her business suit clung to the beautiful curves of her body. He loved the way her eyes danced when she laughed and how she nervously bit her bottom lip when he asked her something that made her go shy. He also loved her carefree attitude. B said what she felt, making her more attractive to the chiseled Scot.

"I would. Like that, I mean. I just dinnae think I can handle waking up to you gone again," he sighed.

"How late are you planning to sleep? I'm viewing a house at eleven and if you're not up by then, I will bloody abandon you again."

Taking her hand, he gazed at her, chuckling again. Inside, he was dancing. B had returned from signing her contract with a beaming smile and the fire back in her eyes, and Zander loved it.

"I thought you dinnae sleep with the same guy twice?"

"Fine. If you're not up to the job, I'll have another shot." she teased, asking Neil for yet another round and raising her glass to him with a devilish smile on her face.

Zander took the glass from her, knocking back both shots, much to B's amusement. "How about you stop drinking this fire water now, please? And for the record, I was born up for it!"

"It's you that needs to stop the shots, sunshine. I'm Welsh. Drinking is our birth right. Anyway, I think I'll head off. The good stuff is calling me. Night Scottie," she teased as she rose from her bar stool.

"Teasing again Welsh Cake? That won't end well for you darling."

B smirked, taking his hand, and sliding a room key into his grasp. "Ten minutes. Room 206. Leave your clothes at the door, Scottie, and if you're really good, I'll let you have the good stuff," she said as she walked away, leaving Zander breathless.

A short while later, Zander entered B's hotel room. The penthouse suite was enormous, with a king-size bed, and a living and dining space that led onto the balcony where B was standing in nothing but a silk, white shirt.

Zander was nervous. He had never felt so excited. Light-headedness struck him as he steadied himself on the door frame, captivated by her beauty.

B hadn't heard him come in, so he stripped off just as she requested and headed onto the balcony to join her, wrapping his hands around her waist to greet her.

"Whoa! you look incredible, darling! said the Scot with excitement as his erection pressed against her.

B turned, pulling him in close, devouring his mouth with bold strokes with her tongue, making Zander moan with pleasure.

"Whoa! Welsh Cake! Where did you learn how to kiss?"

B laughed, "We get taught right in Wales, my lovely, but I have to say Scottie, smoking is bad for your health."

"So are you, darling, but I'm no' giving you up."

B took his hand and directed him to the balcony's daybed.

"Sit, good boy," she requested as Zander watched her retrieve the bottle of good stuff from the table.

Approaching him with the bottle in hand, his eyes fixated on her as she straddled him.

Zander took a deep breath. Still feeling lightheaded. "I'm no' gonnae last two minutes with you tonight, am I?"

B grinned at him, eyes like wildfire once again. "Scottie, you better prepare yourself. I'm celebrating tonight. Now would you like a taste of the good stuff before I ruin you?"

"Christ. Yes," he said as he watched her take a sip of the whiskey before covering his mouth with hers. "Fuck, you taste delicious."

"How about you remove my shirt and I'll let you lick it off my breasts?"

Zander ripped off her shirt, quick as a flash, panting with excitement as he watched B pour droplets of the amber liquid over her chest, allowing him to feast upon them, licking, sucking and tracing his teeth along them as he did so.

"Easy tiger. Pace yourself. We have all night remember," she teased as she placed the bottle on the side table.

"Christ. I cannae, darling! I need to be inside you. I'm going to explode," he moaned as he gorged on her breasts, his cock twitching with excitement.

"I suppose I have made you wait a couple of weeks," she teased, before lifting her hips and lowering herself down onto him, her hands gliding through his hair with force and her mouth covering his as she accepted every inch of him.

Zander moaned in delight as he filled her. His chest still pounding as she rode him as he gazed into her eyes, surrounded by nothing but the midnight sky.

He moved his hips to match her rhythm and cupped her breasts, squeezing them as she went to work.

"Darling, what are you doing to me? I'll no' last much longer with you riding me like this," he said, moaning into her mouth. His spine tingling with increasing pressure as he ascended into her with every thrust.

"You better, good boy," she moaned.

Zander fisted her hair, bringing her in closer to him, allowing her to nip his ears with her teeth, tracing along his neckline, nipping his skin as she increased her tempo.

"Christ, darling, I'm there. Let me look at you whilst I come."

B raised her head, and the pair locked eyes as she continued to please him. Gazing back at her, Zander's body took over, his jaw clenched, body jerking as she rode him hard and fast. The electrifying pressure proved too much for him as he released inside her.

"Oh, Christ!" he gasped as she continued to ride him through his climax, with Zander crying out, trembling, and dripping with sweat.

Collapsing onto her breasts and holding her tight, Zander watched as she slowed to a stop. Breathing into her chest, he gushed. "What did you do to me? I'm sorry darling, I couldn't last. That was immense. I thought I was gonnae pass out!"

"Don't worry, big guy. We have all night!"

Feeling her fingers run through his hair once more, she lifted his head to look at her. Zander couldn't help but gawk as her body glistened under the balcony spotlights. She was smiling down at him, looking pleased with herself, her eyes sparkling with delight.

"I missed you, Welsh Cake."

"I can tell, good boy," she said, giving him a wink.

He traced his hand along her back, caressing its length as he laid a row of soft kisses on her chest, before swinging his legs over the side of the daybed.

"I'd like to take you inside and make love to you, nice and slow. To thank you for that fucking, mind-blowing experience."

B shook her head at him with demonic eyes. "I don't make love, Scottie. I fuck! You can take me to bed and take me but, no slow ride or misogynistic bullshit from behind. Fuck me hard without trying to control me."

It took Zander back a little. His brow furrowed as he looked at her. He wanted to make love to her. He wanted to be slow and sensual. To take his time with her, please her beyond her wildest dreams like she had pleased him tonight and on the first night they spent together.

Swallowing his disappointment, he whispered to her. "I won't do anything you dinnae want me to."

"Oh, I want you, good boy, just on my terms."

"No compromise?" he asked, hopeful, trying not to push his luck.

"No, I just pleased you, now you can please me, and I'll be extra nice to you afterwards."

Zander couldn't help himself. He was desperate for her, gazing upon her, his body fueled with excitement. "Then, you better brace yersel' darling, because I'm gonnae please you until you can't take any more."

Much to his surprise, they cascaded into a luscious romp, and he allowed B the control she desired as she guided him through unique sexual positions. He loved that she wasn't afraid to show him what she wanted and was happy to teach him things he had never experienced before. She was experienced beyond his wildest dreams, and he reveled in the pleasurable learning experience she provided.

They spent most of the night entwined and exploring each other. Zander didn't push her into anything she wasn't comfortable with. He knew she had to always maintain control and tried not to push the boundaries as he took her hard and fast in the soft king-size bed. Zander loved being inside her, feeling her body tense as she screamed through her orgasms, and he couldn't comprehend how she took his breath away every time she pleased him. He had just finished taking her in the missionary position when she pulled him up off the bed.

"Darling, I may need a moment to recover. I've never had so much sex in one night," he said as he kissed her lips.

Watching her eyes flicker in amusement, she teased him again, driving him wild.

"I thought you were a Celt, good boy. Do I have to train you up and remind you how us Celts do it?"

Zander pulled her into him, making her gasp. "Listen here Welsh Cake, as a fellow Celt, I think we both know I can more than hold my own and I can assure you I'll never disappoint. Lead the way and I'll give you the ride of your fucking life and I promise you; you will love every minute!"

"We'll see, Scottie. We'll see."

Zander's jaw ached. He'd never smiled so much in his life and loved the increasing warmth in his heart. Frozen for so long, the new feelings engulfing his body were exhilarating. Tonight was more special than the first night they spent together because he was getting to know B beyond the bravado. Although she tried to hide behind it, Zander could see right through it. He knew there were some deep-rooted insecurities within B's soul, and he wanted to explore them and help her grow. He never cared enough about a woman to allow them to know him before. Everything had been meaningless sex until he met B. Now, as she took his hand and led him into the bathroom, he gazed upon her flawless body, desperate to experience as much as he could with her.

They entered the bathroom with B pulling him into the walk-in shower. It was larger than your average shower, as Zander assessed its size and décor.

"I've never had sex in the shower before. I've always had trouble fitting inside them."

B smiled. "Who said anything about sex?"

Zander wrapped his hands around her waist and buried his head in her neck.

"You need to stop teasing me. I promise you; I will not hold back with you if you dinnae."

B laughed, turning to him. "Not all pleasure is about sex. I know you're tired and that's okay. I'm a hard woman to satisfy. But right now, I'm going to wash you from head to toe, help you relax, and show you that intimacy comes in many forms. I expect nothing else from you tonight."

Her words took his breath away. Zander thought he knew it all when it came to sex. He had pleased hundreds of women since he came of age, yet tonight had been an education for him. B hadn't let him take her in the rough-and-ready ways he was used to. He hadn't got to throw her around the bedroom or bend her over and make him his. He couldn't stamp his authority over her and rule her, like he did with other women, nor had the night been derived from grief and lusty passion. Tonight, was real to him. He felt it with every fiber of his being, and Zander knew, if he wanted a relationship with her, he would have to be patient. But in this moment, he would allow her to do whatever she pleased.

Enamored of her, Zander allowed B to pull him under the shower, his eyes fixated on her as the water soaked her sun-kissed skin. He caressed her cheek with the pad of his thumb, staring into her eyes.

"You're so fucking beautiful."

"You're not bad yourself. Now, hands off until I tell you," she said raising them above his head.

"That's going to be hard."

"You'll get your turn. I want to know that I can trust you."

Zander's heart melted as he pulled her into him placing a firm palm on her ass. "You can trust me Welsh Cake."

"Then show me by keeping your fucking hands to yourself whilst I work, good boy."

Zander threw his head back in a growling laugh, removing his hands. "There's that 'take no shit attitude' I love."

Unable to take his eyes off her, he traced her movements as she pumped shampoo into her hand. Rubbing them together, she ran her hands through his hair, raking through it, washing it as Zander closed his eyes and moaned in satisfaction.

"Whoa,"

She then let the shower rinse his hair before reaching for the conditioner, repeating the process. Her touch incapacitated him as her hands glided through his low hanging beard.

She mesmerized Zander, intoxicated him even, as his body relaxed under the soft strokes from her delicate fingers.

"Hands behind your head," she instructed as she lathered him with shower gel, her fingers caressing his muscular body like silk brushing over his skin.

"God, your touch is electric!"

"I'm just getting started," she teased, rinsing him off and taking her lips to his pecs.

Zander closed his eyes to bask in the experience until her gasp interrupted him.

"He got you too! Why didn't I notice that before?" she said, showing to the claw scars on his back.

Zander studied her strained face, watching her chest rise and fall in rapid succession, showing both concern and shock.

"Aye," he said, finding himself feeling uncomfortable. The scars left by his former Prez still angered him.

"I knew he hurt Ari but not you too."

"Aye, but mine's no half as bad as Ari's or Noah's."

"Noah's?" she questioned, eyes widening in disbelief.

Zander raised his eyebrows. "You dinnae know? But he swam in your pool. He told me so."

"With a rash guard, yeah. I never saw him topless."

It was then, it dawned on Zander that Noah was telling the truth. Zander's body flushed with relief. *He never touched Welsh Cake.* Zander always wanted to believe his best friend, but doubt always reared its ugly head as desperation to be with her crept in.

He refocused his attention to find B still glaring at the scar, showing her fiery dragon eyes.

"Hey, hey, I'm fine," he said, cupping her cheek and kissing her lips to bring her attention back to him.

"No hands, Scottie," she teased, as if she had flicked a switch to turn her attention back to him. Traveling kisses down his body, she reached his midline, dropping to her knees.

"Sweet Jesus!" he gasped as her tongue traveled along the length of his shaft, kissing him until he found his hands grasping a handful of her soft hair.

Tilting her chin to gaze at him, he moaned with pleasure. "Oh, darling. Your lips are amazing around my cock, but I'm gonnae take my turn now. You've given me enough pleasure. It's high time I showed you my appreciation tonight."

Zander pulled her up to her feet, kissing her and grabbing the shower gel in one swift movement. He lathered her body as she had his, caressing her, listening to her soft moans. As he watched the steamy water wash away the bubbles, he planted kisses in the crease of her neck, traveling down to her breasts as B's moans became louder.

"Oh, Scottie, that's amazing!"

Zander felt excitement rush through his body as she became vocal at his touch. The ecstasy coursing through his veins as he traveled down her torso with his lips, kissing her bikini line as his hands massaged her ass with his firm hand. Kneeling before her, he exhaled. "Jesus, darling, I cannae wait to taste you. Tell me it's okay to kiss you here."

"Yes!" she panted.

Zander pulled her close, bringing her to his mouth, tantalizing her with his lips, delivering elegant strokes to her clitoris, as B writhed in his grasp. He became hard as she pulled him closer. Her breathless whimpers, music to his ears as his tongue stroked her opening, flooding his mouth with her arousal. Zander became relentless with his tongue as the experience became too intense for him and he began relishing in her excited screams.

Feeling triumphant from her pleasurable cries, he had an urgency to show his expertise. He found the thought of being inside her overwhelming.

"Fuck, darling, I'm desperate to please you with my tongue, but I need to enter you now. Tell me you want me. Let me take you here and now?"

"God, yes! Scottie, please?"

Zander shot to his feet, pinning her against the wall in an instant. His chest crashed into her as he picked her up. Lowering her onto him, he penetrated her hard, impatient as his desires took hold.

"Oh, God. Yes!" B cried and Zander lost control, filling her with every inch of himself. His solid chest rattled against her bare breasts as he ploughed her hard against the wall. He couldn't control himself as he lost himself inside her.

"Oh Scottie, don't stop!" she pleaded, desperate for more, as he increased the tempo, giving her everything he had.

"Oh, Welsh Cake, oh darling," he moaned, his cock throbbing deep inside her as he felt her quicken.

"Don't stop! I'm so close," she begged, biting into his shoulder as he penetrated her. The vulnerability in her voice making him feel like a God as agonizing pressure built up inside him.

"Harder Scottie. I need you!" she cried.

Zander hung on for life, the pressure sweeping through his body like a tornado. He became desperate to feel her release, pumping her until she couldn't take any more, and one final mind-blowing thrust provoked her trembling body into an explosive orgasm. Clenching all of herself around him, releasing the pressure, B's body demanded his climax. Screaming in unison, Zander continued to take her hard against the wall, until he unburdened himself with a desperate climax of his own. After ensuring he left everything inside her, he slid down to his knees in exhaustion, holding onto her tight.

Kissing her lips, he rested his forehead against hers as the hot shower water continued to fall from above like a waterfall.

"Welsh Cake! Where the fuck have you been all of my life?"

B panted, her body trembling in his arms as she stared at him with piercing blue eyes as Zander remained paralyzed by his emotions as he knelt motionless for a while.

"Let me wrap you in a towel and take you back to bed, sweetheart," he said as he kissed an exhausted B.

Turning off the shower, he grabbed a towel from the rail, wrapping her up and carrying her back to bed. After drying her off, he climbed into bed next to her, stroking her back as they made small talk about B's tattoos. A dragon grasping a daffodil on her ribs, a blue butterfly on her right thigh, and a Scottish thistle traveling down her back, which caught Zander's eye as he looked at it curiously.

"This tattoo is beautiful. What made you get it?" he said, running his fingers over it.

"It represents me, my home, and my family! It represents every fiber of my being."

Scottie continued to stroke it. "How?"

"I was born in Wales, but Scotland gave me a home and made me the person I am. My boys are half Welsh and half Scottish. These tattoos represent me, them, and everything I hold dear!"

"Aye, I noticed their accents."

B shifted her eyes from his and started playing with his chest hair. "I was married to a Scot for 17 years. We met young and had the boys and we got divorced about six years ago."

"What happened?"

B laughed a mocking laugh. "I came home to find him screwing a young tart in my bed, so I ended it! He has since shacked up with her and a little one despite not wanting any more kids with me. I begged him for ten years for another child and got nowhere, and after giving him everything. Bloody hell, I was a submissive to him, a doormat even. My blood, sweat, and tears went into a controlling, unhappy marriage and look what I got for it."

"Shit! I'm sorry darling! Do you still love him?"

B cackled, glancing up at him. "No Scottie I don't! I am the happiest I have ever been since I left him. I am strong and independent. No man will break my spirit and control me again."

"Well, he must be a fucking moron. How could anyone leave you? You are perfect!"

"Scottie, you have known me for five minutes. You don't know what I am capable of. My desire to be in control leads me to fuck things up. Hence the no dating rule."

Scottie pulled her in closer to meet his gaze.

"And how's that going for you?"

"Great until tonight when I broke my own rules of engagement."

Smiling at her, he was desperate to dig deeper. "What was so different about tonight? Why did you choose to break the rules for me?"

B lowered her eyes, looking away from him. "I saw you and every inch of me wanted you to be quite honest with you."

Zander bit down on his bottom lip. "Will you send me away now that you've had me again?"

"Do you want me to send you away?"

"Of course not. I have had the biggest crush on you for months. I begged Noah to take me up to meet you, but he wouldn't and when you sent me that Christmas hamper, I was hooked. Your generosity stunned me. You sent a stranger a thoughtful gift containing everything I missed for the last twenty years. It must have cost you a fortune to mail."

B kissed his chest. "I receive a delivery once a month. I don't want the boys to forget their roots, so I make a point of cooking Welsh and Scottish dishes every week, along with celebrating St David's Day, Burns night, and Hogmanay. We are proud Celts Scottie and I wanted to do something nice for a fellow Celt. Noah never shut up about you, nagging me day in, day out to meet you."

"Then why did it take so long?"

B gazed at his chest again. "Do you remember you made Noah video call me last Christmas? Do you remember our first conversation?"

Zander smiled, inhaling the smell of her hair as he kissed her head. "I remember every word, darling. I thanked you for my gift and I wanted to come up and meet you, but I never received an offer."

"No, you didn't."

"Why?"

B propped herself up on her elbow meeting his inquisitive stare. "I told you! Scots are like Kryptonite to me! When you spoke to me with all that swagger, I assumed you were just another guy wanting to use and abuse. I'll never be a notch on a bedpost, and I won't subject myself to the misogynistic ways of the club. I'm broken Scottie. I'll never be an old lady, and I won't be controlled or feel less than, again. That's why I never get attached to anyone. I visit the Sultry Slalom, taking what I need with no expectations of anything else. I fuck and I run. That's who I am, I'm afraid."

"No' tonight, you aren't. Tonight, I saw you and you're not fucked up or broken. You're just scared, a little insecure even, and that's alright because I'll never hurt you."

B dropped her gaze. "Scottie, what do you see in me? You can have anyone, and most women would bend to your will. Why waste your time on someone who can't give you what you need?"

Zander's firm jawline softened. He hated the way she talked about herself, when deep down he knew she was driven by fear.

"Darling, you came into my life like a fucking bulldozer, smashing all of my walls down, thawing out my icy heart with your fiery Dragon's eyes and that Amazonian warrior vibe you got going on. No one, and I mean no one, has made me feel like you have." He rolled on top of her, careful not to make her feel trapped. "Let me tell you something. I used to think vulnerability was a weakness. Then I met you and you've just fucking schooled me in a lesson of intimacy, for fuck's sake. So, dinnae put yersel' down. I want you! I dinnae want anyone else. So, please give me a chance?"

"I'll just push you away and we're going to be working together soon. What happens if we fall out?"

"Never gonnae happen, darling."

"Don't be so naïve, lovely boy. I'm a dragon and you're a wolf."

"Yeah, and we'll make a fucking amazing couple, given the chance. Can we see where this goes, please?"

"I'm not sure I can. My head is telling me to walk away, and my heart is pulling me toward you. It's driving me mad."

"Well, tell your head to fuck off and let your heart rule you because I need you, Welsh Cake."

He watched how she battled with herself. Her dragon eyes reared their ugly head again.

"Hey, put the dragon eyes away, c'mon. Give me a Welsh Cake smile, please?"

His dimples curled into a devilish grin as she flushed with embarrassment, flashing him a timid smile.

"That's better. Look, I like you and you like me, right?"

"Scottie."

"Right?" he reinforced again.

"Right," she muttered.

"So, like we say at the club. 'Baby steps,' darling. We take things slow, allowing you to get comfortable being with someone who finds you irresistible. Yeah?"

B closed her eyes and pursed her lips. "I'll put you through hell, Scottie. You don't know what I'm capable of. Besides, my boys always come first. My working week involves doing my job, ferrying them to a multitude of clubs, cooking and, if I have any time left in the evening, cwtching up on the sofa with a good book. Then on the weekends, I let my hair down. That's my life! I can't be someone who's out every evening like the club's old ladies. Can you honestly see yourself doing any of that with me?"

Zander smiled, tracing her lips with his index finger.

"Darling, the idea of being part of that sounds incredible. I've been miserable for years. The idea of coming home to a woman like you is out of this world. Understand, I want you, get it in your head. I'm no' letting you push me away when I know you want me too, so take a telling will ya!"

B smiled before reaching up to kiss him, planting a soft kiss on his lips, making Zander moan.

"I'll take that as a yes," he said, rolling onto his back.

B nuzzled into his chest, closing her eyes.

Zander's heart skipped a beat. He loved to hold her. It made him feel safe as she once again snaked herself around him and drifted off to sleep. He had never wanted to sleep with anyone before B. He would send his previous conquests packing as soon as he had his way with them, but B was different. Good different. He gazed upon her as her warm, soft breaths tickled his chest as she slept, thinking how his life would be with B by his side. Thinking of coming home to her on cold winter nights after spending so many alone.

Zander had spent years feeling lonely despite having his brothers and he was envious of the patched members with their old ladies to look after them. He thought he would never find someone to settle down with. Decent women didn't give one-percenter's a chance. Yet, as he gazed upon his sleeping dragon, he wanted the life she didn't think he could accept.

CHAPTER TWENTY-EIGHT

It's Me or B!

Mack arrived home past midnight, drunk as a skunk, waking Ari as he fell into bed.

"Jeez, Mackie, you smell like a brewery. How much have you had?" Ari said, sitting upright in bed in frustration.

"Not enough."

"Oh, what's happened now? I hate it when you pout."

"Dragon. She's fecking destroyed me again. I have to go to Sunnyville tomorrow to sort it out," he slurred.

"What are you talking about?"

"Dragon and Noah. They were in cahoots. I think she's leaving me, and I can't have that. It's not safe there. Why would she do that to me, Ari?"

"Who told you this?"

"Jimmy. He needs our help. The club has money trouble and Dragon hasn't invested yet. She was supposed to help them get back on track. I demand to know what's happening. When she's back, I'm having it out with her, and she'll never leave Uskiville again."

"I think it's a little late for that, honey."

Mack shot up in bed, sobering up in a flash as he stared Ari down.

"You know something, don't you? Tell me now Ari, or so help me God, I'll lose my shite."

Ari pressed her lips together, her eyes unable to meet Mack's as she hugged her knees to her chest.

"She's leaving Uskiville. She left today to sign a new contract in Sunnyville. You pushed her too far Mack and truth be told; I don't think she's ever got over you going black."

Mack's face turned purple as he dived out of bed, staring at her in disbelief.

"You fecking knew. You knew all along and kept it from me?"

"No, honey. She told me just before Noah died and I thought she would change her mind considering his death, but she didn't. She's more determined now than ever."

Mack punched a hole in the bedroom door. "Why would you keep this from me? You're supposed to be loyal to me, not Dragon!"

"Why do you think? She's not your prisoner, and she certainly isn't your old lady. I am in case you have forgotten."

"Oh, here we go again, always jealous of my dragon. I told you; jealousy will never look good on you."

Ari dived out of the bed to confront him. "Jealousy doesn't fucking come into it, you asshole. I sat by and watched you ogle her, then take me to bed. You say you're done with her, but you're lying and I'm not playing second fiddle anymore. She doesn't want you. She never did. The only thing I take comfort in is that she is oblivious to how you feel. Do you know how hard it is to watch you look at B in ways you've never looked at me? How much it fucking hurts? No, you don't, because you are a selfish prick."

Mack's face softened. "Ari, I..."

"Save it! I'm fucking done," she said throwing her hands in the air. "Why do you think I tried to set her up? I wanted her to be unavailable so I could have you to myself, and despite my broken heart, I tried to tell her not to do this. I didn't want to lose my best friend, but I want my Prez for myself. I want you to look at me like you look at her. Any self-respecting woman would have left you, only I'm in love with you. Well, now it's decision time, honey. It's me or B."

Mack stood gobsmacked. His hand rubbing the back of his neck. He never imagined Ari would ever make him choose. He loved Ari, but this was his Dragon they were talking about and now he would have to choose between them.

Dumping himself down onto the bed, he looked at her face as she tried to remain stern. Her face trying not to crumple as she sat next to him, fighting back her tears. Reaching for her hand, she pulled it away.

"Oh, Ari. What the feck have I done to you? You don't deserve this, baby."

"No, I don't! You have been a shit partner. When you claimed me, you promised it was me and it would only ever be me and you fucking lied."

"I'm sorry!"

"No, you're not and I'm fucking sick of sorry. I'm sick of being your reserve. Now Dragon is moving to Sunnyville and you're going to let her, otherwise I'm leaving you."

"Ari, baby. You can't. I claimed you."

"I don't give a shit. You've hurt me for the last time. Dragon is suffocating here. You are suffocating her and hurting me. She likes Zander and he can look after her down there. I'm not saying you can't be friends; I'm saying you need to let her go. It's what she wants and what I want."

Mack dropped his head in despair.

"Ari, she's my family. It won't be the same without her here, and if she goes, we could end up homeless. We don't know her plans yet?"

"Mack, do you really think she would make us homeless?"

"I don't know anymore. She's been so distant since she met Noah. It breaks my heart knowing she kept this from me."

Ari climbed back into bed, fluffing up her pillow. "Now you know how she felt when you met me. You did the same! The difference is, Dragon isn't selfish, and I know she'll do right by us."

"Ari, I love you and I want you, not Dragon. You won't believe me when I say that, but it's true. I just can't live without her here, and I can't bear the thought of her getting hurt in Sunnyville. She brought me back from the depths of despair, Ari and I just want to protect her. It's the least I can do."

"Stop lying to yourself, Mack. I know you want her and yes, I believe the rest of what you say, but understand this, Dragon has to go if we're going to last." Her voice trembled. "I love you, Mack but you need to show me some respect now and choose. Do you want me or Dragon?"

Mack shifted toward her, staring at her as his eyes filled with tears. Gritting his teeth to hold them back, he took her hand.

"I want you! I need you. I just need some help letting her go. She's become like a drug to me, and I can't shake the need for her."

"Then you must let her go, for all our sakes. Otherwise, you'll lose both of the women you love. I'll help you but you need to help yourself."

"Ari, she will die if Blaze finds her, and no one there can protect her. Not even Zander. I have to go to Sunnyville tomorrow. She needs to stay home until he's found. I know you think I'm mad, but he's coming for her. I know he is."

"Then we'll go together."

Mack's stared, slack jawed. "Really? Ari, you haven't been back since..."

"You can't do this alone, and B's already in Sunnyville. There was no conference. She left this morning to sign her new coaching contract. She'll probably head to the MC tomorrow if she hasn't already."

Mack dragged his hand down his beard. "Why am I not surprised? Is she with him?"

"Not that I'm aware. B was adamant this was a business trip. She's fond of him Mack."

Mack nodded. "You should remain in Uskiville, I don't want it to upset you, baby. You've been through enough."

"Which is why I need to go."

"Okay, but she won't be happy with us showing up and dragging her home."

"She'll hate us! We better keep Frankie in the dark for this. He will fight for her freedom at every turn, even if it means she's leaving him, too."

"I'll tell him we're going down to see Jimmy and staying in a hotel. I'll bring Scampers and Rudy with us."

"Fine. And Mack, I promise you there are no more chances after this. I mean what I say. It's Dragon or me."

"I know baby. I'll let her go as soon as she's safe."

"Fine. Now I'm going to sleep!"

CHAPTER TWENTY-NINE

The Morning After

B sat on the balcony's breakfast table, tapping the keys on her laptop.

"Morning darling," Zander said, greeting her with his presence, as he wandered naked onto the balcony.

B glanced up from the laptop, taking in Zander in all his glory as he sat and leaned in to kiss her.

"Morning," she said with a smile.

"Are you expecting anyone? I can get dressed and head out if I'm imposing," he said salivating over the banquet set out in front of them, complete with a full English breakfast: pancakes, continental goods, tea and coffee.

B laughed, closing her laptop, and setting it aside.

"I figured you might be hungry after last night."

Zander raised an eyebrow, flashing his smile. "Did you order everything on the menu?"

"Almost," she said reaching for her cutlery.

"Thank you. This is great!" Zander said, diving into his plate.

B flashed him a smile as she tucked into hers. Spending the entire night in Zander's arms filled her with content. She had never wanted to share her bed with anyone until she met him, and she found the morning after a little nerve-wracking. They had shared a passionate and exhilarating experience in B's eyes. She enjoyed his company afterwards too as he stroked her back until she fell asleep, and now she was in unfamiliar territory as he joined her for breakfast. Stealing glances as he became engrossed in his breakfast, she chuckled to herself, making him turn to her wearing nothing but a cheeky grin.

"What?"

"Nothing," she laughed. "You worked up an appetite last night, by the way you are eating."

"Sorry, it's rare I get to sit in a fancy pent-house suite and enjoy a feast like this."

"Don't apologize. I'm a foodie, too, and I like a man who enjoys his food. Cooking and baking are my things, and I'm always feeding my family and friends. We couldn't be friends if you didn't eat," she teased.

Zander smirked, biting down on his fork. "Friends? I'm curious, Welsh Cake. Do you treat all your friends the way you treated me last night?"

B choked on her tea, making Zander belly laugh.

"I'm only kidding, darling, but I have to be honest with you. When I opened my eyes this morning, I thought you had abandoned me again."

B's face hardened a little. She felt guilty for leaving him without saying goodbye before.

"Sorry. I'm viewing a house today, followed by a press conference later, so I slipped out to get ready without disturbing you. If I didn't have a busy schedule, I would have stayed in bed."

"That's alright. You can always make it up to me later," he teased, giving her a wink.

"What makes you think I'm staying?"

"You have an enormous suitcase with you."

"Very observant."

Zander sipped his coffee and reached for a croissant.

"So, are you? Staying I mean?"

"I'm staying here until I fly out tomorrow."

"Fly out?" he gave her an inquisitive stare.

"Yeah, I'm going to New York for a week. My boys are with their dad, and I want to clear my head before I inform Mackie about my plans."

"What's in New York?"

"Well, it's a big, fast-paced city and—"

"No, smart ass. Who are you visiting?"

B shrugged. "Nobody. I need a break. I usually go closer to Christmas, as it's my favorite time of the year, but I'm free for a week and fancied the trip to celebrate my new contract."

"You know, you could just stay here with me."

B flushed again. She hated he could make her do that. B had an answer for everything until she met him. She wasn't sure why she reacted to him so willingly, although he was naked next to her with the sun shining down on his big, God-like body.

"What happened to baby steps?" she teased.

Zander smiled, taking her hand. "I know. I just dinnae like the idea of you going alone. A beautiful woman like you could get hurt wandering the big city alone."

B laughed. "You have a lot to learn about me, lovely boy. I've told you. I'm no damsel in distress."

"So, everyone says. I just see an alluring Welsh Cake who's scared to show her vulnerable side."

"That's both lovely and deep. Now shut the fuck up and eat your breakfast."

To B's surprise, Zander stood up, scooped her out of her chair and carried her to the daybed behind the breakfast table. Laying her down, he kissed her before meeting her gaze.

"That smart mouth of yours is gonnae land you in trouble with me, darling. I'm no' used to taking orders from a lassie."

"I hate to break it to you, sunshine, but I own your club, the surrounding area and if you're not careful, I'll own you," she said as she swept him onto his back.

Looking down at him wearing a devious smile, she followed his eyes as they met with hers. Breathless, B witnessed both shock and excitement wash over Zander's face as he reached up to kiss her.

His lips covered hers as his tongue applied delicate strokes, making her taste him. Gasping for breath, he pulled away and whispered into her ear. "God, you're gonnae be the death of me woman. I think I may have to strip you naked and take you right here."

B's heart skipped a beat. She wanted his body on hers: she was desperate for his touch, his kiss, his everything.

"That sounds amazing, but I have to view a house," she said as she climbed off him, swishing her hair over her shoulders.

Taking a moment to indulge in the sprawled out, naked Scot, B couldn't help but marvel over his perfect physique.

"Can I come with you? I can keep you company and tell you if the area's nice or if the house is dodgy. I know this town like the back of my hand," Zander said, snapping her attention to him.

"You want to view a house with me?" B asked, with amusement in her tone.

"If you will let me? I want to get to know you better."

"It could be handy having a tour guide."

"Great, then I better get dressed," he said, pulling himself to his feet.

B placed a palm on his chest. "Slow your roll, tough guy. I have conditions."

"Which are?"

"One, we take my truck…"

"And two?" he asked.

"We come back here later so I can teach you more from the karma sutra before I go to my press conference and meet up with your Prez."

Zander's lips curled into the naughtiest looking smile that B had ever seen.

"If I die this weekend from all this pleasure, I will have died a lucky man."

B laughed. Turning to stack the breakfast plates, welcoming his warm hands around her waist.

Nuzzling into her neckline, he said to her; "I need to know your intentions for the club too, though, darling. Everyone is panicking, and I'd like to help you complete yours and Noah's plan. You and Noah cooked up something special with that contract, but Mack is dangerous, and I dinnae want you getting hurt. Noah asked me to look after you, and that's what I intend to do."

"And I will explain everything and get the ball rolling once we meet with Jimmy. I respect the chain of command despite not being a member of the club. Speaking of… Why didn't you become the Prez? Why remain a VP when you could lead?"

Zander turned her to face him. "My days of leading are over. People die when I lead, and I cannae have any more blood on my conscience. And, like I said, I promised Noah I'd look after you."

"Ah, your betrayal story, no doubt. Were you in another MC before moving to Sunnyville?"

"No! I went into private security after leaving the military. I led a team that protected people in power and money."

"You were white?"

"White?" he questioned.

"Like a knight in shining armor. Good and pure?"

Zander laughed. "Uh, I think they only exist in story books, my love. I tried to be a decent guy, though."

"I'm guessing something went wrong."

Zander rubbed his beard. B could tell it troubled him, pertaining to the anguish on his face, before turning away from her.

"Hey," she said, taking his hand and interlinking her fingers with his.

He turned to her; the color drained from his face.

"Sorry, Scottie, I didn't mean to pry. I am no good at this stuff. This is unchartered territory for me. I have found my mind and body responding to you, confiding in you, telling you stuff I've not told anyone, and to be honest, it scares me. We don't have to talk about it if you don't want to."

Zander kissed her forehead. "No need to apologize. This is my cross to bear. People died because I didn't see my best friend double-crossing me. As a leader, I should have seen it coming, but I didn't because I never thought my best friend would betray me for money. Because of my negligence, my client and friends died, and my so-called best friend got away with a shit load of cash. Nobody would employ me after that. Nobody wants to hire someone who lets everyone die."

B could hear the hurt in his voice and see the struggle in his face as he battled his inner demons. She didn't enjoy seeing him hurt: her heart sank, breeding an unfamiliar, searing pain: her head confused why she cared so much about a man she hardly knew.

Reaching up, she caressed his cheek through his beard and placed a soft kiss on his lips as he stood there, frozen in anguish.

"In my experience, the people we care the most about hide in plain sight as they wreak havoc in our lives. You didn't see it because you trusted him, but not everyone has a good heart, Scottie. People are driven by wants, needs, jealousy, and materialistic objects. Their desire makes them lust over them and forget about what and who matters to them. I don't know you that well, but it's that big heart inside your chest that attracts me to you more than anything. So, never lose sight of who you are deep down because that's a quality money can't buy."

Zander pulled her close, his chest heaving as he stared deep into her eyes.

"How do you do that? Take something bad and turn it into something positive? I've never let anyone in, but there's something about you that makes everything feel right. You make me want to tell you my deepest, darkest secrets. You, my darling, are white and pure, and I'm so glad I met you."

B smiled, feeling heat radiate through her face as she placed her lips on his. Feeling his hand reach for the back of her neck, pulling her, welcoming her into his grasp. Captured in the moment, she basked in the passionate clinch of mutual understanding as the two broken souls became one.

Coming up for air, they gazed upon each other, mesmerized, and a little shocked and confused. They were both experiencing powerful new feelings like magnets pulling them toward each other.

B, a little nervous by this morning's interactions, spoke first.

"I think you better get dressed, lovely boy, unless you want us sharing your room at the club. I don't want to miss out on the house of my children's dreams."

"Ooh, I think we could make it work."

"Come on, hot stuff, move your bloody ass!"

As B and Zander headed to see the house, Zander asked her questions about Mack.

"B, have you tried talking to Mack?"

B laughed as she stared into the open road. "Whenever I mention a new start or a new contract, he shoots me down, saying it's a stupid phase. I had no choice but to do things my way because he had sabotaged contracts before.

"So, what's the plan, darling?"

"Like I explained to Jimmy. I own the club and land next door. My gym, day nursery, bistro, shake shack and food bank are complete. Noah also wanted the club to have its own medical room, which will be in my gym. I'm building a steak house and open mic house next to the club. It'll serve food by day and house the latest talent by night. Noah and I planned everything, and I have contractors coming to look at the club soon. The planning has been approved and if we do this right, we can change the narrative of the club. We can make it a profitable business."

Zander's eyes widened.

"Problem good boy?"

"You're serious about this, aren't you? You're going to honor our contract?"

B shot him a devious smile, before turning her eyes back to the road. "I don't joke about business, Scottie. I promised Noah I'd help the club and I'm going to finish what we started together. He had such a beautiful vision for the club. The only thing I didn't agree with was his plans to step down and make Jimmy Prez.

"Noah told you about that?"

"Yeah, he would never lie to me. He knew how I felt about lying. Jimmy will be a problem for me, and Noah would have got him on side. He always told me that Jimmy was Team Mack, and I was counting on him to steady that ship."

"I can talk to him."

"No. I'm not having you fall out with anyone."

"Nae worries there, darling. I'll no' fall out with him, but what about Mack?"

B checked her mirrors and shrugged. "I'm just going to tell him when I get home, get it over and done with. I'll tell him the contract is signed, so I have a legal obligation to fulfil it now. He'll be pissed, but I'm going to give him forty percent of the business in Uskiville."

"And how do you think he will take it?" Zander asked.

"Not well, but I'm hoping the business will bring him around. An annual salary to forty percent is a huge jump. He'd be stupid not to take it."

Zander burst out laughing. "Mack's on a salary? He said you are partners!"

"No, I'm not that fucking stupid. He had to earn this," B scoffed, flicking on her indicators to make a left turn.

"Well, no wonder he wants you close. He's nothing without you, but forty percent? Are you certain you want to do that?"

"It's a small price for my freedom. Besides, he's still my family."

"Jeez, you must be desperate to escape if you're willing to give up so much. But listen, in my experience, the more you give, the more Mack will take. He'll have a bigger hold over you than he already does. I love Mack. He's my brother, but he will control you, darling. Trust me!"

"Well, what would you do?" B asked, looking intrigued.

Zander traced his thumb and forefinger along his lip line. "You want my opinion?"

B nodded, "Yep, let's hear it."

"Twenty percent. It's enough of an incentive and it doesn't have a big impact on your finances. But the bigger problem is getting free of him. He needs you. That's why he tells everyone he has 'the all-powerful Dragon,' a powerful shark of a businesswoman who's ruthless, dangerous and knows everything," he laughed.

"What?" B chuckled, shaking her head.

"Oh yeah! No wonder he's kept you hidden because no offence darling, as much as you are a goddess in the sack, I can see you are far from dangerous," he chuckled.

"No, I'm a great fucking businesswoman, but I am also a coach, and a mother! Why has he been lying?"

"To keep all of us other clubs in line."

"Bloody hell! I'm going to have half the MC world after me with that gobshite spouting that to everyone who'll listen."

Zander's tone became serious. "Dinnae worry. I promised Noah, I would keep you safe and I will."

"I don't need a bloody bodyguard, thanks, good boy. I just want to live in peace, without drama."

"Well, whilst you're here, I'm no' letting you out of my site and I'm gonnae look after you whether you like it or no'."

B rolled her eyes at him.

"Whoa! Did you just roll your eyes at me? I should make you pull over, so I can put you over my knee."

B laughed. "When you're big enough, lovely boy. Now let me concentrate or I'll miss my turning."

"Ha ha! Where is this house, anyway?"

"You'll see," B said as she turned down a dusty track.

"Uh, I think you may have taken a wrong turn. There's nothing down here, unless you are planning to buy that huge thing there," he said, pointing to an enormous, renovated farmhouse, complete with swimming pool, jacuzzi and basketball court.

B grinned at him.

"No way!"

"Yeah," she sighed. "It wouldn't be my choice, as it's too ostentatious for me, but it's the only thing the boys have ever asked for, and it's the least I could do."

"Your laddies are lucky; it's massive. The entire club could move in, and you'd still have space."

"Yeah, I hate big places. I like to feel cozy and secure. cwtched up, as us Welsh say it."

"I get that. Then maybe you should work on growing your family," he said, giving her a cheeky wink.

B laughed at him. She loved his wit.

"What?"

"You make me laugh. I like it. Now, tell me about this house?"

Zander directed her attention to the huge farmhouse ahead. "Well, it's been empty about a year. The owner's business went bust, and they moved back to Germany. That's all I can tell you. Why do you ask?"

"It's over-priced for its size and location and I'm not paying over the odds for it."

"Fair enough. The real estate guy is a bit of a snake. You wanna watch he doesn't rip you off?"

"That's what you're here for, lovely boy," she said with a wink.

"It'll be a fortune!"

"On the contrary Scottie, the houses here are much cheaper than in Uskiville and I promised the boys more space in our next house."

"Well, they will certainly get that!" said Scottie, looking a little inadequate.

CHAPTER THIRTY
Planting The Seed of Doubt

Blaze sat in his office staring at his phone, willing it to ring. He was expecting a call from his little spy, who was half an hour late. His patience was wearing thin when the call came through.

"You're late!" he growled.

"I know. Lot's happening here today."

"Go on."

"Mack is coming down to discuss the club's future. Everyone is a little nervous. The club will consider drug runs again if Mack or Dragon don't come up with the green. Jimmy has requested Dragon come through with the deal her and Noah agreed to."

"What else?"

"Zander is still AWOL. He went to Karaoke and hasn't returned. He hasn't been right since Dragon left without saying goodbye."

"She's a character, that one. I can't wait to get my hands on her."

"Do you want me to do anything?"

Blaze sat back in his chair, twirling a pen between his fingers. "No. I still want all the information I can before I act."

"You got it, boss!"

"Are you still planting the seed of doubt like I asked you to?"

"I'm working all of them. Don't worry about it."

"You better be. I want to make sure Dragon is exactly where I want her when I break her."

"You can count on me boss, I'm not fooled by her, not one bit."
"Good. Now keep it that way."
"You got it! I better get off; eyes are everywhere now."
"Right. Keep me informed," Blaze demanded.
"Will do!"

CHAPTER THIRTY-ONE

You're A Lover Not A Fighter!

B drove up to the ostentatious looking house to meet a tall, slim realtor, who showed them around. The house was full of character, with high ceilings and natural brickwork, and to B's surprise, she fell in love with the place. The cozy sitting room with a stone fireplace sealed the deal for her. It reminded her of home, and she could imagine herself sitting in front of the fire on snowy days.

"It's been on the market a long time, hasn't it?" B asked the realtor.

"Yes, that's correct?"

"Why's that? Any structural or other issues?"

"No. I think you'll find the market price is a steal."

"Then why hasn't it sold?"

"Because nobody can afford it here. People dinnae make a lot in Sunnyville," Zander said.

"The owners are waiting for the right buyer. The house means so much to them," the realtor said.

"Don't piss down my back and tell me it's raining, good boy! I know the details surrounding this house. So, I will put in an offer thirty percent below the asking price and sign for it today. Your buyers won't get an offer better than that. Now, make the call, Boy-oh," B said.

"Understood," said the realtor, walking away.

"Wow! You're a shark Welsh Cake! Remind me never to do business with you," Zander teased.

"Sorry, good boy, but I've already arranged a business meeting with you and your Prez today, in case you've forgotten."

"Then we're screwed!" he said as he pulled her in to kiss him.

"You are when we get back to the hotel."

"I would like to remind you I have no qualms about bending you over and fucking you in front of the real estate guy, darling."

B bit her lip and chirped back, running her hand along the inside of his shirt. "Sorry, good boy, I do a lot of things, but a threesome isn't one of them! I don't like to share; I am very greedy."

"Welsh Cake, if you carry on teasing me darling, I will put you over my knee and spank you until that beautiful ass is red raw."

"I think you'd prefer my lips around you, though."

Zander's moan echoed around the empty sitting room as B nibbled his ear again.

"Welsh Cake, I'm hard again now and it's all your fault."

"You need to pace yourself, sunshine. You'll burn out at this rate!"

Zander gritted his teeth, pinning her against the wall and kissing her hard. "You realize, if this house becomes yours, then I plan to take you all over it."

"Good, I can imagine us having rampant sex in front of the fire."

"Welsh Cake, I swear to God. I'll no' be responsible for my actions if you keep teasing me."

"Oh, I'm sorry, Scottie, I can't help it. You bite so easily! I'll behave until we reach the hotel," she said, aware of the footsteps coming back toward the room.

Releasing herself from Zander's grip, leaving him standing there hard and breathless, she turned to the man in the suit.

"You have yourself a deal! Shall we start the paperwork?" the realtor asked.

"Yes, please!" B replied.

"Uh, is your husband, okay?" he asked, showing concern to Zander standing with his back to them, and his palm against the wall as if he was steadying himself.

"Yeah, he gets a little breathless, that's all. We'll follow you out if that's okay?"

"Of course! Take your time. I'll wait outside," he said, closing the door behind him.

B approached Zander, stifling a giggle. "Are you okay, Scottie?"

"Nope!" he said as he looked down at his crotch.

"Oh Scottie, I love how you react to the smallest things. You're going to need to control yourself if you're going to keep up with me," B said over her shoulder, as she walked out the door.

B followed the realtor and signed the paperwork for her new house before taking Zander for lunch. She didn't mind him asking a million questions: she loved how interested he appeared. Following their lunch, they headed back to the hotel, where neither of them could wait any longer. They were desperate for each other as Zander pinned B to the bed, pressing his erection against her firm body as he devoured her mouth.

Pulling at his jeans to release him, B couldn't wait for him to take her.

"Jesus, darling, how the fuck are you doing this to me? I'm so hard for you. I'm determined to make you scream my name, and I promise you'll fucking love it!" he said through rugged breaths, pulling her out of her jeans with anticipation when there was a knock at the door.

Showing concern, Zander asked her. "Are you expecting anyone?"

"Not for another hour and nobody else knows I'm here besides Ari."

Zander climbed off the bed, pulling his jeans back up with haste, his war face stern.

"Go into the bathroom and lock the door. Let me see who it is. I'll call you when it's safe."

"Scottie."

"Do it now or I swear to God when we're done here, I'll tan your ass, woman."

The urgency in Zander's words took B back. They were unnerving to her. Hesitant at first, B observed Zander's expression until there was another knock at the door.

"Please?" he asked.

B pursed her lips before picking up her clothes and heading into the bathroom to get dressed. Locking the door behind her, adrenaline pumped through her veins as she threw on her clothes.

Hearing voices through the door, concern grew inside of her puzzled mind.

Who does Scottie think is at the door? What is he not telling me?

"Welsh Cake, your lawyer friend is here," Zander said through the door, emanating a low growl.

B could sense Zander's frustration with the interruption as relief washed over her. An episode of lusty sex combined with a potential intruder had sent B into fight or flight for the first time since her fall out with him in Uskiville.

Opening the door, Zander appeared a little embarrassed as she glared back at him.

"What the bloody hell was that about?" she whispered.

"I'm sorry darling, I just wanted to keep you safe. I thought it might have been Mack."

"For fuck's sake Scottie. How many times must I tell you? I'm no damsel! And if it was Mack, I would have kicked his ass already."

Zander kissed her cheek. "Oh, darling, that's cute. You may have a little sass, but we both know you're a lover, not a fighter."

"I almost broke your face, didn't I? You need to stop underestimating me, Boy-oh. I can handle myself just fine," she said, feeling insulted as she went to greet Spencer.

"You're early."

"I wanted to check on you, make sure you were okay. Your phone keeps going to answer phone."

B picked up her phone, tossing it back on the bed. "Shit, it's dead. Sorry. I'm fine."

"Oh, I heard how fine you are," he teased, shooting Zander a smile.

"Are you jealous, my lovely?"

"Having a big biker between your legs who can make you moan like that. Damn right I am."

To B's surprise, Zander flushed in embarrassment, making her grin.

That'll teach him to stress me out.

"Spencer, you're a married man!"

"I can window shop."

Zander shook his head as B watched in amusement as he gathered his things.

"Uh, maybe I should head off and leave you to your business."

"Embarrassed Scottie?"

"No!"

"You should be flattered. He likes big biker men," she teased.

"No offense darling, but I'm a boobs and pussy man and yours is all I need," he said, pulling her in to suck on her mouth.

B smiled, kissing him back and embarrassing Spencer this time.

Pulling away, Zander gazed into her eyes. "I'll let Jimmy know you're coming to the club later and dinnae worry, I'll take care of you."

"I can take care of myself, but thank you," she said pressing her point home, and ushering him out the door.

"Dinnae make me wait too long, and Welsh Cake... I will make you scream my name one day!" Zander teased, closing the door behind him.

As an embarrassed B turned, Spencer pounced, grabbing her hand, dragging her onto the sofa.

"Start talking, baby girl, and don't miss a beat."

"What? There's nothing to tell and I need a shower," B said, trying to get up.

"The hell there is," Spencer said, pushing her back onto the sofa. "I heard the pleasurable moans from the elevator, and I've never seen you allow someone to kiss you like that. Now tell me everything."

"We had sex, that's it! Now I'm going for a shower," she said, shrugging off the situation.

"You like him, don't you? This wasn't just sex. You feel something for him. Shit, the rough-and-ready biker rattled that cage your heart sits in, didn't it?"

"Shut the fuck up, Spencer. I'll be out in a minute."

"You keep lying to yourself, baby girl. I can see it a mile off and I'm damn sure he can, too."

CHAPTER THIRTY-TWO

What The Fuck Jimmy!

Zander hit the road on his motorcycle, the sun blazing down on him as he headed back to the club. He couldn't help but grin as he thought about his time with B, how their bodies moved together, with synchronized wants and needs. He had spent weeks pining over her, and now he had her back. This time, Zander was determined to keep her, and the thought of seeing her later made his body brim with excitement. The thought of her moving to Sunnyville blew his mind as he imagined himself spending cozy nights beside the fire with her and doing things that other patches do with their old ladies.

Parking up, he glanced over to the building site next door, imagining how it would look upon its completion. B wanted the club to be involved in the empire she was building, giving Zander some much needed hope.

Heading into the bar, Glen and the bunnies looked busy cleaning up as Jimmy propped up the bar.

"Well, where the fuck have you been? We all thought you were dead when you didn't come home last night. Found some pussy to get over, Dragon, did we?" Jimmy teased.

Zander grinned, sitting next to him at the bar.

"I was with Welsh Cake all night. I've no' long left her."

Jimmy's smile vanished.

"You went to meet her, and you didn't tell me?"

"Aye. Sorry pal. Ari rang yesterday, saying Welsh Cake was in town to finish some paperwork. She wanted me to look after her and send her back to Uskiville. We're still going ahead with the contract, Jimmy, and she's heading over here for a meeting soon. So, you might wanna call everyone to church and let them know."

Jimmy slammed his newspaper onto the table. "Why didn't you tell me last night? It's too fucking late now! I've told Mack about Noah and Dragon being in cahoots. I haven't disclosed any details. I just told him we need help. He'll arrive within the hour."

"What the fuck Jimmy? We had a deal! You said Monday!"

"It's the right thing to do. Mack is the Founder. We shouldn't have gone behind his back."

Zander punched a hole in the wall next to the bar. "Are you shitting me right now? We promised Noah we would look after her and now you've gone and thrown her to the wolves. What do you think will happen when Mack finds her here? Do you think she's gonnae help us when she finds out you've shafted her?"

"Mack will help us; we don't need Dragon."

"Welsh Cake offered us a golden fucking ticket, Jimmy, and how the fuck is Mack going to help us with no green?"

Jimmy scratched his cheek. "What do you mean?"

"She pays him a wage. He doesn't own shit. He's been lying through his teeth. She was going to give him a percentage when she told him, keep him sweet, but you may have fucked all that now. Mack is nothing without her and when she finds out the Prez has screwed her here, we'll get nothing too."

"Mack won't let that happen," he said, sipping his coffee.

"You don't get it Jimmy. She needed to sign the deal this weekend before Mack found out. Ari's been helping her, and she doesn't want to get her in trouble. You know she has massive plans for Sunnyville and now she's walking into a trap you've set!"

"It's not our problem! She should have been honest with him."

"Oh yeah, and how would that end? *Oh, sorry Mack, I'm feeling trapped and want to move on with my life. I know I'm your fucking cash cow but be a darling and let me leave!*" Zander mocked.

"She's more than a cash cow to him. You know that!"

"No' anymore! She's mine!" he growled, punching another hole in the bar's wall showing his contempt.

Jimmy rose from his chair as club members urged the bunnies to disappear, fearing the worst. "Did you listen to a word Mack said to you, or is your head filled with Dragon pussy? He will never let her leave! Mack has been in love with her since the day they met. He explained this after killing The Mauler. Whatever happens next won't be good, Zand, because he can't get Dragon out of his head. Mack's besotted with her in a totally fucked up way! Now, how the fuck do you want to play this?"

"Shit!! He'll fucking kill her and Ari if he finds out they have both been behind his back. I'll ring her and warn her."

Zander pulled out his phone to get through to B, only to reach the answer phone. The desperation evident in his tone as he spoke.

"Welsh Cake! Mack is arriving in Sunnyville, and he knows you're here! Please call me, so I know you're safe."

"Trust you to find a woman with so much baggage it compromises the club. Only you could do that! I gotta hand it to you fella, you sure can pick 'em," Jimmy said, trying to make light of the disastrous situation.

"This was Noah's dream. We knew he was dealing with her, and I'm glad he did. You read the contract. Her plans for this club are fucking awesome, and she is fucking amazing, pal." He dragged his hands down his flustered face. "I'm intoxicated by her, and last night was something else. My feelings for her frighten the life out of me and I know Welsh Cake feels the same. We both want this, and the club needs this! I cannae explain it and I know you think I'm crazy because I've only spent a couple of nights with her, but I'm telling you there's something between us!"

Jimmy hesitated before placing his arm around Zander's shoulder. "Zand, let's get real for a second! Mack won't let her go and we have a club to think of. We can survive without her help if we remain loyal to him. Do you want to jeopardize that for a woman you barely know?"

Zander shrugged away, his anger consuming his thoughts. "I'm no' planning on jeopardizing anything. I'll find a solution. He shouldn't trap Welsh Cake. She's a good woman, and she is moving to Sunnyville whether he likes it or no'! I'm telling you, Jim, she's no' stupid. She knows him, and I know she will have a plan of sorts."

"Okay, but both parties are heading here, and we can't be Switzerland. We have to put the club first because if we cross him, we're fucked!"

"If it comes to it, then I'll just tell him straight. We made a promise to Noah and I'm keeping it!"

Zander felt hopeless as he stared into his whiskey handed to him by a nervous Glen. Impatiently, he paced, agonizing over the forthcoming confrontation. Anxiety ripped through him at the thought of Mack spotting her in Sunnyville, with the pair amid chaos elsewhere, where he couldn't help either of them. He felt torn between his club and B, stuck between a rock and a hard place.

Zander knew how desperate B was to break free from Mack's shackles, but he also knew how important she was to the survival of the club. Phone in hand, he continued to dial B's number, hoping she would answer, wondering if he should look for her. His anxious mind envisioning chaos erupting in his absence, and Zander would never forgive himself if B got hurt. So, he remained at the club, waiting for them to arrive.

CHAPTER THIRTY-THREE
Betrayed?

B had just finished a press conference at the school with Spencer. She couldn't wait to arrive at the club, the excitement almost overwhelming her as her mind wandered into the future. She had offered the club an incredible deal, with terms that forbid them from returning to crime. As she drove along the sun-soaked town center, she imagined how peaceful it would be to live in Sunnyville, away from the constraints of Mack and Ari.

Turning into the club's compound, B's thunderstruck face grimaced, causing her to dig her nails into the steering wheel. She couldn't believe what they were seeing as Spencer gave her a sympathetic glance.

Shaking her head in disbelief, she attempted to shake the vision away, as if she was trying to wake from a nightmare. B's heart palpated, cold sweat washing over her as Zander, Jimmy and a group of burly bikers stood talking to Mack and Ari.

B couldn't believe it. She felt betrayed, stitched up even. *Was this just one big setup? Did Ari inform Mack of my intentions? Did Mack send Zander to keep an eye on me?*

So many questions raced through her mind. It was the biggest and most unforgivable betrayal, for everyone she loved and cared for appeared to have betrayed her. Hurt transpired into anger with a beat of her palpating heart.

After all she had done for Ari and Mack, ever since Ari's attack, ever since she had walked into Mack's life, and Mack, she took him in off the streets, gave him a home and this is how they repaid her? Trying to trap her in a world she didn't belong, keeping her miserable, allowing them to live off the fat of the land, her land, and then there was Zander. The man she allowed into her life, into her bed and into her mind.

Why would anyone be so cruel?

Spencer gasped. "What the?"

B swallowed her hurt. "Oh, bloody hell, Spence! How foolish I've been. I should have known that it was too good to be true! Mack has put him up to this! I am such an idiot!"

"Look B! If that's the case, fuck them all! You don't need anyone to be successful. Tell them all to fuck off! You owe them nothing and you deserve so much better than the hand they have dealt you. Now be the fucking dragon they portray you to be and sort this!"

B pulled up outside the club and as she stepped out of the truck, Zander walked over to approach her.

B shook her head at him. "How much did he pay you then, Scottie? I knew this was too good to be true! Jeez, I made it so fucking easy for you, didn't I? To think I fell for everything that came out of your mouth?"

"No Welsh Cake, wait! You've got this all-wrong. I've been trying to call you," he said reaching for her hand.

"Yeah, right Scottie! Convenient how Mack arrived when I've come to town. Oh wait!" she said pointing to Mack and speaking rhetorically. "There's my best friend and what are you doing here?" Turning back to Zander, she hissed like an angered snake. "I thought I could trust you. Seems I can't fucking trust anyone anymore."

"Welsh Cake, listen to me! I dinnae know what you're talking about. I've been trying to call you. If you just check your answer phone, you'll see."

"Piss off, Scottie! I'm done with you!"

Zander took hold of her waist. "Please, just listen one God dam, minute. When I arrived back at the club, Jimmy told me he told Mack everything and Mack was coming to town. I tried to ring you to sort this mess out. Mack and Ari have just arrived and dinnae know what the fuck is happening now, but I didn't deceive you, darling. I dinnae lie to you. This is a series of unfortunate events. Please, you've got to believe me."

Just then, Mack approached them, his anger splashed across his face. "Dragon, we need to talk."

B's face screamed in confusion as Zander gave her a sympathetic stare releasing her from his grip and squeezing her hand, no doubt letting B know he was there for her.

"You need to tell him everything now, darling. I dinnae stitch you up. He's in the dark, but now he's here. You need to tell him."

"Tell me what?" Mack asked. "Wait! Are you two still sleeping together?" he growled, and before either of them could answer, he threw a right hook at Zander, sending him crashing to the ground.

"I'll kill you, you bastard!" he screamed, lunging at Zander. Jimmy and B dived in between them as Zander pulled himself up to his feet, shooting Mack a look that could kill.

"What the fuck is wrong with you, Mackie? This has nothing to do with him!" B screamed.

"You fecking promised me, Dragon. You promised you would never sleep with a wolf and here you are, fecking my friend again. I thought the first time was just grief and I let it slide. Do you know how betrayed I feel right now?"

B flew into a rage, standing a breath away from him. "Who I fuck is my business, Mackie, and Scottie isn't the reason I'm here! This is all mine now. I bought this land. Sunnyville offered me an amazing deal here, and I've accepted."

"Dragon."

"Not this time, Mackie. I need to get away. You're suffocating me and this past year has been horrendous. You've had me followed, you question everything I do, and I can't fucking breathe. And as for you," she turned to Ari. "Every week I finish work to discover another potential suitor, like I'm fucking incapable of finding someone myself. You both fucking dress me up and try to control every aspect of my life. For fuck's sake, you don't even have a meal in your own house anymore and your kids might as well be mine because you don't fucking bother with them. You're both just so suffocating. It's like I'm married to the two of you and I have tried to tell you countless times, but you are both so selfish, you won't listen! I can't take it anymore. I want my life back, so I'm leaving!"

"Jesus Dragon, I..." Mack tried while Ari appeared numb. Only for B to continue, gesturing to Zander.

"And as for Scottie, I met up with him in my hotel last night. Let my hair down and yes, I took him to bed, and if I want to sleep with him, I will because you don't fucking own me! You've driven me away and now I'm going to live my life my way! I'm sorry Mackie, but I'm done!"

The gathering crowd in the parking lot fell silent. Everyone was stunned by B's outburst. Nobody dared question the Founder. Men had lost their tongues for less in previous years, but an outspoken woman; that was unheard of. Their eyes fixed on Mack, waiting for a response.

Mack stood, eyes bulging, and wide mouthed, glaring at B in disbelief. "Shite! You're leaving me?" he asked with his voice trembling. "Dragon, I'm sorry! I know things have been tense lately but please. You can't leave!"

"I can't do this anymore! Everything's changed and I need to do what's right for me now. I love you both, but this is killing me."

Mack covered his mouth with his hand and burst into tears to everyone's disbelief. B's face hardened as she too tried to fight back the tears. She wouldn't allow herself to shed a single tear over a man again, and today would be no different. B had never intended to hurt her best friend but needed him to understand her choice for freedom. Taking his head in her hands, she placed her head to his forehead, giving him a sympathetic look.

"Mackie, I'm a ride away. This will be good for us! You and Ari need quality time, and I need to do this for me and my boys, okay?"

"You can't leave me! Please?" he begged, gripping her blazer.

"Mackie, please be happy for me. You are my best friend and I need you to let me do this, okay?"

Mack shook his head in devastation.

Ari stepped forward, taking his hand before addressing B.

"He can't let you go, because he's in love with you and he has been since the day you met!"

B pulled away from Mack in an instance: her brain unable to comprehend Ari's statement.

"Wh-what?" She grimaced. Allowing herself a split second to digest her new reality.

Mack wiped his tears on the backs of his hands. "It's true! When I told you how I felt all those years ago, I meant it and I've loved you ever since. I know you've never felt the same, so I never mentioned it again! I would never try anything, and I love Ari and would never hurt her. She knows that, but she understands I still need you in my life."

The parking lot gasped as B's dragon eyes engulfed in flames. The crazed expression washing over her made Ari take a step back. "What the fuck, Ari? And you knew?"

"He told me the day we met. He told me a large part of his heart will always belong to you, and I understood that, and it never bothered me because I knew you'd let nothing happen between the two of you. God, I see the way you treat him. I know the feeling isn't mutual, and I know he loves me as much as his heart allows."

B shook her head in disbelief. The uncontrollable rage ripping through her body like a Californian forest fire. "Do you know how sick that sounds? What is wrong with you both?" She paced, her brain working overtime. "Oh my God! I allowed you to grapple with me every day; you've seen me in the pool half-naked. You've put sun cream on my fucking back because I thought we were friends, but all this time you were getting your fucking thrills. And what's worse is you're happy with that?" she said, gesturing to Ari.

"She doesn't have a choice. My heart will always belong to you, Dragon," Mack said.

B grabbed her head in despair. "This is so fucked up! What did you think would happen, Mackie? I'd roll over and become yours and we'd live in some fucked up paradise you've built up in your head? Fuck my life. This is infuriating!"

"B, it's not like that!" Mack shouted, as B became worked up. Her chest rose and fell in rapid succession as she continued to pace the parking lot.

Mack attempted to put his arms around her.

She swiped his hands away. "Don't fucking touch me, you sicko! I feel fucking violated. I thought you were my friends, my best fucking friends, my family. But you've both spent years using and abusing me! You must have had a right laugh. Taking me for everything whilst you tried to build your sick little happily ever after. You disgust me!"

"B, please? Let us explain," Ari begged.

Turning to Ari with a face like a possessed demon, B snarled. "I think we're bloody past that, good girl! Hey, at least now I know why you were desperate to set me up with someone."

"I just wanted you to be happy," Ari said, bursting into tears.

"Oh, wipe the fucking crocodile tears away. Neither of you could give a shit if I was happy. You've both just spent forever trying to cage and fucking control me! You've watched me build my business from nothing, giving you a life you would never have had, and this is how you repay me?"

"Dragon, we're so sorry! We never meant to hurt you! Let's go home and sort this out, yeah?" Mack pleaded.

B saw red. "Are you fucking serious? We're done! You're not going to fucking manipulate me and there's no patching this shit up! You've fucking opened Pandora's box and expect me to put that shit back in so that everything can go back to normal. Fuck you! Now get the fuck off my property before I remove you myself!"

The parking lot gasped! No one dared to speak to Mack with such contempt. Not even his worst enemies.

"I'm not going anywhere without you! Just calm the feck down and we can sort this out!" he demanded.

B stepped toward him; her fists clenched. "Calm the fuck down! Really! You drop this shit on me and expect me to be calm? You need to fucking leave, good boy, before I fucking end you."

"Hey now come on. This is getting out of hand! Let's sort this out inside over a beer, shall we?" Zander interjected.

"Stay out of this, Zand. This is between me and my Dragon. Just because you had a taste of her, it doesn't mean she's yours," Mack slammed.

Zander attempted to lunge at Mack, taking both Jimmy and Tiny's strength to contain him.

"Calm down, brother," Jimmy whispered. "Think of the bigger picture. You said she was smart right, so let's see what she does."

"If you lay one finger on her, I'll destroy you, Mack!" Zander bellowed.

Mack continued, despite Zander's outburst. "Okay, Dragon, why don't we have one last grapple for old time's sake? If I win, you stop this bull-shite and come home so we can sort this out. If you win, I will let you walk away! Deal?"

B snorted. "Fuck you Mackie! You think you're in control here? I'm not playing anymore. The way I'm feeling right now, I'll tear you from limb from limb. So, don't fucking test me!"

"Try it! Dragon," he slammed with the evilest look in his eyes.

B took off her Blazer and handed her phone to Spencer.

"B don't do this! I don't want you getting hurt," Spencer pleaded.

"I'll be fine! But get the fuck out of here if it goes south. But only if I'm unconscious you hear me!"

"B, please!" he pleaded.

"I have to end this, Spencer! Trust me, please?"

Spencer nodded, trembling as B gave him a cheeky wink.

B approached Mack, fueled by the fire in her belly. She was going to fight for her freedom, even if it killed her.

Mack sneered, "Are you ready?"

B glanced over to a bellowing Zander, attempting to free himself from the grasp of the club members restraining him.

B approached him, placing her hand on his chest, "Scottie, I am so sorry for all of this! But I need you to trust me, okay?"

Zander's purple face and concerned eyes stared into hers. His angry tone conveying his frustration. "I dinnae fucking care how long I've known you. I will no' stand around and watch him hurt you!" Turning to Mack, he snapped. "Besides, it's in the fucking charter, asshole. No woman to be harmed by a wolf. Do you remember that? Or have you forgotten why you created it? I'm sure Ari hasn't, and now you're gonnae hurt the lassie because she dinnae love you back?"

Mack laughed maniacally. "This is a grapple brother, nothing more! To save this fucking club and FYI, she's no woman. She's a fucking dragon, not a cute little Welsh Cake like she'd have you believe. Besides, it wasn't so long ago *you* made her bleed!"

Turning to B, Mack growled, "make your choice, Dragon!"

B glided her hand through Zander's hair, pulling him in for a long and passionate kiss. Releasing him, she gave him a wink, "I'm no damsel, remember?"

"Your safety is paramount, darling," his face strained, no doubt fearing the worst.

"They don't call me Dragon for nothing, big guy! I got this!"

Walking away from him, B swallowed bile in her throat. The horror in Zander's face made her uneasy as the rest of the club formed a ring around them, and B was desperate for freedom.

Opposite to where B stood, Ari turned to Mack. "Please don't do this. She'll make you look weak."

"No, baby. It'll make her look strong and show everyone she's not to be messed with. The only way she will be safe is if they fear her. Now she is going to destroy me, and I deserve it. But I can't let her walk away because I'll look weaker than if she beats the shite out of me. She has to have an out! Now, just do me a favor, please? I know she is hurting and angry, so if she has the chance, she will take my arms and if she does, I can't ride, and I'm finished. Please don't let her break my arms? She's too angry to see the wood from the trees right now and as much as she hates me, I know it will haunt her if she hurts me."

"Okay!" Ari nodded in tears.

"And Ari, I'm so sorry! I do love you and don't deserve your love! But I promise I will spend the rest of my life making it up to you!" he said as he entered the center of the make-shift ring.

After pushing her way through the circle, Ari found Zander. His satanic expression suggesting he wanted to murder someone. Dragging him from the circle, Ari explained the likely outcome to the grapple before they pushed their way back to the front of the ring.

Mack and B had agreed that whoever submitted first would lose. Just as they did back home. And as soon as Jimmy started the grapple, the pair locked horns.

Mack was twice the size of B, but B had years of experience. Mack was a fierce street fighter who grappled, and he wanted to make sure B could look after herself. B hated guns, and Mack thought grappling was their way forward. It also meant he could spend more time with her, so every morning at 6 a.m., they would grapple together. B would win one round and Mack would win the next, and the cycle would continue until B would annihilate him. But this was different. B was grappling for her freedom and wanted her life back. She could feel it with every fiber of her being, hearing her heart race as they grappled on the cold, hard concrete parking lot.

The floor was hard, roughing up B's skin: a far cry from her gym mats back home. Despite this, B got Mack in her guard, wrapping her legs around his waist, and Mack stood to detach her from him, but she dropped her hips between his legs to elicit a takedown, sending him crashing onto the concrete with a thud. Clashing heads, he winced in pain as B clambered on top of him, the anger searing through her bones, before she took hold of his arm. Tightening her grasp, B knew she'd won and before the grapple had even started. Mack had always been too impatient, trying to win the grapple with his might rather than his brain, allowing B to gain an advantage over him. Mack tried everything to free himself, rolling over and crashing B down onto the concrete, splitting her elbow open.

B grimaced, gritting her teeth, the impact with the concrete making her feel queasy as she refused to release Mack's arm. Instead, she adjusted her hips to initiate an arm bar. B knew it was Mack's biggest fear, to have his arms put at risk of damage as she squeezed her hips, forcing Mack back on his back.

Sneering at him, B's anger took control: no amount of tapping would make her stop hurting him now that she had him. B intended to snap Mack's elbow to teach him a lesson, as she relished being in control.

She wrenched his arm, making Mack scream in pain as he tapped out in surrender. Only B wasn't playing by his rules anymore. There were no submissions today. B intended to put an end to Mack's control once and for all as she became consumed by anger.

"Dragon, please don't do this! You're going to break my arm!" he cried.

B's face appeared unremorseful. The red mist had taken over, unable to hear him through her rage. Mack screamed once more, as B wrenched his arm some more, as horrified faces glowered back at her. She wanted to hurt him like he had hurt her, forcing her hips higher, squeezing them until she heard an almighty crack.

"Argh!" he wailed, as B felt his arm go limp and his body shudder beneath her.

Ari raced to his side. "B, please?" she pleaded upon death ears.

B's rage made her oblivious to the Founder's cries. She was far from done with him until a familiar hand cupped her face.

"You can let go now, darling; he's done!"

B woke from her rage, shaking her head. She didn't want to stop. She wanted to hurt him for what he had put her through until Zander knelt and kissed her temple, softening her senses.

"Please Welsh Cake, he's had enough, and I know you don't want to hurt him. You're angry and you have every right to be, but please don't hurt my brother anymore."

B released Mack's arm and stood up to watch a sea of club members rush to the aid of their Founder, shooting her disgusted looks. She dragged herself to her feet, walking toward her truck, leaving the parking lot stunned. The vacant expression disturbed them. She even heard one biker shout, "Zander, that chick is crazy, man!" as she opened the truck door.

"Hey, dinnae leave! Let me look at you. You're bleeding, darling!" Zander said, taking hold of her bloodied arm.

B peered down at herself. Her shirt was scuffed and torn, and she appeared oblivious to the blood pouring from her gashed elbow.

"Please Scottie, go back to your family."

"Hey, dinnae be like that. I know you're mad, but they are still your family too, darling," he said as he rubbed her shoulders.

B pulled away. "No, they were! Goodbye Scottie, look after yourself, okay?"

"Welsh Cake, please? Let's sort this out," he pleaded as she unlocked the truck.

B climbed into the truck, wincing in pain as everything hurt, leaving Zander to watch as she closed the door and lowered the window.

"Scottie, do yourself a favor and get yourself out of this shit! You are too good for this life. Too good for a motorcycle club and too good for me! You are a lovely guy, and you deserve more."

Turning on the ignition, her truck roared to life and B headed out of the parking lot, accompanied by Spencer.

Looking in her rear-view mirror, Zander appeared to be devastated as he watched her drive away. B knew his heart was pure. She believed he deserved better than her.

CHAPTER THIRTY-FOUR

They're Unravelling!

Blaze answered his cell phone with an inquisitive tone. "This is unexpected. I thought we were due to update tomorrow."

"I know, boss, but shit just got real here. Look, I can't talk for long as they're unraveling. Mack confronted Dragon, and they had a scrap in the parking lot. She busted his arm so badly; he's been taken to the hospital. That chick is nuts. She has disappeared with her fancy pants lawyer and Zand is on the warpath after she left him hanging."

Blaze removed his last cigar from his desk drawer. He had been saving it until he took control of Sunnyville again, only the timing seemed appropriate. The man who shot him and his brother's killer demoralized by a woman was the best news Blaze had heard in a long time. Lighting the Cuban, he took a long drag. "What went down, and don't skip a beat?"

"All I saw was Mack slug Zander for sleeping with Dragon and Dragon shouting at him. She lost her shit with both him and Ari, wanting nothing more to do with them. Some kind of fucked up love triangle and Dragon appeared disgusted by it. They had a scrap, and she's gone. I don't know, but I think she's finished with all of them, and Zander looks broken by it."

"Good. Maybe that son of a bitch is getting his karma after shooting me. Do you have a location on her? This could be our chance to convince her to switch alliances, and if she doesn't, we'll take her by force."

"No boss, but as soon as I do, I'll give you a ring, but fair warning, there's something about her. She's fucking dangerous."

Blaze puffed away on his cigar as if he was celebrating a victory. "Ha! Come now, boy! She's a piece of ass trying to have enormous balls in a man's world. She needs broken in with a firm hand, that's all."

"I dunno, boss. There's something not right there. She's a siren! Look, I gotta go. I'll keep you updated on what transpires."

"I know you will! Excellent work. That VP spot is looking more promising. Keep up the good work."

"Will do. Thanks boss."

CHAPTER THIRTY-FIVE

Broken and Angry

The drive to the hotel was quiet. Spencer's eyes remained fixated on B's desolate stare as she drove down the main street.

"What can I do?" he asked. He had never seen B so vulnerable.

"Can you grab me something to patch myself up with? There's a pharmacy nearby."

"Yes, but that's not what I meant, and you know it."

B stared into the road, desperately trying to keep herself from unravelling. "I'm going to New York as planned. Everyone can piss off now."

"What about the new business, the contract? B you're free but you can't run away until you sort this out!"

B thumped the steering wheel. "No! I need to clear my head! I need your help, Spencer. I have no one else to turn to now!"

"Okay, tell me what you need, and I'll do it! Just say the word. You know I'll always have your back!"

"Thank you!"

After their stop for medical supplies, they headed back to B's hotel room. Spencer couldn't look at B, who sat on the sofa, bloodied, battered, and drinking the good stuff.

"How did you meet the perfect guy, sign a contract to create a fresh start and fall out with your best friends in one weekend?

"Just displaying my talents, Spence," B joked.

"Stop it, baby girl! You can't hide this shit from me."

B winced, knocking back her whiskey to dull the pain. "I despise myself for losing control in front of Scottie. The way he looked at me, pleading with me to release Mack's arm, made me feel like a monster: a bloody dragon. I'm not a dragon, Spence, but that's all they see. Fighting and fortune. Scottie isn't like the MC he belongs to. He deserves better."

Spencer sat next to her, taking her bloodied hand in his. "Bullshit. I can see the attraction sweetness, but it's you who deserves better! B, if there's something between you, then fight for it!"

"It's best I leave."

Spencer became frustrated. "Okay. Lick your wounds, regain your strength and I'll sort the wayward bikers until you return. You're onto the 04:03 a.m. flight to New York City, right? I'm pretty pissed you're going, but I know how reckless you are when you're angry. So, I support your decision. Any last instructions?"

"We continue as planned. The gym, shake shack, bistro, day-care center, and bar are close to completion, and I'm the owner, after all. The rest, we'll take care of in due time."

Spencer studied her and held her hand as she poured another whiskey. Her body was covered in cuts and bruises, but at least her elbow had stopped bleeding. The black eye she must have endured during her grapple shone through her evaporated eye make-up and a slice across her eyebrow had sealed itself. He removed a stray hair from her face, as she met his gaze with a sigh.

"Look at the state of you, baby girl. You need looking after! I don't want to wake up to a call informing me of your death. Witnessing your bad ass bitch mode scared the hell out of me. Fighting with a man twice your stature: you're lucky you only picked up scrapes from bumping heads and crashing on concrete. Let's get you cleaned up."

"I can't face the shower right now. I need to collect my thoughts for a minute!" She said as her knee twitched furiously.

She trailed off, deep in her thoughts, when Spencer interrupted them.

"B, everything is in place for you leaving, except one thing."

B's puzzled face stared back, enquiring to know more.

"For the love of Christmas. Call him! I know you like him B and judging by the look on his face when you left, he likes you. He doesn't have my seal of approval yet, but I hate seeing you like this. Don't leave it like this."

B shook her head placing her whiskey glass to her forehead. . "I've done enough damage for one day, Spence. Scottie is Mack's friend and, frankly, he's too good for me."

Spencer stood waving his hands in contempt. "B, he's a fucking ex-con! He probably thought he hit the fucking jackpot meeting you and let's be honest, before the chaos, so did you. I just think that you'll regret it if you don't call him."

"It's for the best."

"For whom? Because from where I'm standing, you're both losing out."

"Please Spence. I can't take any more heartache tonight. I hurt his friend, and that's all that matters. It's 'Bros before Hoes' at that club."

"Right fine! Whatever! But for what it's worth, I think you are making a big mistake. Now give me your phone so I can call the office. My battery is dead," he said with exasperation.

"It's on my dresser charging. He was telling the truth, you know. I listened to his messages. He was trying to warn me."

"Then call him," Spencer yelled from across the room, knowing she wanted to see Zander.

"No, I'm going to shower and get to bed soon. The sooner I reach New York, the better."

Spencer shook his head, snatching the phone from the dresser before heading onto the balcony, closing the door behind him. He knew B almost too well, aware that she hated the thought of Zander thinking she was an idiot, a crazy person for her actions today. Leaving her alone wasn't an option. B would drink herself into unconsciousness, unable to protect herself if the club retaliated.

Spencer dragged in a breath from the cool night sky.

Screw it!

He raked through her phone book. There was one person who could help B tonight and Spencer was making the call.

CHAPTER THIRTY-SIX
Psychopath!

Back at the club, everyone was still in shock following what happened to Mack. Jimmy had him whisked off to the hospital, fearing the worst about his arm. Jimmy had never seen him in pain before. Hearing him scream in agony as B tried to break his arm made his stomach turn.

Following x-rays, Mack required surgery on his elbow. B had damaged his tendons and they would need to be repaired straight away. So, Jimmy stayed with Ari whilst Mack was in surgery.

They sat drinking coffee whilst Jimmy questioned Ari about the whole situation.

"Can I ask you something?" he said to an exhausted-looking Ari.

Ari nodded. "Sure."

"When did you learn Mack was in love with B?"

"The day we met. He explained how she rescued him off the streets after he had to leave your club. He told me they had become besties despite B being very closed off. You're aware, B brought Mack into the business on the condition he stayed law-abiding or white as she calls it, and he fell in love with her?"

"Yeah, he told me she turned him down and broke his heart. But why stay with Mack if he loves her?"

"Because I love him more," Ari murmured.

Jimmy rubbed her back. "He loves you Ari. He told me so. Mack's always been governed by his heart. He'll never change, even if it kills him. I believe he's in love with both of you."

"God, yes! He loves her and the boys. They mean the world to him. Burying his feelings has destroyed him. It's why we connected the way we did. I was a battered and broken mess, and he was heartbroken. It just brought us together."

Jimmy took a large gulp of coffee. "Do you think anything ever happened between them?"

"You saw how disgusted she was tonight, right?"

"True! She was psychopathic, scary even."

Ari tilted her head with raised eyebrows. "That's B. I think it's why he loves her. Mack insisted that nothing ever happened with B, and I believe him. And after a messy start with a very defensive B, B and I became best friends. I knew Mack wasn't her type. Until The Mauler's death, I assumed he'd gotten over her. They act like brother and sister together. They grapple and bitch, but deep down they love each other. God, they used to drive me mad when they disagreed over something until Mack eventually gave in and admitted he was wrong, which he always was, of course."

"Glad to see that some things haven't changed," Jimmy chuckled.

"That's the problem Jimmy. Everything changed after that. He wouldn't let B out of his sight, had people follow her everywhere. He paid me plenty of attention, but something wasn't right. Mack believes Blaze is coming for her. He's terrified she's going to get hurt and the more he stressed, the more paranoid I became. I knew they wouldn't hurt me, but their connection scared me and that's why I started setting B up. Every Friday, I had a different guy waiting for her at the bar."

"Oh, I bet she appreciated that?"

Ari burst out laughing. "She was so polite at first. Then, after about the third guy, she lost her shit and I mean, she went mental. It took Frankie, Mack, and Scamper to calm her down."

"Shit, and she's moving to Sunnyville..."

Ari shrugged into her grin. "She's your problem now, Prez! Out of all the people she connected with, she chose Zander. I should have known. Noah even said the same after he met her. He gave us a row for trying to 'cage Dragon.' He said it would bite us in the bum in the long run. Explaining only another Celt could tame her."

Jimmy shook his head in despair. "Well, Dragon is well and truly out of her cage now, and I'm concerned for Zander's welfare. I'm sorry, Ari, she's a whack job! She wanted to hurt Mack tonight."

Ari jumped to B's defense. "Listen Jimmy, I love you, but you've got B all wrong. She is the nicest person you could ever meet in your life, believe it or not. She looks after anyone she allows into her life, and we just fucking took advantage of her. We treated her like a slave now I think about it. She paid for everything, gave us a home, worked so hard to provide. She did everything for us and asked for nothing in return. We took advantage of that, screwing her up with our own insecurities."

"I'm afraid I've not seen that side of her, and I'm not putting my club at risk. She'll have to earn my trust."

Ari placed her hand on top of Jimmy's. "Jimmy, I'm just glad she made us take notice today. And if Zander has a brain cell, he'll fight for her, because I have never seen B look at anyone how she looks at him.

Jimmy nodded. "Fair enough! Typical of Noah, though.... still trying to teach us long after he passed. Mack kept her under lock and key, according to him. As he became friends with her, he was angry with you both because he believed Zander and Dragon would make a perfect couple."

"That doesn't surprise me."

"You know, Zand fell in love with her the night The Mauler died. We all witnessed the instant attraction when he saw her picture. Today they seemed connected as she tried to calm him earlier, and he was ready to kill Mack for her," he said, playing with his empty coffee cup.

"It must be one hell of a connection! I mean, could you imagine it, two crazy intense Celts with all of their baggage going at it!" Ari chortled.

"I'm surprised either of them survived it," Jimmy blasted, joining Ari in a fit of laughter, which was interrupted by the surgeon who had just completed Mack's surgery.

He explained that Mack's surgery was a success and, although it would take a while, he would have full use of his arm again. Relief washed over Ari as she thanked the surgeon as Jimmy attempted to inform the club to let them know the good news.

CHAPTER THIRTY-SEVEN

I'm Infatuated!

A disheveled looking Scottie answered the call from Jimmy as he sat at the bar, distraught. He headed to the shower after relaying a message regarding Mack's successful surgery. His head was banging. Exhaustion set in, but sleeping was impossible, with worry consuming him. He attempted to ring B several times, only to be met with endless ringing.

A couple of nights with her and I'm head fucked. At least her phone is on. I can get Gnarler to locate her. I'll know she's safe even if she refuses to talk to me.

Stepping into the shower, the water bounced off his muscular torso, his mind racing with images of their rendezvous the night before. The torment cascading into frustration thinking about how perfectly entwined their bodies were as he took her against the shower wall. He ground his teeth, banging his forehead against the wall in vexation. The rage consumed him until he couldn't breathe.

This crazy, yet beautiful, woman has infected me with her love and compassion. I've never felt like this before. I want her!

Zander wished he could hold her, comfort her. He hated seeing her so broken before she left today, blood oozing from her battered body. He wanted to kill Mack for putting her through trauma to maintain face with the club. Zander didn't agree with Mack's method for keeping B safe. The Celts differed from one another. Mack was more brawn than brain, whereas Zander was fortunate to have both.

As he rinsed his chiseled body, his phone interrupted his thoughts.

The flower of Scotland ringtone echoed from his bedroom: the ringtone he assigned to B's number mere hours before. His heart skipped a beat as he flew out of the shower, answering with a little excitement in his voice.

"Welsh Cake. I'm so glad that you called, darling…"

"Ah, steady on their rough and ready. It's Spencer, B's lawyer! I'm calling because I want to know how you feel about my friend. Do you like her, or is she just a fuck to you?"

Zander's temper rose as he white-knuckled his phone. "What's it to you? Now is she alright and why do you have her phone?"

"Just answer the fucking question, will you? You're not going near my friend until I understand your intentions."

Zander, dripping wet and a little stunned, answered.

"I'm infatuated with her. There's something between us. I cannae explain it, but she belongs in my arms, pal."

"You should come see her," Spencer demanded.

"Why? What's happened? Is she alright?" he said with concern in his voice.

"She's flying to New York City in the early hours, and I don't know when she's coming back. Now I know she wants to see you, but she's so damn stubborn. She doesn't want to come between you and Mack. She thinks you are too good for her. Zander, please understand. B doesn't let people in and she's different from you. I think you should just talk to her."

"Where is she?"

"She's in her hotel room. She never left town, but you can't tell anyone else. I need your word on that."

A rush of relief flooded Zander's body. "Aye, I won't. I just want to see her. Make sure she's alright!"

"Look, I'll leave the spare key card at the desk for you, as I won't be here when you arrive. So, I'm trusting you. She's my closest friend, so please don't hurt her!"

"Why the fuck would I hurt her? I really like the lassie."

"Just promise me you'll look after her and make sure she gets on that plane. She needs to clear her head."

"Aye okay pal!" he sighed. "Oh, and Spencer, thank you."

"I'm doing it for B. Not you!" Spencer said, before ending the call.

Zander tossed the phone onto his bed, allowing excitement to course through his veins like molten lava. He threw on his clothes and aftershave, slipped into his socks and boots, grabbing his keys and phone as he headed to the bar. His body was now quivering with adrenaline.

"You're in charge, pal. I'm heading out," he said to Tiny, slapping his back.

"Hang on a minute, you're not meeting that psycho after what she's done today, are you? She's a siren, brother!" Tiny shouted.

Zander felt his body burst in a fit of rage. Flying at Tiny, who was the opposite of his namesake, gripping him by his throat and slamming him onto the floor. Glen shuddered from behind the bar slack jawed as the rest of the club raced to pull Zander off him.

"Call her psycho one more time, I fucking dare you!" Zander slammed through gritted teeth, his eyes black as coal, as the same red mist that came over B earlier engulfed him too.

Tiny's terrified eyes stared back at a fuming Zander, before his brothers dragged him away, pleading with him to calm down.

Zander shrugged them off. "Let me tell you all something. None of you no shit about what happened here today, so if I hear one more word slating that poor fucking lassie, I will bury every one of you! Now I'm fucking going out and you better watch the club. Do you fucking comprehend?"

The men nodded in agreement, muttering in acknowledgement at their VP. Zander didn't wait for a response. He rushed outside, jumping onto his motorcycle. His thoughts pertaining to B's welfare, only.

CHAPTER THIRTY-EIGHT
I Got You!

Spencer left for home a short while after his phone call with Zander, leaving an exhausted B alone in her thoughts. B's bone-tired body complained of her mistreatment as she dragged herself to the bathroom to freshen up.

B knew a nice hot shower would make her feel better as she tugged at her clothes, wincing while her body cried out in pain. Mack wasn't a small guy; in fact, he was huge! This wasn't an issue in Uskiville because they would grapple on thick gym mats and not a concrete parking lot.

Dropping her once white shirt to the floor, she traced her fingers over the bruises decorating her torso and discovered the same onslaught on her legs after removing her jeans. Stepping into the shower, she let the water nourish her broken body, watching the water turn red as she washed her blood-soaked skin.

Closing her eyes, she let the water run through her hair, allowing herself to clear her mind of her horrific afternoon. It didn't take long for the raged-filled dragon fire to return to her eyes and the anger to engulf her mind once more.

B's choleric disposition transcended into fury as betrayal pumped adrenaline through her veins, igniting a fire in her soul. Clenching her fists in a fit of rage, B lashed out at the white tiles with her fists, roaring in anger to expel her all too consuming rage.

Startled, B felt familiar hands grasp tight around her from behind, weakening her defenses as Zander breathed into her neck.

"Hey, hey, come on, I got you darling," he said, wrapping one hand firmly across her chest and the other unclenching her fist, to thread his fingers through hers.

"Scottie," B said through gritted teeth.

"Breathe, I got you."

B tried to resist him, trying to break free of his loving grasp. The fury was too much for her. Her attempts were hopeless as Zander maintained a firm grasp, his stature preventing her from lashing out.

"I'm no' letting you go darling, no' letting you hurt yersel'. You can beat the crap out of me, but you're staying here until you calm."

Growling, chest heaving, B lashed out with repetitive kicks at the wall. The frustration too much, as the unfamiliarity of a calming influence bred contempt.

Zander kissed her neck, his lips applying firm pressure to her jugular, stopping her in her tracks. B's free hand coiled around the back of his head, pulling him in harder, letting him know how much she required his presence.

Hands still firm across her chest, Zander trailed down her neck, his lips and tongue applying a pressure-filled trail down her back until she turned into him, guiding him to a passionate clinch.

Zander pulled her broken body into him, making her exhale the carbon dioxide residue in her lungs. Breathless, she sank her teeth into his chest. Biting, sucking and kissing his pectoral muscles in a lusty rage.

Zander grabbed her ass, lifting her enough to wrap her legs around his waist as he pinned her against the wall.

B hissed at him, fisting his hair, tugging on it, pulling him back to suck his lips.

"Christ darling, I'm gonnae slip inside you and fuck the rage out of you. I'll make you come until you return to me. I'm gonnae extinguish the dangerous dragon fire in your eyes."

B pushed back against him, anger vanquishing her as he filled her. Gritting her teeth, her face raged like thunder as Zander took her hard against the wall.

Angry lusty growls created acoustic sounds as Zander reciprocated her movements in a rampant entanglement.

"What the fuck has he done to you?" Zander seethed.

B clawed at his back, her body, trembling through her all-consuming rage, trying to fight her impending orgasm as he pulsated through her.

"Don't you dare fucking fight it, darling. I feel you fighting the urge to tighten around me. Let go, let me free you from your pain."

B gritted her teeth, "No!"

"Darling, I'm no' letting you go until you release around my cock. I'm relentless. I'll fuck you until you're free. So, let me take you so you can release."

"Fuck Scottie," she growled, turned on by his demands, chest still heaving.

"Let everything fucking go," he demanded once more.

B screamed into his mouth, her body convulsing, unable to compose herself.

Zander cried out, reciprocating her impending release, drilling her hard and fast against the wall. "Christ darling, lose yersel', I got you!"

B's heart burst in a rush of release, with Zander's words ricocheting around her head like a pinball, freeing her from her rage and allowing her to release.

"Scottie," she cried, relinquishing control, spiraling into a chaotic orgasm, forcing Zander into an uncontrollable sprint of erotic thrusts.

Tensing and writhing, B's body responded to his commands, instigating his release and B became lost in his eyes as he battled his ejaculation, roaring in relief.

"Welsh Cake. Fuck!"

B, still contracting around him, moaned into his ear as her broken body calmed, listening to Zander's rugged, satisfied breaths. Debilitated, B held onto him tight, burying her head in his chest until Zander slowed to a stop. His chest crashed against hers as she remained pinned against the wall. Dragging in the steamy air, B felt Zander loosen his grip, allowing her to breathe.

"Feel better darling?" he asked.

B buried her head further. She didn't want to talk, she was confused and hurt, and Zander's chest was fast becoming a place to confide in. A place where she felt safe to rest and Zander allowed her time to collect herself. Locked in an embrace, they stood in silence, listening to the shower dance upon their glistening skin.

Zander pulled away first, "let me look at you."

B's head remained buried in his chest. Embarrassment corrupting her mind, unable to meet his gaze as he studied her graze filled body.

Shaking his head, he lifted her chin. "Hey, look at me darling. You are worth more than how Mack made you feel. A beautiful lassie like you should feel loved. An old lady should feel honored and cherished. And before you tell me you're no' an old lady, I'm telling you, you will be one day. You're fucking amazing!"

"Scottie, I'm—"

"Let me stop you there. I shouldn't have let things transpire today. I should have hit him myself! Look what he's done to you!"

B gazed into his big brown eyes, "No Scottie, I didn't want that! He's your brother. I did enough damage by turning up at your club today. I fucked everything up and I'm so sorry I involved you. You must think I'm a fucking psychopath after today!"

Scottie chuckled as he kissed her cheek.

"No, you were upset! I just know no' to mess with you in the future."

B allowed a wincing chuckle to escape her embarrassed lips.

Scottie gave her a concerned stare. "Hey, let me clean you up," he said, caressing her broken body.

B relaxed under his smooth hands, soothing her whilst he tended to her cuts and bruises, checking each one before wrapping her in a towel and leading her to the bedroom. Insisting she ate something, Zander ordered B's favorite dish. BBQ pulled pork, loaded fries.

B fixated on him as he tended to her elbow, applying cream and dressings that Spencer had bought for her.

"There, all better. Now come and cwtch," he said, kissing her forehead and guiding her into his embrace. B's head once again rested on Zander's chest as he stroked her back. She was just drifting off when Scottie interrupted her.

"B, there's something you should know, but dinnae go bat-shit at me for telling you."

B bolted upright, showing to her concern.

"Mack asked you to grapple today to provide you with an out. As the Founder, he couldn't just let his biggest asset walk away. You left looking like a force to be reckoned with, and he had to create a situation to make that happen. Mack knew you would win, but he dinnae account for how mad you were. He asked Ari to make sure that you dinnae damage his arms. She explained everything as you grappled. He never did it to hurt you, darling. Mack believed it was the only successful outcome, so the club dinnae think he'd gone soft and was accepting of club rules."

B sat in silence for a moment. "And did I? Damage his arm, I mean?"

"He had to go in for surgery to fix some tendons, but it went well, so I'm sure he will be fine," Zander explained, stroking her shoulder, trying to reassure her.

"You should go to him, Scottie. I don't want you in trouble if you are supposed to be there supporting him. I know how the chain of command works."

Zander's puzzled expression confused her. "I'm no' going anywhere unless you want me to leave, that is?"

B shook her head. "I just don't want to cause any more trouble for you. My fight is between me and him, and I don't want you and your club getting caught in the crossfire."

Zander threw a look of distaste. "You still dinnae get it, do you? I like you! In fact, I am hooked on you!"

"Scottie, stop!"

"No, darling, listen. The day we video called; you took my breath away. I was terrified for the first time. I knew you were special then, and I dinnae care how much money or baggage you have. Everyone has a story, and I promise you, Mack won't be a problem. That man owes me more than you know!"

"Because of what you did for Ari?"

Zander cast her an inquisitive stare. "What do you know about that?

"You're the Scot that saved her and that evil bastard that mauled you all died of a heart attack. I was relieved when Mackie told me he'd met his maker. He sounded like a sadistic son of a bitch."

"Aye, he was," he said in a nervous tone as B nuzzled back into his chest.

They talked for hours, wrapped up together in bed, filling in blanks for one another regarding how B met Noah. Zander explained how Noah knew B would grow tired of being imprisoned by Mack. He believed Mack was treating his friend like a caged animal.

B regretted declining earlier meetings with Zander, with Zander easing her conscience, explaining how Mack tried to keep her from club business for her own protection. Listening to Zander's relaxing tone, B's eyes became heavy, now content in Zander's arms. She had almost drifted off to sleep when Zander made her panic.

"B, I want you to be my old lady. I want to put the club patch on you and make you mine."

B played with his chest hair, fighting the urge to gather her things and leave. "I can't Scottie. I'm sorry, but I'll never wear that patch."

"Why?"

"Because I'm white and the patch is black."

"I dinnae understand."

B sighed. "Scottie, I see the world differently to you. I have to! My mind can't comprehend the colors and emotions of the world. I live a white life and by that, I mean law-abiding, honest, and somewhat dysfunctional. My world revolves around truth and honesty, and I can't falter on that. I trust very few people and even the ones I do, I keep at arm's length."

"Darling, I—"

B gazed up at him, caressing his cheek. "Look. I'm forever broken, and that patch of yours... Well, it's fortified with drama and crime. As much as I love it, I could never wear it. To me, that patch represents pain, betrayal, deceit, and a cascade of lies I never understood. It keeps me up at night thinking of the darkness it brought when it used to bring me so much pride. It represented a better way. A white and pure way, but Mackie made it black, and I'll never embrace it again."

"That's a dangerous perspective, Welsh Cake. The world isn't as simple as black and white. The shades will bleed into one another, eventually. No one can be black or white alone. I like to see everyone as gray. Gray is a healthier way to live."

"Well, my world *is* that simple, Scottie. If it isn't something you can get behind, you can leave," she said, pulling away from him.

"Hey, hey," he said, pulling her back into his chest. "Come on, calm down! I didn't come here to fight. I came here to comfort you and make sure you're okay. Please let me be here for you. I want you to run to me, not away from me."

"It's my MO Scottie. I fuck and run, remember?"

"No' anymore, you dinnae. You let me hold you. We'll figure the rest out together."

B studied him for a moment. His determined eyes and stern jaw drew her back to him, allowing him to comfort her once more. Nestling into his chest, her blood pressure threatened to rupture the blood vessels in her nasal cavity, as she tried to calm herself and Zander's soft hands continued to caress her back until she fell asleep.

Sunrise woke B as it rose into the cloudless sky. Wincing in pain, she turned onto her side to discover the naked Scotsman lying next to her, admiring his muscular physique as he slept.

Bloody hell, he's a handsome son of a bitch!

Allowing herself to indulge in his masculinity, she reminisced about his caring and loving persona the night before, until sheer panic set in.

Shit! How could I be so fucking stupid? We're not doing this! I can't come between him and Mack. I need to fix this, not make it worse. Besides. The Gray Wolves are black, and I don't think I can change that.

Slipping out of bed, ensuring not to wake Zander, B, rushed into the bathroom. Gathering her things as quickly as she could, she slipped out unseen to leave for New York City. The guilt consumed her as she checked onto her flight. Leaving without a trace wasn't her intention. The gratitude she held in her heart for Zander filled her with warmth, but her natural reflexes kicked in, convincing herself she would make everything worse within the club.

B knew they had shared something special, but she couldn't bring herself to trust anyone. Zander was a one-percenter. Black to B's white, no matter how good he appeared to be.

Placing her belongings into her truck, B left for her flight, convinced she made the right decision and glad she had a week to forget about Zander and the Gray Wolves MC.

CHAPTER THIRTY-NINE

Abandoned Again!

Zander woke shortly after B left.

"Morning, beautiful," he said, rolling over to embrace B to discover she wasn't there.

Dazed and confused, he stumbled into the bathroom, hoping to find her. Panic spread across his face as he realized her belongings had gone, leaving him devastated. He felt used after believing he and B had shared a precious moment together.

Moping, he dressed himself, scooped his keys and change from the bedside table, shoving them in his pocket.

Why does this keep happening? Have I got this woman all wrong?

Placing a cigarette behind his ear, he stared at the messy bed, reminding himself of what he'd had the night before. Frustration plagued him.

Damn you, Welsh Cake! He left the hotel room, slamming the door on his way out.

The club members were waiting for him, upon his return to the club, proceeding to tease him about his whereabouts. Unimpressed, Zander's patience wore thin; he was hurting and refused to entertain them.

"Somebody looks knackered. Wore you out, did she?" Jimmy teased.

"No' now Jimmy. I'm off to bed," Zander said, entering his room.

Kicking off his boots, he dialed her number on his cell phone and waited for her answer phone tone.

"Hey, darling. Why do you keep doing this? I know you're struggling but please stop pushing me away. Call me back, please?"

Tossing his phone on the bed, he unraveled, throwing his hands through his hair before turning to his electric guitar. Picking it up, he smashed it against the floor in a fit of rage. Unable to comprehend why B abandoned him again, he smashed his beloved guitar to pieces.

Jimmy and the others heard the commotion as Zander moved onto his lamp, launching it against the wall, and just as Jimmy opened the door.

"Shit man, what the hell's happened now?" Jimmy asked as the others froze in the doorway.

Zander dropped onto his bed with his head in his hands.

"She left again! Dinnae say goodbye. Just like last time. Jesus Christ, we have these perfect fucking moments. Then she gets scared and leaves without saying a word. Who fucking does that?"

Jimmy sat next to him, placing an arm around his shoulder.

"I'm sorry Zand. Look, it's none of my business, but you're like fire and ice. Maybe it's a good thing she's done this. We can hit town and grab a new hottie. You could pick up a new one every week with no stress."

"Christ, I dinnae want anyone else, Jimmy. Welsh Cake is the one. I need her! If she would just let me in so I can help her."

"Noah said it wouldn't be easy."

Zander pinched his nose between his thumb and forefinger. "Aye, I know, but she's gone to New York for a week now and won't answer her phone."

"Well, Mack's in the same boat. She won't answer his calls, either. I spoke to him earlier. He's getting out of hospital and recovering physically. Mentally, he's all fucked up over her."

"He's no' fucking having her! I'll kill him if he even looks at my lassie."

What is it with her? She has both your balls in a vice. I don't understand it, and I'm not having her tear this club apart! Promise or no promise. Now that lawyer friend of hers called last night. He's coming by on Wednesday. Maybe he can get her on the phone."

"Aye."

Jimmy's eyes darted to the doorway of weary bikers. "Right, where's Tyr? Tell him we need a ride out today. This one needs it."

"I'm no' in the mood pal."

"Tough shit! I'm the fucking Prez and you'll do as your told. Get your shit together and I'll get a prospect to tidy your room. You don't want a bunny in here?"

"No, I fucking don't."

Jimmy stood to leave. "Move your ass then. We leave as soon as you're ready."

CHAPTER FORTY

Blaze

"What do you mean, she's in New York City? With whom? God dammit!" Blaze said, throwing his empty whiskey glass at the wall.

"I don't know, boss. It all happened so fast. VP is a broken mess and Mack is the same, apparently. This is our time to strike. They're vulnerable. Let's take our fucking club back!"

Blaze rolled his eyes. "And then what? Dragon returns with her smart-ass lawyer and we're all serving life for murdering the pack? Think, stupid! We can't do shit without that Dragon whore. Any ideas at all where she's staying? Family? Anything?"

"Nobody knows, boss. She left VP high and dry this morning."

"Right! Fuck it! The hunt is on! I'll send a team to track her down. That bitch is mine! I'll make her scream for mercy after she signs over her assets using her blood. You stay in your lane until I tell you otherwise, and if she makes contact, I need to know."

"On it!"

"Don't let me down! I don't want to choke you to death."

"Never! Pitbulls forever!"

"You got that right!"

CHAPTER FORTY-ONE

Condemned!

Zander had spent the past three days unable to sleep as he stared at his phone, waiting, and praying B would call. Nothing could take his mind off her, despite Jimmy and the MC members' best efforts to appease him with ride outs, poker and pool nights.

Spencer arrived at the MC the following Wednesday to meet the building surveyor and smooth things over with the club. B had provided him with strict instructions regarding Sunnyville. She had been gone since Sunday, intending to stay in New York for a week, and the MC was once again questioning the club's future.

After meeting with the building inspector, the two men proceeded with the inspection whilst Jimmy and his club members waited in the bar. After watching the two men inspect the building, Zander sensed the club had problems. Spying on the conversation, he witnessed a frustrated-looking Spencer shake the building inspector's hand before watching him leave. Releasing an enormous sigh, he headed toward them.

Spencer explained the inspector had condemned the club due to structural issues and he would have to contact B to find out how she wanted to proceed. Zander witnessed the panic engulfing the bar. The club was home to most of the senior patches and now they feared being homeless and jobless unless B provided aid.

"Hey, now. Don't panic! Let me call B and see what she wants to do. She'll have a solution, I'm sure," Spencer said.

"I hope you're right, otherwise we're out on the streets!" Jimmy stated.

"B won't let you down, Jimmy. I'll ring her now. She's not up to much today, anyway."

"Is she still in New York?" Zander asked.

Spencer provided a sympathetic nod, shoving his hands in his pockets. "Yeah, she needed it, Zander. You know she did."

"When is she back?"

"I don't know," Spencer said with uncertainty in his voice.

"So, she's pissed off and left you to handle everything?" Jimmy asked.

"Hey, I'm just helping my friend, that's all," Spencer stated as he dialed her number.

"Put it on speaker phone please, pal, so we can hear what's going on," Zander suggested.

"I'm not sure that's a good idea. B values her privacy."

"It is if you want to keep your teeth," Zander said, eyeballing a worried-looking Spencer, who followed Zander's instructions, allowing the dialing tone to reverberate around the desolate bar.

"Hello, my lovely," B said upon answering. "Everything alright?"

"Hi baby girl. You're on speaker phone at the club, and we have a big problem."

B released a long sigh of despair. "Go on."

"The builders have condemned the building because of structural issues. I'm guessing Noah didn't mention these. You have a choice between shutting the place down or more builders on Monday."

Disconcerting bellows rattled the bar like thunder in the midnight sky, showing to the dismay among the patched members.

Spencer stood to attention, losing his grip, flapping his arms around and releasing his wrath upon the hostile crowd. "Alright, alright! I warned you about the speaker phone. This conversation needs to happen. Now knock it off so I can hear my friend."

"Quiet!" Jimmy asserted. Demanding silence.

"Shit!" B cursed

Spencer sat once more, leaning into the phone propped up against a glass on the table. "Yeah, sorry to add to your problems, baby girl. Only the fellas here don't have anywhere else to go or the funds to move."

"Any good news for me?" she mocked.

"Afraid not."

"Right! Well, I can't exactly make them homeless, so the original offer still stands. However, I haven't explained all the details pertaining to my proposal and I have grand plans for Sunnyville. If there's no bullshit and they will do honest business, then we'll proceed. In the meantime, I'll need to talk to Jimmy to sort accommodation."

"Are you certain that you want that? I mean, you've just freed yourself from Mack and his crap?" Spencer asked, forgetting where he was.

With that, Zander kicked him under the table, his stare menacing, showing to his outrage.

"I understand your concerns, Spence, but making them homeless isn't an option. Despite previous impressions, I'm not a callous bitch, and I get the potential haters after the Mack incident, but it's the decent thing to do."

"Solution then, baby girl?"

"I need to know what Jimmy requires from me at present. Is he there?"

"Affirmative. He can hear you loud and clear," Spencer said, giving Jimmy an encouraging smile.

"Tell me what you need, Prez. You have to vacate so my guys can step in. Are we talking cash for rental, temporary RVs, or what?"

"Oh, there she is," Jimmy mocked. "Don't worry. No apology needed for taking the cruelty cleaver to my best friends or kicking us out of our home. I get that we're bums to you, or black as you call it, but respect is important to us Doll Face."

The bar fell silent, anticipating B's response, the color draining from Zander's face as he buried his head in his hands.

The sound of B clearing her throat transpired through the phone. "That works both ways, good boy. Shit went down on both sides, and I'm guessing you informed Mack of the contract. If you had faith, it would have been different."

"That wasn't an option, following your radio silence. We have mouths to feed here. Noah may have put all his faith in you sweet cheeks but I've yet to see the amazing Dragon he made you out to be."

B snapped back with elevated aggression in her tone. "Right back at you, sunshine. When Noah explained his wishes for you as his successor, he mentioned greatness, not a whiney, impatient bitch."

The undeniable gasps around the bar demanded a response from the Prez. "Let's get one thing straight. I'm the fucking Prez..."

"Let me stop you there, good boy, because I couldn't give a shit who you are. The sole reason I'm still entertaining this shit show is down to Noah. I made a promise I intend to keep and it's my name on the deeds. The potential in Sunnyville is outstanding if everyone plays nice, and I have the capitol to pull your club from the shitty black world it's drowning in."

"You're one harsh bitch, Dragon!" Jimmy sulked, snatching his coffee from the table.

"You don't get anywhere in this world being nice, Prez! Now you have two choices: take my help or piss off and let me assure you when I say my patience is wearing thin with the masculine bullshit driving the Gray Wolves MC: something I never saw in Noah. So, forgive me for not bending the bloody knee, but I intended to do business with my friend, not you or anyone else."

A sea of scattered sorrow washed over the bar with the raw reminder of their fallen friend. Zander remained mute, the hurt in his heart mirroring the hurt in B's voice as his sympathetic glare met Jimmy's sullen stare.

"Okay, Dragon. Let's try Noah's plan. Give me the deets!" Jimmy said, calming.

B explained she would never place herself in the situation she found herself in with Mack and Ari and there would be a multitude of clauses within their potential contracts. Both parties agreed on the MC partnering with B to manage the entire business with Jimmy running the bistro, Eddie, Tiny, Tyr, and Sandy running the bar with Glen the prospect helping. Gnarler would head security, Hyde would manage the Shake Shack and act as an onsite doctor, and Zander and Sims would manage the gym and foodbank with B, which was orchestrated by Zander through writing on a note pad demanding so.

Zander didn't feel comfortable conversing in a room full of his brothers, nor did he want to pressure B. This was club business, and his feelings could wait.

"I'm not sure Zander will be happy working with me at the gym. I think I've pissed him off enough, as it is, Jimmy."

"Yeah, his favorite electric guitar is in pieces after you left without saying goodbye again, but he will be fine. He's been trying to get hold of you. So do me a favor and answer your phone, please?"

B's voice went quiet. "Uh, I'd rather talk to him face-to-face, Jimmy. Seen as I was a complete asshole to him by leaving like that. Upsetting him wasn't right, and I didn't want to cause trouble with the club by placing Scottie in an awkward position."

"And what about Mack? Are you planning to talk to him face to face because we can't do business with you unless we have his approval? I hope you can understand that Dragon. He is the founder, after all."

B went silent for a second before responding, "I will talk to Mack when I return."

"And when are you planning to return?"

"Tomorrow at dawn. I'll come to yours first so I can sort the contractors, but I would appreciate it if you didn't mention that to Mack, as I would like to talk to him myself."

"Does that mean you'll sort it out with him?" Jimmy quizzed.

"I will make him an offer, as I have with you. It's up to him if he takes it."

"You smooth things over with him, sort us out some trailers and promise to talk to Zander, and we have a deal."

B allowed a sigh of relief to transpire down the line. "Great, and I'll need you to come to Uskiville next week. I'm off to the UK for four weeks, so I'm only returning for a week and a half. I need to be confident you know what's expected of the club whilst I'm away. There's a lot of money riding on this. You'll also see how I run my business in Uskiville. My boys are home this weekend, so I'll join you in Sunnyville the following weekend."

"No problem."

B continued. "When you come up, you can stay with me and I will transfer you some money for expenses, to tide you over until we complete the deal."

"Thank you. And you promise that you'll talk to Zander when you arrive tomorrow?"

"Jeez, yes! You're as bad as Noah for nagging; I understand why he wanted you to be Prez now."

Jimmy belly laughed. "I'll take that as a compliment and Dragon, he's hurting, wandering around here like a lost fucking puppy. As Prez, I don't enjoy seeing my best friend like that."

Zander threw his hands in the air in despair, before B added, "I'm sorry I hurt him, Jimmy."

Zander stared at the phone, awaiting her next sentence.

"He is a lovely guy, and I'll apologize upon my arrival," she spoke in a low voice.

"Do you want me to pass on a message?" Jimmy asked, grinning at Zander.

"If you could ask him if I can talk to him when I see him tomorrow, please?"

"And what time are you arriving? I'll have him unlock the gates and let you in."

"That's unnecessary, Jimmy. Four a.m. is too early to wake you all. I'll park out front until the contractors arrive and talk to Scottie when he wakes."

"On the contrary, Dragon, despite what you have done to Mack and Zander, they're still worried about you and Mack has asked me to monitor you. Zander will be at the gate to ensure your safety."

"Fine," she huffed.

Jimmy gave his brother an encouraging smile and a nudge before continuing to converse with B, making all the arrangements for her arrival. After Spencer left, Jimmy returned to the table where Zander sat, staring into his coffee whilst the rest of the members chatted between themselves.

"Are you alright, man?" Jimmy asked.

"Aye!"

"Look, I was only trying to help earlier. I'm sorry if I overstepped brother."

"No, you did, great pal, and I appreciate it. It's just, hearing her voice has made my head spin again."

"You really like this chick, huh?"

Zander nodded his weary head. "I do, aye! Ridiculous, huh? There's something there, Jimmy, I just cannae get my head around her leaving without saying goodbye."

"Oh brother, it had been a hell of a night for her. She may have thought you would change how you felt the next day. Who knows what goes on in a chick's head and let's be fair, Dragon's different!"

"Aye, she is indeed."

Jimmy placed his arm around Zander's shoulder.

"Zand, I am trying to understand what you're going through. This was Noah's forte. I've never seen you struggling with feelings and shit. It's unnatural for you to behave like this. You've never been like this with anyone in the years I've known you, man."

"Then it should tell you how special she is to me."

Jimmy sighed. "I have to be honest. I'm still not convinced you and Dragon are a good fit. Dragons treated you and Mack like shit and, as an outsider looking in, I'm not a fan. Noah must have seen something I'm not brother because I have a hard time seeing you both together."

"Then why help me out with her today?"

"Because I fucking care, and as much as I don't agree with it, I want you to be happy."

"Well, I'm no' giving up on her. I know she likes me, she's just scared," Zander said, retrieving a cigarette from behind his ear.

"Well, whatever happens, you can't let your relationship affect the club, especially since we'll all be seeing a lot more of her now."

CHAPTER FORTY-TWO
Re-connect.

B hurried through the thick steel gates guarding the clubhouse, her heart crashing into her sternum with rapid thuds. Zander raised his hand, directing her to a parking space in the far corner of the parking lot, enabling her to capture a glimpse of his rugged handsomeness.

Switching off her engine, she just sat there in silence, attempting to calm herself despite the enervating guilt that had consumed since her departure the previous weekend. B was nervous, fidgeting in her seat as a heavy-footed Zander approached. Tapping the window, he indicated for her to open the door, her fingers fumbling as she did so.

"Hey, darling," he said with half a smile on his face. "Let's get you in out of the cold, aye?"

B's eyes remained in her lap, afraid to meet his gaze. "I think it's better if we talk out here, Scottie."

Zander's brow furrowed in confusion. "What! Why? You'll freeze out here."

"I'll be fine. It's not long until the contractors arrive. Besides, I don't want to cause any more trouble. I've done enough to hurt you already and..."

"Hey, hey, what you talking aboot? C'mon, let's get you inside, aye?" Zander interrupted, interlocking her icy fingers with his.

"Scottie, I know I hurt you when I left. Jimmy told me so and I'm so sorry. I don't want to come between you and Mack. I've done enough."

"So, that's why you deserted me in the hotel?" Zander said, exhaling with a smile on his face.

B pursed her lips in frustration, before stressing, "Yeah. I'm no good at this stuff: I keep fucking up. I just need to sort the business out and I'll be on my way."

Zander edged closer, the proximity almost too much for her as she savored the familiar scent of lavender, vanilla, chestnut, and tobacco. Her breathing quickening as he ran his gentle fingers through her hair.

"And what if I dinnae want that?" he whispered into her ear whilst inhaling her.

"Scottie, please? I'm trying to be sensible here."

"Look Welsh Cake, meeting you was the best thing that's bloody happened to me, and I know deep down you're scared of Mack, darling. But comprehend this, I used to outrank him, and I will happily put him back in his box if he starts. He's on my shit list for what he's put you through."

B raised her head, fixating on his chiseled jawline. "Being at logger-heads because of me isn't what I want. I need to create harmony between Sunnyville and Uskiville again. I have arranged to meet Mack tonight to propose a strategy that will benefit everyone, just like I explained last weekend. No more arguments, please."

"Okay darling, whatever you want. Now please come inside?" he said, pulling her close, to kiss her button nose.

B dipped her head, burying it into his chest and threading her arms under his to clasp his back. "Scottie, if I go inside with you, we're going to become entwined again and I'm not in a clear frame of mind. I don't want to hurt you again."

"Welsh Cake…"

B gazed up to find Zander staring back at her with a troubled expression etched across his face. She could see the torment in his eyes as he cupped her cheeks.

"You need to stop worrying about everyone else and let me take care of you for a change. I'll no' make you do anything you dinnae want to do. Understand, I like you and that's no' changing for me."

Exasperated, he continued preventing B from commenting further. "I'm no' wanting to put any pressure on you, darling. I know you're going through the mill right now and I want to help, okay?"

B nodded, as Zander tugged her into his embrace, a pleasurable moan escaping him as he wrapped his heavy arms around her.

"Right, I'm no' taking no for an answer, we're getting out of the cold," he said, removing her from her truck and setting her down to retrieve her suitcase from the trunk.

Taking her hand, he led her into his trailer with the warm air from the heater washing over them as they stepped inside.

The trailer was larger than your average two bed trailer, with a large seating and dining area, a generous kitchen, bathroom and two bedrooms.

B had almost relaxed when a volatile snore of echoes escaping from the first bedroom startled her.

"Hope you've slept. Jimmy drank half a bottle of cheap whiskey. We'll no' hear anything but snoring until sunrise," Zander joked.

"Good. I can't face him right now. He's Team Mack, and that's fine, but I'm too exhausted for his crap. I just want to rest my head and close my eyes for one minute to collect myself."

"Dinnae worry, I got you darling." Zander said, leading her along the small corridor into his bedroom.

The bedside lamps provided a warm and cozy appearance, providing enough light to illuminate the room. Red satin bedding decorated the double bed, accompanied by a wardrobe and vanity section which housed all of Zander's hair and facial products in the room's corner. It pleased B that Zander took pride in his appearance. It was one of the many things she adored about him.

Zander placed her case against the wardrobe before pulling her to sit down on the bed next to him. Mixed emotions ran through her head. She wouldn't ordinarily allow a man to exert any control over her. B had to feel in control, always, but not with him. It was different. She relinquished as much control as she could muster, allowing herself to trust Zander just enough to provide comfort and pleasure, freeing her from her troubled mind.

The thought of relinquishing total control terrified B. She was privy to the club charter, which stated *a wolf must exert total control over his mate, taking her from behind to make her title as an old lady official. Further stating, an old lady must forgo all control to serve her patch, allowing him to control every aspect of her life. An old lady should be seen and not heard, addressing a patch only when spoken to.*

To B, the club charter was outdated and disrespectful to women, despite Mack informing her that MCs had enforced similar rules long before him. B's anger and distaste caused a stir the night Mack presented her with them, and B initially thought Mack was pranking her, until his eyes turned stern.

Astonished that her best friend was capable of in B's eyes, such disrespect, B lost her temper, allowing her fist to collide with Mack's nose in disgust in a vibrant clubhouse.

B was the only woman ever to escape unscathed from assaulting a Prez, but B didn't play by Mack's rules. It was her name on the door, so she wouldn't answer to anyone, especially her best friend, with misguided beliefs regarding women.

It took Mack almost three weeks to convince B the charter rules were important foundations to an MC, and they soon agreed to disagree on the matter, allowing Mack to continue building his MC as he saw fit, as long as it stayed, law-abiding and white, as B called it.

Zander sat, staring into B's eyes with a smile on his face. His dimples lighting up his face like a kid in a sweet shop. B had grown fond of him, after discovering his remarkable qualities and kind heartedness, despite his past life choices. However, B knew in her own protected heart, she would struggle with long-term intimacy. She had been so broken by her ex-husband's infidelity, it destroyed her confidence, leaving her unable to trust again.

It convinced B that she would never allow a man to steal her heart again. It wasn't worth the pain, and she barely recovered the last time. B's grueling divorce destroyed every fiber of her being, stripping her soul bare and making her devoid of feelings.

B's survival mode forced her to lock her heart away, where it had remained untouched ever since. Yet sitting before Zander, an exhausted and terrified B bared her all to the rugged biker staring deep into her soul. It was as if he was searching for answers to who she was deep down.

"B, how do you feel about me?" he whispered, rubbing the top of her hand with the pad of his thumb, showing to his nervousness.

"Scottie, I like you," she replied, "Only…"

"Please dinnae say anymore! I just needed to know I'm no' all up in my head. You're hurting and everything is upside down right now. No doubt confusing the shit out of you.

B swallowed hard against a boulder-like lump in her throat. Having an attractive man understand her both excited and frightened her. For once, B wanted to feel and show Zander how she felt. She was desperate to uncover who she was, only fear prohibited it, crippling her from within. The fear B unearthed was of hurting Zander when she struggled with her emotions again, and fear of future rejection if he ended their relationship.

B wouldn't recover from heartbreak again, not since she made herself a formidable force to be reckoned with these past years.

Zander once again interrupted her thoughts.

"Do you trust me, darling?"

"I'm trying to," she whispered, squeezing his hand with hers.

"Then allow me to help you."

B's eyes narrowed in confusion.

"I want you to close your eyes and dinnae open them again until you feel one hundred percent comfortable, okay? I'm gonnae ask you some questions and I only want you to answer, 'yes or no' darling is that okay?"

Still a little confused, B nodded.

"Ready?" he asked.

"Ready," she said, closing her eyes and taking slow, deep breaths to calm herself.

Come on B, get your shit together. You want this. Get out of your head and trust him.

Zander's hands caressed her cheeks, diverting her attention from her thoughts as he drew her in to his soft lips. The warmth of his lips beckoning her as his moist tongue seduced her mouth and his divine taste awakening her senses.

"Is that okay, darling?" he asked.

B's eyes remained shut, the fear of the unknown caused her erratic breaths. "Yes."

Zander moved down to explore her collar bone, kissing every inch, and expelling soft moans of his own. B knew he enjoyed kissing her there. It had become his go to every time they embraced.

"And what about here?" he whispered, struggling to control himself by the sound of his own rugged breaths.

"Yes," she moaned as Zander placed his hands under her sweater, lifting it over her head to remove it.

Proceeding, he left a trail of tender kisses over her chest, unclasping her bra before lowering her down onto the bed. "And this?" he asked, as if he was fighting to compose himself.

B nodded; eyes still clamped shut with pursed lips. Her ability to speak escaping her.

Zander continued to kiss her, traveling down past her navel, and hovered over her pubic bone after releasing her from her black denim jeans, sliding them down along with her red thong until they reached her ankles. Zander removed her boots and the last of her clothing and marveled over her naked body.

"God, you're beautiful."

B remained mute, her chest rising and falling, expecting his next move until his silk-like hands caressed her body, his touch refined as if he feared breaking her. His heavy breaths tickled her torso as he slid her legs open with his own, covering her lips with his. His tongue explored her mouth as he shifted his hips, placing the tip of his hard cock at her entrance, and his chest compressing hers as he released low growls of arousal.

B gasped with pleasure as he entered her, penetrating her with every inch of himself, her body betraying her as she gave herself to him with every thrust. Her hands grasped his tight ass, inviting him to give her everything as she bared all beneath his durable physique.

"Do you want me darling?" he struggled.

B opened her eyes to meet Zander's eyes smoldering with desire: evident he was enraptured by her approval as he fixated on her.

"I want you!" she said with desperation in her voice.

Zander's face softened, acknowledging her request. His eyes now ablaze with passion as he delved deep inside her, devouring all he could as he delivered slow and forceful thrusts.

Zander demanded all that she offered, rejoicing as B cried out through each long and hard thrust, threatening him with her impending orgasm.

B could feel Zander reciprocate every twitch as she writhed beneath him, allowing her hands to discover his body again. Exploring him, her nails dug into his back, enabling her to bite down on his neck as she struggled to endure his forceful thrusts.

Zander let out an almighty growl, taking her hard, allowing B's pleasurable screams to rattle the RV as he continued to tantalize her G spot.

"Oh God, Scottie!" she cried, struggling to compose herself, witnessing his beautiful bug-like eyes glaze over. Threading his hands under hers, he forced his tongue into her mouth with urgency as he continued to penetrate her with God-like strength.

B's exhausted body coiled into him as she released her orgasm as Zander's erratic rhythm and heavy thrusts became too much for her. Crying out in pleasure, B came undone. Zander bellowed a manly cry, his face confirming the intensity of B's orgasm as she became lost around him.

Their bodies trembled with immense satisfaction as Zander continued to thrust rhythmically until his soft moans intensified into a guttural cry of relief.

Collapsing on top of her, he gushed "Christ. I dinnae know what you do to me but it's fucking awesome."

B couldn't help but laugh, experiencing an unfamiliar ache in her jaw from an enormous smile, as Zander grinned from ear to ear, looking pleased with himself.

"Feeling better, darling?" he asked.

Embarrassed, B nodded as Zander, once again wrapped his enormous arms around her, holding her tight. She couldn't explain why she felt so safe in his arms, it was as if their souls were supposed to be together.

"Here, let me capture this moment," he said, reaching for his cell phone. Retrieving it from the bedside table, he snapped a picture of their embrace. B's doughy eyes became heavy from exhaustion as Zander continued to caress her and she drifted off to sleep.

CHAPTER FORTY-THREE
Truth and Lies

The sun rose, meeting the clear blue skies with B's alarm, waking them from their warm embrace: an abrupt reminder of B's meeting with the contractors this morning. Zander didn't want to release B from his embrace as she stirred, reaching across to hit the Snooze button whilst remaining nestled into his chest. It amazed Zander how peaceful she appeared. The once daunting, hard-faced dragon appeared soft and kitten-like as she purred against his skin. He wished they could remain in the moment forever. Only B had business to attend to before her return to Uskiville.

Rolling her onto her side, he kissed her lips to wake her.

"Morning beautiful, aren't you meeting the contractor soon?" he asked.

"Ugh! Five more minutes, Scottie, please? I don't want to adult today."

Zander flashed a smile, kissing her shoulder as he ran his fingers down her arm to take her hand.

"I'd rather stay in bed with you, darling, but the quicker you sort this, the quicker I can have you all to myself."

B raised her weary head, propping herself up on to her elbow to look at him.

Stroking her cheek, he tracked her movement as she brought her head to meet his hand.

"Can I borrow your shower, please?" she asked.

"As long as you bring it back."

B laughed, leaning in to kiss his lips. "Are we able to fit in there?"

"We can try," he said, giggling like a naughty schoolgirl and pulling her onto her feet.

"Here, put this on," he said, handing her his checkered flannel shirt, burying her in it as he pulled on his boxers before leading her into the bathroom.

After a tight squeeze in the shower, Zander left B to dress whilst he made some tea, to be confronted with Jimmy's glare in the kitchen.

"So, I see she got her claws into you again," Jimmy said as he sipped his coffee, half naked at the breakfast table.

Zander ignored him and continued to make tea for himself and B.

"Look, I know I said I'd support you... I'm just saying I think Dragon is crazy and I think you're out of your depth. She drops and hurts you and then, as soon as she feels like it, she picks you back up again. Shit, I know you don't date brother, but surely you can see you're just a bit of rough to her?"

"Jimmy, I love you, but you dinnae know what you are talking aboot. I convinced her to come in. I waited up for her like you arranged, and I brought her into my bed because I wanted her there. She's broken, she's hurting, she's been through a hell of a lot with Mack and Ari, and for fuck's sake, stop calling her Dragon. I don't like it!"

"Oh, so she's a damsel in distress and you're her knight and shining armor? Trust me brother, pick another damsel! Besides, have you ever thought about what happens when she's all healed and no longer needs fixing? She might not need her bit of rough to comfort her then. Stop being so fucking pathetic."

"She's no' like that!" Zander slammed. "Mack and Ari have controlled her for the last couple of years. Ari told you that. The lassie wants her life back just like we did under Uncle Mauler. Or have you forgotten that?"

"Oh, so she's a sympathy fuck, too? Why don't you just admit she has you under the thumb?"

This angered the Scot, who slammed a carton of milk down on the counter, flying into a fit of rage.

"You just dinnae get it, do yer, pal? I like her! Jesus, before I met her, I was uncomfortably fucking numb: despised everything about myself. A ruthless killing machine with no future, and I never looked forward, drinking and fucking anything in a wee skirt. My life was meaningless. I felt meaningless," he said, frustrated as he looked at Jimmy before continuing. "Then when Noah died, I fell deeper into the rabbit hole, and it was dark and horrible. I was on the verge of doing something stupid, but when I saw her standing at the church doors, something changed," he said as he pointed toward the bedroom door where B was getting dressed. His bold and bright eyes beamed as he continued to convey to Jimmy how he felt about her. "As soon as she opened her mouth and that fucking sexy Welsh accent fell out, I knew she was my person. I mean, what are the chances of someone like me finding a fiery, fucking beautiful Celt?" he laughed, shaking his head in disbelief.

"I get it. She's different, but that doesn't mean she's right for you, man."

"Make up your fucking mind, Prez. You're hot and cold all the fucking time. I get you're Team Mack. I understand your concerns for the club but you dinnae know her, and believe it or no', before all the shit with Mack kicked off, I got a glimpse of who she is and let me tell you Jimmy, she is the kindest, funniest, and most intelligent person I have ever met, and it drives me fucking bat shit crazy."

"Zander, c'mon" Jimmy pleaded, but Zander cut him off.

"No Jimmy, listen, please? When Welsh Cake first took me to bed, she transported me to places I've never been before, taught me things beyond my comprehension! She is thawing me out, Prez, and that's no' a bad thing. To you, she might seem fucked up, broken and dangerous, but I see her: she's got a beautiful heart. I know she dinnae want to hurt me or the club. So, for the love of God, please give her a chance? That's all I'm asking,"

Jimmy's eyes widened: a huge grin cascaded across his face.

"Well, fucking hell! You are human, after all!" he spewed. "Okay, we will try it your way, but understand this. Zand, I don't give a fuck about her and frankly, I don't like her for what she did to Mack. I'll do this for you, not her. I'll welcome her, be nice or whatever the fuck you want me to, but the minute she puts a foot wrong, and she will, I won't hesitate to put her back in her box," he said, shaking his head.

As he approached his room, he saw B leaning against the bedroom door, glaring at him.

"Eaves drop, much," he said, snapping at her.

B scowled at the half-dressed pot-bellied man. "I understand your concerns Jimmy, but understand, you have witnessed one tiny episode in an enormous series of my life, and I respect that your loyalties lie with the club. I am not your enemy or anyone else's, nor am I out to hurt anyone."

Jimmy stood speechless at the powerful woman who had now switched out one of her many hats for her business hats, staring him down, before continuing.

"There are always two sides to a story, but I understand you're not interested in mine, and I couldn't give a shit. I don't care that you dislike me or for your misguided concerns. What does concern me is your professionalism because that affects my business and has a direct impact on the future of my children. What you should be concerned with is whether your club can commit to legal business practice and deliver on the proposed contractual obligations."

"Uh. um. I am."

"Good, because Noah entrusted us with the club's future. Now I have a meeting to attend and when I return, you'll look like a business owner, ready to talk business like an adult. But if you continue to piss me off, then I will turn into the angry, bloody dragon you perceive me to be. Oh, and trust me, Prez, what I inflicted on the Founder is child's play compared to what I'm truly capable of," she said, walking straight past him, wrapping her arms around Zander, who hadn't taken his eyes off her the whole time.

"I'll not belong, handsome," she said, giving him a farewell kiss and collecting her mug of tea as she left.

"Aye," Zander managed in a gruff voice, as he watched her leave.

Turning to Jimmy, he said to him: "She doesnae see me as an ex-con. She sees me as a real person. Makes me feel like I can be more than a criminal. I see a future with her instead of the torment of my past."

"Is she prepared to know who you really are? She hasn't learnt the truth about Uncle Mauler yet, and that implicates you, too. Now, she's ready to crack and discovering the truth could push her over the edge," Jimmy said in an exhausted tone.

"She'll be fine! I'll explain everything in time."

"Wake- up, Zand. You are from two very different worlds, and I'm not sure you're cut out for hers."

"You're wrong!"

Jimmy tied his scruffy hair into a man-bun using the hair-tie around his wrist. "We are ruthless killers! Do you honestly believe she's capable of seeing past the murder, lies and deceit? No brother! When she discovers the truth, your fairy-tale ends."

Zander turned away from his best friend. The bitter truths piercing his heart. Running his hand through his hair, he looked at Jimmy. "I'm no' that man anymore. Given the chance, Welsh Cake will see that for herself. You'll see!"

"I hope you're right, brother, for all of our sakes!" Jimmy said before returning to his room.

CHAPTER FORTY-FOUR

Call Back the Spies

"Hey boss, call back your spies. Dragon has returned to Sunnyville, and it's business as usual."

Blaze washed his face in the kitchen sink, waking himself from his slumber. "Hell, what's going on? I can't keep up."

"She's back and patched things up with Zander. I don't think Jimmy is too happy about it, either."

"How so?"

"Think about it... A smart-ass bitch rolling up on your club, calling the shots. He looks weak."

Blaze dried his face in his off-white hand towel and smoothed down his wet moustache. "Don't underestimate Jimmy. I had high hopes for him back in the day. He was my brother's prospect. If he's letting her play little miss bossy bitch, it won't be for long. Jimmy's clever, he'll have his eyes on the prize, like us."

"Understood. What's the play here?"

"Find me a situation where she's vulnerable. I want her alone so the spies can drag her ass here. I'll break her in! She'll be sucking cock and giving me the financial freedom I require, making Sunnyville the most feared club stateside in a week. I'll own that bitch, and those traitors will rue the day they ever crossed me."

"I'll try, boss, it'll b—"

"There's no trying here, boy," Blaze clipped. "You'll deliver because your life depends on it. Now I don't give a rat's ass how you do it. I need a five-minute distraction. The spies will take care of the rest."

"But boss—"

Blaze's impatient tone reverberated down the line. "Listen, I dragged you from the depths of hell and I can just as easily toss you back there. I want that bitch and my club, and I won't rest until the rivers run red with my enemies' blood. Do you com-pre-hend?"

"Yes boss. On it!"

"And don't think of double-crossing me, asshole. History should explain I always win."

"I won't let you down. You can count on me."

CHAPTER FORTY-FIVE
Teeth

Zander led B across the parking lot where B noticed Glen sitting near the other MC members, B waved, much to Zander's dismay, who growled in distaste. Zander's body fueled with rage, despising other men looking at her. He hadn't claimed her, so, to them, she was free for the taking and Zander was ready to kill anyone who glanced at her. She was his, even if she wasn't ready to be claimed yet.

Tightening his grip on her hand, he led her to church where the rest of the patched members waited. They sat around a rickety table that was removed from the clubhouse, creating a makeshift church in the parking lot. Zander introduced B to all the patched members. All members gave B a warm smile and a wave. Gnarler, the Sergeant of Arms, was to the right of the Prez's seat, followed by Hyde, the new resident doctor, Tyr, the Roadie, Tiny, the club's enforcer, Sims, the club secretary and Eddie, the treasurer and chaplain. Jimmy had yet to arrive.

Holding her hand, he gestured for her to sit after removing his chair.

She raised an eyebrow. "A seat at the big boys' table?"

"Don't get used to it Dragon, we want your money, that's all. You're just another piece of ass to us. You may make his dick hard, but your dragon charm won't work on the rest of us," Tiny slammed.

Zander growled, stepping in front of her, livid Tiny had the audacity to speak to his woman like that.

"Watch your tone, brother, unless you want to lose those pearly whites," he growled.

Tiny raised his hands. "Sorry VP, it's just we're not used to having a woman tell us what to do. They serve us, remember?"

B burst out laughing. "For fuck's sake, you gotta be kidding me. It's 2023, asshole."

"Yeah, and we're one-percenters. We don't take orders from a woman, especially in church. You shouldn't even be here."

Zander's nostrils flared, his hackles up. "We're no' one-percenters and I mean it brother, one more word out of your mouth and I will crucify you!"

"And I'm paying for this fucking church of yours and I don't work with fucking one-percenters. So, I'll just take your fucking club and turn it into something else," B snapped.

Zander grabbed her waist. He could feel her heart race and her Dragon's eyes burn as he held her close.

"Ignore that prick, darling. We're clean. We killed every deal at Noah's request months ago, and please dinnae disrespect my club. He's just trying to get a rise out of you."

"Oh, he'll get something else out of me if he opens his mouth again."

Zander's lips curved into a smile. "I dinnae doubt it. Now please, put your dragon eyes away and wait for the Prez?"

Zander waited for her to take a deep breath as he felt her soften in his arms.

"Yeah, be a good bitch and listen to VP, and if you behave, he'll share you with the pack and let a real man taste you!"

"Fuck!" Zander spat, feeling B's rage in his arms.

"Fuck you, you fat prick!" she yelled.

Zander released her, turning toward Tiny in haste, punching him in the face, knocking his two front teeth out.

Gasps rattled the gazebo, leaving wide mouths around the table.

"I warned you, brother," he said as he wiped Tiny's blood into his jeans. "Now carry on and I'll end you!" he said, fueled with adrenaline. He needed the hit after seeing the contractors' leaching over B earlier, and Tiny just walked right into it, in his opinion. Turning back to B, he expected her to be furious with him, to discover her smirking with a hand on her hip.

"I can handle myself, you know," she said.

"Aye, I know, but you would have killed him, and I only knocked his teeth out!" he said, giving her a wink.

B shook her head as Tiny made for his trailer with haste, catching the blood in the palms of his hands, almost bumping into Jimmy.

"What the fuck has happened now?"

"Ask that bitch," Tiny spat.

Zander saw that Jimmy was seething at her. It angered him, urging him to defend her once more.

"Your handiwork again, Dragon?" Jimmy snapped entering the gazebo.

"No! Tiny needs to know his place! He needs to get right with the fact that we're no longer one-percenters. He's gonnae be trouble if he doesnae get his head right," Zander explained.

"Did you need to knock his teeth out, though?"

"He warned him Prez! He was disrespecting Zander's old lady," Hyde chirped in.

Zander raised an eyebrow, grinning like a Cheshire cat at Hyde's acknowledgement that B was his property, despite knowing B would be livid.

"Funny, I didn't know he claimed her," Jimmy clipped.

Zander growled, "She's off limits!"

"Calm down Zand. No one else could handle her anyway," Jimmy said.

"Uh, I am bloody here, you know!" B snapped.

"We're well aware of that, Dragon. You've more than made your presence known, so how about we sort the plans for our ride out to Uskiville before Zander knocks someone else's teeth out," Jimmy said as he took his seat at the table.

Zander sat in his seat, this time pulling B onto his lap as the others smirked. He wanted the members to understand she was off limits. The fire in her eyes was visible as B displayed her disapproval.

They spent the next hour discussing the trip to Uskiville and B's expectations of the club's new role in Sunnyville. B sat in Zander's lap with his arms wrapped around her through the duration of the meeting, and Zander loved every minute. He even tried his luck by traveling his hands under her shirt until B took his hand and gave him a devious look.

"Scottie, if your hands travel anywhere other than around my waist whilst I try to conduct business again, you will lose them, good boy."

Patched members attempted to tease him, oblivious to him as he bit his lip. His eyes smoldering, acknowledging he was pushing his luck with her. He couldn't help himself and once again, allowed his hands wander to her breasts to experience a searing pain in his wrist. B proceeded to wrist lock him.

"Ow!" he said, laughing into pain.

"I fucking warned you good boy!" she said as she stood up with her hand locking his wrist. "Now piss off, otherwise we're not doing business together. Any kind of business!"

"I'm sorry! It won't happen again. Please dinnae break my wrist with your ninja shit," he said, chuckling at her and raising his free hand, much to the amusement of the rest of the patched members.

B released his hand and stood to continue her conversation with Jimmy, and Zander couldn't help but marvel over her curvaceous body. Reaching for her hand, he squeezed it, giving her a wink as she looked down and rolled her eyes at him.

Shit! I'm in trouble.

B squeezed him back, as Zander sighed in relief.

Zander continued to witness her business prowess as she engaged everyone on a personal level, making sure each patch was financially stable. Their employment contracts wouldn't be ready for a while yet.

Despite Tiny's outburst, Zander noticed B seemed to get along with the other members. They seemed to like her, moving past her treatment of Mack. B was letting her guard down, showing her softer side, and after a few laughs, even Jimmy was warming to her.

The meeting concluded, leaving everyone in a better headspace regarding the club's future and they set everything for the MC to take a road trip in a couple of days, leaving B ready for her drive back to Uskiville.

Back in the trailer, B was collecting her things as Zander propped up the doorway sulking. Zander didn't want her to leave. He wanted to unpack her things, keep her close to him, and if it was up to him, he would.

As she readied herself to leave, Scottie stopped her in her tracks, pulling her close to him.

"Are you sure you won't let me come with you?"

"I'm sure! I'll sort this shit out and we can take more baby steps," she said, pecking him on the cheek.

"And you promise I can come up on Wednesday?"

B looked at him with a nervous smile and nodded. "Yes! But baby steps, remember? My kids haven't seen me with anyone other than their dad and I don't want to panic and push you away again!".

"Best behavior, I promise! Now, are you sure you won't stay another night? You've no' slept much," he said, trying to convince her to stay.

"I can't Scottie, the boys are home tomorrow, and I need this sorted before then. I don't want them dragged into my mess!"

"Then please let me come with you. I know what Mack's capable of even with one arm."

B shook her head. "Scottie, if he sees you, then it'll just make things worse and…"

"You dinnae need to fear him, darling," Scottie interrupted.

B stood back in surprise. "I don't!"

"Bullshit! Look, all I mean is that you dinnae have to do this alone. I dinnae want you getting hurt. I'll go to the ends of the earth for you, darling."

"I know Scottie, but I got this, and you need to trust me. Besides, if he tries anything, then I'll break his other arm," she stated in a casual tone.

Scottie's eyes widened in concern.

She wouldn't.

B's lips turned into a wry smile. "What, too soon?"

Scottie breathed out a sigh of relief allowing a chuckle escape. "Fucking hell. You're killing me."

B gave him a cheeky grin. "I don't know what you mean. I'm an innocent, relatively young Welsh woman."

"Innocent my ass!" he said before pushing her down on the bed and climbing on top of her.

"You are a fiery Celt, and you drive me fucking crazy. I dinnae know how I'm gonnae get through the next couple of days without you," he said, leaning in to kiss her. Only to be thwarted by her sweeping him onto his back, pinning him down on the bed, exerting her dominance over him.

Zander loved her strength, and how she took control, lowering herself down to bite his ear lobe.

"Oh, God! Welsh cake! I dinnae think I can let you leave," he said breathlessly.

B flashed him a naughty smile, before diving up off the bed in an instant, leaving Zander wanting more. "Now that I've given you food for thought, I need to go."

CHAPTER FORTY-SIX
Mack and B

B parked on her drive and headed inside with her things. The house was quiet, and she wasn't used to it. Even when the boys were at their dad's, the house was vibrant with Mack and his family, or Frankie would sit at the breakfast bar helping himself to whatever baked goods B had made that week.

B mourned for her lost family. Yeah, she had her boys, but she'd lost her best friend in the entire world. Mack was her person until he hurt her. She'd also lost Ari, and despite still holding resentment toward her for changing Mack and birthing a cascade of lies, they had still become close, close for B anyway.

B had also lost Noah and didn't even know if Frankie hated her. He'd not called or texted since she lost it with Mack. Frankie was like a big brother to her, and he'd not even bothered to check if she was okay that week.

B shook her head in despair.

What a bloody mess!

B was so angry with everyone and everything and couldn't bear to stay in her empty house another minute. She headed into the kitchen and retrieved a bottle of Welsh whiskey from the countertop.

B only felt comfortable in one spot: at the top of the hill behind her house. It was somewhere she could breathe and release her troubled mind. She would head up there by herself whenever life threw her a curve ball, sitting there for hours.

B enjoyed watching two striking gray wolves frolic in the valley. They were beautiful, with piercing blue eyes, they never deviated from the opposing hill. They would howl at the moon in the black night's sky and B would become lost in the picturesque story unfolding before her.

B headed out and up the path. She knew the forestry like the back of her hand, reaching the top of the hill in no time, using her phone torch to light her path.

When she reached the clearing, she headed toward the edge of a small ridge to her favorite spot overlooking the valley. Not close because of her fear of heights, but close enough that she could capture the valley in all its glory. Propping herself against a large stray boulder, she unscrewed the cap on the amber liquid, sipping and allowing it to warm her palate.

"Bloody hell, I've missed this," she told herself as she stargazed alone in the dark. Being alone didn't faze B. She welcomed it, closing her eyes and relaxing into the rock behind her. She zipped up her jacket, burying her face in it so that the cool breeze could no longer tickle her face. She was just beginning to unwind when her whiskey was torn from her hands. Opening one eye, B looked up to see Frankie staring down at her with a friendly smile on his face.

"Mind if I share your rock?" he asked.

"Knock yourself out," B said, budging up a little to allow him to sit next to her.

"Thanks," he said swallowing a big gulp of whiskey. "You alright B?"

B pursed her lips and nodded, "Yeah, you?"

Frankie released a roaring sigh. "Great, until I found out shit hit the fan in Sunnyville. Finding out from a bar boy that my two best friends were trying to kill each other, made me feel like a mushroom; fed shit and kept in the dark."

"Hey, that's my line."

"Don't do that with me B, don't deflect. You're like a sister to me, so I deserve to know the truth. Mack and the wench ain't saying shit."

"Don't call her that. You have to accept she is part of the family."

"She's not family, she's a home wrecker, and that's all she'll ever be to me. She took your bond with Mack and severed it to get her claws into him, and I'll never forgive her for that."

"There is no bond now and for once, it wasn't Ari's fault."

Frankie looked at B. "what do you mean?"

B told him everything and witnessed Frankie sink a third of the bottled whiskey. His eyes grew wide, and his temper flared.

"You can't leave. This is your home. They can leave!"

"No Frankie, I want this!"

"Then, I'm coming with you. Where you go, I go!"

B shook her head, "No, he's your best friend. I'm not taking you away from him. He needs you!"

"The hell he does! He's barely acknowledged my existence since he's been with her and I'm not fucking staying to put up with their shit. Besides, I have old marine friends near Sunnyville."

B rested her head on his shoulder. "Frankie, I am hurting everyone. I put my best friend in the hospital. I can't take his best friend, too."

"He did that to himself with his cascade of lies. I knew he loved you B, doing the whole of his head to yours thingy that you do. I just didn't realize he was getting his jollies off at your expense. To me, he violated you, broke your trust."

"That's what I said and then I snapped. Good and proper! I couldn't put the dragon back in her box. I wanted to hurt him like he hurt me and now I'm a monster!" she said, picking up the whiskey and knocking back a glug.

Frankie took the bottle from her again. "You're not a monster. They have lied to you, and Mackie broke your rules and your trust. Just say the word and I'll drag his black ass out of Uskiville."

"I can't do that to him, not with the kids. It's their home, and I made a promise to Junior."

"B, he broke the rules. Black and white, remember?"

"Yeah, I know," B said shifting her body to sit cross-legged and face him. "But I won't do it to them, and he won't be in my life once I'm in Sunnyville, so black and white still stand. I'll check in once a month. I can't take his lies anymore."

"So, what now?"

"I need to sort things out with Mackie so he can run the retreat. I also need to ask if you'll remain here until he's competent. To keep an eye on things."

"Fine," he sulked. "I'm not fucking happy about it though!"

"I know Frankie, but I'm desperate! This is such a bloody mess!"

Frankie put his arm around her. "And we'll sort it. I would follow you off this ridge if you asked me to. I will always have your back. You are blood to me. B, you took me in and made me a man again. Whatever you need, consider it done."

"Thank you, Frankie. I'm sorry I didn't tell you; I just didn't want to come between you and Mackie."

"B, I think somebody beat you to that," he sighed.

The pair sat guzzling the good stuff and stargazing.

"How about you and VP? I didn't see that coming, B in a relationship. Well, fuck me sideways!"

"Neither did I. It just bloody happened, came out of nowhere," she laughed, choking on her whiskey.

"Not like the usual Sultry Slalom shenanigans then?"

"Christ no! It was like we connected somehow. I can't, I mean I don't understand it. It's just one big mind fuck to me."

"He's broken your one and done rule."

B nodded. "Yeah! He's a beaut; so black to my white. I shouldn't let him in."

"But?" Frankie asked, smiling at her.

"I can see a light inside of him. There's something telling me he's good. He has such a big heart under that black frame, Frankie, and he's so bloody passionate, he makes me want to scream."

"I bet he does," Frankie teased, giving her a wink.

"Piss off," she joked, nudging him.

Frankie nudged her chin. "Look, if it feels right, do it. Life is too short for anything else. Just take baby steps and if you don't like it, then he's done."

"But what if he corrupts me like Ari has done to Mackie? What if he turns me black? I can never go black, Frankie. Remaining white and law abiding maintains my moral compass. I never want to be black. It's why I made those rules."

"Blethen Arianwen Jones, I hand on heart promise you I will never let that happen. Now come on, let's get off this rock. I'm freezing my nuts off here."

"Okay, let's go find Mackie and get the ball rolling. The sooner I move to Sunnyville, the better," she said as they headed off back through the clearing to B's cabin.

As they entered B's warm cabin, Mack had perched himself on her sofa with his arm in a sling. His eyes likened to a deer staring into a headlight.

"Hey," he muttered.

"Hey," she said, stopping in her tracks and shoving her hands in her back pockets. B hated seeing him so broken, knowing she caused his pain. It didn't matter how he'd betrayed her; she broke her friend, making guilt flood her veins.

Frankie pushed her toward the sofa. "I'm just in the kitchen making tea. Now put this to bed."

B approached Mack, sitting on the sofa opposite.

"Does it hurt?" she asked.

"No more than I deserve!"

"I shouldn't have done that to you, Mackie. I'm sorry! Your honesty fueled me with rage, and I couldn't see the woods from the trees. If Scottie hadn't stopped me, things would have ended worse for you."

Mack shook his head. The disgust visible on his sulking face. "I can't believe you're with him, Dragon. What does he have that I don't?"

"He's different Mackie. Like no one I met. He's one of the very few people I've met that asks nothing from me."

"Oh, he wants something from you, Dragon. He's a one-percenter! They all want something."

"Mackie, Scottie's made me feel again. That's huge for me."

"He's not good enough for you!" Mack spat, his temper rising.

B laughed. "He's probably too good for me! You said it yourself; I need to settle down. Maybe this is me trying!"

"No! not him. Anyone but that fecking mouthy Scot. Dragon, please stop this."

B moved to sit next to him on the sofa. "Mackie, I'm moving to Sunnyville. I want this and I'm not playing anymore. I didn't tell you because you sabotaged my last deal and Sunnyville is an opportunity of a lifetime."

"No, it's not! We still don't know what happened to Noah and you're moving there. What happens if whoever killed Noah saw you together? What if they come for you?"

B dragged her hands down her face. "Mackie, I'm going into business with your brothers. Helping them, just as you wanted. Frankie is going to flit between Sunnyville and Uskiville, ensuring my safety, and I'll return once a month for the weekend to discuss our business going forward."

"Dragon, please? Go to New York, Utah, fecking San Francisco, just don't go to Sunnyville. It's not safe and I don't want to bury my best friend next."

"You're being paranoid; besides I've signed the contract. The deal is done. I've even bought a house. I'm sorry Mackie, I'm moving to Sunnyville, and you need to get right with that."

Mack took her hand. "How can I? I love you; God damn it! You own my fecking heart and soul!"

"Mackie stop please!" B said pulling her hand away. "I can't create feelings I don't have, and you have a wife for crying out loud. How is this affecting her? You can be better for Ari if you let me go."

"Feck! I can't Dragon. I need you! Believe me, I know I've fecked up and I'm sorry! Please, please don't leave," he said as tears streamed from his eyes.

B placed her arm around him. "Look my lovely, I bloody love you and adore you and despite our recent fall outs, you'll always be my best friend. I'm doing this with or without your blessing. You need to let me go!"

Mack sobbed into her chest, clinging onto her with his good hand. "I don't know how."

"Baby steps, good boy. Baby steps."

Mack snorted. "That Scot is rubbing off on you already."

"I like him Mackie."

"I don't! He's betrayed me by stealing you."

"Mackie, if you love me, you'll not interfere with my relationship with him. He's your brother and I'm your Dragon. Two people you love have connected. I know you never wanted me with a wolf, but I can't help what's happened between us and I don't want to. I'm tired of pointless sex, and it's different when I'm with him. Good different. I have a long way to go before it becomes a thing. Hell, I'm unsure if I'm capable of a relationship, but for the first time since I was married, I want to find out.

Please don't ruin this for me. We both know I'll probably do a good job of that myself."

"And you're okay with this?" Mackie said to Frankie as he entered with three mugs of tea and some cookies wedged under his arm.

"B can do whatever makes her happy, and we both know VP would die before he let anything happen to her. Look how he guarded her at Noah's funeral. He became human, for fuck's sake; besides, I think they could be good together."

Mack took her hand in his once more. "If he fecking hurts you, he's dead. You understand me, Dragon? No one, and I mean no one, will ever love you like I do, and I know in my heart he's not right for you. Even if you don't feel it now, I know we will be together one day and I'm saying this when I love Ari. Dragon, our fate is aligned. I know you'll come back, so I'll let you go for now."

Although confused by his response, relief swept through her, grateful for Mack's release. "Thank you, Mackie. I am sorry, you know. I'm sorry I don't feel what you feel or what you want me to feel. It must have been difficult for you to live with this. Watching me sleep with other men. Please know, I never meant to hurt you. Had I known..."

"You would have cast me out. I know it, you know it. I couldn't risk losing you. Not that it matters because I've lost you now, anyway," he sighed.

B opened the packet of chocolate chip cookies, taking one out and dunking it into her tea. "Mackie, you've not lost me, good boy. You never will. I'll always be your Dragon. Even though you piss me off, I will always be there for you, and I'm always gonna wanna talk to you and I still need you in my life."

"How? You're leaving!"

"Well, who do you think is gonna run this place whilst I'm gone?"

Mack's stunned expression almost prevented him from speaking. "What?"

"Mackie, I'm giving you twenty percent of the business, and I want you to run things here."

"You're going to trust me to run this place? Do what you do on my own?"

B laughed, licking the excess cookie crumb off her lips. "It's time you had your piece of the pie, Mackie. You've earned it, sunshine."

Mack's jaw dropped. "And I can run it how I want?"

"Within reason, yeah. I mean, I'll still own eighty percent, so any big decisions still go through me, but I'm keen to hear your ideas going forward."

Mack picked up his tea, shaking his head. "Feck! You're serious?"

"Yeah! You know it's gonna be a hell of a lot more work, and I'm gonna need Frankie with me soon, so you'll not be able to rely on him forever. Pick your team sunshine and organize your affairs."

"You think I can do this?"

"I know you can, so don't bloody let me down."

Mack's eyes turned serious. "Just promise me one thing?"

"What?"

"You won't break my other arm if I feck things up," he teased.

"Mackie, if you fuck things up, your arm will be the least of your worries, good boy."

"Come here, you," he said, placing his forehead on hers and pulling her into his embrace. "I fecking love you, Dragon!"

"I love you too, Mackie!"

CHAPTER FORTY-SEVEN

B's House

On the ride up to B's house, Zander stopped to pick up some red roses at the local grocery store, much to Jimmy's disgust. However, Zander was determined to make the right impression. It had only been a couple of days since he had last seen her, but he missed her.

Upon arrival, Mack greeted them in the driveway, embracing them with his good arm whilst the other sat in a sling.

Stepping inside the warm house, aromas of a Sunday roast tantalized their nasal cavities, it smelled mouth-watering and reminded Zander of his childhood home. Excitement gathered as he entered the plush kitchen, dining area, giving him flashbacks of the night The Mauler died. Of course, B was unaware he'd ever been inside her house, but as his eyes scanned the room, he experienced the same cozy vibe that attracted him to her.

Brimming with excitement, the roses trembled in his hands with his eagerness to see B.

The sound of laughter came from the basement as they put their bags down.

"Come on then, let's go say hi, then I'll show you to your rooms," Mack said, ushering them downstairs.

Following him down, they were met by a choir of laughter. Zander could see the tears of laughter roll off B's cheeks as she held her sides, making him experience another new feeling of warmth and happiness. He wasn't used to feeling the whirlwind of emotions sweeping him off his feet. He found them invigorating, as if he was being awakened for the first time.

Interrupting his thoughts, Mack bellowed in a playful tone. "What's going on down here?"

"Aunt B is ruining jokes again, Dad," Junior said, chuckling to himself.

Zander's eyes darted across the room to B, forgetting what she said regarding the requirement for baby steps, provoking her personal space to embrace her and planting a kiss on her lips.

"Hey beautiful. I missed you!" he said.

B shirked away, flushing all shades of scarlet. "Uh, hey!"

Zander caught the attention of the room. Multiple shocked eyes fixated on him, along with a menacing stare from Mack. Awkwardly, he handed her a dozen roses. "Sorry! Here, I got these for you. I hope you like them," he said as he awaited her response.

B curled her lips into an enormous grin. "Wow. Thank you, Scottie. They're stunning! I haven't received roses in a while."

"And they're your favorite," Madoc teased.

"They are indeed," B said.

Zander breathed out a sigh of relief, trying to contain his nerves. "Uh, I'm glad you like them,"

"I'll pop them in a vase," she said as she headed off, a little embarrassed.

"Right, let's show you to your rooms, so you can get ready for dinner," Mack said, leading them back upstairs.

Entering the kitchen again, Zander saw the vase full of roses on the breakfast bar, before turning to see B prepping vegetables.

"I'm so sorry I took hold of you like that; I dinnae think. You asked for baby steps, and I should've respected that."

"It's fine."

"Is it though, because if a woman says it's fine, then it's far from fine."

B grinned at him, pulling him in to devour his mouth.

"Is that fine enough for you?"

"Fuck, yeah it is! Missed you darling! Two days apart is too long."

B wrapped her arms around his neck as he held her waist.

"Play your cards right, good boy, and you won't have to wait much longer," she whispered.

Zander held her close. He wanted her there and then as his soft lips glided into her mouth once more.

"Fecking hell, do you two ever come up for air or what?" Mack snapped, disturbing them from their clinch.

"Calm down Mackie. I've not seen him in a couple of days, and I don't call you out every time you and Ari go at it. How many times have I caught you two fucking?"

Mack growled. "Well, there are kids around. So, put him down."

"Charming," Jimmy and Eddie chimed in unison.

"Right. I'm here if you need anything else. Dinner is in thirty minutes," B said, addressing the three men and releasing Zander from her grasp.

"Let's go guys," Mack said, ordering them from the kitchen.

Zander glanced behind him, giving B a cheeky wink as he headed down the hallway parallel to the kitchen. Mack stopped at the first door.

"Right Jimmy, this is you, matey," he said as he opened the door.

Inside, the beautifully decorated bedroom encased fitted wardrobes, a huge king-size bed, draped with a cozy duvet that B had purchased back in Scotland. A new plush-looking dressing gown, a set of clean towels sat on the bed with a bottle of Welsh Whiskey and a fresh glass sat on an oak bedside table.

Jimmy peered into the Jack and Jill bathroom, complete with a walk-in shower, oversized bath, a toilet, and wash basin. The sleek black and white, marbled tiled bathroom provided a hotel-like vibe stocked with masculine essentials.

"Whoa! This is awesome!" Jimmy gushed. "And where does this door lead?" he asked, referring to the adjoining bathroom door.

"That would be Eddie's room," Mack confirmed.

"Nice!" Eddie said as he entered the room and dived onto his bed.

"Get settled and head back to the kitchen when you're done. Food won't be long and believe me, you won't want to miss B's cooking."

Leaving the room, Mack spoke with venom in his voice, eyeballing Zander. "This way, pal!"

Zander smirked, ignoring Mack, who led him to a lone door at the rear of the house, gesturing to Zander to head inside.

Scanning the room, he placed his bag onto the bed, realizing Mack had directed him to a guest room. Wreaking with disappointment, he opened a door revealing another Jack and Jill bathroom.

"Where does that door lead?" he asked.

Mack glared as if his hackles went up, releasing a disappointing sigh.

"That would be my Dragon's room, but let me tell you now, if you step one foot inside it, there's gonna be hell to pay," he said through gritted teeth in his thick Irish accent.

Zander's lips curled into a sinister smile; his eyes lit up as if he was accepting a challenge as he faced off with his MC brother.

"Why no' let the lassie decide whether she wants me in their brother," he sneered. "Besides, you're a wee bit incapacitated to be throwing your weight around."

Mack flew into a fit of rage, standing within an inch of Zander's face, invading his personal space with his one good fist clenched tight, ready for action.

"Ya no fecking good for her, Zander!" he spat, almost foaming at the mouth.

Zander laughed, "and you think you are? Jesus, man, she's just spent months trying to get away from you! You made that lassie sick to her stomach grappling with her, pretending it was brotherly love just to get your dirty cheap thrills! You disgust me. You have a wife and kids, yet you lust over someone who dinnae want you!" he said, shaking his head in disbelief.

"Watch your tone VP."

"Fuck you, Irish! You're just the same old street rat you were when I met you. You're no' Prez of mine after what you did to her. It's fucking disgraceful how you hurt her."

"That's none of your business, brother!"

"Oh, but it is! Mind that night you were getting yer operation? I went to her hotel room, and she was fucking broken as I cleaned her wounds."

"And I was just fecking fine after what she did to me?"

Zander grabbed his jaw, squeezing it. "You tried to cage a dragon brother and you got burned! What is it? If you can't have her, nobody else can? You'll be trying to lock her in a tower next, like some fucking captured princess."

Mack swiped his hand away. "Feck you! I'm trying to stop her from getting hurt. Making a mistake she'll regret!"

"What? By moving or by sleeping with me? Because let me tell you Mackie boy, I've spent many a night inside her and I dinnae hear her complaining about it! She likes me and I'm already falling for her, so why can't you be happy for us?"

Mack burst into a maniacal laugh, leaving Scottie dumbfounded.

"Oh, my days! You honestly believe that don't cha?"

"You silly bastard! Dragon doesn't stay with anyone. You're a means to an end and once you've signed that deal, there will be no more riding my Dragon because my dragon isn't capable of anything more than rough sex! You know why she won't trust you or let you in?"

Zander glared at him. His temper boiling like a melting pot as his patience wore thin.

"It's because she can't see anything other than BLACK & WHITE! And let me tell you, you're black and she's white. You're an ex-fecking-con who thinks he can have a beautiful white dragon, and it's so fecking funny you can't see the woods from the trees!"

"She's no' like that!"

"Oh, this is priceless!" he laughed. "Oh, but she is! And when she discovers who you are and your sinister past, she'll cut you loose, because there are two perfect humans at the center of her world. She would never compromise them for a criminal like you. Do you seriously think she wants to play happy families with you? Wake up, Zander!"

"Well, she did with you, ye prick!"

"Yes, but I've not done half of what you've done. I mean, you're a fecking killing machine, for heavens sakes. Let her go before someone gets hurt."

Zander shook his head in disbelief. "Fuck yersel! The only reason you're saying all this shit is 'cause you're scared. Scared of losing yer cash cow and scared of losing the woman you love. You just cannae stand the fact that she lies with me!"

Zander's nostrils flared. His eyes were as black as coal, face fire red as he stared him down. His frightening demeanor provoking Mack to step back in caution, with fear written on his face.

Stepping into Mack's personal space once more, he continued. "I dinnae give a fuck what you think anymore, brother, or what mind games you are trying to play because I know she wants me and believe me when I tell ye, I satisfy her in ways you could only dream of. See, we've connected; I feel it and she does too, and for as long as that keeps happening, brother,

I'll no' be going anywhere! Oh, and if you ever hurt my Welsh Cake again, I'll tear yer wee head off yer fucking shoulders."

Mack composed himself as he watched Zander storm out of the door.

That works both ways, brother.

Zander headed back to the kitchen to find B placing an array of vegetables and sauces on the decorated table. Following her back to the kitchen, he couldn't help but lust over her as her dress clung to her curves. He wanted her even more, now Mack had stated his disapproval of their relationship. B was stirring the gravy on the stove as he approached her, desperate to hold her but remaining reserved, remembering what she said about taking things slow around the boys.

"Hey, can I help at all?"

"No, we're just about ready to serve. Can I?"

Zander's bewildered gaze met hers. "I dinnae follow."

"Are you okay, Scottie?"

"Uh huh."

B raised an inquisitive eyebrow. "Maybe tell your face that."

Zander bit his lip displaying a cheeky grin. "Nothing gets past you, does it?"

"No, now tell me what's bothering you."

Zander scratched his chin as he gazed upon her. He didn't want to appear ungrateful or curse about Mack, but he hoped he'd at least share a bed with her. Whispering into her ear, he said to her: "I know we're taking things slow, and I respect you want to keep your distance because of the laddies. It's just, I dinnae expect to be in the guestroom. Being honest, the thought of you no' being in my arms tonight makes me sad."

Taking a step back, B glared at him.

"What are you talking about? I just need you to hold back on the public displays of affection around my boys. They know I like you and they're okay with that. If you want to be with me, accept that my boys come first."

Zander leaned into her, trying hard not to touch her: it was killing him.

"Understood, darling, and I'm fine with it. Does that mean I need to sneak into your room via the bathroom tonight? Am I your secret hook up?"

He watched as she turned the stove off and poured the gravy into two gravy boats, before turning to him. The confusion on her face growing into concern.

"Why do you need to sneak in?"

"I'm sleeping next door," he said as he witnessed her face turning purple with anger.

"Take these to the table for me, please," she seethed.

"Okay, where are you going?"

"To move you into my room and maybe castrate Mack."

"Right," he said as he watched her storm past Mack, whispering into his ear, before shaking her head and storming toward her bedroom.

Zander placed the gravy boats onto the table as a sheepish-looking Mack directed everyone to their seats, placing him at the opposite end of the table to B.

Zander was losing patience with the Founder, his hackles stood up like a wolf ready to attack. Sitting himself at the table, he grimaced as Mack grinned at him.

Zander clenched his fist under the table.

Keep it up, motherfucker. Keep it up!

He hoped B would step in when she returned, as he didn't want to cause a scene in front of everyone.

If I lose my cool Welsh Cake will end us. I have to be smart here.

Zander found his blood pressure rising as Mack joked with Jimmy and Eddie, like a king sitting at his throne.

Christ! I want to wipe that smile right off his face.

"Hey, VP. I think we are in the wrong seats," Frankie said, removing the fork from his grasp and directing him to the chair next to B's.

Zander hadn't realized he was holding the fork as if it were a deadly weapon, releasing it in an instant and standing up to meet Frankie's gaze.

"Thanks pal. I appreciate it."

"Play him at his own game. Don't let him get to you. If you lose it in front of Rhys and Madoc, she will never trust you."

"Aye, he's pushing my buttons though."

"Then push his by showing him you and B are a formidable force. Let him be the bad one for a change," Frankie said, providing an encouraging slap to his back.

"Aye. Hey, Frankie, why are you no' supporting your Prez on this?"

Frankie smirked. "B is my best friend too, you know. In fact, she's my sister, and for whatever reason, she's taken a liking to you. I've seen a side to her I didn't know existed since she met you and it's doing her a world of good. You're humanizing her VP and none of us has ever managed that. Now go on, don't keep her waiting."

Zander glanced across the table to see B studying him from her seat.

Sneaky! She must have slipped by whilst I conversed with Frankie.

"Thanks brother."

Frankie nodded, before taking his seat and Zander made his way to B. She looked radiant as she joked with Ari and the boys. Her smile lit up the room as she met his gaze.

"Let me guess, another Mackie intervention?" she whispered into his ear.

"Aye."

"I'll talk to him."

"No need, darling. Leave him to play his games. I'm no' interested. All I want is you," he said, slipping his hand onto her thigh.

"Then you'll be happy I've moved your things into my room."

"You sure you're happy with that?"

"Yes, now shut up and eat your haggis," she teased, directing his attention to the array of dishes on the table.

Zander's jaw dropped.

"No way! Haggis and steak pie. Wait! Haggis is illegal here?"

"It is. Only you told me these were your favorite at Christmas?"

"You remember that?"

"I remember everything, Scottie," she said with a smile and a wink.

"You made them for me?"

"And my boys! You're not the only Scot here, good boy. There's also lamb, hence the lamb roast on my plate. Help yourself to whatever."

"Spoken like a true Welsh Cake. What is it with the Welsh and lamb anyway?' he asked as he helped himself to a bit of everything.

"I can't speak for all Welsh, but it's our national dish. Well, cawl is anyway. It's like a lamb stew and my favorite meal."

"Aye?" he said with a smile.

"Yes, it is as it goes. Now eat your bloody food!"

"Yes, Ma'am."

Zander tucked into his food; his palate seduced by the meal B spent hours preparing. He placed his fork on his plate, clasped his hands together, and gazed upon her, grinning from ear to ear. B didn't look at him as he watched her flush with embarrassment, smiling out the side of her mouth.

"What?" she asked.

"You've just taken me back home. I've no' eaten haggis and steak pie in twenty years. It's better than my mother's and hers was awesome."

"Maybe you'd forgotten how it tastes."

"No. It was delicious. Thank you!"

"You're welcome."

Zander shook his head at her. "Is there anything you can't do, darling?"

B burst into a fit of laughter, catching the table's attention, making Mack grimace.

"Bloody plenty Scottie. I can't sing, dance, or play an instrument. I am clumsy. The list goes on,"

"And she is rubbish with electronics. She struggles to turn the tv on some days," Rhys teased.

B laughed again. "Fair play, he's right."

"Ah, it's all coming out now," Zander teased, before whispering in her ear, "but if you're trying to put me off, it's a little late. I'm hooked, darling, and now I know you can cook like this; you'll never get rid of me."

"I thought you were attracted to me and all along it was my cooking. It makes sense now, Scottie. I won you over with that Christmas hamper, didn't I?"

"My attraction began long before that. All I needed was one taste of you to confirm what I felt. The cooking talents are the icing on the cake," he whispered, glancing along the table to see Mack giving him a death stare.

Fuck you, Mack! He smiled and waved.

The evening wore on as everyone overindulged in food and drink. The teenagers cleaned up the kitchen, leaving the adults to continue their evening on B's decking.

Zander despised how Mack waltzed around as if he owned the place, showing off her outdoor bar and wood burner as if it was his own. They had all been sitting for a little while when Zander discovered B hadn't joined them outside. It made him uneasy not knowing where she was. The vibrant house made it hard for him to steal a moment with her.

There was a relaxed energy in the air and Zander envisioned a future with B, after seeing her relax today. She was a different person, so chilled as she went about her day. B's laughter filled the air as she joked with the family, highlighting her radiance, making Zander desperate to get to know her further.

Lost in his thoughts, he missed her exiting the back door, startling him as she tickled his neck.

"Sorry darling, I was lost in translation then," he said as he watched as she plonked herself on his lap, making everyone stop and take notice.

Flooded with warmth and adrenaline. Zander couldn't comprehend what was happening as she kissed and leaned back into him.

Wrapping his hands around her waist, he whispered into her ear: "What happened to refraining from public displays of affection?"

"The boys are in bed. I'd like to be, too."

"Ready when you are. I can't wait to get you alone."

"I can tell," she teased, giving him a seductive look.

"Sorry, I can't help it. I've been rock hard since seeing you in that dress. I've had to stop myself from hitching it up all afternoon."

"Should we say goodnight to everyone?" B asked.

Zander could hardly contain his excitement. "I'd like that, just understand. I've been like a man possessed all day, demonstrating a lot of restraint. I'll no' be able to stop myself from taking you hard and fast when I take you to bed."

"Ooh, promise?"

"Go warm the bed and keep the dress on."

B smiled, bidding the others a good night.

Zander watched her leave, his eyes following her as she headed inside.

"Somebody's got it bad," Ari said.

Zander chuckled. "I do!"

Mack and Zander stared each other down, eyes narrowed, and jaws clenched. The tension in the air like thick smog engulfing their lungs, intoxicating them with contempt for one another.

Mack's eyes were evil, following Zander's refusal to stay away from his dragon, poisoning her with his black scent. He'd stolen her away from him, and Zander realized it was the ultimate betrayal in Mack's eyes.

"VP knows this can't go any further. He's not good enough for her," Mack growled.

Gasps rattled the decking.

"That's up to her, and if you dinnae mind, she's waiting for me," Zander said as he rose to his feet.

Mack stood to meet his gaze. The testosterone in the air wreaking of disdain.

"This is your final warning, VP," Mack snapped.

"What are you gonnae do, Mack? Cast me out? Lock her away? We want this, she wants this. Let her be happy because she needs this. I need this. So, do the right thing."

The two men stared each other down.

"C'mon fellas, it's been a good day. Let's not ruin things now," Jimmy interjected.

Zander shook his head, grimacing at Mack, eyes narrowed, and fists clenched. He was ready to fight for B, and Mack was just a jealous bully to him. A bully who needed to be set straight. Only Zander knew if he caused a commotion, he would lose her.

Breathing heavy he thought of how B calmed him on the night of Noah's funeral and attempted to calm himself.

"Can I ask you something? Did she look happy to you today?" he asked Mack.

Mack glared at him. "She's not thinking straight."

"Bullshit. Yes, or no? Was she happy?"

"It doesn't matter what she looked. You're not right for her."

"That's your opinion and there lies the problem. See, I know she wants me, and she's asked me to go to bed with her tonight and I'll no' let the lassie down. This isn't some cheap hook up. I've wanted her since the moment I laid eyes on the picture I saw the night we helped save your family and I've no' said a word about that to her. But I promise you, if you fuck with me on this, I'll tell her everything and your little nest egg here will be gone. Noah didn't like how you treated her and I sure as hell don't."

"Is that a threat, brother?"

"No, it's a promise! Look, I'm no' interested in her money. I like her and I'm no' gonnae keep her waiting any longer," he said, turning to leave.

Mack stood up and grabbed his arm, making him growl at him.

"You hurt her, and I'll kill you."

Zander removed his hand. "That's your MO brother, no' mine," he said as he headed off to bed.

Zander entered the spare room and emerged in the bathroom doorway. Stopping in his tracks, he allowed himself a moment to capture B's beauty. Her bright blue, crystal-like eyes beckoning him as she smiled at him.

"You sure you want me in here, beautiful?" he asked.

"Come here," she said, holding out her hand to reach for him. "You know you're the first man to share this bed with me," she said as she watched him strip off and climb in beside her.

"Then I am one lucky guy!" he said to her as he leaned in to kiss her lips. They felt like silk as he pressed his to hers.

"I've enjoyed watching you with your family You look so happy and relaxed. It's attractive."

"That's because I *am* happy and relaxed here. It's my home! It's where I feel safe and content. The residents live in my world. I can trust them; they have my back, and I have theirs. It's what I'm hoping to create in Sunnyville."

Zander's eyes widened. It pained him that B viewed the world through a trauma telescope. To him, she was a beautiful butterfly trapped in a cocoon of black and white madness, and he wanted to release her to the colorful world she'd hidden from.

"I cannae wait until you move into that big house of yours. It's been torture, being away from you. he said, making her smile as she laid kisses on his chest.

"Scottie, I must say, I love that you wear my patch on your chest."

Zander peered down at her, eyes narrowing and lips curling into a wry smile.

"Your patch?"

B propped herself up on his torso to look at him, head in hand, with a bashful smile beaming at him.

"Yeah, I came up with the design. Mackie loved it and made it the club patch."

"You're serious?"

"Yeah! We were up on the ridge behind my house one night. It was a shit day, so I escaped with a bottle of good stuff. I enjoy getting lost up there. My brain shuts down and I can just be—"

Zander brushed her cheek with his fingertips, hanging on to her every word, grinning at her, ecstatic she was opening up to him at last.

B froze. Her face hardened as she closed off.

"Forget it. You think I'm daft!" she said, recoiling back into her shell.

"Hey, hey, no I dinnae! Tell me, please?"

"You do! You're looking at me as if I'm a loon," she said with hurt in her voice.

"I'm smiling because I'm happy! You are opening up to me, and I love it. You're telling me something real for a change instead of brushing me off? And no, I dinnae think you're crazy. Now please finish your story."

"Okay, I was lost in the view when Mackie found me. He attempted to get me to confide in him, but I didn't talk to Mackie like that. I don't talk to anyone."

"No shit! Really?"

"Fine! Fuck you! I'm not telling you shit now. You can fuck off!" she snapped in an angry tone, kicking the cover off and storming into the bathroom. "Prick!" she spat over her shoulder.

Zander chuckled to himself as he dived out of bed after her, picking her up from around the waist, and pinning her to the bed in an act of playfulness.

"Aww, I'm sorry darling! Of course, I want to hear your story. I'm just so fucking happy and I love that you're letting me in. It's amazing! Thank you for today. It's been great!"

"Well, you can't bloody love it that much, good boy because you won't let me finish. Now get off me. I hate being restrained."

Zander's heart pumped fast in his chest. He loved being in control for a change as his body pressed against her. Feeling her chest revolt against his as her heart rate rose, turned him on.

"Welsh Cake, I'm gonnae keep you here until you finish your story and I promise I will listen to every word that escapes your irresistible lips."

B's pained face hardened, her eyes once again like wildfire, and voice stern. "Scottie, I'm not finishing my story unless you get off me, and I've told you; I don't like to be restrained or controlled. Now remove your hands or I'll remove them for you."

Zander's eyes knitted in confusion. He'd become so content and lost in the moment; he hadn't heard what B was trying to convey. It hadn't occurred to him how uncomfortable she had become with his playful demeanor. It was clear B didn't understand his humor, making her feel threatened as he felt her push back against him with concern etched over her face.

Zander released her in an instant, allowing her to breathe.

"Sorry darling, I got carried away playing with you, and I promise I will never try to cage or control you. Look, I'm no' Mack and I'm no' your ex. Understand, I want you to feel comfortable with me."

"Promise?" she whispered, trying to clear her throat.

"Aye, I promise. I want to make you happy darling," he said, kissing her forehead as she watched him like a hawk watching its prey.

Zander traveled down her neckline, feeling her pulse quicken. Her chest rising and falling in rapid succession as his plump lips pressed against her breasts.

"Trust me darling, please? I got you," he whispered as his trail of soft kisses reached her chest, his hands to trailing over her lace dress, traveling underneath to remove her panties.

Sliding them off, he locked eyes on hers to find her staring back at him with uncertainty.

"Please dinnae look at me like that Welsh Cake. Let me remove this dress and show you how sorry I am for making you feel uncomfortable," he asked, sounding like a wounded puppy.

Waiting for her answer, he observed as she sat up to meet his gaze, running her hands through his hair, pulling him in to cover his mouth with hers with a slow and hard kiss.

Zander was determined to spend the night making her feel comfortable again.

CHAPTER FORTY-EIGHT

Goodbye Uskiville

B and Zander spent the next few days inseparable as both the Uskiville and Sunnyville charter worked together to create a brighter future for the club. Astonished gawks met as they walked around the retreat, hand in hand out of view of the boys. B was still getting used to having someone in her life again and tried to break free of his grip every time someone flashed them a look. Zander had other ideas, smirking as he maintained a firm grip and occasionally, pulling her in for a romantic kiss, where B would melt.

Mack threw himself into his new role as he showed Jimmy an example of B's expectations in Sunnyville and provided a few tips regarding B's temperament: even Frankie tossed in some advice for good measure. B enjoyed cooking in the evenings, with Jimmy offering a helping hand ready for his new role as bistro manager, whilst Zander got to know Rhys and Madoc a little more by playing guitar with them and talking about music. B would steal a glance from the kitchen often as she watched her boys' bond with the man who was capturing her heart. By nightfall, they were desperate for intimacy, spending the night exploring one another. B developed feelings she never knew she was capable of, and it scared her to death.

Weekend came and B rushed around ensuring the boys packed everything they needed for the weekend with their dad as well as what they needed for their trip back home to the United Kingdom.

They would spend the weekend with their dad before flying out with B. They would spend four weeks with B in Wales and four weeks with their dad in Scotland. She suffered from terrible separation anxiety when her boys were away and she dreaded the thought of leaving them in the UK for four long weeks, but she knew it was unfair to deny them of the trip.

After Rhys and Madoc said their goodbyes to Mack, Ari, and the boys, they headed off, leaving Mack's family despairing over their departure. Their pained hearts and tear-filled eyes weighed heavy on B as she slumbered back inside to finish packing.

Thank the lord I'm only taking clothes and personal items.

B was leaving the cabin in Sunnyville furnished for when they visited, breeding new furniture for her home in Uskiville which Frankie agreed to handle whilst she was away. That way, she could move in when she arrived back from Wales.

Zander stayed and helped her pack whilst Jimmy and Eddie headed back to Sunnyville. B insisted he left too, but Zander's relentless determination to support her posed too much for an exhausted B, allowing him to remain by her side.

The office was the last room to pack and after spending the morning reminiscing, everything overwhelmed B. Troubled, she sat on her brown leather sofa with her head in her hands until Zander, who had gone to fetch some more tape from her truck, found her.

"Are you alright, darling?" he asked, cradling her in his arms.

B sat bolt upright, inhaling long and hard. "I'm fine."

"Second thoughts?"

"No. It's just, I never imagined leaving here. I can't wait to start fresh in Sunnyville..."

"But..." Zander tilted his head to enquire.

"It's scary doing this on my own again."

"You're no' on your own darling. You have me and Frankie and a giant club behind you and you never have to be afraid, okay? I'll no' let anything bad happen to you or your boys. I promise!"

B caressed his cheek, her eyes sincere. "Fear doesn't come into it but thank you, Scottie, for everything. I'm gonna miss you when I'm away."

"And I'm gonnae miss you, too! Look, let's head back to Sunnyville and lock ourselves away until you leave?"

"Sounds great, handsome."

"Good, now move your ass," he teased, pulling her to her feet.

The pair finished and packed the last of the boxes into B's truck and prepared to leave as Ari stood waiting.

"Where is everyone?" B asked.

"Mackie's in the bar, he's devastated. He says, he can't watch you leave. Come and say goodbye please?" Ari asked as tears ran down her face.

B hugged her before they entered her truck and drove the short distance to the bar while Zander followed on his bike.

Walking into the bar, she squeezed Zander's hand. She hated goodbyes.

Zander squeezed it back and whispered in her ear. "I got you darling," before planting a kiss on her cheek for encouragement.

It was eerily quiet as she walked through the bar door, only to be met with a full bar screaming at her.

"Surprise!" they yelled, making her jump out of her skin.

The whole retreat had turned up to say goodbye, lavishing her with cards and gifts to wish her luck and B was taken back.

As she readied herself to leave, Frankie hugged her tight, explaining her house would be in order and he would be waiting for her when she arrived in Uskiville the next month. Exhausted from holding back the tears all day, B needed to escape before they consumed her. Turning toward the exit in haste, she felt an arm snake around her shoulder.

"You didn't think, I'd just let you slip away did you Dragon," Mack said embracing her.

"I was kind of hoping you would."

"No fecking chance, good girl," he teased impersonating her Welsh accent before handing her a jewelry box.

"What's this?"

"Open it and find out."

B opened the box and gasped at what he had gifted her. It was a silver necklace with a dragon holding a shamrock.

"Mackie, it's beautiful. You shouldn't have."

Mack smiled a bashful smile. "Do you like it? I had it handmade for you. To wish you luck."

"It's stunning! Thank you! I'll cherish it forever," B said, clutching it to her chest.

"Promise me one more thing."

B nodded.

"Promise me you'll wear it once you get back and never take it off. It will keep you safe and look, I have one too," he said, showing her his.

"Promise, I'll even put it on now."

Mack placed his hand over hers, stopping her in her tracks. "No, don't wear it until you get back. I'm scared you'll lose it over there. Please put it in your safe until you return?"

"Okay, fine! Now, say the words and let me go."

Mack put his forehead to hers and closed his eyes. "Best friends never quit!" he said as a single tear rolled down his cheek.

"Your damn fucking right they don't!" she said pulling away and wiping his tear-stained cheek.

Mack nodded as B watched Ari place her hand in his and Frankie put a hand on his opposite shoulder, giving her a wink. It was obvious Mack was struggling to hold it together as she backed out of the door.

Exiting the building, she heard Mack break down and cry, shattering her heart into tiny pieces as guilt ripped through her body. Frozen to the spot, her jaw clenched shut as she squeezed Zander's hand.

"You wanna turn back?" he asked in a low voice.

B shook her head. "I'll just make things worse."

"Hey, that's no' true darling. You've made my life so much better now you're in it. In fact, it's perfect."

B managed to smile before climbing into her truck.

"Are you sure you're okay to drive? It was a bit of an emotional roller-coaster back there."

B sighed. "I'm fine Scottie. let's go, okay?"

"Understood, darling. Scamper and the boys are waiting at the gate. They'll escort us as far as Portland where the Sunnyville chapter will meet us. You alright with that?"

"Yeah."

Zander planted a soft kiss on her lips. "I'm sorry you're hurting darling."

"I'm fine."

"Bullshit Welsh cake. You know you dinnae have to be brave around me."

"Keeping everything locked up is the only way I survive," she whispered. The hurt consumed her heart and soul.

"No' anymore! We're gonnae work on that. I'm gonnae free you from all this pain you hide inside and make you feel. It will hurt like hell at first but then you won't suffer like you do."

B started her truck. "I'm not suffering Scottie."

"Yes, you are, I can see it in your eyes, and it hurts me seeing you like it. I've got you darling and I'm no' letting go. No' now, never."

B nodded before kissing his cheek. "Thank you, Scottie, now go on, get on your motorcycle. We need to get out of here.

The sun had faded into the night sky as B arrived in Sunnyville. Zander parked his motorcycle and headed to B's truck to help her with her case. Opening the door to greet her, B met him with a desolate gaze.

"I knew I shouldn't have let you drive on your own. Are you okay," he said gliding his hand to the back of her head and kissing the top of her head.

B brushed his hand away. She wasn't used to letting anyone see her like this.

"I'm fine! Had something in my eye is all."

"They're called tears Welsh Cake. You're allowed to cry."

"I wasn't bloody crying Scottie." B huffed. "Now can we go to bed please? I'm exhausted and I'm meeting the contractor in the morning.

Zander shook his head at her. "Whatever you say beautiful."

CHAPTER FORTY-NINE
Acceptance & Rebranding

B woke in Zander's arms, refreshed and ready to seize the day. With a full itinerary ahead of her, she slipped out of bed unheard by a sleeping Zander. After getting washed and dressed, she exited the trailer, careful not to wake her new MC family, and headed to the bar to meet the contractor. The sun rose in silence as she crept along the parking lot, allowing the contractor to escort her into the bar.

B had led Jimmy and the other members to believe there was a structural issue with the club, convincing them to move into temporary accommodation so she could implement Noah's plans.

Spencer had followed her wishes at his last meeting with Jimmy. She knew Jimmy didn't trust her enough to allow her to make the necessary upgrades required to transform the club into a profitable business, even if it was Noah's dream.

B wanted to ensure Noah's plan was complete. It was his legacy, and it started with the club. She wasn't sure if the patched members would like it, despite Noah's notebook detailing the expected input from each individual patch. The anticipation of their reaction made her tummy churn, but it was done, and Noah's wishes were coming to fruition.

Entering the building, B gasped. It was just as Noah described in his notebook, with waves of red and black draped across the bar. The secret interior designer had done a grand job of smuggling in new furniture to match the incredible decor. The bar had an array of new draught beers, which reflected off the black marble countertop with red leather bar stools beneath it.

A perfect blend of red and black leather couches, tables and chairs took their place throughout the bar next to brand new pool tables, dart boards and a jukebox to complete the MC vibe. The refurbished kitchen bore a new sleek white and red finish, complete with new appliances, and the wall of fame was decorated with past and present club members, with a framed picture of Noah, dead center.

"This is perfect! Thank you so much!" she said to Mike, the interior designer.

"You owe me big time B. It's not been easy pretending to be a contractor and smuggling in furniture: removing MC stench was hellish."

"Sorry Mike. They just wouldn't have allowed me near the place if I'd told them."

"Well, they better bloody appreciate what you've done to their new home. The place required transformation from a maggot to a beautiful butterfly. Come on, let me show you their sleeping quarters," he said as he took hold of her arm and escorted her down the corridor.

B's eyes scanned everywhere in astonishment, with each bedroom decorated and furnished with new furniture, electronics, bedding, towels, and hygiene products, all embroidered with the Gray Wolves patch.

Mike had even added framed pictures of classic motorcycles to the presidents' and vice presidents' rooms and added a few extras to set them apart from their subordinates. They had their rank embroidered into their new belongings and an oak king-sized bed with the MC badge carved into the headboard and their own unique colored bedding. They also had a new leather cut and a bottle of good stuff placed over their bedside table.

Running her fingers over Zander's silk bedding, she turned to Mike. "And church? Is that complete?"

"Exactly as you requested," he said, grinning like a grinch at Christmas, urging her to follow his lead.

Church was situated behind the bar in a big, rectangular office. It had a huge window looking into the bar so the members could see potential intruders while having their meetings. The club couldn't afford a special club table since rebranding as the Gray Wolves until B and Noah ordered one to surprise them.

B had no doubt that the room looked glorious as the hand-carved table illuminated the room. The varnished oak glistened under the lighting: the Gray Wolves patch, carved into its center.

Casting her mind back to the day Noah saw the finished article, B smiled, remembering his kid in a sweet shop demeanor. He was so excited, it rendered him speechless as he stood with his hand covering his goofy grin.

It was one of her fondest and happiest memories with him. They had lunch together and picked out business suits for each club member. Noah had taken all their measurements so B could order them, complete with club ties.

They had both agreed they needed to change the narrative in Sunnyville to ensure the townspeople knew they weren't one-percenters anymore, with B explaining the requirement to look and act like professional entrepreneurs.

Inhaling sharply, B mustered the courage to open the oak church door. Her heart sank as she saw the beautiful table, complete with hand carved chairs and a gavel to match.

There was also a crystal whiskey decanter full of the good stuff. with matching glasses and over each chair hung two business suits for each member and B couldn't help but run her fingers over the fine material.

"What should I do with these?" Mike said, holding Noah's suits.

"I'll hang onto them," B said, with thick hurt in her voice.

"That's everything. Do you need me for anything else?"

"No thank you. You've outdone yourself, and I can't wait to see what you do with the bar and grill when it's complete,"

Mike gave her a hug. "Call me when the real contractors finish the extension and I'll come do my thing."

"Thank you, Mike. For everything," she said, ushering him out of the building and waving him off.

Turning on her heels, she discovered a curious looking Jimmy and Zander waiting for her.

"I was wondering where you snuck off too!" Zander said, scooping her up in his arms to kiss her.

"Haven't you two had enough yet?" Jimmy teased.

"Oh, we're just getting started, Prez," Zander gushed, setting her down.

B stood, biting her lip.

"Oh shit! What's happened?" Zander asked.

B gulped. "I need you both to look at this and when you're done, meet me in the bar," she said, handing Jimmy Noah's notebook.

Jimmy and Zanders stared in fear at the ruffled notebook.

"B, why do you have this? Jimmy asked.

"Noah kept it at mine in the months leading up to his death. He didn't want to ruin the surprise and now I'm giving it to you. So, look at it and when you're ready, I'll be in the bar," she said before entering the club, leaving Jimmy and Zander with their bewildered expressions.

B poured three whiskeys and sat on the plush new bar stool, tapping on the countertop, waiting with her nerves, and after a short while, they entered the bar.

"What the..." Jimmy managed as he threw Zander a look.

"Jesus!" Zander gasped, his eyes darting around the bar.

B took a sip of her whiskey to calm herself, unsure of their reaction.

Jimmy was the first to speak. "You did all this?"

B nodded. "Noah wanted to surprise everyone. He explained your hopes and dreams for the club. He said you all designed it together."

"Aye, we did!" Zander managed, running his hand along the bar.

"I'm sorry I lied about the building being unsafe. You all hated me after the Mackie incident, and I knew you wouldn't trust me with the club. I had to do it my way."

Jimmy snorted. "You're probably right."

"You should go to church first. Noah picked out something special for you all," B said.

The two men nodded. They were speechless as they headed behind the bar into the church. B sipped her whiskey until they returned, shaking their heads with soaking wet eyes.

Zander squeezed her into his grasp, knocking back his whiskey.

"You two did all this for us, made it all happen?" he said, taking her chin between his trembling thumb and index finger.

"I wanted to do something special. Finish what Noah and I started together. We planned so much for the club."

Jimmy placed a hand on her shoulder.

"Darling, you have a big fucking heart locked away in there," Zander said, tapping on her sternum. "We're blown away. Thank you so much."

"You're not mad, I redecorated?"

"Hell no! This place was a shit-tip. I'm surprised we all didn't catch foot and mouth disease living here," Zander joked.

"Go explore the rest of the club. Here are the key cards to access the club and your bedrooms. I upgraded the security around here. Only Jimmy and you can access church. The others have access to the bar, kitchen, store cupboard and their bedrooms, of course."

Zander and Jimmy took their key cards, grinning like a possum eating a sweet potato.

"Come with me," Zander asked.

B shook her head. "No, go look yourself first, please?"

Zander pulled her in for a long and heartfelt kiss. "Thank you."

"You're welcome, Scottie."

After exploring the club. Zander and Jimmy called an emergency church meeting, demanding all members meet at the club, and they did with haste. Jimmy led them into the club while B worked out front in the sunshine.

A short while later, they emerged, wiping the tears from their eyes. The cluster of laughter and pain in the air echoed as they cursed about Noah's surprise in disbelief, taken back regarding his plans for the club.

B smiled, allowing the happy glow inside to sweep through her, proud of herself and proud of Noah for what they achieved today. He'd brought unity to the club and B experienced so much gratitude, partaking in the journey with them.

Working away, she hadn't seen the members head her way with a whiskey offering until they reached the picnic bench, she was working at.

"Listen up!" Jimmy growled, demanding their attention before turning to B. "The boys and I would like to thank you, sweetheart. What you've done here will never be forgotten. Yes, we've had our differences, but after spending time in Uskiville and seeing what you've done here for us today, I want you to know I wiped the slate clean. I'd like to start over if you'll give me the chance?"

B couldn't hide her shock. "Thank you, Prez. I'd like that. Noah and I put plans together to ensure the club's future and I have always had the best intentions. I know, I'm a little intense sometimes, but I didn't become successful by being a push over. I want to continue with our plan if you'll let me. No secrets. It's all in his book."

"We'd like that," Jimmy said, handing her a drink.

"To Noah, Welsh Cake and a new era for Gray Wolves," Jimmy toasted.

B tipped her glass to the sky giving a smile and a wink.

Step two in our long and illustrious plan complete, Baby Face.

Zander pulled her into him. "Come here beautiful," he said, devouring her with his lips and tongue to the sounds of cheers and wolf whistles.

Zander smiled through their kiss, sticking up his middle finger to his brothers as Jimmy wailed.

"Right, call your old ladies, we got a party to sort tonight!"

After partying the night away, B's alarm went off at 2:15 a.m. B shut it off quickly, trying not to wake Zander. He was a heavy sleeper and B loved observing his rugged handsomeness whilst he slept. Sneaking into the bathroom with her clothes, she readied herself for her flight. and upon her return, a half-awake Zander sat half dressed, raking his hand through his bedhead.

"Please tell me you weren't gonnae leave without saying goodbye, beautiful?" he asked.

B placed her hands on his warm cheeks. "I'm not good with goodbyes Scottie."

Zander scooped her up in his muscular arms, planting a soft kiss onto her cold lips. "Please dinnae go!"

"I must, Scottie, I'm sorry! Staying isn't an option. I need to clear my head, get clarity, so I can focus on the future. I can't afford to keep making stupid mistakes."

"Is it necessary to travel halfway across the world?"

"Yes! This trip was planned months ago, and my boys need some mother and son time."

Zander closed his eyes. His Adam's apple bobbed as he swallowed against the obvious feeling of emptiness.

B understood his hurt, she experienced similar herself, and Zander had been acting differently toward her this past twenty-four hours, more protective, almost scared to let her out of his sight.

Dipping his head, he nodded in comprehension before kissing her once more. His voice was low as he spoke to her. "We better get you to that check-in desk, darling, or I'll struggle to let you leave."

"Wait. I want you to have this…" B pulled out a large bundle of cash and placed it in his hands.

"What's this?" he asked in confusion.

"This will keep you afloat until I get back."

"I'm no' taking your money, darling. That's no' what I'm about. I dinnae care about your money, and I'm no' worried about the club. I want you and nothing else!"

"I know. I just don't want you to worry about finances whilst I'm away. Please take the money, Scottie."

"I cannae do that Welsh cake! I want you and I dinnae want there to be any confusion. I'm no' Mack, darling. I want you, no' your bank account."

B kissed him long and hard. "I know that handsome and I appreciate that. See it as an early wage. I need you guys to keep the club secure while I'm away, make sure that nothing gets damaged or stolen. Can you do that for me, please?" she asked as she pushed him down on the bed before nibbling on his ear, whispering, "Please, Scottie. I need to know you're okay whilst I'm gone."

Scottie moaned, breathless beneath her. "Christ! You're driving me nuts! I dinnae want you to go. We're just getting started!"

"I know! I'll make things special once I get back. That's if you still want me?"

Zander frowned in disgust. "Hey, of course I'll want you! Welsh Cake, you're like cocaine to me. It's only been a few weeks and I'm already addicted! I've waited a hell of a long time for you. I can wait a little longer because I'll have forever with you."

B sucked back her hurt with sharp inhalation. "Thank you, Scottie! For seducing me when we met, for the wild sex, for looking after me. For everything! You are perfect and it frightens the hell out of me! I don't want to leave, but it's necessary for you, the club, and my family."

"I know, darling! Let's get one thing straight, though. You seduced me, intoxicating me with your gorgeous body and cheeky smile. When you bit your lip for the first time, I wanted to explode. I needed the beautiful and crazy woman who thawed me, and now I cannae be without you! I do, however, understand you need to get your head right. So, come on! You'll miss your flight!

B gathered her things with Zander's help, placing cash into his hands.

Sighing, he glanced at the rolled banknotes. "I really dinnae want it, darling."

"That's why you need to take it, handsome, and we need to leave."

Zander stared at B with longing eyes as they embraced near the airport's check-in desk.

"Now promise me you will ring me when you land so I know you are safe, yeah?"

This took B back, who nodded before he continued.

"It's typical. I find the women of my dreams and now she has to leave."

"Sorry, Scottie," B whispered.

"I cannae wait to continue this when you get back Welsh Cake, so dinnae go meeting some fancy businessman over there?"

"Hmmm, I can't promise that," B said, watching his face drop in disappointment.

"I'm joking, ya dafty," she scoffed.

Zander let out a huge sigh of relief and scooped her up to kiss her.

"I thought you were serious then! I thought you'd had your bit of rough and was done with me."

B looked at him, a little frustrated. "Don't call yourself that and no I've really enjoyed spending time with you. You are pretty damn amazing."

Zander's reddening face boasted a huge grin. "Why, thank you very much. You're awesome, yersel', and I am pretty sure some of the things you taught me last night are illegal in some countries."

"Well, I didn't hear you complaining, Scottie."

"No complaints here, darling. In fact, you are by far the best I've ever had, and I am praying you won't change your mind about me. You're so special to me!" he said, squeezing her waistline.

"Oh, Scottie—"

B's flight was announced, and Madoc and Rhys appeared with their cases, interrupting them.

"Hey mum, hey Zander," Rhys yelled from the airports entrance.

B waved back. Returning to Zander's gaze, her voice trembled in unfamiliarity. "That's me, handsome."

"Aye," he said, kissing her cheek and watching her leave.

B glanced over her shoulder; her eyes stung an unfamiliar sting as her heart rattled in her chest. The events of the last few weeks striking her like a storm. Four weeks to collect herself appealed to her, four weeks without the chiseled Scot. Well, that was another thing entirely.

CHAPTER FIFTY

Be Ready!

"What the fuck do you mean, she's in the UK?" Blaze seethed, kicking the worn-out rug in his office as he headed to his filthy couch to grope the woman waiting for him. "I can't fucking keep up with her. Who the fuck does she think she is, flouncing around like some fancy fucking jetsetter?"

"She's left for a month, boss. What do you want to do?"

"I want to drag her ass here. I want my revenge and I want my fucking club. Now tell me how I'm supposed to achieve that when she's across the fucking pond?"

"Uh, I dunno, boss!"

"I'm fucking living off scraps here while you lap up the life of fucking Riley," Blaze snapped, slapping his latest piece of ass across the face in a jealous rage. Her cries reverberating through the phone.

"Sorry boss, she was calling the shots and Zander didn't let her out of his sight."

"Hmm, smart! I wouldn't either. I've lost all patience with Sunnyville. This has to end!"

"Say the word and I'll start shooting. I'm ready boss!"

"Nah! I need your eyes and ears. I'll come up with something for her return. Look, we won't survive a month. You will need to give some of your recent wealth to the club."

"I have three G saved. It's all yours. Usual drop off?"

"Yeah, and listen. I'm not waiting any more. The minute she lands, her ass is mine. I'll message you the details when you provide a return date, so be ready!"

CHAPTER FIFTY-ONE

Missing You!

An exhausted Zander slumped over the club's bar. Consumed by her touch, and the feel of her skin, B was all he could think about, and the unfamiliar sting in his chest incapacitated him.

Pouring whiskey to numb the pain and drown out his troubled mind, he tossed the fire water down his throat.

This is torture!

Two weeks had passed, and Zander had spoken to B almost every day! He enjoyed following her social media, studying at all the videos and pictures of B that her family had tagged her in.

He loved to see her happy. Missing her was suffocating him, and his brooding was clear within the club. Zander became less tolerable, moping at the bar, staring at his phone. His brother's attempts to cheer him up were in vain, although he tried to act interested. His mind was elsewhere: it was with B where it belonged, intoxicated by her. Zander wondered if this was what addiction was like, desperate for another hit. His hit was B, and he wanted her home.

"Are you alright, man?" asked Jimmy, sitting at the bar.

"Aye, pal, why do you ask?"

"You're grumpy, distracted, disengaged from the club and you've not shaved in weeks."

Zander spun his whiskey glass on the countertop. "Sorry pal. I'm fine, though, honest!"

"Are you sure, man? We're worried about you!"

"I'm fine. Give me two minutes and we will have a drink."

Jimmy left Zander to compose himself, only Zander didn't feel like socializing. He wanted to be alone with his thoughts. He knew his brothers were trying to ease his pain. Ingesting a deep breath, he removed himself from his perch to join them.

Faking a laugh and a smile, ticking the relevant check boxes was all that he could muster before heading back to his room to video call B.

"Hey, are you alright? It's late where you are."

"Hey beautiful! I needed to hear your voice, is all."

"Are you okay? You sound fed up," B said with a concerned tone.

"Missing you, darling. I cannae wait to see you!"

"Oh, I'm looking forward to seeing you, too."

"I'm not sure how I'll get through the next two weeks. I am struggling. This is the first time I have felt this way."

B released a huge exhalation of pent-up breath. "You are so sweet, Scottie, and if it's any consolation, I would much rather be there, but there is so much you don't know about me. I don't want you to be disappointed when I return.

"Aww, you could never disappoint me. You're perfect!"

"That scares me! I am crap at this sort of stuff!"

"Hey, I'm in unknown territory, too. Dinnae allow our separation to fill you with fear. Why no' come home early, and we can explore this together?" Zander said, adjusting a squint, framed motorcycle picture on the wall.

"I can't, handsome! If I leave now, I won't see my boys for six weeks instead of four, and four weeks will destroy me as it is. Not to mention that I am missing Madoc's birthday! I can't wait to get back, but I have to stay the course."

Zander dropped his head to his chin. "No need to apologize. Your laddies come first. I would never interfere in your relationship with them. I see how much you love them. Remember, I'll be there the whole time they're away to cuddle you, okay?"

"Thank you, handsome, but there's one problem with that."

Scottie panicked.

Does she not want me?

"What's that then, darling?"

"The Welsh don't cuddle, I'm afraid."

"Oh, alright, I'll bloody cwtch you, good girl," he teased, attempting a Welsh accent.

B chuckled. "Only the Welsh can cwtch! I can teach you if you are nice to me."

"I am always nice to you!" he chuckled.

He loved B's quirky sense of humor! Every time they spoke, he got a glimpse into her soul. She gave very little away when they conversed and always deflected anything real, so Zander talked about himself.

B remained guarded, scared to let anyone in, and Zander didn't press, allowing her to remain comfortable. He didn't want to push his beautiful, funny, and intelligent woman away.

"Can we lock ourselves away for a couple of days when I return, and you can be as nice as you please?" B asked.

"That would make me the happiest guy on the planet!"

"Well, I aim to please," B said as she bit her lip.

"Oh, now that's not fair, is it Welsh Cake? You're biting your lip again, knowing I can't do anything about it. You are teasing a very frustrated Scotsman."

B's hearty laugh echoed from his cell phone. "It's called revenge, sunshine. You tease me every day."

"How's that?"

"Well, you video call me every day from your bed, baring all. Now that's teasing!"

Zander grinned from ear to ear. "Sorry, I had no idea the effect I have on you. Shall I keep my clothes on in future?"

"No, thank you! Frankly. I'm disappointed you're clothed tonight."

B's quirkiness drove Zander mad. He was so lost in conversation he didn't see Jimmy appear behind him.

"Hey Jimmy!" B said, excited to see him.

"Hey, Doll Face! How's it going? Do me a solid and return soon. This one's been a miserable bastard since you left."

"Piss off!" Zander scolded.

"Sorry Jimmy. I'll come home soon. Promise."

"At least we know he's human now! We were worried for a bit. Listen, can I be cheeky and steal him? We are waiting to play cards and the animals in the zoo are getting restless?"

"Of course. Don't let me stop you!"

"Thanks, Dragon. Come on, Romeo," he gestured to Zander.

"Aye, okay, I'm right behind you."

Jimmy walked away, allowing Zander to release an exacerbated sigh. "I'm happy talking to you, darling. I'm in no mood for cards."

"Hey, I'm happy to talk to you all night. It's just, I don't want your brother's thinking I'm a bad influence. They will hate me if they think I am coming between you. Please play cards, Scottie."

"I dinnae care what they think!"

"Well, I do!" B said demonstrating her dominant voice. "They are your family. Now go on and we'll talk later."

"Yes ma'am!"

"Bye handsome!"

"Bye, beautiful, have a lovely day."

CHAPTER FIFTY-TWO

Coming Home

Another long week passed, and Zander's turmoil bled into the club.

The brooding hadn't gone unnoticed by the men at the club, noticing the excitement exuding him every time his phone vibrated. They had never seen him like this, and they feared he would get hurt.

It was a sunny Sunday morning when Zander's cell phone rang.

Jumping off the bar stool, he headed outside to answer it, whilst the men teased him.

"Oh, here he goes. Jeez, you're whipped man," Tiny said.

"Hey, tell her to come back to sort you out. We can't take you taking your serial frustration out on us anymore," Eddie teased.

"Leave him be lads." said Jimmy.

It frustrated Zander. He ached for B and couldn't wait to see her again.

You got this, Zander. One week left.

"Hello, darling."

"Hey handsome, how's it going?" B asked.

"Better now I see your beautiful face."

"Aww, Scottie. Listen, I need a favor, please?"

Zander grinned. "Oh, Aye, what's that then?"

"I am having something delivered to the gym ready for me coming back and it's arriving soon. Spencer is popping by to drop you off the keys and security pass, and I was wondering if you can take it into my office, please?"

"Aye, no bother. Shall I just take it in my room until you get back?"

B pursed her lips in embarrassment. "Uh, it's a little big. It's my new bed! When the boys are with their father, I'll stay at the office."

Zander's grin grew wide. "Oh, really."

"Yes, really." B chuckled. "Once you are in the office, you need to use your security band to enter my room. There is a security button on the top shelf on my bookshelf. If you swipe it across the top, my bedroom door will open."

"You're serious? You have a hidden bedroom in your office?"

"More like a hidden panic room I'll use as a bedroom."

"Wow! Okay! Do you want me to put it together for you?"

"No, don't trouble yourself. I can do it when I return."

"No trouble, Welsh Cake! Besides, I am looking forward to seeing you in bed again."

"Easy tiger," B joked. "Can you just promise me that nobody else will use that bed in my absence, please?"

Zander narrowed his eyes. "I dinnae follow?"

"I mean, I don't want you sleeping with anyone else in my bed."

Zander's stomach churned as if someone had kicked him.

"Do you think I'd do that?"

B shrugged. "No, it's just, I've been gone three weeks—"

"So, you think I've been with other women?"

"I didn't say that!"

"You dinnae have to."

"I didn't mean it like that," she said, her tone apologetic.

"And how did you mean it? No, let me ask you something. Have you been seeing other men back home?" he said through gritted teeth, rage consuming him with each inhalation.

"No!" B slammed.

"Then, why would you assume that about me? Jeez Welsh Cake, I have spent three weeks tortured and tormented by your absence."

"I'm sorry Scottie, I didn't mean to offend y—"

"Look, I gotta go, Prez is calling."

"Scottie, wait! Please let me explain," B said in desperation.

"No need, I get it, Welsh Cake. I gotta go."

"Scottie..."

Zander hung up; distraught, B thought that of him. His heart palpated and his chest heaved, bottling up the rage that continued to consume him.

"Get your Welsh Cake fix, mate?" Tiny teased as he entered the bar.

Zander saw red, losing his cool, throwing a right hook to Tiny's stern jaw.

Tiny flew across the bar, skidding across the floor before landing in a heap. Zander raced toward him. He wasn't done and Tiny had it coming.

The patched members pounced on him, attempting to restrain him as he pushed through them to reach his prey.

"Hey, hey, calm down. He's teasing you," Jimmy said.

"Well, no fucking more! It's pissing me off!"

"Okay, okay," Jimmy said. "Why don't we take a walk, yeah?"

After brushing off the three men holding him, Zander walked out the door and as he stepped outside, Spencer emerged from his car.

"Spencer! You got something for me, I believe."

"I do! I'm a bit surprised she's trusting you with her pride and joy. Here," he said, handing Zander an envelope.

Zander nodded.

"Oh, and Zand, all our compasses are finally facing north, so please don't fuck this up!" he said, before speeding off in his flash car.

"What was all that about?" asked Jimmy.

"Welsh Cake has asked me to take in a delivery," he said before retrieving his vibrating phone from his pocket.

B again. I can't face her right now. My current temperament will make things worse.

"Are you not going to answer that?" Jimmy asked.

"No!"

"Is everything alright man? You were okay until you spoke to her and now you are beating on Tiny again and ignoring her calls."

"I'm fine," he growled. "Sorry pal! I need to sort this; I'll be back soon." He turned in the direction of the gym.

"Yeah man, no worries! Do you need a hand?"

Zander shouted over his shoulder, continuing toward the gym. "I may do when it arrives. I'll call you."

Zander walked the small distance to the gym. Retrieving the security card and keys from the envelope, he disabled the alarm using the instructions on the envelope and let himself in.

Not too hard, so far.

Admiring the flashy gym equipment, he made his way to the office and let himself in. Approaching the white bookshelf, he did as B instructed, swiping the top of the bookshelf, unlocking the panic room door to B's room.

The room was a large, well decorated and furnished living space with bedside tables, a built-in wardrobe, small kitchen area, balcony and ensuite bathroom. It was a perfect pad, although he wondered why B didn't just work from home.

Despite the hurt in his heart, he reached for his phone to call her back, longing to fix things and hear her voice again. He hated falling out with her.

B's phone went straight to voicemail.

Sighing at his phone, he discovered an answer phone message.

Hey, I'm sorry about what I said. I didn't mean it the way it came out!

All I meant was, I wouldn't blame you if you went with someone else. I've been away so long, Scottie, and as much as I'm excited to see you, I wouldn't expect you to wait. You could have your pick of women!

Anyway, I was trying to tell you I am coming back tomorrow instead of next week. I want to see you. I'm fed up with being away. Hence getting my room sorted for my return.

Please don't be mad! I tend to fuck things up, like a lot.

Anyway, see you in the morning if you don't hate me.

Zander froze in shock that B showed some insecurity. He'd seen snippets of her vulnerability, but she remained tight-lipped most of the time. Listening to the message again, he wanted to ensure he heard correctly, and B was coming home tomorrow.

Excitement overwhelmed him, only he was desperate to patch things up before she arrived home.

Shit! She'll either be at the airport or on a flight already.

Dialing her number again, he waited for the answer phone.

Welsh Cake, I want to apologize for being a total asshole earlier. There's been no one else, darling. Understand, I am besotted with you and I cannae wait to see you.

I am so happy you are coming back early. Let me know when you get this.

Bye for now.

Zander's insides danced with excitement as he waited for B's delivery, spending the rest of the morning putting the king-size bed together.

Glancing around and raking through cupboards, he searched for a duvet and duvet covers but couldn't find them. Consequently, he borrowed the club pickup truck and drove half a mile to the local mall to pick out some classy bedding.

Upon his arrival back to the MC, his brothers congregated outside, basking in the glorious sunshine with a cold beer.

Stepping out of the pickup, he approached a nervous Tiny.

"Hey pal, I'm sorry about earlier. Something pissed me off and I took it out on you! It won't happen again."

Tiny stood up, towering over Zander, bringing him in for a man hug. "All good, brother. I'm sorry I have been busting your balls over Dragon. She's alright when she's not beating the shit out of the Founder. I'll dial it back, okay man?"

Zander nodded and proceeded back to the truck to retrieve the new bedding.

"Everything sorted now?" Jimmy asked.

"Yeah, thanks pal."

Jimmy scanned the shopping bags in Zander's hands. "New bedding. You're keen?"

"Aye," he chuckled.

"Just what was the delivery?" Jimmy asked.

Zander grinned. "A new bed."

"Your face says you can't wait to test it?"

"Correct. B's back early. Flying in tomorrow."

"Thank fuck for that! Does that mean you'll stop being such a broody bastard then?"

"Aye."

Zander's anxiety approached breaking point as he waited the rest of the day for a reply from B to no avail.

Christ! I hope I've no' fucked things.

The unresolved drama ate away at him. He wanted her home to ease his mind.

He'd hardly slept since B's departure, spending the long nights thinking of her. Sat at the bar, plying himself with enough alcohol to fill a brewery, paranoia set into his exhausted mind.

What if I created this in my head? I mean, we talk every day, and she knows how I feel about her. Well, I thought she did! What if she comes home and ditches me? No, she told me on the answer phone she wanted to see me.

He was stuck in a negative feedback loop, desperate for a response, confirmation that all was okay, anything.

His brothers witnessed Zander agonizing over it. The desperation written over his face as they watched him guzzle a bottle of whiskey and attempt another.

"Why don't we call it a night, Zand?" Tiny said.

"I'm alright pal, thanks," Zander slurred.

"I got him, Tiny," Jimmy said, placing an arm around Zander's shoulder. "Hey man, let's get you to your bed. You've got a big day tomorrow with Welsh Cake coming home. You don't want to look terrible when she arrives?"

"Aye, you're right, Prez. Can you help me to my bed, pal?"

"Yeah, I got you, come on," said Jimmy, helping him to his feet.

"I fucking love you, brother!" Zander slurred as Jimmy guided him to his bed.

"Ooh, you're gonna hurt in the morning, man."

"Who's hurt? Welsh Cake? Where is she?" Zander said in a drunken panic.

"No, no, brother." Jimmy said, easing him onto his bed. "She's on a plane, remember? Now get some rest, otherwise I'll get it in the neck tomorrow. Dragon fucking terrifies me!"

"She's no Dragon, Jimmy. I told you. Welsh Cake is a f-fucking Q-Queen and I love her," he gushed before losing his battle with alcohol and exhaustion.

Jimmy returned to his bar stool, laughing to himself.

"Is he alright?" asked Tiny.

"Yeah. His hard shell is cracked right open. Gushing about being in love with her. He'll be sheepish tomorrow."

"No way. VP, for real?" Sandy asked.

"We've never seen him like this," said Tyr.

"He's never felt like this before," said Jimmy. "The minute he laid eyes on her, he was hooked, and he doesn't know how to handle it."

"Well, let me tell you now, I'll be having words with Dragon if she thinks she's going to fuck him about," Tiny said with concern in his voice.

"Let's see what happens when she gets back. Should we need to step in, I'll deal with it? She's flying in first thing tomorrow morning," said Jimmy.

"Understood, boss," Tiny said.

Zander woke the next day ready to vomit, the stench of cigarettes and whiskey making him wretch as he dragged himself to the bathroom.

Staring back at himself in the mirror, his bloodshot eyes and overgrown beard stood out from his weathered face.

What the fuck did I drink?

Casting his mind back, trying to recall why he'd gotten himself in such a state, he realized.

Christ! Welsh Cake! How the fuck did I forget?

Excitement engulfed his weary body, making him tremble in the hot shower. The day had arrived. B would be back in his arms soon. He brushed his teeth and shaved for the first time since before B left, making himself presentable again. Satisfied with his sleek appearance, he made way for the bar where Jimmy was serving breakfast.

"Here. This will sort you out. Nice to see that you've showered and shaved for the lady."

"Cheers pal."

"You feeling alright? You were spewing some heavy shit last night?" Jimmy said, as Zander tried his best to finish his breakfast.

"How so?"

"You told me you love me," Jimmy teased.

"Get to fuck!" Zander said chomping down on his bacon.

"You did! You also informed me you're in love with Dragon."

Zander dropped his fork. "For fuck's sake, it's Welsh Cake! She's no' dragon!"

"Okay, Welsh-fucking-Cake. And do you? Love her I mean?"

Zander swallowed hard. "I—"

"Help! Help!" a woman screamed, interrupting.

The MC members scrambled to their feet, racing outside to discover an onslaught for which they weren't prepared. B was racing to dive at an unknown male attempting to strike Sandy's five-year-old son, Joey with a baseball bat as his mother and baby brother screamed in horror.

B slammed Joey's attacker into a wall as the frightened boy screamed.

Everyone rushed to Debs and her boys.

The attacker was bundled into a red chevvy by two other men. The tires screeching while fleeing the parking lot.

After checking on Debs, realization struck Zander like a bulldozer. B hadn't got up after saving Joey's life.

CHAPTER FIFTY-THREE

B.Sixteen Hours Previous

B boarded her flight, tight-chested, following her conversation with Zander. Her tendency to overthink getting the better of her.

Great work B! After years of being alone, you sabotage something beautiful. Well done, good girl!

She didn't sleep a wink on the plane and, to make matters worse, she had packed her portable battery in her suitcase and not in her hand luggage. B was a nightmare for allowing her phone to run out of charge, believing it was a deliberate act of her subconscious mind to encourage her to unplug from time to time.

Tossing her dead phone into her bag, B pinched her nose between her thumb and forefinger.

Bloody hell, B. Get your shit together. This isn't you.

She was desperate to return to Sunnyville to make up with Zander.

After their third week in the UK, both B and her boys were bored. They agreed the boys would go to their Grandparents and meet their dad earlier than planned and B would go home to Sunnyville to ready everything for Rhys and Madoc's return.

B understood an extra week apart from her boys would be difficult. However, she was eager to see Zander and start fresh in Sunnyville.

B longed for Zander's hands on her body and his lips on hers. She was determined not to mess things up again, should he give her another chance. Her tired mind fantasized about their reunion, their embrace. B would make everything right again when she returned to the club.

B woke from her slumber as the plane connected with the tarmac. Excited, she couldn't wait to get to her truck, hurrying through baggage to collect her case.

B was thirty minutes from seeing the Scot.

Retrieving her charger from her case, she plugged it into her truck's charging slot and the phone came to life, pinging with familiar message tones and an answerphone message. B's heart melted listening to Zander's message with the weight of the world tumbling from her shoulders and relief washing over her.

Twenty minutes until I see him.

B attempted to ring him to inform him of her imminent arrival to be met with his answer machine. No matter, she would arrive at the Gray Wolves Motorcycle Club in no time.

CHAPTER FIFTY-FOUR

Something's Not Right Here!

Upon arrival at the MC, B's face drew into an inquisitive stare as she pulled into her parking space.

Daybreak had just arrived when she witnessed three menacing looking men approach a young mother retrieving a baby and young boy from her car. They appeared suspicious, approaching the car from different directions.

Something's not right here. They're not Gray Wolves, they're too thug-like.

B's uneasiness quickened, her dragon fire looming in her stomach as she switched off her engine.

Keeping a watchful eye, B's eyes roared into flames as one man retrieved a baseball bat with a blade embedded into it from behind his back.

Shit.

B's instincts took over when she realized the man was about to strike the woman carrying her young baby. Diving from her truck as the man swung his bat, B planted herself between the woman and her attacker. The bladed bat struck B's left triceps muscle in a crushing blow, splitting her skin open as the blade embedded itself into her arm.

Crying out in a gut-wrenching squeal, as the torn flesh wreaked havoc on her pain receptors, the reality hit home. B was fighting for survival.

Snapping herself out of her pain in her adrenaline filled consciousness, B gritted her teeth in anger, taking her good hand to the bat and her bloodied hand to the man's throat, forcing him onto the car bonnet.

Blood poured from her wound as she used her knee as a lever to force her attacker's arm into hyper-extension until she heard a pop. He wailed in agony as she wrenched the bat from his crippled hand. Wrenching his broken arm, B noticed a familiar tattoo on his arm: a red, angry Pitbull.

"Who are you, asshole?" she screamed, positive she had seen it before, until her attention turned to another attacker.

"Wanna play with the big boys, sweetheart? Let's dance?" her tubby attacker spat.

B's anger spread through her body like wildfire, retrieving the bat as he approached at speed. B's instinct took over. Tightening her grip on the bat, B timed his run like a baseball approaching from a pitcher. Keeping her eyes locked on his, she swung as he reached mid-stride, swinging the bat into his side.

Her attacker gasped, knocking the air out of him, and dropping him like a sack of potatoes. B was baying for blood, kicking him in the ribs while he seethed in pain. Epinephrine passed through her like wildfire as her eyes darted around, attempting to make sense of the situation.

B looked at the mother and her children, spotting the third man. Grinning at B, with his backswing in full force, ready to strike the young boy.

No!

The color drained from B's face as the young mother screamed in horror.

B threw herself at the man, smashing them both into the wall before crashing to the ground, leaving the mother and her children unscathed.

B drifted in and out of consciousness as her mind attempted to comprehend reality.

"Grab her," a voice called as she tried to regain her vision.

"Shit. No time, we fucked it! The wolves are coming. Get him in the car now. They can't catch us here," another attacker yelled.

"What about the plan?"

"We'll come back. She's vulnerable now. Now let's go!"

B became weak, losing the battle between her body and mind. She was shutting down as scrambled voices rushed to her.

The MC guys had heard the noise and ran out of the club.

B attempted to move her weak body when reality kicked in.

Shit. I'm bleeding.

Blood gushed from her open wound, her yellow vest now a deep shade of red. Shock took hold of her battered body as she heard Zander's voice.

CHAPTER FIFTY-FIVE

Distraught!

"Oh no, darling!" Zander cried. "Prez, Welsh Cake is bleeding pretty bad! She needs to go to the hospital."

"Okay, man, get her in her truck," Jimmy demanded.

"Dinnae worry darling, I've got you," he said as he cradled her limp body and placed her on the back seat of her truck.

Climbing in beside her he rested her head on his lap whilst Jimmy handed him a first aid kit to tend to her wounds. Elevating her arm, he applied firm pressure and a tight bandage, trying to stem the blood flow.

"Dinnae go to sleep darling, you need to stay awake for me. We are taking you to the hospital."

B's eyes rolled in uncontrolled waves as her consciousness continued to falter with Déjà vu, slapping Zander in the face. B was the second bloodied female to leave the Sunnyville parking lot in haste.

"Is she alright?" asked a worried Jimmy.

"Aye, she's gonnae be fine, aren't you Welsh Cake?" Zander said, throwing Jimmy a look of growing concern.

"Right, we need to sit you up, darling. Try to keep you awake," Zander said with a concerned tone.

Keeping her arm elevated, he held B and attempted to scoop her up against his chest.

Waking to her trauma, B screamed in anguish, and it was then Zanders eyes traced a secondary injury on B's ribs. Zander assumed the blood on her yellow, blood-stained vest was from her arm and the slight cut above her right eye from her battles. However, when he reached under her vest, a thick two-inch wound pumped blood like a volcano.

"Shit!" Zander gasped as he packed the cut with remaining dressings from the first aid kit.

"You need to step on it now Prez, Welsh Cake has a blade wound. It dinnae look deep, but she's lost a lot of blood."

"Five minutes out, man," Jimmy said.

"Scot—" B mumbled,

"I got you Welsh Cake. We're almost there, darling."

"No, m-my boys, in the UK. They can't know, you can't worry them. Don't let the hospital ring them, please," B managed.

"Dinnae worry about that, darling. I'll sort it."

"Promise?" she whispered.

"Promise, I'll no' tell the boys a thing."

"My phone, they will be worried w-when I don't answer," she said, attempting to get up. B was becoming delirious in her state of low consciousness and as she moved, more blood pumped from her wounds.

"Hey, hey, it's okay, I'll sort it," Zander said, cradling her, "just stay still until we arrive at the hospital."

Zander's heart palpated as Jimmy slowed with the traffic. "We don't have time to sit here, Prez."

Jimmy started slamming on the horn before trying to maneuver around vehicles.

"Got you, man," he said, swerving in and out of traffic to echoes of angered drivers.

B's exhausted body slumped in his arms. She'd lost too much blood and lost her fight with the conscious world.

"Welsh Cake, stay with me darling!" Zander cried as he tried to jostle her awake, but B was unresponsive!

"Welsh Cake wake up!" he pleaded. "She's unconscious and I barely have a pulse."

Jimmy swerved straight into the ambulance bay, tooting the horn to attract the medics' attention.

Leaping from the truck, Jimmy flung open the door to an apparent horror scene. The back seat was covered in blood as a blood-stained Zander cradled B in his arms.

Zander sat numb with shock, until he was brought back to reality by a stern voice.

"Get a trolley now!" shouted a small but fierce doctor.

Loading B onto a trolley, they hurried into the hospital as Zander followed.

"Are you a relative, sir?"

"A yeah, her fiancé," Zander said. The words falling out of his mouth.

The doctor quizzed him as they hurried down the corridor. He had remembered every little detail from the time they had spent together, informing her that B was a picture of health, yet he stared at her broken body, feeling scared and hopeless.

"Right, we got it from here sir, she's in excellent hands. My colleague will direct you to the waiting room," the doctor explained.

The nurse led Zander down a narrow corridor to a small private room. The sun shone through the window onto his blood-stained, flannel shirt. Dazed and confused, he stood, trying to make sense of what had just happened.

Jimmy entered the room and stared at his brother, who ordinarily showed no feeling, who just got the job done. But this was different! Zander stood drenched in blood, looking broken.

"Hey man, why don't you take a seat and I'll get you a coffee?" Jimmy suggested. His words falling on deaf ears as Zander stood there uncomfortably numb.

Jimmy put his arm around him, guiding him to his seat.

"You alright man? The docs will fix her up, you'll see," Jimmy said.

Zander cradled his head in his hands. The familiarity of emptiness lingered in the stale hospital air, just as it did when identifying Noah's body at the morgue. The dreary shadow of helplessness casting over him and now, he was more lost than ever. It was bad enough that he had spent the last month pining for B. Now, their reunion was stolen from them.

They sat in silence. Zander had no words. His troubled mind stewing over the unforeseen attack.

Jimmy sat with him for a while before getting up to buy some coffee.

"I promised her I would keep her safe," Zander whispered as Jimmy opened the door.

"This ain't on you man," Jimmy said, closing the door again.

"Aye it is."

"We couldn't foresee this! Jeez, who could? Besides, B threw herself in the way of Debs and the kids. If she hadn't done that, they would be dead now. She took on three men to keep them safe, for fuck's sake. She could have screamed for help, stayed out of it. It was her decision and the right decision. What she did today for Sandy's family was some superhero shit and you should be proud of her, brother!"

Zander stared at his blood-stained hands in silence.

"You've really fallen for her, haven't you?" Jimmy asked.

Zander remained silent.

"Listen, I don't know what's going on between you and Welsh Cake, but I saw it, man. From the first time you laid eyes on her, you were hooked. We've all seen a difference in you this last month. You're excited when she calls. You have become more human since you met her and I know right now you are hurting, so talk to me."

Zander tussled his hair, releasing a tormented sigh.

"I dinnae know what the fuck is happening with me! I went weak at the knees when I first saw her. She is everything I've ever wanted. Something beautiful emerged from all the crazy shit that went down with Uncle Mauler and Blaze, and yeah, I am in love with her."

"She's good in the sack, then?" Jimmy teased, attempting to make light of the situation.

Zander remained serious; the passion burned in his eyes as he gushed about her.

"Prez, I'm serious. I dinnae just mean the sex. She's amazing and I know a guy like me probably has no chance long term with her, but I feel like I have known her forever."

"Whoa man, you have got it bad. But listen, don't talk shit about yourself. You are good enough for her. Besides, I get the distinct impression the feeling is mutual. I mean, she was pissed and soon as the handsome Scot opened his mouth, she softened. You looked at each other like you were the only ones there amidst all the chaos with Mack. Maybe it's a Celt thing, but man, I have seen for myself, she adores you."

"You reckon?" Zander said, tapping his foot in a nervous disposition.

"Yeah, man. Welsh Cake wants you, and let's be honest. She had a dog's life at Mack's. She's much better off with you."

"I dinnae think so, pal. I should have kept her safe."

"Listen, you need to stop blaming yourself for what happened today.

Oh, and no more keeping shit bottled up. I have seen you deep in thought since she left. You come talk to me, alright?"

"Yeah pal, thanks," Zander said, extending his arms for a hug. "You are a good friend, Jimmy."

"Too good," Jimmy joked. "I'm going to get us some coffee. Oh, and I brought Welsh Cake's phone in. I know she was worried about the boys, and it hasn't stopped ringing."

Zander attempted to check B's messages, to discover it was locked. He would have to wait until the boys rang to talk to them. He would need to think of an excuse to reassure them that B was okay, and low and behold, Rhys rang minutes later.

"Hello, mum?"

"Oh, hi pal, Zander here," Zander cleared his throat. "Your mother is in a meeting with the big boss. Her phone died on the plane, and she left it with me to charge whilst she attended the meeting. She said she would ring as soon as she's done."

"Okay! Can you let her know I called, please?" Rhys asked.

"Absolutely pal! She may be a wee while, but I will get her to call you the minute she comes out, alright?"

"Thank you!"

"No bother wee man! Speak to you later."

The guilt swept through him. He felt bad for lying. What was the alternative?

Sorry laddie, your mother is busy bleeding out in hospital?

"Well, at least you bought her a couple of hours," Jimmy said, returning with two coffees in his hands.

"What will I do if she dinnae pull through? How can I look those laddies in the eyes knowing I let this happen to their mother?" he said, taking a coffee from Jimmy.

"Hey! What did I say? This isn't on you, damn it, and Welsh Cake will be fine. Besides, Gnarler sent the security footage from the club and Jeez, Welsh Cake can fight! I mean, I know she handed Mack's ass to him on a platter, but she took out three fucking guys!"

"What?"

Jimmy continued. "I mean, you can't get a clear visual, but the wolves are positive the pimp sent them after Debs again!"

Zander shook his head in confusion.

"Look! Just watch it!" Jimmy demanded, pressing play on his phone. The phone showed the whole thing, leaving the Scot gobsmacked! He watched as B took down the attackers one by one.

"What the…"

"I know, man, she got some mad ninja skills!"

"Christ."

"Ya see. She'll be on her feet in no time."

A knock at the door interrupted them, with Zander hopeful of an update on B's condition, only to witness a hoard of wolves. All his brothers were there except Sandy, who was getting his family checked out.

Zander stood in surprise. "Guys, you didn't have to come."

"Like hell we didn't! We look after our own! You hurt one of us and we all feel it. We're here for you, brother, and it's the least we could do after what Welsh Cake did for Sandy's family."

"Cheers guys," Zander managed, choking on his feelings.

"Anyway, when's the wedding? We heard you told the docs that Welsh Cake is your fiancée," Tiny teased.

"Fuck off!" Zander chuckled.

"She must have something on you to make you propose so soon," Eddie chortled.

A glint of a grin flashed across Zander's face. He puffed out his chest, proud as punch. "Let me tell you all something. I would marry that lassie tomorrow and give her the most beautiful fucking Celt babies, no questions asked. She's amazing! No other woman comes close. I love her alright! So there, I fucking said it! Now you can all get over yersel's."

The room erupted in cheers. After years of watching him become a killing machine, he stood before them with a heart full of love. He had grown, and the pack was happy.

"Ahh, VP is loved up," Tiny teased again.

"Aye, alright you've had yer fun, now fuck off the lot of you!" he said, leaving them in fits of laughter until they were interrupted by a knock at the door.

The doctor entered, and the room fell silent.

"Gentlemen," she said, before turning to Zander. "Zander, right? Can I talk to you for a moment, please?"

"Is everything alright Doc?" Zander asked in a concerned tone.

"If you could just step outside a second, please?"

"Listen Doc, this is my family, so just tell me, is Welsh Cake alright?"

"She's stable!" The doctor said. "She has lost a hell of a lot of blood, and we feared that she had ruptured the brachial artery in her arm. However, when we took her to surgery, we found that wasn't the case. We also feared she was suffering from a punctured lung from the wound to her ribs. This also wasn't the case. Your fiancé is an extremely lucky woman."

Zander hunched over, resting his hands on his thighs to release a huge sigh of relief as the doctor continued.

"She is on oxygen and receiving a blood transfusion. However, she is still unresponsive. Do you know if she hit her head?"

"I dinnae think so. I've checked the security footage."

"Okay, well, she's been through a lot."

"Aye, she's just off a plane from the UK too," Zander explained.

"Well, we'll know more when she wakes."

"Can I see her now, Doc?" Zander asked.

"Yes, by all means. We are placing her in a private room. You can see her shortly."

"Thank you," Zander said, slumping down into the nearest chair to compose himself.

"See, what did I tell you? She's a warrior, that one," Jimmy said grasping the back of his neck.

A short while later, a nurse led Zander to B's room, followed by his entourage. They approached the room and Zander could see B lying there unconscious, with her left arm elevated in a sling, and a blood bag next to her bed.

His heart broke. Tears rolled down his cheeks as guilt flooded him. He didn't care his brothers could see him cry. He had fallen in love with her and wanted her to wake up. He kissed the top of B's head and sat holding her hand, staring at the bag of blood coursing through her veins.

The doctor, already in the room tending to B, placed her hand on his shoulder. "In most cases, the patient makes a full recovery. She is in excellent hands."

This brought no comfort to him; he was inconsolable as his brothers attempted to console him. The doctor left and Zander's upset turned to rage.

"The pimp dies for this!" he said through gritted teeth.

"I think Sandy has already called dibs on him, VP," said Tiny.

"Well, Sandy's woman isn't lying in a fucking hospital bed, is she? He will die by my hands."

"What the fuck happened today, anyway?" asked Eddie.

"The pimp sent three men after Debs. He still can't handle her leaving the game for Sandy," Tiny said.

"It's been six years, for fuck's sake," Hyde said.

"Well, she was his best girl," Tyr said.

"Listen, I dinnae give a flying fuck why it happened. That prick dies," Zander slammed.

Jimmy nodded in agreement. "Well, it looks like the boys are going hunting. Ed, Tyr, and Hyde are with Tiny. I will stay here and guard with Zand. We'll keep you updated."

Zander nodded in approval and the wolves embraced Zander, followed by a kiss on the forehead for B, before heading out the door.

Tiny called Jimmy into the corridor, "Prez, I'm worried about him. In the years I've known him, I have never seen him like this before. Especially not over a woman."

"He loves her man; I'd be the same if I was in his shoes. I'll keep an eye on him."

"Understood, boss. See you later."

Jimmy returned to the room, picking up a rucksack he retrieved from Tiny, handing it to Zander. "Here. Go clean yourself up."

"I'm no' leaving her side," Scottie said.

"The bathroom is three feet from her bed. If she wakes, I'll call you. Clean yourself up, for crying out loud. She doesn't want to see you soaked in her blood when she wakes."

"Aye, okay," Zander said, wiping his nose on the back of his hand. He picked the bag up and headed into the bathroom, returning ten minutes later as clean as a whistle.

"Thanks pal. Listen, you dinnae have to stay," Scottie said.

"I'm not going anywhere. I've grown fond of her."

A slight smirk flashed across Zander's face as he rested his head on B's bed, taking her hand in his. He was exhausted and within minutes, he'd fallen asleep. Jimmy turned off the lights and covered the Scot with his jacket before settling himself into the spare seat and drifted off to sleep.

CHAPTER FIFTY-SIX

In Love.

B regained consciousness whilst Zander remained sleeping. Jimmy reassured her and left to fetch the doctor.

The doctor arrived and examined B, explaining the procedures taken to save her life and provided her with some much-needed pain relief.

B was hurting as she tried to get comfortable and trying not to wake Zander, who slept next to her.

"How are you feeling?" Jimmy asked.

"Like I've scrapped with three guys," she joked, wincing in pain.

"Well, I'm glad your sense of humor has remained intact. This one has been worried sick about you, though," he explained, showing to Zander.

B gazed at Zander, still holding her hand.

"Is he okay?" she asked.

"He was in a right state. In fact, he was in tears earlier. You know he is besotted with you Doll Face?"

"I wasn't sure if he gave a shit until I heard his voicemail. I fucked things up yesterday. Hurt his feelings."

"Oh, he gives a shit! He was fucking frantic, thinking he'd lost the woman he'd fallen in love with."

"He said that to you?" B asked in apparent shock.

"Yeah! And he's blaming himself for not keeping you safe."

B's face hardened. "Shit! Sorry. I couldn't sit there and watch those psychos hurt that poor family. As stupid as it sounds, I didn't think. I never do. I just fucking react and worry about the consequences later. I should have rung you guys to come out, and I sh—" B couldn't finish her sentence; she was getting angry.

"Hey, hey, come on now, sweetheart. What you did was heroic. You were brave to put yourself between Debs and the kids. If you hesitated, they would all be dead."

"Thanks Jimmy! I don't understand why anyone would harm a mother and her children. It's heart-breaking!" she said shaking her head in disbelief.

Jimmy then explained to her that Debs was a hooker and Sandy was one of her regulars before they fell in love, and he got her out of the game. Jimmy explained how they settled down together, but her pimp couldn't let it go and had attempted to hurt her in the past.

They were chatting for a while when the conversation returned to Zander.

"B, can I ask you something?" Jimmy asked.

"Sure."

"Do you love him? I mean, I know it's early days and your relationship hasn't had a chance with all the crazy, but I have to know! See Zand is my best friend and I've never seen him like this before. He's invested and I'm scared he's going to get hurt and, frankly, I don't think he could take any more trauma in his life."

B froze in silence and Jimmy continued. "I guess what I'm saying is, if you don't feel the same, then I'm going to need you to end the relationship. Because let me tell you, sweetheart, that poor sucker is all in. He's ready to spend the rest of his life with you, and if you don't feel that for him, I need you to let him go so I can help him through it."

"Jimmy, I—"

"Zander's been through a lot, shutting himself off from the world until he met you, and now the floodgates have opened. See, Zand's just not used to feeling and since he's met you, it's all he's done."

B closed her eyes and pursed her lips. "Jimmy, I wanted him the moment I saw him and like Scottie, I too shut myself off from the world until I met him and now it's so fucking scary. I'm experiencing feelings I never thought I'd ever feel! Everything is amplified with Scottie. I am falling for him, and I'm scared when he gets to know me a bit more, he'll not want me."

Jimmy patted her hand. "He worships you."

"Jimmy, I'm no biker chick. To be honest, bikes and guns terrify me. I'm a businesswoman, and I'm scared I won't be enough for him. He is gorgeous, kind and so loving. He could have anyone. So why choose me? I'm nothing special, but he is. He's the reason I'm back earlier than planned. I love him, Jimmy and you may think that we are both stupid, but there's an intense chemistry between us I can't explain."

"Oh, I see that," Jimmy laughed.

"Jimmy, I can promise you this. He will break my heart before I break his."

Jimmy put a gentle hand to her shoulder, careful not to hurt her. "Welsh Cake, you both have something special, yet so fragile. You're both the most dysfunctional and emotionally crippled, yet beautiful people I've encountered. You found each other in amongst a load of crazy, a shit storm, Doll Face. You're so in love with one another yet terrified of hurting each other."

"Fuck, I don't know what's happening to me," B said.

Jimmy grinned, shaking his head. "B, Zander said the same thing whilst you were in surgery. I don't know, you Celts are so fucking passionate! I think if you give Zander a chance, you'll do beautiful things together. What you have is special and I'm talking from experience here. So, please, for the love of God, hold on to it tight and don't let go. Don't make the same mistakes I did."

B smiled with endearment, "Thank you Jimmy! Scottie is lucky to have you in his life and so am I! Thank you for sticking around to look after him."

"You're welcome. Now get some rest so we can take you home, okay?" he said as he gave her one last kiss on the cheek and left the room.

CHAPTER FIFTY-SEVEN

Blaze's Fury

Blaze's veins protruded out of his forehead. His face was beetroot red as he bellowed in anger. "How did she beat the three of you? She's a piece of ass for fuck's sake. You had one job, and you fucked it up! I should kill the lot of you!"

"Boss, please! You don't understand. The woman is a fucking beast! She snapped my arm like a twig," said the greasy, one-armed man.

"Yeah boss, she's tapped. She looked possessed or something."

Blaze paced his office, holding onto his braces. "So, Dragon likes to fight back, does she? Ooh, I like a feisty bitch. It'll be more pleasurable when I make her squeal for mercy."

"Boss, you better be careful. I don't think you'll fair well against her and you're the most dangerous man I know."

"Is that a fact?" Blaze sneered, removing his gun from his holster, and shooting the terrified man in the head.

The two other attackers trembled as Blaze continued.

"Now, does anyone else think I'm incapable of slaying Dragon?"

"N-No boss!" the men chimed.

"Get this asshole out of here. His negativity infuriates me," Blaze spat, returning his gun to its holster, as he grimaced out the window.

Glancing out to the distance, he raged.

Your time will come, Dragon, and everything that's yours will be mine!

CHAPTER FIFTY-EIGHT

The Gray Wolves Are White, Asshole!

Zander woke hours later to his hair being ruffled. Lifting his weary head, he met B's gaze who had since been taken off oxygen.

"Welsh Cake, you scared the living daylights out of me," he said, reaching up to kiss her.

"You don't get rid of me that easy, Boyoh."

"How long have you been awake?"

"A little while. I didn't want to wake you, and Jimmy kept me company. He filled me in on what I have missed."

"Has the doc seen you yet?" Zander asked.

"Yeah, she is coming back soon," said Jimmy. "I'm off to get a coffee, you want one?"

"Yeah pal. Thanks."

Zander didn't wait for Jimmy to leave before he kissed B again, stroking her cheek and kissing her hand, relieved she was okay.

"I am so sorry I let this happen to you, darling," he said.

"This isn't on you, handsome, so stop blaming yourself, okay?"

"But—"

"No buts. It wasn't your fault. Look, Scottie, I'm sorry about our last conversation."

Zander closed his eyes, shaking his head into a smile. "Dinnae worry about that. Jeez, I am just glad you're okay. How's it you came back early?"

"We were bored, and I missed you, so I came home early. Shit, the boys! They're going to be frantic," B said as the panic spread across her face, as she searched for her phone.

"Hey, it's okay," Zander said, caressing her face. "I spoke to Rhys earlier and told him you had a meeting and would call him back."

B let out a sigh of relief and dialed Rhys's number. "Thank you," she said before Rhys answered his phone.

The hospital discharged B after spending the night. Arriving back at the MC, she headed straight for the shower, guided by Zander.

"I'm fine!" she stated.

"Aye, I know darling, but I want to make sure," he said, removing her clothes.

Taking her hand, he led her into the shower to wash her bloodstained body. B steadied herself by keeping a hold of his muscular biceps, watching him wash her. Zander had missed her, and this was far from the reunion he imagined.

Zander was aware of B studying his every move, biting her lip drove him wild, but he knew he had to show restraint, given what she had been through.

"Almost done, darling," he said, meeting her gaze.

"Kiss me Scottie," she asked.

Zander smiled. "You never need to ask" he said, delivering a careful kiss to her lips.

B's hand slid down to his firm backside as she tried to pull him closer to her.

"Mm, Welsh Cake, I want this, I do, but I dinnae want to hurt you, my darling. Let's wait until you're recovered."

B looked him in the eyes. "Please?" she whispered.

Zander saw desperation in her eyes as he met her gaze. He didn't want to hurt her, but he really didn't want to upset her, either. Taking her head in his hands, he kissed her.

"Darling, I've just got you back. I dinnae want to lose you again by filling you. We have all the time in the world. Now let's get you back to bed."

B glared at him. "You're telling me no?"

"I just dinnae want to hurt you. You're not well!" Zander whispered.

"Then fucking leave! I don't need a man telling me no. What is it, Scottie? Too busted up for you now, am I? Well, I had that with my ex. Brushing off my advances because I was no longer fucking good enough, despite giving him everything. Been there, done that! No fucking thank you!"

Zander shook his head in disbelief. "It's no' like that."

"The hell it isn't. Just leave Scottie. I can't be around people who think I'm not good enough," B said, turning her back on him.

"Jesus! Is that what you think? Fuck me. That ex of yours did a fucking number on you, didn't he? Well, I'm no' him. I thought I'd fucking lost you and you want me to take you against the wall when you can hardly stand? Christ on a bike. I dinnae know whether you're fucking mental or just don't give a shit about yersel'," he said, turning off the shower to leave.

Gliding his wet hand through his hair he stared at her, his frustration almost overwhelming him. "I'll do anything to make you feel good about yersel'. Make you feel happy, but never accuse me of thinking you're no' good enough. That is all I think about. Now you might not comprehend this because that prick of an ex has clearly corrupted that beautiful fucking mind of yours, but I will never, ever tire of you. I love you!"

B stared at the floor. "Sorry, I love you, too. I need to rid my mind of what happened. I hate it! Scottie, I only know how to turn fear into fire. I don't know what else to do with it."

He placed his forehead to hers, staring into her terrified eyes. "Embrace it, stop fighting it, and let it wash over you. If you take away its power, you're free darling and I promise you, I'm no' going anywhere, and I'll let nothing happen to you again. Now back to bed. You need to heal."

Zander left B sleeping as Hyde, the new club doctor, watched over her. Tiny had messaged him, informing him he caught the pimp and was bringing him back to the MC. Zander walked the short distance across the parking lot and into the club.

"Where is he?" he growled as he entered the bar.

"Store cupboard. Your toolbox is ready, VP."

"Good. Turn the jukebox up to drown out the noise. I'm gonnae take my time with him. He's going out in pieces."

Tiny hesitated. "You sure you want to do this VP? It breaks all of Welsh Cake's rules, and Mack is on his way."

"I'll make sure I'm done before he arrives. This fucker needs to die," he said, pushing the door open to the poorly lit store cupboard.

The pimp sat tied to a chair, bound and gagged. The sweat poured from his sleek black hair as the terror in his eyes blinked back his tears.

Zander entered the room, composed and silent as he opened his toolbox, laying down a blow torch, a hammer, five nails and a pair of pliers. His jaw line firm as his raged consumed him.

The pimp started to moan and bob in his chair, a feeble attempt to break free in Zander's eyes.

"No point trying to break free, asshole. Your fate was sealed the minute your guys hurt my old lady," he said, removing his blade from its holder. "I mean, what stupid prick thinks it's wise to step into our compound and hurt our loved ones?"

The gagged man cried, shaking his head, his words incomprehensible as his pants flooded with urine.

"Oh, pissing yersel' is the least of your problems. I'm gonnae rip off your fingernails, one by one, and take a fucking blow torch to your eyes and that's just the beginning.

The pimp wailed through his gag as Tiny turned up the bar's jukebox volume.

"Now before I rip out your tongue, I want to hear you apologize for ruining my reunion with my woman," he said removing the pimp's gag.

"It wasn't me, man, I swear," he cried.

"Lies, lies, lies," Zander said in a calm tone before delivering a fist to his jaw.

"Argh."

"Oh, I think I just fractured your jaw, fella. Did it hurt?"

Blood poured from the pimp's mouth, dripping down his chin. "I w- was at the cop shop. I lost three fingers the last time I fucked with you, please? I'm not stupid enough to challenge the Pitbulls again."

Zander picked up his blade, jamming it into his thigh. "We're the Gray Wolves, asshole. The Pitbulls are dead."

"You're wrong. They're still alive and back in town."

"And what makes you think that?" Zander said, gripping him by his collar.

"Bec—"

"What the fuck are you doing?" B bellowed from the doorway.

Zander's head spun around to see a furious B standing and glaring at him.

"This piece of shit is gonnae die for trying to hurt Debs and the boys, darling."

"Release him now."

"Welsh Cake—"

"Release him now, or I'll tear you and this club apart. The Gray Wolves are white, asshole."

Zander growled. "I cannae do that, darling. He's gotta atone for his sins."

"Then we're done, and by we, I mean you, me, and this club. Gather your shit and leave," she said, storming out of the door.

CHAPTER FIFTY-NINE

The Dragon and the Gray Wolf

Scottie stormed into B's bedroom a little while later to find her standing naked with her good arm propping up the wall. He looked at her beaten body and it enraged him.

Approaching with caution, he attempted to hold her.

"Don't fucking touch me, you piece of shit. You're supposed to stay white, not attempt to murder someone on my property," she said, battering his chest with her good hand.

"Whoa, stop it! Stop it, God damn it."

"You're fucking black as night, Scottie. I trusted you," she wailed, striking him again.

"For fuck's sake! Mack was right about you! Black and white? The world isn't like that, darling," he said taking hold of her waist. "Trying to see it as anything different is naïve and that's what's gonnae get you hurt, my love. Not me. Not the club. That narrow-minded way you see the world. So, for the love of Christ, open your fucking eyes and step into reality. Hell, you might enjoy being something other than white!"

B batted his hands away. "See, that's what you just don't fucking get, lovely boy, I can't! And you don't get that because you don't have kids. You can't go murdering people you don't like. Honestly, Scottie, we should just call it a day. I'm white, you're black, so let's end this now!"

Zander's brow narrowed, stopping him dead in his tracks.

"Let me spell it out for you. If you get arrested, it'll devastate me when you go down for attempted murder. Scottie, I lose! I lose you, then my prick of an ex-husband sees I'm not fit to be a mother for mixing with criminals and he takes full custody of my boys. My fucking world collapses and I'm left with nothing and all to get payback for some bull shit attack. We don't even know if the pimp was involved!"

B's words stung like a bee. He understood she feared losing everything, but questioning whether the pimp was involved was ludicrous. There was no other explanation.

"What do you mean? Of course, he was behind it. Jeez, what is in your head now? I cannae keep up. I wish you would let me in so I can see how your world works because I'm fucking exhausted!" he shouted as he threw his hands in the air in frustration.

"Then leave."

Zander took a deep breath to calm himself. "Look, darling. When you got hurt and were lying in my arms, fucking lifeless after I'd just gotten you back, it damn near destroyed me. I thought I'd never see you again, thinking you'd been taken away from me. I wanted him to hurt as much as I was hurting."

"I don't care! Get out!"

Rage filled him as captivated images of her broken body flashed through his mind. His blood pumped through his veins with contempt. The familiar rush of adrenaline feasting on his veins like a parasite. He'd felt it a thousand times before in the army, and when he was beating the living daylights out of opposing MC members, he couldn't control it. Just like B when her fiery dragon roared, Zander had something lurking of his own, only he had less control over his than B had of hers.

The sheer disbelief of the words that escaped her mouth, as she stood, eyes wide and scary, struck him at his core.

"See what you dinnae get, darling? Is that before I met you? I was cold like ice, a nasty bastard. Then I met you and I started to fucking thaw. You made me feel again and I love how you do that to me because you give me hope. You make me believe I can be a good person. But when you got hurt, I realized how dangerous that is. Now, I'm defrosted, raw, and you want to end things? How fucked up is that? I fucking love you! Can you no' see I did this for you? They hurt you, Welsh Cake!"

B glowered at him. "Do you think I want this? You killing anyone who hurts me? Seriously, it's bloody dangerous and reckless, not to mention idiotic. You'll get us all killed! And whilst you're so bloody sure that the pimp was behind the attack, let me tell you, Boyoh, I'm not, because the man who I disarmed first wore MC branding. His mark, his bloody birth right, right there on his wrist," she said, pointing at her own. "The same bloody branding as Noah. So, tell me, Scottie, do you still think he's behind this?" she screamed.

"Mack was right! I'm not bloody safe here. It was stupid of me to think I could leave Uskiville. I don't even know who I can trust anymore. I'm done, we're done," she said, filling her glass with whiskey.

Zander's head pounded as he tried to make sense of B's rant.

"What branding?"

"What does it bloody matter now? You're all the same. Beat first and ask questions later. So bloody stupid."

Zander flew into a fit of rage, grabbing her injured arm, as if possessed by something. His jaw tensed as he spat through gritted teeth, "What fucking branding?"

An intimidated B shouted. "His fucking red Pitbull," she said, slapping him across the face, "and never lay your bloody hands on me."

Zander grabbed her by her wrist to stop her, his face filled with evil intensity as B struck him again and again.

"Stop it," he growled.

Only B didn't stop, with fear-filled rage enticing her to continue.

Zander grabbed her to stop her from reigning down on him until B broke free, striking him again, and splitting his lip.

"For fuck's sake, stop it, you're hurting me" he shouted as he continued to hit him, lost in a current of resentment toward him.

"Argh! I've fucking had it!" he snapped as he grabbed her waist. Lifting her up in the air, he sat on the bed and threw her over his knee.

"You dinnae get to beat the shit out of me, darling. It's no' fucking happening. You need to learn a lesson," he said as he spanked her hard across her backside. He had no idea why he spanked her. He didn't want to hurt her. It was the only thing he could think of to keep him in control.

B screamed as his palms struck her bare skin, the pressure of his thighs pressing against her wounds evident.

"Scottie, please!"

"I've never struck a lassie, but I am gonnae spank your ass until you learn never to fucking hit me again. You understand me?" he shouted before spanking her again.

B screamed in agony, so Zander struck her again and again.

"Scottie, please, you're hurting me."

"Oh aye, but it's alright for you to hurt me, is it? No, you need to fucking learn. Act like a dragon and I'll fucking treat you like one," he shouted as he spanked her again.

Zander enjoyed punishing her, relishing being in control for the first time since they met and then losing himself in the moment. Intoxicated by the power he had over her, he grabbed her around her waist to bend her over the bedside cabinet, to witness her slump to the floor in a heap.

What the fuck have I done?

"Oh, fucking hell! Shit! Darling, I am so sorry! I dinnae mean to hurt you," he said, snapping himself out of his cold rage and dropping to his knees to check if she was alright.

Nausea swept through him, staring at the red-raw handprints on her backside, and perfect droplets of blood escaping her split stitches on her ribs.

"Shit, Welsh Cake, I am so sorry I got caught up in the moment."

B was too exhausted to move, so Zander carried her to the shower to clean her up. She could barely steady herself against him as he washed the blood from her body. She winced in pain.

After putting her to bed and sealing her wounds, he gazed upon his broken woman Holding back the tears, Zander knew he had hurt her far more than he had realized. He wasn't used to self-control.

Whenever he fought, he fought for his life, striking people for survival. He didn't intend to hurt B tonight. He just wanted to make her stop hurting him, but he broke her just like everyone else had done before him.

"B," he said in a low, gravelly voice. "I'm so sorry," he said as she pulled her duvet over her chest. Her eyes looked like glaciers as she fought back the tears. She would never cry in front of him.

"Darling, I'm so fucking sorry. I never meant to hurt you. I just wanted to make you stop hitting me. Please, please forgive me."

Zander stared at her distraught face, stroking it as she stared into nothingness. He bent down and kissed the top of her head, sitting beside her for a moment. He grabbed her hand, his tears falling down his face until they got lost in his beard.

"What I just did to you, losing control like that, was wrong. The disturbing thing is, I liked it!"

Watching her sit upright, he could see the confusion in her face.

"You enjoyed hurting me, Scottie?" she asked, voice low and trembling.

"No, darling, I just liked the control. I fucking hate that I hurt you. It fucking damn-near destroyed me. But for a split second, I felt in total control, and it felt good," he said, shaking his head, looking disappointed with himself.

"Oh, Scottie," she said, drawing him in closer, but he jerked away from her.

"No, darling, you were right. As much as I love you, we shouldn't be together. You need to stay white, and I'm blacker than black. Trying to pull you into my world is so very wrong of me. You should be with someone more deserving of you. Someone with a big fucking heart, who wants to do good things. Me, I tried and I'm no' good at it and I cannae give you that right now."

B turned her head away, making Zander lift her chin with his index finger, turning her to face him. "I want to be the man you want. but right now, I need to be black. Do you understand that?"

B shook her head. "No, I don't Scottie, because I don't want you trying to become something you're not, just to please me. I want you to live the life I know you can have. There is good in your heart. I just don't understand why you need to be black. What are you not telling me? Please? I don't understand!"

"And you never will, darling. Because you're too good for me. Your mind could never reach where mine lives. Just know I will always love you. Now, I've got to see Jimmy and Mack, okay?"

"Scottie, please don't go! We're not done here!"

"Oh, darling, but we are," he said as he kissed the top of her head and dragged himself out of the office.

CHAPTER SIXTY

Changed Your Tune

Jimmy, Mack, and Frankie sat at the bar drinking whiskey when Zander stormed in like a man possessed.

"You three, church now!" he growled, pointing at them. The three men studied Zander in confusion as he stood covered in blood.

"What have you fecking done?" Mack shouted, rising from his seat.

Zander ignored him. "I said fucking right now!" he bellowed as the entire bar stopped in silence. The three men entered church with Mack grimacing at Zander.

Zander turned to see Ari standing in the bar's corner looking nervous.

"You too, princess, dinnae think you get to wriggle away. This all fucking started here with you!" he sneered as he watched her march into the room.

Grabbing a bottle of whiskey, he tore off the cap and guzzled a third of the bottle before following them and slamming the door behind him.

Zander dragged the bottle of whiskey along the oak table. His gaze met with fury, panic, and fear as they waited for an explanation.

Mack was the first to rant, his eyes fixated on the blood-stained clothes. "If you've fecking hurt my dragon, I'll end you, brother. Now where is she and what the hell have you done?"

"What's going on Zand?" Jimmy asked.

He sank into the seat in front of him. "She dinnae trust us anymore, and I dinnae think she ever will, unless we tell her the truth."

"Zander, what do you mean?" Ari asked.

"She said so herself, she dinnae know who to trust anymore. She noticed it with you, Mack. She said you changed after we ended The Mauler's reign, and now with me. So, I ended it, so I dinnae have to lie to her."

"Oka—"

"You know, all that lassie wants is for people to be honest with her, and after all that she's done for us, I think it's the least we can do. I love her and I wanna be the man she deserves, but with this cascade of lies bullshit hanging over us, we dinnae stand a chance."

"Jesus, VP. Tell us what's happened. Is B, okay?" Frankie said with concern written across his face.

"I dinnae think either of us will ever be okay after tonight," he said as he ran his hands through his hair.

He turned to Jimmy. "It wasn't the pimp, and I dinnae think they were after Debs and the kids. No, I know it was just a bullshit ruse we all fell for, but not her. She's so fucking clever. It's unreal."

"Zander w—" Mack tried.

"The man that wedged the bat in Welsh Cake's arm was branded," Zander shouted. "His red Pitbull decorated his fucking wrist like a badge of honor. I think they were really after Welsh Cake, and boy, did they get more than they bargained for," he said with a laugh.

The room fell silent.

"She told you this?" Jimmy asked.

"Aye. We were arguing. She was mad at me for beating down on the pimp. Spitting fucking feathers, she was. Telling me how reckless I was and how she thought the pimp wasn't responsible because her attacker wore the Pitbull patch on his forearm. Welsh Cake is no' as fucking naïve as you all think she is and now she dinnae trust anyone."

"Shite!" Mack said.

Zander continued, pacing. "Welsh Cake lost it tonight and the scary, fiery dragon came out to play. She started hitting me aboot the head."

"And what did you fecking do?" Mack hissed.

"I fucking lost it! And I dinnae want to hurt the lassie. I love her. I just wanted her to stop, so I put her over my knee and fucking spanked her until I realized I hurt her."

Jaws dropped in disbelief.

"So, is she okay?" asked Ari.

"Aye, I told ye, I dinnae damage her. I mean, I spanked her and split her stitches and I'll never forgive myself for laying a hand on her, but she was beating the shit out of me. Spanking her was the only way I could stop myself from losing it."

"What about the blood?" Mack growled.

"I told ye. I split her stitches wide open. There was blood everywhere! But dinnae worry, I cleaned her all up and put her to bed before I left," he said with a casual tone.

Sighs of relief flooded the room. They had all witnessed Zander's artistry as he ripped his prey apart with finesse, relishing in his victims' pain.

Zander looked at them in sheer disbelief, "Wait a minute. You thought I'd killed her?"

"You've killed people for less," Jimmy said.

"I've no'!"

"You fecking have! I should kill you now for laying a hand on her, but I think you're torturing yourself enough," Mack snapped.

"It's just you came in frantic and covered in blood. We thought—" Ari began.

"That I fucking killed her?"

"Well, yeah, VP," Frankie confirmed.

"Jesus Christ, I'm telling you she's in danger, and no' from me. Someone knew she was coming home early and used Deb's routine as a piggyback and cover to get to her. Only I dinnae think they knew enough about her to know about her fiery fucking dragon tendencies!"

"Oh, so you're allowed to call her a dragon, but nobody else is?" Jimmy teased.

"What the feck are you talking about? She's my dragon," Mack interjected.

"Will you two shut the fuck up and let me explain," Zander slammed.

"I think someone from the old days is trying to catch themselves a dragon."

"Zand, that makes little sense," Jimmy said.

"I know, none of it does. But why would Welsh Cake be so fucking concerned about that tattoo and no' trust anyone, unless she thinks Noah's death was no accident? She's suspicious someone close to her is responsible for all of this. I'm sure of it. Think about it for a second. Noah and Welsh Cake were friends. They had been talking to each other for months before Noah passed. They planned an entire business together. What if Noah told her things?" Zander hypothesized.

"She would have told me. My Dragon keeps no secrets," Mack said.

"She kept a whole move from you, asshole. And another thing. When I beat the crap out of the pimp today, he told me the Pitbulls are back! That wee prick looked me right in the eyes and pleaded innocence, and now I fucking believe him!"

"Shit, this is not good!" Ari cursed as she panicked. "Look where lying got us the first time around? Mack had surgery on his arm and B left Uskiville. If we lie to her again, we won't just lose our friend, we'll lose everything."

"Aye, we need to tell her! I've ended things with her because I cannae lie to her anymore. I'll no' hurt her more than I have already. It's no' fair, and she deserves better."

"Have you two taken fecking silly pills or something?" Mack snapped with Irish venom. "You have fecking met her, have you not? You tell her this, she will lose it. She will take the lads, sell everything, and leave, and not before she tears everyone apart who has ever hurt her. Jeez. You think a damaged arm is bad, let me tell ye. This is nothing compared to what she'll do if she finds we betrayed her twice. It's too risky."

"Mack's right!" Jimmy agreed. "If they're after her, then telling her and letting her leave is too dangerous. This could all be a coincidence."

"This is no fucking coincidence, "Zander growled as he guzzled more whiskey. "The Red Pitbulls are back."

"If that's true, they'll be making a play for the club, and Welsh Cake is the only one standing in their way. They're not stupid, they've done their homework, leaving us on the back foot. They will know Dragon owns the keys to their castle and they'll come for her again when we least expect it," Jimmy stated.

"But who, though? Who would have the balls to come?" Ari begged the question.

"Blaze!" Zander yelled. "With Noah gone, Sunnyville is for the taking. It's clear as day. Revenge is achieved by taking the person who means so much to everyone. The person with all the power. My guess is, he took Noah out too."

Turning his attention to Mack, he shook his head. "You yer tit, have spent forever bragging about yer precious dragon, and if he's been plotting this whole time, or had anything to do with Noah's death, then it's no' just our precious dragon who's in danger, it's all of us! Blaze is the nastiest mother fucker I have ever encountered. He is more sadistic than Uncle Mauler himself."

"I say that we take the fight to them and surprise them," Mack said rising from his seat.

"We don't know where they're located," Jimmy stressed. "Noah, Zander, and I spent months searching for him and his spies and came up empty. We just assumed they bailed.

"Aye! And what about my fucking Welsh Cake? I'm no' leaving her behind, putting them in danger!" Zander said.

Frankie steepled his fingers and interjected, "You're all forgetting one thing, gentlemen," addressing Mack, Jimmy, and Zander, oblivious to the fact that Ari was still in the room. "Few people knew B was coming home early. It'll be the reason she feels she can't trust anyone. B knows someone in Sunnyville is against her, and now, so do we. There are several issues to address here."

"Shite."

"One," Frankie continued, "Who and why the fuck is anyone feeding back to Blaze? And two, what do we tell B to ensure she trusts us enough to keep her close and *ALIVE*?"

"Frankie's right!" Mack intervened, "and we need to keep this between us until we find the spy. I mean, we've had a lot of unknown faces come through our ranks since relieving The Mauler of his command."

"But how do we keep Welsh Cake from catching on? She clearly worked this out way before us. Are we meant to sneak behind her back until we learn something new? She needs to be guarded. Her boys are back next month, so how on earth are we going to guard them without her getting suspicious? Jimmy asked.

"That won't be a problem," Frankie explained. "B will close ranks now. She doesn't trust anyone. She will turn to me and Mackie again, it's all she knows. I'll talk to her, keep her right."

Zander leaped up out of his chair, slamming his hand down on the table, "Yer no' taking her away from me! The only reason I ended it with her was to keep her safe."

Frankie sat unfazed by Zander's outburst. "Maybe you should rethink that VP. B's safer with you, and right now, she's over there on her own."

Zander calmed again, returning to his seat. "Aye, but I dinnae want to lie to the lassie anymore. This cascade of lies just keeps coming back to hurt her. It's no' fair. When this shit is over, I wanna be with her."

"But that's just it, Zander. She won't be with you if you don't keep her safe. And yes, if she discovers the truth, she will be on the war path. But at least she'll be alive. Dragon loves you man and she'll forgive you once I tell her this is all on me," Mack explained.

"We'll you've changed yer fucking tune, pal. What happened to black and white?"

Mack approached Zander, sitting down next to him, and taking a big gulp of whiskey. "Look, I was wrong, okay? I was jealous and angry that she picked you. I always told myself she didn't want me because I'm an ex-con, because I'm black and she's white. But once she slept with you, I understood it had nothing to do with how she sees me in the world. It was just my character she found unattractive," Mack said, releasing an enormous sigh.

Zander put his arm around Mack's shoulder, giving him a tight squeeze, "She loves you pal, just no' like that. You're her family and I never wanted to come between you. But by Christ, you're right about black and white" he sighed as he took the whiskey away from Mack and finished the dregs in the bottle.

"Well, maybe you're the wolf to change the narrative, make her see color," Mack said.

"I dinnae think that's possible, pal," Zander said, looking defeated. "All I know is, she keeps getting hurt and I witness another wee piece of her break," he went on, "I know I've no' known her that long, but when we met, she was a beautiful, fiery fucking dragon, and now I'm seeing her spark diminish. I hurt her tonight, and I dinnae think she'll want me back now."

"But if you love her like you say you do, then you have to try," Jimmy advised.

"Look, I've known Dragon for years, she has a huge dragon heart of gold and when she finds something she loves, she doesn't let go," Mack said, "She even threatened to end Ari and that was way before she tried to kill her that night."

Ari glared at Mack. "You never told me that."

"Well, I didn't want you to run off. We were just starting out," Mack said, before returning his attention to Zander. "She loves you, brother. We all see it!"

"He's right, man," Jimmy stated, with Frankie nodding in agreement.

Mack continued. "Dragon has never looked at anyone like she looks at you. Hell, we'd never even seen her in a relationship before you," he laughed. "So, I'm telling you, brother, you have something special there. Now go and fecking talk to her, will you, ya Scottish prick?"

"Right. I'm getting her back!" Zander said, standing to leave, only to be stopped in his tracks by Frankie palming his chest.

"Whoa, slow your roll, rough and ready, we need a plan first, so we know what you're going to say to convince her to trust you and the rest of us again."

"Aye. You're right," Zander agreed as the group put their heads together to formulate a plan.

Meanwhile, back in the bar, Glen served drinks to the rest of the club members.

Peering through the bar's window into church, he asked the question in everyone's mind. "So, what do you think's happening? Zander was covered in a lot of blood there and where's B? Hey, you don't think—"

"Shut the fuck up, prospect, it's none of your fucking business," hissed Eddie.

"Jeez, sorry I spoke," Glen huffed as he put away the clean glasses.

"Leave him alone," snapped Tiny. "He's only curious, just like the rest of us are."

"Yeah, and we'll know when they tell us and not before. It's the chain of command," Eddie explained.

"I don't know. Ever since Dragon showed up, there's been nothing but trouble. Just because she owns the place, it doesn't mean she owns us. Why are they listening to a woman? She's a piece of ass, for Christ's sake," Tiny said with contempt in his voice.

"Maybe because she is the owner and the only person willing to aid Noah trying to stop the club from dying out. Oh, and she's the love of Zander's life and Mack's best friend," Eddie said.

"So," Tiny spat.

"With the manpower behind you, you can do what you want. Those men would die for her. She's that important," Eddie explained.

"This is BS. I'm going for a ride," Tiny said, picking up his keys and heading out the door.

"So, she controls everything?" Glen asked.

"Yes, you fucking idiot! Now shut the fuck up. You have work to do," Eddie bellowed, losing patience with him as the sound of nearing footsteps approached from the hallway.

Moments later, Mack, Ari, and Frankie appeared at the bar. They were laughing and joking as if nothing had happened. Zander emerged soon after, showered and changed. He had a quick drink with them before he headed out of the door.

"Go get her, tiger!" Mack teased as Zander backed out of the door. He laughed at him and flipped him the bird.

Zander was nervous as he walked across the parking lot to the gym. They had just spent the last hour discussing how they were going to keep B safe, leaving Scottie exhausted. He didn't want to hurt B and feared he was about to put more distance between them.

Christ! I just want to be honest. Be the man she needs. But the truth will endanger her. No, stick to the plan.

They decided the club couldn't risk B freaking out, as she did with

Mack just a few months ago. They came up with a half-baked version of the truth where they would explain protection was required as a precaution. B would listen to that as she worshipped her boys. After all, it was she who raised the concern.

Zander cracked his knuckles. It was becoming clear that Mack and Ari's cascade of lies was becoming more damaging. Noah was dead. B had been attacked, and Zander didn't want to lie anymore. He wanted to be honest. He wanted to be white, not black, so B could love and trust him with no doubt in her mind. But for now, Zander hoped B would forgive him and love him for who he was.

Zander pushed open the bedroom door, expecting to see B sleeping, only to find an empty bed. Her cases were still there but there was no sign of her. Filled with dread and panic, he ran to the parking lot to find her truck still there. B was gone!

Frozen to the spot, Zander couldn't breathe as he dropped to his knees, clutching his chest.

Fuck, not again!

Mack and Jimmy had stepped outside for a cigarette when they saw him and raced to his side.

"What's happened? Have you been shot? Where's Dragon?" Mack asked.

Zander shook his head. It was all he could manage as he tried to breathe.

"Gone," he muttered.

"Shite! Jimmy, call an ambulance. I think he's having a heart attack and tell Frankie to find Dragon."

"It's one of those panic attack thingies. He's had a couple of them of late."

Zander tried hard to breathe as Mack took his head in his hands. "Look at me, brother. You need to clear your mind and concentrate on your breathing. In and out. Come on. Believe me, I know it's fecking horrible, but you got to breathe so we can find Dragon."

Frightened, Zander mustered all his courage to drag some air into his lungs. Closing his eyes, he tried to cast his mind back to the night B helped him, the instructions she gave and his breathing steadied.

"That's it brother. You're alright. Come on now, keep breathing, it'll pass for sure," Mack said, putting his arm around him.

Zander sat on his backside. "Fuck, this is hellish."

"I know, man. I've been there, but it'll pass. Keep breathing. You'll be alright."

Zander calmed, gathering his bearings. "She's fucking gone!"

"I know. Don't worry if anyone can find her, it's Frankie. He's a born tracker, that one."

Zander tried to stand as Mack grabbed him. "I need to go help find her. I need to make things right."

"You ain't going anywhere yet. Anxiety messes you up. You need to pace yourself in case another one hits you like a freight train. Trust me, VP. I live with that shite daily."

"What if something happens to her?"

"I've just seen Jimmy and Frankie leave with ninety percent of the MC. She hasn't been gone long, so they'll find her. Now let's get you inside. We look like a pair of tools, he said, pulling him to his feet.

"Thanks, Prez!"

"All good, man. Frankie will return her in no time."

CHAPTER SIXTY-ONE

The Easy Way or The Hard Way!

B walked across the grocery store parking lot, her frantic mind in overdrive as she grabbed a shopping cart. She had slipped out of the gym's entrance unnoticed and left for her new home. Her stomach churned as she wandered around in a trance, filling her cart with random items. She was on autopilot. After purchasing a handful of groceries, she placed the small, brown paper bag under her good arm, wincing with pain as she did so.

B'd had enough of bikers today. She wanted to curl up in her cinema room with a cup of tea. She longed to feel settled after spending weeks away, and as she exited the store, she was greeted by a familiar face.

"What are you doing, woman?" Tiny said as he sat perched on his motorcycle, flipping his flick knife between his fingers.

"Not now Tiny. I'm tired, so do me a favor. Refrain from your bullshit and leave me be," she said as she walked past him.

Tiny chuckled. "That sass will land you in trouble, woman. Now get on my bike."

"Piss off! I'm going home. I've had my fill of Gray Wolves tonight."

"In case you haven't noticed, we own you now. You may be little miss money bags, and your name may be on the door, but your ass belongs to us. You're an asset, and we don't allow our assets to stroll around unprotected."

B stopped in her tracks, infuriated. "I belong to no one, asshole."

Tiny stood to approach her, towering over her. "Look, Dragon. We can do this the easy way or the hard way. I have no qualms about throwing you over my shoulder and dragging your ass back to the club. Or you can give me your candy and get on my bike?"

"You can try, asshole."

Tiny chuckled. "Have it your way."

"Wait. Fuck! I can't have my wounds open again. Here," she said, slamming the brown grocery bag into his chest and heading to his motorcycle.

"Excellent decision."

B climbed onto the back of his motorcycle while Tiny stuffed the paper bag into his cut.

"You're taking me to my new home, asshole."

"Absolutely, Dragon."

After punching in the front gate's security code, B instructed Tiny to drop her off at her front door.

Handing her the brown bag, he grinned at her, shaking his head.

"What's so funny, asshole? Don't think you're stepping over my doorstep. I'm good. Now you can fuck off!"

"That's gratitude. Are all women across the pond like you?"

"Piss off," she said as she opened the door.

"You're not going to offer me in for coffee?"

"Nope."

Tiny stepped off his motorcycle to be interrupted by his phone ringing.

"Hey, boss."

B rolled her eyes. *Great, more assholes. Give me a break!*

"Absolutely. Thank you."

B watched the color drain from Tiny's face.

"What's happened?"

Tiny shook his head, covering his mouth with his hand.

"Tiny. Are you alright?"

"Go in and lock the door. Don't open it to anyone other than Mack,

Frankie, or Zander. I need to leave now," he said, turning to his motorcycle.

B grabbed his arm and Tiny grimaced over his shoulder. "What's happened?"

"It's personal."

B circled him, standing between him and his motorcycle.

"I know a scared face when I see one. Now tell me!"

"It's nothing to do with you," he said, attempting to step beyond her.

B palmed his chest. "See, that's the problem with you wolves. You're happy to keep me in the dark, but demand to know all *my* shit. I want to know what happened."

Tiny laughed. "You got balls, Dragon."

"Bigger than yours, sunshine. Now, let me in."

Tiny rolled his eyes. "Fine. It's my mother. She's had a fall. I have to leave to sort things. She's another woman who doesn't take a telling."

"Is she alright?"

Tiny kicked the ground. "I think so. She hasn't been the same since my dad passed and she thinks she can run a ranch singlehanded. She's a pain in my ass, just like you're being now."

"Sorry. I didn't mean to pry. Wait! You refer to your mother as boss?"

Tiny leaned against his bike, chuckling. "No, I was talking to Prez."

"You didn't say you were with me. I thought they had sent you to collect me."

Tiny pulled a joint from his shirt pocket, lighting it with his fancy MC lighter. He took a long drag while B waited for him to answer her. "No, I was escaping just like you. I'd just finished talking to my mother when I saw you walk into the store, I realized you were alone."

"I don't understand. Why didn't you inform Jimmy I had left?"

"Oh, he knows, you have the entire club searching for you."

"Then why not say you have me?"

"Dragon, you're a nightmare and go against everything I'm used to, but even you've had enough shit for one day. I haven't seen you and you were never on my bike, understood? Zander will castrate me if he ever finds out."

B smiled. "Thank you."

"Fuck. A smile and a thank you. Steady on, there, Dragon. You'll make me hard."

"Piss off," she laughed.

"Look, I meant what I said. Go in and lock the door. There's some unease in the air tonight, and while I'm not privy to the information, I know it's not safe for you to be alone. Now get inside."

B nodded, squeezing his arm before stepping through the front door.

Tiny climbed on his motorcycle, waiting for her to close the door.

"You know. I know a place in Uskiville where your mom could be happy. Home away from home. Plot 23B is available if you wanted to convince her to move closer."

"I appreciate that. Now, lock the fucking door."

B laughed and closed the door, applying the deadbolt and setting the alarm system.

B woke the next morning to Frankie cooking breakfast and singing along to the radio. She couldn't resist the smell of bacon wafting into the room. Stumbling into the kitchen, she rubbed her eyes, trying to rid them of the crusty, sandpaper like clusters trying to make her sleep. She'd slept well, just not well enough, as she continued to wake her weary head.

"Morning B. Take a load off," Frankie said to her as he served her up some bacon, pancakes, and a cup of tea.

"Thanks, Frankie," she said, giving him half a smile.

Nudging her face with his fist, he said, "Cheer up. It might never happen."

"It bloody already has," she said as she stuffed half a pancake in her mouth.

"VP told me what happened. You alright? I would fuck him up, but he's doing a damn good job of that himself."

B sipped her tea. "Is he alright? I pushed him too far, Frankie. Made him snap. I'm just sick of all the bullshit, the drama. It's like I'm bloody cursed."

"You're not cursed, B. You have a knack for attracting broken soles, and you get dragged into their shit.

"No kidding."

Frankie sat next to her at the large, wooden dining table. "Listen. VP's a good man, he has a heart full of love for you. Don't let your insecurities fuck this up. You need him and he needs you."

"He doesn't want me, Frankie, and I'm clearly not cut out for anything intimate. Everything is such a bloody mess."

Frankie stole a piece of bacon from her plate, swallowing it whole. "Now see, that's where you're wrong. VP wants you. He's just scared you're gonna get hurt. It's making him all kinds of fucked up over you. So much so, he collapsed having a panic attack last night."

B dropped her fork onto her plate. "What! Is he okay? Is he at the hospital? Shit! Why didn't you wake me?" she said, standing in a panic.

"He's fine. Mackie talked him through it just like you've done a thousand times for him. What is it with these men? They are all so broken and can't function without you."

"That's not it, Frankie. They couldn't give a toss about me. If they did, they'd give me some answers."

"You want answers? I got plenty. Sit your ass down and eat your fucking breakfast. You'll need your strength after what I'm about to tell you."

B sat in her seat, stabbing another pancake, and throwing it down her throat. "Happy? Now tell me what's happening."

"You sure you wan—"

"Come the fuck on, Frankie. Just fucking tell me."

"Alright, alright. Keep your fucking panties on, woman. Right! The reason VP panicked last night is that you confirmed our suspicions about who attacked you and maybe who killed Noah."

B choked down her pancake. "I don't understand. What do you mean?"

"The Pitbull on your attacker's arm was Noah's uncle's old patch. The patch the Sunnyville chapter belonged to before Mackie patched them over. After The Mauler died, Noah took over, and we believed Blaze, Noah's other uncle, was in the wind. Now, after everything with Noah and now you, we're not so sure."

B's forehead creased in confusion. "But why would he come after me?"

"Because you own his family club. I'm guessing he came back and killed Noah to get to the club without realizing you owned it."

"Shit."

Frankie pinched a chunk of pancake from her plate. "Yeah, shit. We believe the attackers came for you B. I don't want to worry you, but we need to get real for a second. You need to stop running off. You need twenty-four seven security until we sort this out."

"For how long? The boys will be back soon. This needs to be sorted out by then. Now where the hell is he living? If he wants me, he can fucking have me armed with the FBI, the son of a bitch."

"Hey, hey, slow your roll. We have no idea where he is, and the FBI? You know how Mackie feels about cops."

"I don't give a shit what Mackie thinks. If there are psychos out there trying to kill me, I'll call Spencer. He's bound to know an agent interested in someone like Blaze."

Frankie pinched his nose. "B, we don't know how deep his pockets are. He could have rats everywhere, so it stays in-house for now."

"And what, I'm just a sitting duck. Fuck no. I'll find him. Choke him out and drag him to the police department myself. I'm no damsel, Frankie, and I'm sick to the back teeth of all this shit. It's like a cascade of lies again." B slammed her cutlery onto her plate, shoving it across the table.

Frankie draped his arm around her. "Listen. We're going to find the bastard, okay? Let us guard you and have your wits about you."

"Great! I'm a bloody prisoner again."

"No, no you're not. You can go where you like. We just want to keep you safe."

"Bullshit!" B said picking up her mug of tea.

"B!"

"I better go back to my cell. Sleep off this nightmare," she said, getting up from her seat to leave the room. Turning on her heels, she kissed his cheek. "Thanks, Frankie. You're the only one I trust right now, I'm grateful to have you in my life."

"Always!" he said, grabbing her hand.

"Thank you for always being honest with me. I'm beginning to think you're the only one I can rely on."

"You're wrong, B. Everyone bloody loves you, they do," Frankie said in his best Welsh accent, making her laugh.

"I love you, too, big guy."

"Rest up. VP will arrive soon, and you need to talk to him. You got that?"

"Yes sir," she teased.

"Yeah, and don't you forget it!"

The sound of muffled voices in the kitchen woke B from another nap a few hours later. She had just sat herself up when Zander entered the room.

"Hey darling. How are you feeling today?" he asked in a low whisper.

"I'm fine. A visit is unnecessary. You made things quite clear last night."

She watched as he slid onto the couch next to her. "Frankie said he told you about Blaze?"

"Yeah! At least someone has the balls to be honest with me!"

Taking her hand, Zander gazed up at her angry eyes. "Please, Welsh cake. I'm sorry. I dinnae know what happened. I was angry and worried I was gonnae lose you. Things got out of hand, and I never wanted to leave you. I fucking love you and dinnae want to lie to you."

B nodded. "I really want to believe that Scottie. I do bu—"

"Welsh Cake. All I could think about is finding the bastard who hurt you and ending him, so he couldn't hurt you any more. I know you want me to stay white, but I can't let anyone hurt you. You're my fucking world."

B was taken back by his words. "Scottie, I pushed you last night because it frightened me, too. Not knowing who to trust anymore is horrible. I stepped off a plane to this crazy shit, and it's like I'm stuck on a merry-go-round, and I can't get off. Shit seems to follow me wherever I go, and I can't stop it."

"I'm sorry, darling. I'll fix this. Trust me and I promise I'll put an end to all this."

B took his hand and wrapped it around her, resting her head on his chest.

They sat in silence for a moment until Zander opened up to her.

"You know, I wasn't always like this, darling. I wasn't always black. I was a decorated war hero until my pal screwed me over. I had nothing, and the club gave me a home and I will always be grateful. I can't change the past, but I can look forward to the future with you. Welsh Cake, I can be the man you need, keep you safe. Worship you. Make you happy."

"Just promise me no more lies, Scottie, I can't take any more."

"No more, darling. I promise," he said, kissing her head and stroking her back.

B glanced up at him. "You drive me crazy, Scottie. I don't trust myself around you."

"Then trust *me*, darling. I'll keep you right. I promise," he said, kissing her lips.

B welcomed his tongue as she sat up to straddle him, only to be disturbed by Mack and Ari walking into the room.

"For feck's sake! I can't keep up with you two. Dragon, put him down so we can watch some stand-up comedy. God knows we need a laugh. Frankie and Jimmy are bringing the beers in, so budge up," Mack said in a playful tone.

B snuggled up to Zander as Mack and Ari looked on with open mouths. B didn't care what they thought. She was in her happy place.

CHAPTER SIXTY-TWO
Sultry Boy

A few weeks passed, and B and Zander had become inseparable, working, and laughing together before B was escorted home by Frankie at the end of the day. B wanted normality back in her life and stayed at home from Monday to Friday. She would stay with Zander on the weekends despite his best efforts to convince her to be with him every night. B insisted on taking baby steps in fear of messing things up again. She needed calm, as much as she enjoyed learning more about Zander. There were countless times she wanted to embrace him and take him home, but fear prohibited it, and B decided Rhys and Madoc should be informed before she made the terrifying commitment to Zander.

Zander continued to charm her morning, noon, and night. Bringing her freshly baked muffins in the morning, working out with her in the gym, driving her to her new coaching role and working his backside off in the office.

B discovered that beneath all the bravado, he was an intelligent man and a whizz with numbers as he fixed her books, removing her requirement to hire another accountant. B knew she was in love with him, and it scared her. She decided she would talk to the boys regarding Zander becoming a permanent fixture in their lives upon their return.

Zander headed out to the bistro where Mack and Ari sat drinking rum cocktails with B and Jimmy. Once his eyes caught sight of B, she took his breath away as she sat in her white vest, cut-off denim shorts, and biker boots.

Her eyes danced as she laughed, running her hand through her hair to remove it from her eyes. Zander wanted her sun-kissed body on top of his, he longed for her touch. He tried to respect her need for baby steps as his love for her consumed him. B intoxicated his mind twenty-four hours a day, seven days a week, in both his waking hours and in his dreams. He couldn't sleep on weekday nights, the torment of being apart was too much for him.

As he approached the table, B glanced up at him. "Hey handsome, let me fix you a drink," she said, rising and kissing his cheek then heading inside to fetch it.

Mack grinned at him. "You two are still good?"

"Aye. I just hate watching her leave in the week."

"Hang in there, VP. I think she's almost there," Frankie said.

"Aye, I hope so, brother," he said as he watched her emerge from the bistro and hand him a drink.

Whispering in his ear, she said to him; "Hey, can we go somewhere quiet to talk later?"

Zander hyperventilated as Frankie, Mack and Ari grinned at him. "Aye. I'd like that."

"Thanks," she said sitting back in her seat.

Zander smiled, unable to contain his excitement. He had been waiting for this moment. Stealing a glance as she drenched her lips in rum became too much for him, as he white knuckled his seat to compose himself. He wanted her.

Desperate for her touch, her kiss, he became lost in his thoughts until the sound of a phone ringing woke him from his daydream.

"My babies. This should be them calling to let me know when they're leaving," she beamed.

Zander gave her a sweet smile as she passed him, holding her phone to take the call. He was happy for her, knowing how much she missed them. She'd told him that week, she couldn't feel at home in Sunnyville until they were home with her, and now she was fit to burst, as they would soon fly home.

Zander followed her with his gaze as she talked happily into her phone. He couldn't take his eyes off her, mesmerized by her beauty, until he saw her dragon eyes emerge. Hanging up the phone, she ran her hand through her hair and launched her glass of rum across the parking lot.

Mack and Frankie rushed to her aid before Zander realized what was happening.

He was about to go to her himself when Ari stopped him in his tracks.

"You better get used to that. Everyone lusting after her, I mean. Oh, when B has an issue, everyone rushes to save her, desperate to be her hero. You know he still calls out to her in his sleep?" she said, downing another shot of rum.

Zander's upper lip curled in disdain. "Ari, has anyone ever told you jealousy isn't a good look for you? Your best friend is hurting, and you're slating her for needing support from her family. It wasn't that long ago you needed support, or have you forgotten that? And as for Mack. Well, that sounds like a you problem. But let me offer you some advice. Don't ever bad mouth the woman I love in front of me again. It won't end well," he said, getting up to see B.

Walking over to her, he could see the fire in her glowering eyes. Her face strained as Mack and Frankie tried to ascertain what was wrong.

"What's happened, Dragon?" Mack asked.

B stood there, her face broken and mute.

Frankie put his arm around her. "Talk to us, B. We can't help if you don't tell us what's wrong."

B pursed her lips, shaking her head and seeming unable to speak. Zander stood close to let her know he was there for her when her desperate eyes locked onto his and she reached out her hand.

Taking her hand, he squeezed it. "Tell me what you need, darling."

Whispering, she said to him. "I need to leave!"

"I got you, darling," he said, leading her to his motorcycle whilst Mack and Frankie stood stunned.

Placing his spare lid on her head, he could see how much she was hurting, and it tore him up inside. He knew he had to help her, save her from whatever was hurting her.

Climbing onto his motorcycle, he started it up, listening as it roared to life.

"Come on, darling. Let's get out of here."

Zander rode like a bat out of hell with B holding on tight until he saw signs for Portland. Turning onto a quiet and dusty road, he sped up to the top of a huge ridge, pulling up near some gigantic trees. After he climbed off his bike, he helped B off and removed her helmet before taking her hand once more, leading her through the tree line. He remained silent as he led her to his hideout, his place to escape, when the world became too much. He hadn't been there since Noah had passed and as he reached his favorite spot, he could see the empty beer bottles he had left behind the last time.

"Here we are. It's quiet here. You can scream, shout, do whatever. I come here when I'm down. It's a beautiful view."

He watched her sit, overlooking the sea of green and blue, still trembling, rubbing her triceps. The shade from the trees made her break out in goosebumps.

"Hey, come here," he said as he sat behind her, coiling himself around her and kissing her neck.

B softened in his arms.

"That's better, isn't it?" he said, breathing into her neck.

B nodded as she turned into his chest, holding him tight.

"They're not coming home for another two weeks. The boys are frantic and homesick and I'm so bloody angry. Frustrated, because I can't do shit about it!"

"Oh, darling. I'm so sorry," he said, stroking her back. He could feel the tension in her rigid body, and he hated it. His temper rose at the thought of her ex still having some control over her, and after everything he'd put her through.

Zander continued to stroke her, feeling her heart rate slowing as she breathed against him. She had almost relaxed when she snapped herself out of it and pulled away.

Running her hands through her hair, she grew frantic again.

"Hey, come on! Come here!"

B shook her head, shaking and trembling: "I'm sorry Scottie, I'm too fucked up now. My body is on fire. I need to release the rage tearing through me, take control. I mean, what if he keeps them? It will finish me."

Zander placed her head in his hands. "I'll no' let that happen, I promise. I will fetch them myself if I have to. But those fiery fucking dragon eyes aren't helping you, darling. They feed on your need to control everything, suck the life out of you and, as much as they're beautiful, I prefer my Welsh Cake. My soft, intelligent, and funny woman, and I'll do whatever it takes to get her back."

B closed her eyes, grabbing her head and gritting her teeth in anguish as her chest pumped in quick succession. "Fuck! I don't have what I need here to fix this!"

"Yes, you do," he said, curling his index finger around her chin, hooking it to meet his gaze. "I know what you need and why you need it. Noah told me it's why you went to the Sultry Slalom. He saw how wired you became before you took your prey and how chilled you were after. Like you'd freed yersel' by going there. I know what you need, and I want you to take it from me. Get your relief, darling. I'll do anything to make you feel better."

B shook her head at him. "I can't do that to you."

"Welsh Cake, please take what you need from me. Let me ease your pain."

"I won't use you, Scottie," she said, struggling.

Zander kissed her neck, whispering his raw words into her ear. "Oh, but you can, and I know you want to. I know you need to."

"But I don't want to hurt you, Scottie. I'll retreat into myself after, and that's not fair to you."

Zander smiled at her. "I'm giving you one free pass, darling. For one afternoon, you get to do whatever you want to me."

B chuckled a little as he kissed her nose. "See, I'm here for the long haul. I know you'll be my old lady one day. I'm just waiting for you to realize that yersel', so please take what you need from me."

Zander was desperate to help her, and even though it would destroy him when she pushed him away after, he wanted to show her he was willing to hurt, so she didn't have to.

"Scottie, I won't do it. You love control as much as I do. You've shown so much restraint. I see it in your eyes every time you take me."

"Then let me command you. Take me here, ride me here, in my happy place. See it as a business transaction. You do what you need to do, here and now, and the next time those fiery dragon embers ignite, I'll show you no mercy and make you mine. Clear?"

"I'll probably fight you off," she said, pained.

"Then I'll tie you up if I have to, darling," he whispered wearing a devilish smile. "See, I need two things, because like you, I'm hurting. I need to silence that fiery dragon inside you. Put her back in her lair so I can be with my beautiful Welsh Cake, and I need to put my mark on you. Make you mine, because I see the way my brothers look at you, undressing you with their eyes. I see Mack, despite being with Ari, still desperate for your love. They need to know that you're off limits. They need to know you're the property of the VP."

"Scottie, you know I'm open to the sex, but I've been caged for long enough. I won't bow to you, sunshine. Besides, how many others did you make yours before me?"

Zander's eyes softened. Shaking his head, he cupped her face with his hand, brushing her cheek with the pad of his thumb. "None, darling. I've never felt this way before. I told you. My heart was an iceberg until you came into my life. Sex was just a release and I know you understand that. I see you struggle with your feelings for me. All I hope is in time, you'll see that I'm all in. Ready for anything. Marriage, beautiful Celt babies, anything. Learn to trust me and let me in. I hate seeing you struggle, darling, so take me now and you return the favor next time. Let me free you from your inner dragon so we can be together. And for the record, you never have to bow to me, but I'll always drop to my knees for you, beautiful."

B glared at him. Face tense, she kissed him, slamming her lips to his.

Straddling him, she ripped his shirt clean open, sending the buttons soaring into the sky. "Oh, fuck!" Zander panicked. His chest pumping, heart rate skyrocketing as she slipped him out of his shirt.

Pushing him onto his back, she raised his arms above his head, binding his wrists with his shirt. He glanced up at her, and she shimmered as the sunlight struck her: the fiery embers glowing in her eyes like fireworks.

Zander became speechless as she kissed his torso, ravaging his skin with her teeth and nails. He had experienced nothing like this before; the intense pleasure and pain he felt as her teeth and lips devoured him. He stood to attention as she ripped open his jeans, licking his long shaft, as if to prepare him for what he was about to endure.

Trembling with uncertainty, his body shook beneath her as she slipped out of her shorts to lower herself onto him, covering his mouth with her lips.

"Jesus Christ, Dragon," he said through gritted teeth, feeling her moist sex as he filled her.

He was desperate to free himself and ride her into the ground, take what was his, but he wouldn't. She would never forgive him. Her actions informed him the deal was done and if he wanted his Welsh Cake, he had to play Dragon's game. Take what she gave him, let her have her way with him until she freed herself from her rage.

Zander struggled as her submissive. He hated losing control to her. It went against every fiber of his being as she dominated him.

Accepting the situation, he fixated on her fiery eyes. Welsh Cake was nowhere to be seen. The alluring stare of the dragon met his gaze now. Frightening and power-crazed, her malevolent demeanor controlled his thoughts as she rode him. She clawed his chest, and his body screamed in desire as she moaned with pleasure. Dragon was high on control as she took what she wanted.

"Fuck." The only word his brain could muster as B increased her pace.

Zander tried to lift his arms to release himself. He couldn't take anymore.

B pinned them, shaking her head, growling at him. "No, good boy. You're mine right now!"

Nodding breathlessly. he lifted his head to kiss her soft lips as B bit his top lip.

"Christ!" he growled, watching her grin as the pressure mounted in his hard shaft, becoming too much for him.

Defenseless and ready to explode, he bent to B's will, his eyes rolling into the back of his head, grateful for the impending release: the tension consumed him as he shifted his hips to thrust, matching her movements, allowing them to become one.

B's hand pinned his once more as she moved in rapid succession, and that's when he felt it. The ebullience as his body yearned for release. Defenseless, raw, and vulnerable, Zander tried to fight it, but he couldn't stop his body from relinquishing control, bending to her every command.

"Come for me Scottie," she demanded, "come for me now." And just like that, he lost control, erupting like a volcano, sending molten shock-waves through him.

"Holy Christ, fuck!" he cried as he battled against her, trying to free his arms to turn her over and drive into her with lusty control.

B grinned a sinister grin as she conquered him, maintaining her tight hold over him, forcing him to release beneath her.

Zander roared again and again, hammering his hips into her as he responded to her commands.

"Yes, Scottie," she cried as he felt her contract around his heavy cock, squeezing the last of his climax out of him.

"Oh, Jesus, Holy Christ! What the fuck have you done to me, woman?" he cried, staring at B lost in jubilation.

Fuck me! She's frightening and beautiful as she rinses me of my climax.

Regaining his composure, he watched as she came to. Softening, allowing for her perfect crystal eyes to sparkle as the fire left them. Exhausted from the stress, she collapsed onto his chest, freeing his wrists as she did so.

Zander released his hands and placed them on her back, his brain still attempting to comprehend his experience.

"Feel better darling?" he asked.

B nodded; eyes closed.

"Well, that was fucking incredible," he joked.

B's voice was full of remorse. "No, Scottie, I used you. I should never have done that. You're the last person I want to use."

"Well, you can use me like that any time. Christ. I was off world for a second there."

B shook her head, the tension in her reverberating through him. Rolling her over, he studied her. "Hey, dinnae dare feel bad about this. You just blew my mind."

B stared back at him, her eyes narrowed and confused. "Scottie, I'm no good for you. You should find someone who deserves you."

Zander pressed his lips together, "Oh darling, when will you get that my big old heart is forever yours?"

B stared at him; her eyes terrified as her heart raced beneath him. "Don't give up on me," she murmured.

Zander's face softened; his breaths uneasy as he stared back at her. Even when terrified, she looked sublime to him.

"Never Welsh Cake. I want you, now and forever," he said as he leaned in to kiss her. Stopping just short of her lips, he wanted confirmation that she wanted to be kissed, waiting for her to encourage him.

B bit her bottom lip like she always did when she was nervous, before raising her head to meet his lips.

The mesmerizing touch of her lips against his filled him with emotion as he accepted her tongue, massaging it with his own.

"You never cease to amaze me, darling. Every time with you is like the first time."

B smiled at him. "Right back at you! And thank you. I don't know what I would have done if you hadn't whisked me away today."

"Darling, I'll always be there to whisk you away, and I dinnae care how long I have to wait to take the next step with you. You're worth waiting for. Now, how about we head back? It's getting cold, and everyone will be worried sick about you."

"Can we cwtch for a while? Please? My head on your chest is my favorite place in the entire world. It calms my soul. Please, just five minutes?"

Zander stopped in his tracks. He couldn't help but grin as he listened to her soft request. "Anything for you, my love. Come here."

Later outside the club. Zander had just dropped B outside the gym as Mack, Frankie and Ari looked on.

"I'm gonnae tell Frankie to take you home for a few days. Clear your head darling, lounge by the pool, and relax. We can handle everything here.

"Scottie, I—"

"It's okay darling, you need this. Promise me you'll do this for me, please?"

B nodded.

"Go grab what you need, and I'll talk to Frankie," he said before kissing her cheek and watching her head inside.

Zander walked the short distance across the parking lot, approaching Mack and Frankie. His ripped shirt unable to cover the marks of his undertaking with B.

"What happened to your shirt?" Mack asked.

"Nothing."

Mack shook his head at him. "You've become a Sultry boy for fuck's sake. She won't have any respect for you after you let her take you in a rage. You stupid prick and to think I was rooting for you VP."

"It's no' like that."

"It fecking is! I've seen that look a thousand times before. You were supposed to be the one who grew old with her. Now we're back to square one. You fucking disappoint me, brother!"

"Pipe down Prez! Maybe it's a good thing she's ravaged him. She'll have a clear head now. Better to ravage the guy she loves than some fucking Sultry boy," Frankie said giving Zande and encouraging punch.

"Look, the boys aren't coming home for another two weeks, and it's fucked her up. She needed someone and I'm glad it was me. Now, I need to do something. I hate seeing her in so much pain. It's fucking heart-breaking," Zander turned to Frankie. "I've suggested she go home for a few days to clear her head; can you take her please, pal?"

"Impossible! We have other problems," Frankie said.

"What now!" Zanders said, running his hand through his thick black mop of hair.

"Tiny's missing!" Jimmy said.

"What? How?"

"I called his mother; a neighbor answered the call. Some cruel bastard gave her the beat down of her life. She's on life support. Tiny's bike is on the drive and he's in the wind. The police have issued a warrant for his arrest."

"No way. Tiny adores his mother. He wouldn't hurt Selina," Zander said.

Jimmy shrugged. "Then where is he?"

"That's what we're trying to ascertain. The tracker in his phone is down. Last ping was near the ranch," Frankie said.

"Fuck! This makes no sense," Zander said, scratching his head.

"He was a lone wolf. My guess is someone's got to him," Frankie said.

"I dinnae like this, Prez. I'm keeping Welsh Cake here, by my side until we know what's happening."

"Negative VP. B's going home to Uskiville. It's BikeFest 3000, this weekend and B has to be there." Frankie said.

"Over my dead fucking body. She stays with me."

"Oh, you're coming VP. The entire club can have a ride out. We're leaving in the morning to make sure security is tight in Uskiville," Frankie said.

"And Welsh Cake knows this?"

Frankie took his sunglasses from his cut pocket, placing them on his head. "Well, no. She was originally going up with Glen on Wednesday. The prospect is keen to learn more about the business. B agreed to take him along," Frankie said.

"And this is the first I'm hearing about it?" Zander snapped.

"She was supposed to talk to you about it later, but you whisked her off to get her sultry on," Mack said.

"Christ! And how are we supposed to flush out our spy at a motorcycle festival? We've tried everything these past few weeks and nothing," Zander said retrieving his cigarettes he left on the table earlier.

Mack tilted his head. "Maybe it was Tiny, and he cracked. His timing for leaving town was impeccable. He could have easily asked Selina to call the club."

Zander narrowed his eyes in disgust. "What? And then beat her within an inch of her life for cover. No chance."

"Pressure can affect a man, VP."

"I di—"

"That's me," B interrupted, her laptop bag in hand.

Zander's stern face turned to meet her gaze.

"What's happened?" B asked with urgency.

"Tiny is missing, darling. A neighbor found his mother beaten, and he's in the wind, leaving his bike behind. We have nothing concrete, but he could be the spy at Sunnyville."

B shook her head. "No. You're wrong."

"Dragon, you can't stand Tiny. What makes you so sure?" Mack asked.

B pursed her lips. "The night I slipped out of the club, Tiny found me. He had just dropped me home when you called him, Jimmy. He was worried about her. There's no way he's the spy. He could have taken me anywhere that night, but he brought me home at my request and insisted I locked myself in until one of you arrived. He even told me to only allow you guys in."

"That son of a bitch. He took you on his bike?" Zander growled.

"He didn't want me to tell you. He said you'd castrate him."

"Oh, I fucking will, darling." Zander lit a cigarette to calm his anger.

"Okay, let's step back a second. If Tiny's not the spy, who is and how do we catch them?" B asked.

Mack snapped. "I don't know, but Dragon, you don't go anywhere without us. We're heading to Uskiville early. Zander and Frankie will take you to pack your things. We ride out at dawn."

CHAPTER SIXTY-THREE
Ride out!

Morning came with the sun blistering down on the busy parking lot. Tyr the roadie hurried around, ensuring each patch understood the plans for the ride out. Glen assisted B in packing her truck full of the pack's extra luggage while Frankie, Jimmy, Mack, and Zander conversed in a quiet corner of the parking lot.

The excitement in the air spread like wildfire. It had been a while since the Sunnyville chapter had a ride out. The Mauler had killed their potential employment-based ride outs and Noah had always been busy in Uskiville to plan something as big as the venture ahead of them. Old ladies were just as excited, bidding farewell to their children left with grandparents and friends.

B and Glen had just placed the last cases of the good stuff into her truck when Mack appeared.

"Hey, kid. Take a hike," Mack said to Glen.

"Sure, thing, sir. I mean Boss. Sorry, Prez,"

Mack raised an eyebrow at B, presenting his usual devilish smile. "Noah always loved a nervous Nelly. Poor sucker ain't going to make the cut."

"Don't be cruel. He's a lovely boy," she said as she perched herself on the back of her truck.

"Exactly. How many lovely, patched members do you know? He needs to toughen the hell up."

"Maybe he likes to use his brain instead of brawn. We could do with more of that around here."

"Maybe you're right," Mack said as he sidled up next to her. "You alright, Dragon? We haven't talked in a while. I miss you."

B rested her head on his shoulder. "Miss you too, Mackie, and to be honest, I'm exhausted."

"Listen, Dragon. We'll put an end to this."

"It's funny. I thought I'd be free, leaving Uskiville, yet I've never felt so trapped. Mackie, you need to promise me the kids will be safe, no matter what. I understand I created a new life in Sunnyville, but the kids are innocent."

Mack wrapped an arm around her shoulder, kissing her temple. "Always, Dragon. I'll die before I let anything happen to them."

"Promise?"

"Hey, promise. Nothing is happening to anyone. We'll end this and you can live the life you want. Just don't forget what I said back in Uskiville."

B nodded and planted a kiss on Mack's cheek. "Thank you."

Mack's cheeks turned scarlet. "What's that for?"

"For becoming the man, I know you are inside, and for helping Zander. That must have been hard for you."

Mack looked away. "You did it for me, Dragon."

"Yes, because you're my best friend."

"And you're mine."

B turned his head to face her. "Mackie, I'm in love with him and I may not be his property, but I belong with Zander."

"Yeah. I know. He worships you too; you know."

"That'll take some getting used to."

"For you and me, both," he sighed.

B scanned the parking lot. "Mackie. Thank you for helping him deal with his shit. Frankie told me what you did, and I see how much it pains you to see us together. Just know, I'll never quit on my best friend."

"This is on me, Dragon. I pushed you too far. Suffocated you."

B shrugged. "It's done now," she said, catching a glimpse of Zander approaching from afar. Turning back to Mack, she placed her head against his. "Say the words and let me go."

A shocked Mack took a moment to steady himself before closing his eyes. "Best friends never quit!"

"You're damn right they don't," she said as she squeezed him tight.

"Everything alright?" Zander asked in a nervous tone.

"Just catching up with my best friend," she said, giving Mack a smile and a wink.

"I'll leave you two love birds to it," Mack said, slapping Zander's back with encouragement.

B watched him leave, releasing an enormous sigh, as Zander wrapped his hands around her waist.

"Anything I need to worry about?"

"Nope. Just clearing the air. I miss him. He may be the biggest pain in the ass, but he's all I've known for years."

"I get that, darling. As long as he knows you're off limits?" Zander said looking over at Mack climbing onto his bike.

"He knows, handsome. Now I better get in my truck."

"Are you sure you dinnae want to ride with me? I'd rather you were safe, holding onto me."

"Safe? I'm in a big steel box, sunshine. Not dicing with death on a two-wheeled death trap."

Zander opened his mouth, teasing her with a shocked expression. "How dare you call my beloved a death trap?"

"I thought I was your beloved?"

"You are, and so is my bike."

"I'm sorry, Boyoh. You know I don't share," she teased, releasing herself from his grasp.

"You dinnae get away that easily, darling," he said, slamming her into his chest and devouring her mouth. "I'm right beside you, the entire way up the road and dinnae take any shit from the prospect, either. Thinking he can get all cozy with you in your truck."

"He's a boy and he's helping me."

"Fair warning. If he looks at you, I'll chop his wee nuts off."

B laughed. "Jeez! Paranoid much?"

"No' paranoid. Protective."

The ride up to Uskiville was uneventful. Mack and Jimmy led the pack with Zander, Frankie, and Tyr, following behind them. B's truck followed, along with the rest of the pack.

B made a pit stop at the local grocery store in Uskiville to purchase her favorite candy, to the distaste of the rest of the bikers.

"Take no notice, darling," Zander said as he attempted to kiss her upon her return from the store.

"I bloody haven't," she clipped, pushing past him to get in her truck.

Climbing in, she sped off, leaving the gob-smacked bikers in the dust.

The retreat was vibrant upon arrival, with Ari and the Uskiville old ladies directing the Sunnyville pack to their rooms for the weekend.

B wasted no time is scooping up baby Alexandra for a snuggle. She had missed her and couldn't believe how much she'd grown.

"That's a beautiful look for you, darling," Zander said, snuggling up to them on her couch.

"I've missed my little friend," B muttered.

"I think she's missed you, too," he said, allowing the baby to place her hand in his.

B smiled, admiring the little girl who sat in her lap.

"Are you alright, darling? That outburst at the store. What was that about?"

"I'm just tired."

"Have you spoken to your laddies?"

B nodded.

"Oh, darling. I know you're desperate to see them, but maybe it's for the best they're not here. It gives us a chance to find the son of a bitch causing all the drama."

"That doesn't stop me missing them, though, Scottie."

"I know, but I want you to open up to me. Run *to* me, not away from me. I'm all in, darling. So please let me into your frantic mind. Let me be there for you."

"Scottie, I'm trying, and I appreciate you. I really do."

Zander kissed her shoulder as she bounced the baby on her knee.

"I'll no' rush you, darling. Take all the time you need. I want to you to trust me beyond everything. Who knows, I may even convince you to let me put one of our own inside you one day."

B gasped, staring at him with wide eyes.

"Oh, Christ. I've done it again, haven't I?" he said, shaking his head, seething with himself.

B set Alexandra into her stroller before returning to face him with a hard stare and pursed lips.

Zander traced his thumb along her chin. "I feel I say and do all the wrong things. I'm just so happy with you. Being with you makes everything seem possible."

B's eyes narrowed. Her brow furrowed as she stared at him.

"Say something, please?"

B took a deep breath. "You need to stop panicking about being with me. I won't break."

"But—"

B cut him off. Her Dragon eyes lurking. "But nothing. I want a future with you and everything that comes with it. I just can't think about the future with potential danger looming. The Red Pitbulls killed Noah. I'm sure of it and now it appears I'm their next target. So, I won't allow myself to get excited about a future I might not have."

Zander scratched his bearded chin.

"You think I cannae protect you?"

"I can protect myself, Scottie. I'm no dams—"

Zander growled. "Cut the hard bitch act for a second. I know you can look after yersel', but I'm asking you if you trust me to protect you?"

B turned away.

Placing his hands on his thighs, he glared at her. "Right, and why is that Welsh Cake? Why can you no' trust me to take care of you and protect you from the evil coming your way?"

"I want to. It's just—"

"I dinnae protect Noah. Is that it?"

B shot up from her seat. "No. Bloody hell. Why would you say something like that?"

"Because you dinnae let me in. Makes sense though. I let our pal die. So, you cannae trust me to look after you. I get it."

"You're wrong."

Zander stood with expressive arms. "Enlighten me then. What weakness do you see in me that makes me incapable?"

B walked into the kitchen, retrieving a bottle of beer from the fridge. Opening it, she took a large gulp before resting her head against the cupboard door.

Zander approached her, his distraught face almost breaking her heart.

"Tell me. Please? I need to know what's holding you back from me."

B brought the beer bottle to her lips. "You want the truth?"

"Aye, of course," he said, leaning into her.

"Because I know now, you're all still lying to me. I could feel it in my gut and then confirmation sucker punched me in the grocery store today. You've all been holding back, pretended like something big ain't happening. You all keep up the big charade. I can't trust you because you know something I don't."

"B."

"True, isn't it? You never call me B. I understand it's Bros before Hoes, but you can't expect me to place my life in your hands when I know something's off."

Zander took her beer, placing it on the counter. "It's no' what you think?"

"And what am I thinking, good boy?" she snapped, glaring at him. "Just tell me something. Why did I find blood under my garage door when I returned to Uskiville last year? And why did the grocery store owner ask me if I had relatives over again? He said he met you for the second time when you bought flowers for me. Told me a big, handsome Scot visited in off season. Came in for some smokes, saying how he'd stayed at the retreat. "

Zander palmed the cupboards either side of her head to look her in the eye. "Darling."

"No," she said, raising her palm to him. "Why was my cabin so familiar to you when you stayed? You knew where I kept my whiskey, my glasses. You knew where the second bathroom was, and nobody showed you. I keep piecing fragments together, and each one is a great big mind fuck. A red flag, a bloody siren, warning me that something's off."

Zander's face became pale.

"Welsh Cake, let me—"

"Right, come on B, the spa is waiting for you honey," Ari interrupted as she entered the room to collect Alexandra. "And you," she said, pointing at Zander. "Mack and Jimmy are waiting for you. Fishing, remember?"

"No' now, Ari," Zander growled.

"Actually, now is good for me. Enjoy your fishing, VP," she hissed, showing him the door.

CHAPTER SIXTY-FOUR

Fishing

"What the fuck's got you all wound up?" Jimmy asked as Zander entered the truck, slamming the door shut in a rage.

"I fucked up!"

"Feck, you two bickering again?" Mack asked.

"Worse. The grocery store owner recognized me from our pit stop there last year. Told Welsh Cake. It's why she was pissed at me. Oh, and great job on the power wash asshole. B found blood under the garage door when she arrived home after you un-alived Uncle Mauler."

"Shite!"

"Yeah, *shite!*"

"She's never mentioned it. I'll go talk to her," Mack said, ready to exit his truck.

"Nah, leave it. She's no' happy, and Ari has taken her to the spa. She knows we've all been lying to her again. Maybe she'll calm by tonight and we can get our heads together and figure out what to tell her without screwing us all."

"I better at least text Frankie and Ari. Give them a heads up," Mack said, picking up his phone from the dash.

"No, she'll know I've told you then. Just leave it. Now tell me she's safe while we do some boring ass fishing."

"She's not in danger here, man. Uskiville's locked down, and I have briefed my wolves."

"Any word on Tiny?" Zander asked.

"Nothing. Tyr is taking it bad, mind. You know how close they are. He's blaming himself, and he's pissed at me for not allowing him to go to Selina's to look for him," Jimmy said.

"Right move. We don't need another lone wolf going AWOL," Zander said lighting up a cigarette.

"If that's what happened," Jimmy said.

"Feck. When are we going to catch a break?" Mack said, hammering the steering wheel.

"I dinnae know, but by Christ it better be soon."

Mack, Jimmy, and Zander sat at the edge of the quiet creek, staring into the abyss after another long hour of their fruitless labor.

The overcast sky loomed like a wave of depression as the Gray Wolves collected themselves.

Zander was the first to crack, tossing his fishing rod into the water.

"Fuck this! I'm done freezing my ass off while I got shit to sort with my woman. What's the fucking point in fishing, anyway?"

"It's relaxing. Great for taking stock and being mindful. So, pick up your fecking rod, sit down and shut the feck up," Mack snapped.

"Mindful. What bullshit are you chatting now? Fucking mindful. I'll show you fucking mindful," he said, dragging the rod from the water and snapping it with his brute strength.

"Oh, crap," Jimmy said, taking another sip of his beer.

"What the feck was that for? You fecking moron. Look, you're pissed, I get it, but there's feck all we can do about it now. I'll come up with some bullshite story to palm her off a little longer. We're close to flushing out the spy. I can feel it!"

"Zander's eyes became wide in a dumfounded stare. "Have you learned anything these past months? Christ, she knows! That lassie has always been one step ahead of us. She's no' thick! She's aware of our lies and you think we're closer to finding the wolf in sheep's clothing? Wake up, you Irish prick! I told you. I'll no' lie anymore. Christ knows I've fucked it with her. We all have. Chance after chance and we still fuck things."

"Alright, Mr. Fecking Know-it-all. What do you suggest we do?"

A small rustling came from the bushes to the rear, distracting Jimmy from witnessing his brothers bickering. Casting a curious eye over his shoulder, he couldn't make out what was emerging.

"Uh, fellas—"

"Why no' come over here and make me?" Zander shouted, oblivious to Jimmy's cautious tone.

"Feck! What an invitation! I'm gonna enjoy this, you Scottish wanker! You and me, now!" Mack sneered, about to lock horns with his Celtic brother.

Jimmy stood to inspect the disturbance. "Hey, fellas, somethi—"

Jimmy slumped to the floor, snapping the two men from their rage.

"Jimmy," Zander called, rushing to his side.

Turning him over, Zander stared at the military grade dart embedded in his neck. "What th—"

Clutching his chest, Zander's eyes widened into a vacant stare before he too succumbed to the fate of the dart.

Mack retrieved his knife in a panic, knees bent in a defensive stance.

"Come on out, you fecking pussy. What, too scared to face us? You have to pick us off. Show me the man who's too fecking weak to face his maker!"

Rustling sounding from around the creek, with men emerging from all nooks and crannies. Dressed in military wear, complete with war paint that highlighted their menacing demeanors, a team of twelve men stood armed to the teeth.

"Who the feck are you, and what are you doing on my land?"

"Your land, pissant? Don't you mean your Dragon's land?" a familiar voice roared as it edged closer.

Pushing his way through his army of men, Blaze emerged from behind the cabin, his buzz cut as sharp as his sadistic stare as he pointed a gun at Mack's head.

"You!" Mack said, ready to pounce.

"Uh-uh-uh," Blaze teased. "Careful Irish, or do you want to watch your entire empire burn?" he said, waving his gun as his men circled Mack like a pack of ravaged beasts.

Mack bared his teeth, his chest heaving as his hand tightened its grip around his blade.

"See, I was thinking an eye for an eye. You killed my brother, so I'd take your Dragon and your empire. Cushy setup, by the way. I'm impressed a meathead like you could pull something off like this. But now. Now I see what you've built and what's for the taking. I'll allow you to watch while I wipe out your family and not before I ruin your wife and force your Dragon to sign everything over to me. I'll maybe force her to become my old lady while I keep you and Zander alive, torturing you while you bear witness to everything I do to the woman you both love."

"You son of a bit—"

"Night, asshole!" Blaze said, slamming the butt of his gun into Mack's head, knocking him unconscious.

Mack dropped to the ground as the men closed their circle around the three incapacitated wolves. Taking the dart gun from his right-arm man, Blaze shot Mack in the back.

"Let's not take any chances. Now load them up," he instructed, before turning to the cabin.

"You can come out now," he shouted, waiting for his guest to emerge.

"You've done well. I'm proud of you! You've earned that VP spot you've always wanted. Now leave the note on the windscreen and let's go home and celebrate."

CHAPTER SIXTY-FIVE

True Blue and the Note

B attempted a nap on the couch after her spa treatment. It had helped ease her tensions a little, but so many questions remained unanswered. Her head spun like a spinning top as the pieces of a gigantic puzzle came together. There were still so many unanswered questions that made B feel sick to her stomach, forcing her to rest and recuperate. She would seek the answers she required when the untrustworthy trio returned from the creek.

B had fallen into a deep sleep when Frankie rushed in, disturbing her with an almighty war cry. Ari followed, hot on his heels, and Bamfa guarded the doorway, armed with an AR-15.

"B!"

B dived off the couch to be confronted by Frankie, who stood with a gaunt expression. His hand gripped a screwed up handwritten note, and Ari stood by, with a tear-stricken face.

"Frankie, open your bloody mouth and talk to me," B commanded.

"We need to talk. You and me. Not her!" he said pointing to Ari.

"W-Wait a sec—" Ari's voice shuddered.

"Can it. Wench! We're all here because of you. I'm in charge now, so fuck off back to your cabin. Bamfa, drag her ass next door and keep her there. Lock her up for all I care. Just get her out of my fucking sight!" he snapped.

B stood motionless as Ari gave her a look of desperation. "I'm sorry, B. Please, do something."

B's jaw hardened. Her teeth ground as the familiar spikey thorns of her stomach acid tore her insides. She had no clue what Frankie was about to tell her, and she had no words for Ari. The damming words she spoke to her in the year previous, screaming in her troubled mind.

I know exactly who you are and what trouble you bring. Let it be said, the day something happens because of you and your actions is the day I will happily go black. I promise you I won't stop until I end the destruction your dirty little cascade of lies has brought upon my family.

B watched Ari leave with Bamfa as Frankie poured two large glasses of whiskey and tossed them on the table along with the screwed-up note.

"I can't shake the feeling that something black is coming, something so dark that it could destroy us."

"That's what you said when you met that wench, and you were right. Fuck! I hoped it was paranoia, jealousy, anger over maybe losing Mackie, but you had to be fucking right, didn't you? Tell me B, does it ever get exhausting being you? You take every asshole into your life, give them love, a home, and what positivity do they bring to your life? Why? Why can't you just be fucking selfish and look after yourself? You have no idea the danger you've put yourself in. The position you've put me in. Fuck, you're family to me now. I have to help you," Frankie said, knocking back his whiskey and launching the glass into the fire.

B jumped. Frankie had always been Mr. Calm. Nothing faltered him.

B retrieved her glass from the table and handed him the bottle.

"Well, there's a conversation starter. Talk, Frankie. I'm fucking exhausted, and it's high time I had the truth. The whole bloody truth, Boyoh."

"You better sit. Maybe I should tie you up first. Restrain you. This is a lot," he said as he cast his eyes around the room for a potential restraint.

"I let you off before, good boy. You try that shit again; I'll break your face. Now I want to know everything."

Frankie told B about the events that started with Ari and Mack, with everything and everyone's involvement leading up to the most recent event.

"And this happened on my fucking property? My fucking house? My kids could have been here," she seethed until reality struck her like lightning. "Oh, my God. Junior tried to tell me, and you all kept that shit from me. Thought you could sweep it under the carpet. Fuck! First my best friend was in love with me, then I got attacked and now I discover the entire cascade of lies shit rained down in my driveway. And nobody thought I should know this before I moved to Sunnyville?"

"B. I'm sorry!"

B paced the room, her arms flailing dramatically. "Fuck sorry! We're way past that! And Noah and the Sunnyville chapter all in cahoots? Fuck, I'm just a mug to you all. None of you have any respect for me. I'm just a fucking cash cow."

Frankie stood, gripping her shoulders. "No. No. God damn it! Look, there's more! B, you need to listen if we're going to survive. You need to take your fucking anger and channel it after what I'm about to tell you. Now, please listen."

B brushed him off, snatching the bottle of whiskey from the table. Shaking her head, she sat on the couch, letting the good stuff wash the back of her throat.

"You ready?" he said, handing her the note.

B's trembling hands picked up the crumpled piece of paper. Her eyes turned into a toxic stare as she read each word.

Dearest Dragon.

You won't know me, but I know all about the mighty Dragon.

My nephew was very fond of you. However, it appears he and the people you hold dear deceived you.

The club you own is my birth right and my family home.

You will return it to my family.

From one businessperson to another, I propose a trade.

My club for your family?

I only want what's mine.

8 p.m. Noah's childhood home. Come alone!

Old Land Farm.

If you tell the cops, everyone dies.

See you real soon.

Blaze

B stared at Frankie; her teeth clamped tight as the anger spread through her like a disease destroying its host.

Frankie couldn't look at her. "There's more!"

B gripped his throat. "More! Fucking more! What more could there be? I have to walk into the lion's den for people I thought loved me. For people I considered family. For God damn people I'd walk through fire for and if that's not bad enough, you're telling me there's more." B slapped her thighs. "Well, let's have it, big man. Let's add to the ever-fucking over-flowing cup of shit that's become my life. God knows I might not have it for long, but let's at least clear your fucking conscience, sunshine," she said, tossing her arms in the air and standing to create distance between them.

There was a moments' silence before Frankie whispered his next sentence.

"I'm a cop!"

B stopped, thinking she had misheard. Her eyes narrowed and head tilted toward him.

"What?"

"I'm FBI, B. Been undercover for years. I arrived in Uskiville tasked with uncovering the truth about my partner's murder. Infiltrating Sunnyville was impossible. I was too close back then and Mackie became the key to the operation. I went to Sunnyville with Mackie last year expecting my cover to be blown. Fortunately, Zander killed the last spy in the ranks who knew I was blue."

B's stunned demeanor rendered her mute as Frankie sat next to her. B stood, moving away from him. The eerie silence lingering between them before Frankie continued to explain.

"I'd been building a case against The Mauler and the original nine for years, long before Mack and Noah ruled. Part of a team working alongside OCGS. Sorry, Organized Crime and Gang Section. You partnering with Sunnyville was my way of uncovering the truth. That was, until Noah was murdered. He was the missing link present at Rocky's murder. Blaze also knows who killed him. I'm sure of it! His brother confided in him. Killing a cop makes an interesting conversation."

B returned to the couch, her face softening into confusion. "Frankie. I don't understand."

"B, I was going to use The Mauler's murder as leverage so Noah would reveal what happened to Rocky. Cut a deal to keep everyone out of prison. That's no longer an option and my superiors want to set an example. I have to deliver results, and you need to attend that meeting and retrieve the information I need to save everyone."

B stared at him in anger as the overflow of truth poured from his tight jaw.

"B they're looking at a lengthy spell. The wench and even Junior could face charges: his future in soccer ruined. B. I've grown to love everyone. I'm torn between justice and love for my family, and I'm running out of time. I know I've lied, but I meant every word. You're like a sister to me. You turned Mackie and a club of one-percenters into potential entrepreneurs. You are white, fucking good, and I'm honored to be a part of your family, but it's all been built on lies and I need your help to save our family and get justice, my friend."

B furrowed her brow, attempting to digest the information. It was too much to take in.

"B, I know I'm asking you to put your life on the line here, but Rocky and I fought in the marines together, went to basic training together. He didn't deserve to die at the hands of a one-percenter, and I can't allow his mother to die not knowing who killed her son."

B walked to the front door and opened it.

"B. Please! I know you hate me. Betrayal is never easy, but pl—"

"Lead the way, sunshine. You can explain the plan on the way," she interrupted in a slight whisper.

Frankie stood to confront her. "You're going to do this?"

"You were honest to me, big guy. I just want the people I love to be real with me. Yes, you lied to me for fucking years, but for good bloody reason. You're white, Frankie. I've always known it. It's why I've never doubted your trust, and if I'm going to put my life at risk, I'd rather it was for something decent and not for a cascade of fucking lies."

Frankie embraced her, squeezing her tight. "I fucking love you, sis. Thank you."

"I love you too, big guy, and I don't know what you being a cop means for us. For now, let's concentrate on putting this shit to bed."

CHAPTER SIXTY-SIX
Trapped

Zander woke to Mack's gut-wrenching cries. The painful screams pierced his ears as he wailed in agony. Bound to a wooden pillar and wearing a black head cover, Jimmy was just within Zander's line of sight, tied to an opposing pillar, bloodied and beaten.

Mack hung about five feet away from a familiar meat hook, beaten, mauled, and shirtless. The torn, burned flesh across his chest reeked in the atmosphere as it attempted to overpower the smell of stale horse manure.

Casting his gaze around, he established they were in a barn some-where. The pungent air suggested they were somewhere resolute where fields were in abundance.

Fucking think. Zander. How long have you been out? Look at your surroundings. Where the fuck are you?

"Zand," Jimmy mumbled.

"Jimmy. Where are we, pal? You alright?"

"Fucking Blaze, man," he coughed. "Broke my fucking ribs. They're taking a break. You're up next."

"Dinnae worry, pal. That wee bastard's gonnae die."

"Oh, look who's awake," Blaze interrupted, entering the barn.

Zander turned as Blaze approached.

"Now we want to make you look special for your old lady's arrival, don't we? Oh wait! You haven't claimed her yet," he sneered. "Don't worry. I'm going to claim her repeatedly when I get my hands on her, and you can watch as punishment for shooting me, you fucking dirtbag."

Zander raged. "You fucking touch a hair on—"

Crack!

Zander's nose was busted right open. The cracking sound accompanied by the eye-watering pain and loss of blood reinforcing the potency of Blaze's fist.

"You'll what?" Blaze sneered.

"I'm the real Prez, boy! Learn your fucking place. Now, Irish here. Well, he'll never learn. All that brawn has prevented what little brain cells he had from learning his lesson," Blaze said, gripping the jaw of a barely conscious Mack.

"You bastard! I'll kill you!" Zander spat. Blood spatters from his mouth, decorating the hay-ridden barn.

"Oh, come now, Scottie. That's what she calls you, right?" he teased. "You know the end game here. An eye for an eye and then some. That's the price for crossing a Red Pitbull. Now help a brother out. Would your Dragon prefer to be beaten, then fucked, or fucked, then beaten? I want to make a good impression on my new old lady."

Zander foamed at the mouth. He roared, pulling at his shackles to break free, the cast-iron clasps cutting into his wrists as he pulled against them. "I'll kill you!"

Blaze danced toward him in a shadow-box-like dance before delivering blows to his ribs and kidneys. "Oh, I'm so fucking pumped," he said, making his way to an old picnic bench to inhale a line of cocaine. "Ah, fuck yeah!" he cheered before swiping a bottle of cheap whiskey from the table.

"Whiskey?" he offered. "Come on. I'm celebrating! You fuckers are going to watch as I take back my club and ruin the Gray Wolves. Oh, oh, and I have a surprise for you. Boys, bring in their gift," he ordered.

Three skinny spies entered the room, dragging in a bound and beaten Tiny, dumping him before them. He appeared gaunt, weak, and devastated to Zander. So unrecognizable. Fear filled his eyes as he laid before him. Old injuries masked his face as he attempted to speak to his VP.

"VP."

"Dinnae worry, brother. We'll get you out of here."

"The spy—" Tiny said.

"Oh, no you don't. I get to reveal that surprise!" Blaze said, kicking him unconscious.

CHAPTER SIXTY-SEVEN
Little Spy

Frankie pulled up a half a mile from the farm.

"Are we clear on our aim?"

B tied her hair back in a high ponytail. "Frankie. I'm not a bloody idiot. We've been over this a million times."

"And we'll do it again until we're clear. There's no room for error, B. We have one shot."

B threw her hands in the air. "I hear you. Now. Come the fuck on."

"B, promise me you'll show conviction. Everyone has to believe you. Even you have to believe yourself."

"Alright. I get it. Now start the truck. You're making me nervous."

"You should be nervous. It's our lives on the line," Frankie said as he drove down the winding road and pulled up outside the poorly lit farmhouse.

To their right stood a dilapidated-looking barn, with the starry night allowing the barn lighting to shine like a beacon through the holes in the rotten timber.

B and Frankie exited her truck and walked along the gravelly path to the barn. The eeriness made B's neck hair stand tall as she cradled a bottle of good stuff and briefcase, handcuffed to her wrist.

They arrived at the big barn doors just as a familiar face emerged.

"What the fuck?" Frankie growled.

Glen, the prospect, stood to greet them with a familiar, sadistic grin, pointing a gun at them.

"You should see the look on your faces. Your brothers were the same. Poor little prospect's been screwing you all from the inside out. You were so busy looking for the big boys, you didn't see how much I was infiltrating, spinning my webs, casting the shadow of doubt. The pack spilled their guts in that bar every fucking night and you didn't see it coming. My dad, Blaze. He was right. Like you, Dragon. Noah had a soft spot for rescuing people. And what's more depressing than a homeless guy begging for food and shelter? Stupid prick didn't even see his death co-—"

B punched him in the face, splitting his eye wide open. "Shut the fuck up and take me to the organ grinder. I'm not interested in the monkey! And the next time you point a gun in my face, I'll make you choke on it. If you've been listening, little spy, you'll know I despise the damn fucking things!"

"Good start!" Frankie said with amusement.

"You bitch! My dad will have your tongue for that!" Glen cried, cradling his face.

"I doubt that, sunshine. Now lead the bloody way. Time is money to me."

Glen clambered to his feet; his gun clenched in his scrawny hand.

"W-Wait! I need to search you, asshole," he said, waving his gun at Frankie and struggling to see out of his bloodied eye.

Frankie raised his arms in the air, smirking as Glen attempted to search him. "Want me to hold your gun while you frisk me, prospect?"

"Shut up! Right, you're clean. Let's go!"

B stepped forward, making Glen step off. "You not going to frisk me, sunshine?" she asked with humor in her voice.

"Oh, I know you'd never pick up a gun. You think I don't see you trembling in fear of this?" he said, waving the gun around.

"Yet you're still stupid enough to point it at me. Silly boy!" she teased.

"Shut the fuck up. I know you're mocking me. I'll—"

"Show them in, boy. You're fucking embarrassing me," Blaze shouted from inside the barn.

Glen pushed Frankie toward the door. "Move."

B's eyes darted around the putrid barn. Up ahead, Mack hung from a meat hook, conscious but beaten and mauled. Jimmy and Zander had an onslaught of their own wounds. Their faces split and swollen as blood pooled on the floor beneath their beaten bodies, bound to barn pillars. Tiny was bound to a hook on the barn wall, kneeling as if he was begging for mercy. His condition appearing to be almost as bad as Mack's. Only most of his wounds were older. The purple-colored bruising and dried blood on his shirt confirming his prior beat down. His bloodied nose was the only indication of today's beating.

There were no guards or spies accompanying Blaze in the barn. A true display of his arrogance regarding the situation.

"Welsh Cake, No! Frankie, get her out of here," Zander cried as the others looked on with panic-stricken faces.

B's jaw tightened into a grimace. Ignoring Zander as her heart palpated, trying everything to contain the rage ripping through her body. The quiet simmer of bitterness and vexation was present with every step she took.

"I said come alone," Blaze said, wiping his bloody hands on an old car rag and tossing it on the hay-ridden floor.

"I couldn't give a fuck what you said, good boy. Now you've had your five minutes of fun, now let's sort this. My patience is wearing thin."

"Ooh! I see why you like her, boys. She's got spunk, but let's calm the dramatics sweetheart. You ain't convincing anyone with that good girl gone bad shit."

"Oh. Blaze, Blaze, Blaze. You really don't understand what's going on here, do you, handsome?" she sneered, stepping closer to the sadistic Prez.

"Oh, I understand you'll do anything for these traitorous mother fuckers and you're gonna give me everything I want if you want them back alive."

B laughed. Placing the briefcase on the picnic bench, she freed herself from the handcuff before twisting the cap off her whiskey bottle. Her eyes not deviating from Blaze as she took a big gulp.

"Like I said. You don't see the bigger picture," she said, placing the whiskey bottle down and picking up a stray rusty nail from the table. Twirling it in her fingers, she walked along the opposite side of the bench to Blaze to approach Mack.

"Dragon," Mack muttered.

B turned to Blaze. "Now, this asshole has almost served his purpose.

So, torturing him doesn't get a rise out of me," she said, driving the rusty nail into his left biceps muscle.

Mack screamed as Blaze's eyes widened into a curious grin.

"This one," B said kicking Jimmy's shoe. "He's still plenty useful. And this one. Oh, my sweet, gullible Scottie. Well. When you killed my source in Sunnyville. My friend. Your own flesh and blood. I had to get creative with the handsome Scot. Sleeping my way in with the broken but tough damsel act. He bought it. Of course, he did. I kept him entertained and allowed him to fill me enough, knowing he could convince Jimmy to do anything," she said, running her hand down Zander's chest, giving him a wink, watching him crumble.

"You won't mind if I kill them, then?" Blaze taunted.

"In good time, but not until they've served their higher purpose."

"I'm intrigued, Dragon. Here, I thought you'd storm in like a hard bitch and fight for them."

"I fight for myself, good boy. Now keep up. This one. Well, he's special," she said, strutting toward Frankie, standing with his back to the wall. "But you should know all this, right? Mr. Eyes and Ears Everywhere."

Blaze tilted his head, tracking her movements as she traced her palm along Frankie's neckline. Her torso pressed up against his side as she reeled him in to kiss him. Caressing his back and obscuring the view of her enemy, B reached into her waist band, retrieving a small handgun while exploring Frankie's mouth with her tongue, placing the gun under his cut.

"Welsh Cake. No! Frankie, I'll fucking kill you," Zander snapped, jerking from his pillar.

"Oh, this is interesting. Tell me more," Blaze said, rubbing his hands together.

Frankie smiled, winking at B as she released him, turning her attention back to Blaze. "You see, good boy. Nothing is what it seems. Now I understand you have no clue regarding my true identity or intensions regarding Sunnyville. If you did, you wouldn't have been stupid enough to piss me off. So let me enlighten you," she said. Opening the briefcase to reveal one million dollars, in bound fifty-dollar bills.

Blaze's eyes bulged. The banknotes, creating a sparkle in his eye. "What is this?"

"This is the real reason I moved to the States. Cold, hard, beautiful bloody cash!"

"What do you mean?"

"Oh. Blaze. You didn't believe a soccer mom could afford all I have on a coach's salary? Oh, this is priceless!"

Blaze stepped forward. "Don't mock me, bitch, or I'll slit that pretty throat of yours and take your cash."

"Ah, but you won't. See your men who lurked in the darkness outside. They're all dead. Go on, try calling them. They won't answer," she said, giving him a hard stare. The fire burned in her soul as she stepped into her power.

Blaze stared her down before reaching for his phone. Dialing a number, he grimaced as it rang out. "Go find them, boy," he commanded.

"Oh, I wouldn't do that, prospect," she said, stopping Glen in his tracks. "I have a shoot to kill order on anyone emerging from this barn without me giving the okay. Try if you like. You'll only do it once, mind."

"What the fuck is this?" Blaze hissed, his red face like dynamite as B watched his control slip away.

"There's no fun in losing, is there, Boyoh? Now how about you sit your ass down and I'll explain what I want from you. Here, try some good stuff. God knows what that cheap shit you've been drinking tastes like," she said, handing him the bottle.

Blaze snatched the bottle and guzzled the amber firewater, unable to take his eyes off her.

B smiled. "My name is Blethen Arianwen Jones. I'm the illegitimate daughter of the late De Santo Calegari. You may have heard of him? The arms dealer, drug baron and nasty son of a bitch from across the border."

Blaze choked on his whiskey.

"Weren't expecting that, were you, asshole? See, my mother fled to Wales to give birth to me, but daddy dear found me. Paid for a private education, priming me from afar to step into the family business one day. I started small in the UK, laundering his drug money through my many gyms, and all while playing the sweet an innocent soccer mom. Now my father wanted Sunnyville. It's a prime location for drugs and money laundering, but your brother fucked that up while Daddy was alive. So, when I stumbled across a former Red Pitbull in my pool in Uskiville, I thought I'd won the lottery."

Blaze looked confused.

"Stay with me, Boyoh. I learnt everything I could about the Red

Pitbulls from Mackie-boy and kept my eyes on the prize. I mean, he did me a favor ending your brother, making Noah the obvious business partner. See, Noah shared my vision. Make Sunnyville a reformed and vibrant, profitable business as a front for drugs and money laundering. But you, ya prick, had to create chaos in my calm. And every time I move forward, you keep getting in my way like a bloody disease."

Blaze rubbed his chin. "That's why he signed my club over to you?"

"Bingo! You catch on quick! Tell me. Is that why you shot him in the back?"

"He was a traitor!"

"Not to me, asshole. Now, how did Noah not know the prospect?" she asked, doing her best to compose herself.

"Like you, his mother kept him away. I didn't know he existed until he showed up at my door last year."

"Poor fucking kid!"

Blaze rose to his feet, slamming his hands down onto the table. "You're testing *my* patience now, bitch."

"Alright. Keep your pants on. The point is. I need those pricks a little longer and you to stay away from Sunnyville long enough for me to convince the town and anyone else it's legit. My operation needs to succeed here. You do that for me, and I leave this cash as a gift. Maybe even build an empire here on your farm. We work together and once I'm established, you can have your pound of flesh and take over the Sunnyville business."

"And if I say no?"

"Then you die tonight in this barn!" she said with conviction in her voice.

"And how do I know you're not bluffing?"

B gestured to the rickety barn doors. "Step outside and find out. I think you'll find my word is my bond."

Blaze swallowed hard. "What do you have in mind?"

"Well, for starters, I want answers. I know you killed Noah, but I want to know who killed my brother's friend. Blaze, I know you have that information, and I want it. I also want the prospect. He comes with me. You killed Noah. I want your boy."

"B!" Frankie snapped.

B gave Frankie a hard stare. "Shut it! Good boy! I'm working!"

"Noah was killed because he was a traitor. Glen was acting on my orders," Blaze said.

"Yes, and now he's a traitor to me. He'll serve his time under me until I get bored with him."

Blaze turned to Glen. "What else?"

"Dad. You can't!" Glen shouted.

"Shut it, boy. You're an embarrassment. Did you really think I'd make you a VP? Look at you. You're nothing, and you'll do as you're told."

Glen cowered in the corner as Blaze turned his attention back to B. "What information?"

"My brother's friend, Rocky Rodriguez, was murdered in Sunnyville a good few years back. Now, I know most of the details. I know your brother mauled him. I know someone stabbed him in the heart and I'm asking who delivered that fatal blow? A stab to the heart is personal. That was never The Mauler's MO. I want the name of the asshole who killed him. His mother needs closure."

Blaze scratched his head. "Rocky? He was a stinking cop. Deserved everything he got."

"Do you have any idea how many cops, lawyers, and fucking congressmen I have on my books, sunshine? I don't give a shit who he was. I want information. Closure. We need to build trust here, asshole. You need to give me something if you want what I'm offering."

"You won't find him. He's a ghost! He finds you!"

"Name."

Blaze bit his tongue. "Jericho Walters. He was my brother's Sergeant of Arms. He discovered Rocky was a cop, and my brother went berserk. The Mauler dragged him up onto a meat hook and mauled him. Then he demanded Noah finish him."

B's eyes narrowed in concentration, not wanting to miss a beat. "Go on."

"Noah couldn't do it. That's when my brother knew he wasn't cut out for the claw. Jericho stepped up to the plate. Rocky had details on the multiple murders Jericho had committed in Sunnyville. Jericho thought Rocky was a friend. Took his time with his betrayal, slicing off his tattoos to add to his collection of victims on his cut. The stinking cop begged for death in the end, and Jericho plunged the knife through his heart."

"What happened to him?"

"We dumped his body at the local PD."

B rolled her eyes. "Not Rocky, asshole. Jericho."

"Oh, he was getting a bit too big for his boots. Clashed with my brother. Went NOMAD about six months later. Not seen him since. I get a call now and then, that's it."

"If you're lying, and this intel turns out to be shit. I promise, you'll die a horrible death."

"Why would I lie?"

"Because you're a Pitbull, asshole. A sadistic fucking prick missing a few brain cells."

Blaze back-handed B across the face, splitting her lip, sending her back a few paces and throwing concern to the captured wolves.

"I warned you, bitch. I'm not one of your Sultry boys. I don't take orders from women. Did you think I'd buy all that shit?" he sneered. "I know a liar when I see one. You're a cop and if I'm going down. I'm taking you with me."

B wiped the blood on the back of her hand as Frankie stepped forward.

"I don't think so, jerkoff!" Glen said, pointing the gun at him. "Go ahead, Dad, I got him," he said to Blaze.

Blaze turned his attention back to B. "Now, you may have taken my men, but I have a room full of leverage to get myself outta here, bitch."

B grinned into a devilish smile. "It's funny you think you have me, asshole. No man will ever have me."

"Challenge accepted," he said as he lunged toward her, gripping her by her throat and throwing her onto her back.

The captured wolves screamed and rattled their hooks, fearing for B as she landed on the cold floor, knocking the wind out of her. Blaze was bigger than Mackie. His strength was more obvious as he tried to move her kicking legs to get to her.

"I'm going to enjoy this," he breathed, attempting to grab her leg.

"Fuck you!" B said, kicking him in the face, watching a stray tooth fly as the blood spatter followed.

"Bitch!" he said, taking a moment to compose himself while B jumped to her feet.

"Watch him, B. He's a slippery cunt," Frankie said. More grunting and frantic movement as Jimmy, Zander, Tiny, and Mack failed in their attempts to free themselves from their shackles.

Blaze circled her, fist raised and, his evil eyes fixating on her as if she was his prey. "I'm gonna torture the fuck out of you and you're gonna beg for death and not before you give me my club back."

"When you're big enough, asshole."

Blaze lunged again, this time at B's waist. His rough hands were like sandpaper as he gripped her in a bear hug, swinging her around while trapping her body in a vise.

B couldn't breathe, her insides suffocating as she flipped her head back to headbutt him, only Blaze didn't flinch. B became desperate, her ribs struggling to cope with the crushing pressure against them as she used the picnic bench to kick off, sending them both crashing into the wall.

Blaze released his grip in a moment of weakness, the collision with the wall just enough for B to break free and pick up the half full whiskey bottle. Collecting himself, Blaze ran at her growling in anger and B swung the open bottle, striking him in the face. The glass shattered as Blaze dropped to the floor. Conscious but delirious, he attempted to crawl away as Glen watched in horror.

B released her grip on the neck of the whiskey bottle, smashing it into the ground.

This ends now!

"Dad. Get up!" Glen despaired as B approached Blaze.

Threading her arm around his throat, B climbed onto his back, locking him into a choke hold. Locking her legs around his big gut, she rolled him onto his back, keeping him clinched in a rear-naked choke.

Blaze tried to grab at her hair, headbutt her and gouge at her. His now frivolous and feeble attempt to escape obvious to the wide-eyed onlookers. She squeezed tighter and tighter, her chest pressed firmly into his back, her limbs locked in place. Blaze would breathe his last breath tonight.

The turmoil of the cascade of lies overwhelmed her conscience. There was no black and white here, just death and destruction. Blaze would pay for what he did to her loved ones. To Noah, to anyone he ever hurt. B was black now; her family had sealed her fate, and she'd deal with the consequences later.

The world will be better off without you, asshole.

Justifying her actions in her head, B's eyes escalated into darkness. No fiery embers ignited them now as she felt Blaze go limp in her arms. Taking a breath, she tossed him onto the floor like used garbage and stood as everyone watched in horror.

"You fucking killed him," Glen said, scrambling to his father.

Frankie hurried over to check his pulse, glaring up at B. "He's still breathing. But not for long," he said, retrieving the small handgun and filling Blaze's chest with bullets.

"No!" Glen cried, firing his gun at Frankie.

B dived in front of her best friend in a frantic sprint as two bullets struck her chest, with Frankie, sending a shot to Glen's head.

The room fell silent as Glen dropped to the ground and Frankie turned B.

"B, shit. You stupid— why?" he said as blood seeped from her mouth.

Shrieks and cries filled the room with Zander and Mack, lashing out for freedom as Frankie started chest compressions. Tiny and Jimmy sat on their knees in tears. Their Dragon had fallen.

The barn doors burst open with a team of agents sweeping through like something in a movie scene.

"I need a fucking medic. Now!" Frankie said, picking her up as a team of paramedics on standby surged toward them with a trolley and the four shackled men could only watch as the paramedics rushed B away.

CHAPTER SIXTY-EIGHT
Clear!

The paramedics rushed B into an ambulance with Frankie by her side. Her heart had stopped, and the paramedics ripped open her shirt to discover two bullet holes lodged in her bulletproof vest.

They quickly removed it as they gave B a shot of adrenaline. The impact of the bullets proved enough to stop her heart, and force blood from the lining of her chest as the medics began to resuscitate her.

"Clear!" the paramedic shouted as he shocked B with the defibrillator. Her lifeless body jolted into an unfavorable jerk as her body failed to respond to the current attempting to revive her.

"Again," he snapped.

"Come on, B. Don't you dare fucking do this to me," Frankie said, biting down on his fist.

"Clear."

"Nothing," the paramedic said, charging the paddles to bring her back.

"Come on, lady. Come back to us," the paramedic said, taking a deep breath. "Clear."

B's body sprang into life as she coughed and spluttered blood from her throat.

"Welcome back!" cheered the paramedic as B panicked, dragging in a breath. Her eyes searching until she found Frankie.

"Don't you ever fucking do that to me again. You hear me?" Frankie shouted in fear, grabbing her hand. "Fucking hell, B. Way to torture your family, eh!"

"Frankie, what happened?" B murmured, still weak from her ordeal.

"Glen shot his father in a jealous rage before turning the gun on you. I put one between his eyes after he shot you. Remember?"

B glared at him. Her senses returning to her as Frankie nodded. B understood what needed to be done. He was saving her like she had saved him. "Are you—"

"Fine. All good. Now rest. You've had enough excitement for one day."

The paramedics took B to the local hospital where a cardiovascular consultant checked her over. Her heartbeat returned to normal and after a chest x-ray and some further tests, the hospital discharged her.

Frankie debriefed her on the way home, taking a statement and arranging for her truck to be returned to her.

Parking on B's driveway, Frankie switched off the engine and leaned into her. "You gonna be okay?"

B nodded. "I'm always okay, sunshine."

"For real?"

"I killed him, didn't I?" she murmured, staring at her hands.

"No! I did!"

"Frankie, I felt his life leave him."

Frankie took her head in his hands. "Look at me! You didn't kill him and as far as anyone else is concerned, neither did I. Glen did, okay? Now get that shit out of your head," he said as he pulled her into his embrace. "I love you B. I will always be there for you. Never forget that."

B nodded, pulling away. "What now? I mean, you're a cop. Not that it bothers me, but you have a life. Shit, I don't even know your real name."

Frankie chuckled. "B, my name *is* Frankie. Call it a double bluff. Look, everything I told you was the truth. I'm not good at lying either."

"Risky, good boy. You could have been discovered."

"I fucking wasn't, though," he laughed.

"So, do you have a real family?"

"Yeah, I do. You're sitting right fucking next to me and don't you forget it. Look, I need to end this, and I don't care that Mack and the rest of the pack will want me dead. Just understand I want to return home once I nail Jericho. I've loved every minute of being part of your family and I'm done being a cop after this. Just promise me one thing?"

"Shoot."

"Never try to kiss me again. That shit was weird."

B chuckled, coughing as her bruised chest struggled. "I know, but how else could I have planted that gun? I did my bloody best there, big guy."

"You did great! It's just a bit weird being kissed by someone you see as a sister."

"It was bloody gross. Let's just erase that from our minds, yeah?"

"Fine by me," he joked, opening her door.

"Frankie. When will I see you again?"

"Soon."

B wrapped her arms around him, hugging him tight. "Promise me you'll come home for Christmas."

"B."

"Promise me, big guy."

Frankie nodded, slipping out of his cut and draping it over her shoulders. "Here, I think I've lost the right to wear that now."

"I'll keep it for you."

"B, I don't see the club letting me wear it again, somehow."

"Fuck the club and fuck Mack. It's why we're in this mess. They can all go fuck themselves," B said, her temper rising like the midday sun.

"They're your family and they love you, B."

"No, they're liars."

"What are you going to do? You made a deal to keep them out of jail. The minute you agreed to step into that barn, their crimes were absolved. So, what are you going to do when I release them later?"

"Tell them all to fuck off! I'm done, Frankie."

Frankie tugged on his cut, zipping it up to her chin. "B, VP worships you, and I know Mack loves you more than life itself. You can still make this work. The slate's wiped clean."

"Is it? Look what I had to do tonight. I almost died, Frankie, because of their lies. There's no coming back from that."

"Listen, go up on the ridge, clear your head. Please, take some time to collect yourself. I know you love VP. You can get past this. Have a future together."

"I just want to be alone, Frankie. I can't think further than the ridge and a bottle of good stuff."

"Well, go on then. Don't let me stop you. I'll give you some time before releasing them. Now come here, he said, hugging her.

"I'll see you real soon, okay?"

B nodded. "Yeah," she said, getting out of the car.

She walked around to his window. "Christmas," she demanded.

"Christmas." He smiled, leaving the driveway.

Ari raced to B's side after seeing the car on the drive.

"B, what happened? Where's Mack?"

"Fuck off, good girl, before I end you!" B snapped, leaving Ari in her drive.

Jimmy, Tiny, Mack, and Zander were treated for their wounds and taken into custody. They received no information regarding B as law enforcement processed them.

Arriving back at the station, Frankie grabbed a coffee from the machine and walked into the office, receiving a standing ovation from his team.

A little embarrassed, he raised his cup in acknowledgement before being greeted by his superior officer.

"How's B?"

"She'll live."

The superior officer placed an arm around Frankie's shoulder. "I know you've grown fond of her, but remember where you belong, son. I'm proud of you. We've got every officer in the department looking for Jericho. We'll find him."

"Thank you, sir. Have they said anything?"

"No. They'll only talk to you. Their only concern is whether B's alive."

"Did you tell them?"

"Nah, I figured they could stew for a while."

Frankie nodded. "Good. I'm gonna start with the Scot and go from there. He may know something about Jericho," he said, before heading down the corridor to the interrogation rooms.

"You want a wingman?"

"No, thanks. I need to do this."

"Come find me when you're ready. We'll debrief," the officer shouted.

Frankie walked the short distance to interview room two, where Zander was being held. He sat cuffed to the table with a gaunt expression on his face. His knee tapped back and forth as his weary hands cradled his head.

"Here," Frankie said, placing his coffee on the table.

"Where is she?" he grimaced. His eyes were red and wired.

"Safe. She's alive, VP."

Zander inhaled the stale air, fighting back the tears. "How bad is it?"

"She was wearing my vest. The bullets stopped her heart, but the paramedics brought her around. Nothing but betrayal and bruising now. She's probably half a bottle in up on that ridge,"

"And you? You're a cop?"

Frankie nodded. "Yeah, and if you want to keep B safe, you need to give me some answers,"

Zander glared at him.

"I need a statement explaining your account since your abduction, right until Glen shot his father in a jealous rage, before turning the gun on B. You witnessed me putting a bullet between his eyes to save her,"

Zander gave Frankie a crisp nod while Frankie continued.

"B agreed to put her life at risk in a deal, exonerating you all, including past crimes and The Mauler's murder, but I need to know if you know anything about Jericho Walters. You heard Blaze in the barn. I need to find him,"

Zander gestured to Frankie to uncuff him so he could sip his coffee. "I tell you what I know. You let me go. Deal?"

Frankie removed the handcuffs. "Sure. It's all I need,"

"I replaced Jericho. Had his old room. I didn't meet him. He left a few weeks prior to my arrival. Sick puppy, that one. Noah told me he would cut off bits of his victims' skin, tattoos even, and attach them to his cut. Embalm them or something,"

The thought made Frankie feel sick. Rocky's marine tattoos had been removed in the same manner. "You said you had his room. Anything in there that might lead to his location?"

Zander gulped his coffee. "Nah. That place was a bit too theatrical and to be honest, too girlie for me. Art, flower power, and craft, everywhere. I tossed everything in the trash. Wait. There was a postcard from a sister in Tennessee. Tammy, I think. That's all I got."

Frankie nodded. "Thank you. I'll draw up the paperwork for your release," he said, getting up to leave.

"That's it? You're just gonnae leave her? She trusted you."

"And she still does. Keep her safe, VP."

"And all that talk about her being the illegitimate daughter of De Santo Calegari and you and her together?" Zander asked in a concerned tone.

"There is no De Santo Calegari. Blaze knew that. It's why he attacked her, and B's my sister asshole. She kissed me to plant a gun in my waistband."

Zander nodded with a sigh of relief. "You know Mack will want you dead for this betrayal."

"I'm the least of Mackie's problems. Good luck, VP. You're gonna need it," he said, leaving the room.

That's one down!

Frankie interviewed both Jimmy and Tiny with no further knowledge emerging regarding Jericho. He informed Tiny of his mother's safety and informed him that he was no longer a suspect. Following their statements, they too were processed for release, yet they showed no gratitude to Frankie. He was dead to them following his betrayal.

Mack was the final wolf to be interviewed. Armed with another coffee and his paperwork, Frankie entered the interview room.

"Here he is. The fecking pig!" Mack spat. "Where's my fecking Dragon?"

"Safe, alive, and back in Uskiville," Frankie said, placing his coffee and paperwork onto the table.

"You're a fecking traitor. I'm surprised she didn't kill you like she ki—"

"Listen, you piece of shit," Frankie clipped, gripping him by his cut. "The only reason you're breathing is because you're of use to me. Now you're going to shut the fuck up and write a statement explaining how Glen shot B after turning the gun on Blaze. Just like it happened. You get me? Otherwise, I might just put one between your eyes like I did to Glen," he said, his eyes bulging with anger.

Mack eyed him with venom. "I'll do your statement, pig. Then you can release me. I was a victim here."

Frankie released him and sat in the chair opposite him. "Oh, same old Mackie: always the fucking victim. You dragged a decent woman into your sinister world, poisoning her with black. Let her go now, Mackie. Zander can look after her. You and that wench of yours, are just a disease, and B deserves better."

"Feck you! Don't pretend you care. You're a stinking cop. Get back to your badge and remember one day, you'll die by my hands. Me and my Dragon will end you."

Frankie whipped his head back with roaring laughter. "Oh, Mackie. It's sad to see you like this. You think B will allow you back after this. She's pissed! Done, *finito*. She's probably beating down on Ari as we speak. You're nothing now. You'll be back where you started, on the streets because everything you touch turns black. B made a deal to keep you out of jail, but that won't save you. You're nothing but a dead man walking."

Mack's face turned sour as Frankie stood to leave.

"And Mackie. If anything happens to B in my absence. I'll hold you responsible," he said, opening the door to leave Mack with his statement.

CHAPTER SIXTY-NINE

The Return of the Gray Wolves

There was an icy chill in the night sky as Ari rocked on the swing, waiting for Mack to arrive home. Eddie had left to retrieve them hours ago.

The black truck emerged moments later, parking up on the drive.

Zander exited the vehicle first. "Where is she, Ari?" he asked urgently.

"On the ridge, and it's bad. She's drunk and has taken Bamfa's gun, threatening to kill anyone who comes near her. God knows I've tried."

"No offense, but you're the last face she wants to see. This whole fucking mess started with you," Zander snapped heading around back.

"Hey. I know you're pissed, brother, but there's no need for that. Ari's trying to help," Mack spat as he dragged his tired body from the truck.

"Mack. She's going to hurt someone. I'm scared," Ari said rushing to him.

"She's not thinking straight. I'll sort it, baby. Promise!" Mack said, kissing her cheek.

"For Christ's sake. Stop wasting time. I'm heading up there," Zander said, storming off.

"Shite! Come on. He's fit to blow," Mack said, urging the others to follow.

B sat on the ridge. Her tear-stained and bruised face evidence of the torment of previous hours. Plying herself with whiskey, she stared out over the land.

Her head pounded and anxiety ripped through her body as she tried to rid her mind of lies and deceit. Everything that had transpired since Ari entered their lives had caused death and destruction in B's peaceful world. Everything appeared in reverse. Up was down, right was wrong, and black was white, making B's fragile mind implode. She tried to calm herself, but everything she knew had been a lie.

Banging her head on the rock she sat against, she heard rustling from the trees before the clearing.

B picked up the handgun in one hand, holding her bottle of whiskey in the other, dragging herself to her feet.

"Welsh Cake!" Zander shouted as he came into view.

"Stay the fuck away from me, Scottie!" she screamed.

Zander continued to press toward her.

"I said stay away!" she shrieked, firing a warning shot at his feet, stopping him in his tracks.

Zander stood, stunned, to the spot.

"Welsh Cake, please—"

"Fuck you! You're all a bunch of fucking liars. You never gave a shit about me. It's all about money for you. Have a good chuckle with the pack about how you're fucking the club cash cow, did you? Well not, any longer, good boy."

"Darling, no!"

Mack, Ari, Jimmy, and Tiny emerged from the clearing.

Anger tore through B at the sight of Mack and Ari. "Oh, here's the fucking cavalry. Fuck the lot of you, I've had it. I turned black for everyone tonight. You were all going to jail. Even you, Ari, and I know what you endured. But dragging me and my kids into your shit is sick! I took two in the chest because of yours and Mackie's cascade of fucking lies. I told you she would be our undoing, Mackie, and you never fucking listened."

"Dragon. Please? Drop the gun so we can talk," Mack said, stepping forward.

"Don't come near me, asshole," she said, waving the gun and stumbling.

Everyone ducked for cover as B composed herself.

"Was Noah in on this? Did I have anyone real in my life?" B asked.

"Noah intended to explain everything, just like we should have," Zander said, taking a slow step forward with his hands raised.

"Then why didn't you?" she yelled.

"I wanted to, but the club thought it was best to keep you safe, darling."

B's sinister laugh echoed over the valley. "No, the club wanted their cash cow safe. None of you give a fuck about me."

"No, darling. That's no' true!"

"Fuck you! Bros before hoes, right?" she said, waving the gun around again.

Ducking once more, Zander pleaded. "For Christ's sake, put the fucking gun down."

"Why? I'm not scared of them anymore. Two in the chest does that to a woman."

"Can we just talk, please?"

B threw her bottle of whiskey at his feet. "No, no more talking, no more cascade of lies. Fuck you, Scottie, and fuck the Gray Wolves!"

"Welsh Cake, please? I love you."

B growled. "Stop lying, Scottie, you don't love me! People don't lie and put the people they love in danger. God, you—you made me fucking fall in love with you, messed with my head and made me believe I can love again, be happy and trust. What kind of sicko does that?"

The hurt in Zander's face slipped into his throat, came out as emotion. "Darling, I do love you. I've spent months chasing after you, pleading with you to be mine. I could have fucked anything that moved before I met you. You showed me what love is, and when you walked into that barn today, my heart fucking broke."

B pursed her lips together, closing her eyes as Zander continued. "Seeing you fight a monster and get shot right before my eyes. I just wanted to die. Christ. A world without you isn't worth living in. I love you; I dinnae mean to hurt you, darling, and if I cannae be with you, you might as well point that gun at my chest and put me out of my misery."

Zander walked toward her, B's nervous eyes shifting between Zander and the pack. Stumbling backwards, B got closer to the cliff edge as Zander stood in front of her, lifting the gun to his chest.

Gasps echoed around the group.

B's hand shook as Zander gazed upon her with his tear-filled eyes and a swollen face, placing his hands on hers over the trigger.

"It's okay, darling, I hurt you again. I'm sorry, but I cannae live without you. Please put me out of my fucking misery. My heart beats for you. I live for you and only you."

Anger shimmered in B's eyes, her hand gripping the gun tighter. Her eyes shifted to the pack and back to Zander, the pain consuming her. Someone had to pay to help her heal.

Zander pressed his chest into the gun, tears running down his cheeks, "It's okay, darling. I deserve this for allowing you to become black today. Just know, I will always love you!" he said, kissing her cheek.

B glared at the man who had betrayed her. The man she had fallen in love with as he stood broken and willing to pay for his lies, the club's lies. Her bottom lip trembled as her eyes filled, the fiery flames washed away by a sea of hurt. Releasing her grip, she sobbed. Her legs buckling underneath her as everything became too much for her.

Zander caught her midfall, tossing the gun and dropping to the floor with B in his arms. "I'm so fucking sorry Welsh Cake, I wanted to fix you and all I did was break you," he sobbed into her hair.

Their sobs chimed over the valley as Zander cradled B in his arms and her tears soaked his chest as she clung to him.

The pack who had now gathered amidst the chaos didn't move, stunned in place, watching the night unravel under the moonlight. Instead, they sat watching two wolves howl under the moon on the next cliff top, laying everything bare like Zander and B.

Listening to the sobs quiet down, Mack turned to the pack. "We need to fix this shite for them, and I don't mean for the club. For them."

"What do you propose?" Jimmy asked.

"A peace offering and a big-ass I'm sorry."

"Meaning?" Tiny asked.

"Meaning, enough is enough. I fecking love them and they deserve to be happy."

"Honey, you're not making any sense," Ari said.

Mack sighed. "They should be the club's future. Zander is the only one I've ever seen calm Dragon. Like it or not, fellas, without Dragon, there are no Gray Wolves. So, I'm proposing we vote Zander in as Prez. He has my role, with Dragon by his side. Sunnyville calls the shots and Uskiville accepts them as the leading chapter. That would mean stepping down to VP Jimmy."

"Do you think it will work? Dragon may be calming now, but she made it clear she's done," Jimmy said.

"Look at them, Jimmy," Mack said gesturing to B and Zander's embrace. "They love each other. Dragon has let him in and whilst she struggles, I know she can't let him go. He just offered to die rather than live without her. Together, with our help, they will be a force to be reckoned with."

"Zander won't go for it. He hates the thought of leading again, after what happened with his military contract," Tiny said.

"Well, we'll just have to make him see he is giving her the stability she needs. Dragon's head is a mess. We've taken everything that's kept her safe and blew it apart. She'll need us: Zander knows that."

The pack glanced to watch Zander stroke B's head as B clung to him. They sat there in a silent embrace, unable to move.

"Look, I think we need to try this for all our sakes. Dragon believes she's lost everything tonight, and Zander thought he'd lost her. So, let's put it to a vote. Tiny, get everyone at church. We do this now," Mack said.

"I'll get hold of the patches looking after Sunnyville. try to explain this shit and get their proxy," Jimmy said.

"What about Frankie? B took his jacket inside earlier and he headed out. He took off, boss," Bamfa said, appearing from nowhere.

"That's because he's a stinking cop. A dirty stinking rat, and the only reason he is still breathing, is because he helped Dragon and kept us out of jail. He's dead to this club from here on out."

"Shit! I didn't see that coming."

"No one did," Mack said as he ushered the pack away. "Come on, let's sort this."

"Hadn't we better speak to them first, gage their reaction?" Tiny asked.

"Shite, yeah," Mack said, approaching Zander and B.

Clearing his throat, Mack alerted them of his presence. "We fucked up. Let you both down. We want to make it right. Dragon, all of this is my doing. My cascade of lies, as you call it. Everything that's happened is because of me and Ari, and I'm sorry."

B glared at him as she rested her head on Zander's chest. Mack couldn't look at her. His eyes remained fixed on the ground. "Zand, we never should have made you lie to Dragon. She didn't deserve it. Neither of you did. We've ruined everything."

Zander peered down at B, kissing her forehead. "Listen fellas, I'm tired. I just want my woman and I'll do whatever it takes to be with her. If that means burning this patch off my chest and moving to Alaska, so fucking be it. I won't betray her again."

B's head shot off Zander's chest, her eyes wide as she stared at him in disbelief, hands trembling on his chest.

"Darling, I just dinnae work without you, so please? Tell me how to make it right," he said to her, wiping the stray tear from her cheek.

B broke from her stare to glance at the wolves before her. "Let them talk, Scottie,"

Zander nodded, turning his attention to the men towering over him.

"We want you to be the leader of both chapters. You remain in Sunnyville with Jimmy as your VP. I remain in Uskiville under your reign."

A shocked Zander shook his head. "Christ no! I dinnae want to lead again."

"Yes, he fucking will," B said.

Zander looked at her with a gaping jaw.

"You want me to stay, and figure shit out? We need to make big changes. I need to trust this club and I can't with Mackie as Prez. He knows this. That's why he's suggesting it."

"Darling, leading's no' for me."

"Then I'm selling up. We'll sort a deal for each club, but that's it. I'm gone," she said, pulling away.

Zander grabbed her hands. "Darling, I'm no' the man for this job."

"You're the only man for this job. You not wanting it says you are. I can't continue here if you won't step up, Scottie. They know that. I undermine the club because I don't trust or like to be controlled. This is the way to go. I know we have a lot to sort, but if you love me and want me to become your old lady, you'll do this."

Zander took a steady breath. "You mean?"

B nodded. "I'll let you claim me once you're Prez."

"You're serious? After everything that's happened, you still love me?"

B dropped her head. "It's not something I can turn off Scottie, and despite these pricks breaking my heart and lying to me, I love them, too.

I'll probably hate them for a long time, but we're family and if we do this, I have some God damn demands."

"Okay," Zander said with a puzzled expression.

"You or anyone touches Frankie, I kill every one of you. He saved my life and kept you all out of prison. He has unfinished business, but when it's done, he's coming home. Frankie will always be my brother and deserves his place by my side!"

"Dragon, he's a rat! We don't know what he has on us."

"What he has on you, you mean? Mackie, I don't give a shit what he has on you, sunshine. You made your fucking bed, now lie in it. Frankie could have locked us all away, even me, and I didn't do shit. In my eyes, you all betrayed me far more than him. He's the only one who had my back, unlike the rest of you."

"Okay darling. What next?" Zander asked.

"The club stays white, and I want details on every fucking member of both chapters. I want to know who's living in my fucking house. I realized today I don't know any of you, not really, and I can't trust people I don't know."

"Darling—"

"Don't darling me, Scottie. It's true. You've only allowed me to see what you wanted me to see. Just like I've done to you. Maybe that's why we're in this mess. Cards on the table and in return, I hand you Sunnyville. I own it, but you run the club your way. I'll stay in my lane, away from any club business. The club and my businesses remain separate, and you guys get your wage for working for me. Nothing changes there. I become an old lady and a business owner from here on out. Even if it means swallowing those bullshit misogynistic rules."

Zander shook his head. "You dinnae have to do this Welsh Cake. We're in the wrong, no' you, darling!"

"It's called compromise, and it's the only way this works, Scottie. The club can't move forward with a woman undermining club rules, and I can't move forward with Mackie running the club. We need to rebuild trust, so this never happens again! Now I'll leave you all to discuss it. God knows I need a fucking shower and another drink," B said, getting up off the ground and dusting herself off.

"I'll come with you, B," Ari muttered, reaching out her hand.

B pushed her hand away. "No offense, Ari, but I've had my fill of BFF bullshit. I'm gonna need some time before I can stomach you again."

Ari stared at the ground. The cascade of lies had started with her and in B's eyes, that was unacceptable.

Turning to Scottie, she took a deep breath. "I wanna be out of here by noon tomorrow, please. Uskiville is no place for me anymore."

"Aye, okay, darling. We'll leave as soon as you're ready."

B nodded, turning on her heels, making her way back through the clearing and out of sight.

CHAPTER SEVENTY

Make Me Yours

Zander took a deep breath before entering the bedroom. Preparing himself for B. Hours had passed since the vote to make him Prez and Zander had spent the whole time worried about her. He knew he'd let B down and he didn't know if she would ever truly trust him again, despite agreeing to be his. Zander prayed he could make things right, even if that meant spending eternity groveling to build trust. He would do anything to make B happy.

Steadying his trembling hand, he turned the handle and entered the room wearing his Prez cut.

B sat in her rocking chair, wearing a silk dressing gown, staring out of the window. She still looked mesmerizing despite the split lip and the purple and yellow mass of bruising on her chest.

Zander kneeled before her, running his hand through her hair, bringing her to his attention. His face strained with the guilt consuming him as he kissed her cheek. "I'm so, so sorry, darling! I've ruined every-thing, but I promise I'll fix it, okay?"

"Is it done?" she asked.

"Yeah darling, it's done," he said, pointing to his Prez patch on his leather cut.

Watching her take a deep breath, she nodded and rose to her feet, taking his hand to ensure he followed.

Confusion swept through him. He wasn't sure what to expect. B appeared so broken, and he was desperate to fix things as he followed her into the bathroom.

Zander studied her movements as she turned to him, dropping her gown before removing his clothes. He didn't try to kiss her, he followed her lead, scared to make another wrong move.

"Let me clean you up," she said as she led him into the shower.

Zander's body grew numb with shock. She took the tea-tree shower gel and squirted some onto a sponge to wash his blood-stained chest. He watched her face strain as she stared at his broken body. It was all kinds of black and purple from Blaze's beat down. Flinching, he winced as she hit his sensitive spots.

Dropping the sponge, she kissed him as he cupped the back of her neck.

B caressed all his tender spots, traveling across his body ensuring she missed nothing, before returning to face him.

Zander gazed upon her. She looked vulnerable. B was baring her soul for him to see, and only him. It was as if someone had opened her eyes for the first time.

Zander studied her beauty as she wrapped her hands around his neck, invading his personal space, bringing her lips to his. He placed one hand on her backside and one on the back of her head to pull her in close as she kissed him. Kissing her back, he moaned, allowing relief to wash over him as he embraced his woman after all the lies and deceit. He wanted to thank her for giving him another chance. He knew he didn't deserve it, so he tried to show her how much it meant to him.

Lifting her up, allowing her legs to wrap around him, he pinned her against the wall. Kissing her hard, with his lips finding their way to her neck. His haven. Zander loved to kiss her there, listening to her soft moans every time his lips struck her delicate skin.

As he relaxed again, B stopped in her tracks, pushing him away.

Zander stopped dead, devastated by her halting him as he watched her shake her head and turn off the shower.

Taking his hand once more, a confused Zander watched as she dried his bruised body and led him to the bedroom.

Staring into his eyes, she said to him. "Take me, Prez. Make me yours and don't hold back, no matter what!"

All kinds of emotions ripped through Zander's body, his heart pounding out of his chest as a lump formed in his throat.

"You sure you want this, darling? I can wait," he said, voice trembling.

"You can't be a good Prez without your old lady keeping you in check. Take me, please? I want to be yours."

"But all that I've done. How can you forgive me?"

"Because you love me, and I love you. Now it's time to tame your dragon. None of this works unless you make me yours."

Zander nodded, tears running down his cheeks as he kissed her lips. Unable to compose himself, he sobbed as he held her close and whispered into her ear. "I'm no good for you. I'm black as night, and I dinnae want to hurt you anymore."

B threaded her fingers through his. "You're my wolf, and I'm your Dragon. I got you and if you love me and do this for me, I will give you my heart and soul. I will be forever yours."

"Just promise me you're no' doing this out of fear and necessity. Promise me you're doing this because you believe in your heart, I'm good."

"Promise, good boy! No more white, no more black, and no more cascade of lies. Just pure, unadulterated love. You promise me that, Scottie, and we can go home tomorrow and start living the rest of our lives together," she pleaded, with eyes wide like saucers.

Zander stared deep into her eyes with raw emotion. His hand trembled against B's cheek.

"Darling, I promise. I'll do anything for you. I'd capture the moon, so you never have to be afraid of the dark. The sun so you never feel cold again because all I want is you! I promise I will never ever hurt you again. No more lies, just truth and honesty."

B nodded, blinking back her tears, and Zander knew in that moment that was all B ever wanted to hear.

"I love you so bloody much, Boyoh!" she choked.

"And I love you, my beautiful fiery dragon. You know, everything happens for a reason and you're mine. For breathing and for living."

"Oh Scottie, you're mine too. You complete me!"

"What. Like a jigsaw puzzle?" he joked.

B giggled. "Yeah, but way, way better."

After a long embrace, B spoke first. "Well, Prez, are you going to make me yours or do I have to get my fiery dragon eyes out and kick your ass?"

Zander pulled her into him, every cell in his body engulfed with nerves and excitement. "Dragon wants, Dragon gets," he said as he devoured her mouth, sucking her neck, before gorging himself on her breasts.

Picking her up, he carried her to the bed. His erection pressing against her as he laid her down onto the bed.

Tracing his tongue over her breasts, Zander wasted no time in making her writhe as he moved down to her clitoris, forcing her legs to fall open as he delivered slick blows, licking the length of her opening. Growling with pleasure, he listened to her elegant cries.

"You taste fucking amazing," he moaned before sitting back on his knees to admire her.

Stroking his length to tease her, his nerves had all but vanished. "Oh darling, I've been dreaming about this day."

"Take me, Scottie!"

"Call me Zander. I promised you'd scream my name one day, Welsh Cake, and today's the day."

"Zander, please?"

"Good girl. You're about to become my old lady, my Dragon. I know it's hard for you to relinquish control darling, but I promise, you'll enjoy it," he said, teasing her nub with his index finger and making her moan.

"I'm gonnae free you, beautiful. I'm gonnae turn you over and take you until you're mine. You'll yield to me, darling, and I'll free you from the shackles that's kept you locked up for so long."

B's eyes lit up like wildfire, like they did every time she felt threatened.

"Dinnae be scared, darling. I got you!" he said, before showering her body with his passionate kisses.

"I'll start slow, but once I turn you over, there's no safe word. As my old lady, you need to take what I give you. You can scream, shout, bite down, but I need to take you like a wolf takes his she-wolf. Understand?"

B nodded. Zander could see the fear in her eyes and the curiosity that made her body shake. It empowered him as he spread her legs and teased her entrance. His passion burned into her eyes as she displayed her vulnerability beneath him.

"I got you," he whispered as he entered her with a deep thrust.

B kissed him, pulling him close as he allured her with slow thrusts, careful not to put pressure on her bruised chest. Her eyes became cloudy and innocent for the first time since they met.

"Oh, darling. I've missed you," he moaned at the sight of her. Her 'oh' sounds, music to his ears.

Quickening his pace, Zander felt the familiar sensation of her nails digging into his back. "Grrr. Fuck, darling," he said through gritted teeth as his thrusts became harder.

B cried out. "God!"

"Zander, call me Zander. I wannae hear my name on your lips," he growled.

B called out his name with every thrust as if she was struggling to take his masculinity as he drove her into the mattress.

"Oh, darling. It's time! I need to make you mine," he said, removing himself from her quivering entrance.

"Wait. I'm close," she cried.

"And you'll come as my old lady," he commanded, turning her over and pulling her up onto her knees.

Wasting no time, he entered her. "Christ, I love your pussy," he growled, embracing his role as Prez: his first order of business taming his dragon.

B panted as he entered her with a long and forceful thrust. "Fuck, Zander!"

"Dinnae fight it darling."

B seethed, gripping her sheets, her knuckles white as she fought the urge to take back control.

"Easy dragon, relax, enjoy it. Welcome me, knowing you're the only woman I've truly given myself to like this."

"Scottie. I—"

"Zander!" he snapped. Slapping her ass: the excitement from control pulsating through him. "Enjoy taking it as much as I'm enjoying giving it to you, darling," he said as he dominated her with harder thrusts.

B cried out, shaking, unable to compose herself as Zander entered his stride.

"Oh, Zander,"

"That's it darling," he said gripping her hips. "I'm just getting started and I'm no' stopping until you release around my cock and become mine."

B screamed, her hands now grabbing at the headboard.

"Oh, Zander, please. I can't take much more."

"Music to my fucking ears darling," he said as he filled her with every inch of himself, savoring the moment.

B bucked and writhed in pleasure as Zander relished in control. He'd never been dominant with B, and tonight he was making up for it. "I'm gonnae fuck you through your screams darling and I'll no' stop until you're mine."

"Zander, yes!" she cried.

"Fuck," he cursed showing B no mercy with relentless thrusts. His cock suffocating in erotic pleasure as she clenched around him.

B screamed again, this time backing her ass into him, matching his rhythm.

"That's it, I knew you'd like it. Yes Dragon, yield to me."

"Oh, Zander."

Zander almost came with excitement, hearing her cry out. "You like this, dragon?"

"Yes!" B cried out again as he reached a racing pace, opening his stride as if he was racing to the finish line.

"Oh yeah," he growled, lost in the moment. Euphoria swept through him like nothing he'd ever experienced as he tamed his dragon. Tensing, he knew she was close, and it filled him with pride.

"Oh Dragon, I can feel you," he said. His cock fit to burst as he held out for her climax, the pressure immense as she tightened around him, almost too much for his impending release.

"Christ. Dragon," he said through gritted teeth, slamming into her with force until B clamped down hard, screaming and exploding into a rampant and chaotic orgasm, thrashing about the bed.

Zander followed, unleashing himself inside her. "Oh Christ. Oh fuck, Dragon. You're mine!" he cried, pumping her with everything he had before collapsing on top of her.

His chest still heaving, Zander rained a trail of kisses along her back, turning her over to face him.

"Are you alright darling? I dinnae hurt you, did I? I just fucking lost it and took charge. Shit!" he said, wrapping his arms around her.

B shook her head. "No, you were perfect," she said, looking bashful.

"Darling, I can't thank you enough for everything. What we just experienced was incredible, extreme ecstasy. A connection so deep, I felt it with every fiber of my being."

"I felt it too, Scottie. I've been so trapped, and, in that moment, I felt free."

Zander kissed her lips. "Promise me we're good, darling?"

B shook her head. "I'm afraid I can't, Prez."

Zander frowned, "How? What else do you need? Tell me and I'll make it happen," he said concerned.

B's lips curled into a devilish smile. "I want what every old lady wants after her Prez has made her his."

Zander breathed a tremendous sigh of relief, pinning her down on the bed, grinning at her. "Jesus. I should spank your ass for that."

"Go ahead, good boy. I'm sure I'll like it this time round, but I want my ice cream first."

Zander shook his head, grinning at her. "You're gonnae be the death of me, woman."

B smiled. "Maybe. But not for a while. We're just getting started."

CHAPTER SEVENTY-ONE

She's Mine!

Zander emerged from the bedroom, entering the kitchen to find Jimmy, Mackie, and the rest of the MC members having a beer.

Snatching the beer bottle from Mack's hands, he bellowed in a teasing tone. "Jesus! Can't a guy get some privacy?"

"We wanted to make sure you were both okay. You've been through a lot, and we wanted you to know we're here," Mackie said, placing a hand on his shoulder.

"Aye, thanks."

"So, is my best friend, okay?" Mack asked.

"Aye, she's fine and now mine," he grinned, looking pleased with himself.

"Oh, we know that brother. The sounds coming from your room were fucking glorious," Jimmy teased.

"Christ! Seriously?"

"No offense brother, but those cries of joy were heard across the fucking pond in Celt land," Jimmy said.

"Dinnae dare tell my old lady that? She'll crucify the lot of us."

"Congratulations!" Jimmy said, embracing him.

"Aye, thanks!" Zander said, shaking his head. "After all I put that lassie through. She still became my old lady. I'm one lucky son of a bitch."

"It's not luck brother, it's love. She fecking loves you, and you're besotted with her. Seeing you both on that ridge damn near broke us. Noah would be so proud of you, Mack said."

"Thanks, brother," he said, shaking Mack's hand.

"I'm serious. You've both fought tooth and nail for your happiness and now all the skeletons are out of the closet, you can move forward."

"Aye. I'll no' let her down again."

"And neither will we, Prez."

"You bet your ass you won't because I'll bury the lot of you. She's your fucking queen now, lads, and you all better respect that."

Ayes echoed around the room as it filled with sounds of laughter.

"So, what now?" Jimmy asked.

"Now, we move on and become the biggest MC the West Coast has ever seen," Mack said.

Zander removed a tub of salted caramel ice cream, shaking his head. "No brothers. As Noah once said, 'Go big or go home.' Now, with my dragon and my brothers by my side, we become the biggest MC in the country."

"Yeah," the boys echoed, before Mack raised his beer bottle. "To the new Prez, his dragon and the future of the Gray Wolves MC!"

After polishing off a whole tub of ice cream between them, Zander, and B cwtched up in bed together. Stroking her bruised body, he realized the complexity of the woman that laid before him. He gazed at her tattoos amazed how B could be so fierce, yet so gentle. So black yet so white. He realized he hadn't made her black today, nor was she ever really white. She was gray and always had been. Gray was who she was meant to be. She just didn't know it.

"Welsh Cake, can I ask you why you chose these tattoos?" he asked as he continued to stroke her.

B opened her eyes, a little confused.

"I told you before Scottie, remember? They're who I am. They mean a lot to me."

"Aye, but if that's how you see yersel', darling, then I dinnae think you were ever really meant to be white!" he whispered, still stroking her.

B looked annoyed as she furrowed her brow.

"Scottie, I'm exhausted and don't understand what you are saying, my lovely."

"Well, they both represent who you are, darling, but they both also represent black and white."

"How?"

"Power, wisdom, rebirth, resilience. Your tattoos symbolize all of that! The dragon is black, fiery and shows strength, power and wisdom, whilst the flowers and butterfly are white and represent rebirth and resilience. I'm just saying everything happens for a reason and maybe you had to experience black today so that you could be reborn and grow as a person."

"That's mighty philosophical of you, handsome," she teased.

"No. Listen!" he said, tickling her chest with his soft fingers. "You've struggled with black and white since the day I met you, and over the months, I've watched you grow, and you've become more beautiful than ever as you've opened yersel' up to the beautiful colors of the world. I'm so proud of you for that, darling. When that bastard shot you. I thought you were dead," he said, trying to shake the images out of his head. "I under-estimated you. We all did, and we've been doing it since the day we met you. That was so wrong of us. All we saw behind that sensitive smile was an uncontrollable, fiery dragon. We experienced fear. Fear of losing and hurting you as opposed to seeing the strong and resilient woman you are and for that, I am sorry. I promise you, darling, I will never underestimate you ever again."

"I hear you, Scottie. Perhaps you're right and I'm Gray in a world full of color. I've been so exhausted trying to be a good, kind, and honorable person. Struggling to see the world and other people for anything other than black and white, good, and evil, law abiding and criminal, always trying to over analyze every detail, every aspect of my life. Maybe now I'm free from the black and white shackles that tied me to such a narrow-minded life that isolated my thoughts and freedom," she said as a single tear escaped from her eye.

"Darling. The last few months have been grueling. Dragged you from your comfort zone, making you frantic, troubled even. You've fought every urge to run from gray, but now everything is out in the open. I hope you're relieved and never want to run again."

B pursed her lips, stroking his head. "Scottie, for the first time, I feel like I'm exactly where I'm supposed to be."

Zander smiled, kissing the tears off her cheek.

"Thank you, handsome, for who you are and what you've done for me since the day I met you. You've made me feel and pulled me from a dark and desolate world. Dragging me kicking and screaming into a beautiful and bright one. I have fought you at every turn, but your heart remained true to me. Why?"

"Because I love you, darling. I told you; I've loved you since the day we met. You took a big old broken ice block of a man and defrosted him with your fiery dragon heart. You made me feel for the first time and gave me an insight into that crazy yet fucking beautiful world you live in. All I want is to feel intoxicated by you for the rest of my life!"

"But I don't deserve you, Scottie! I'm still broken," she whispered.

Scottie looked at her in sheer disbelief.

"Darling, you got shot twice in the chest for us tonight. On what fucking planet do yer think you dinnae deserve me? And after all my wrongs, too. I told you! I was numb before I met you! If anything, *I* dinnae deserve *you*."

"That's not true."

Zander took her hand, kissing her bruised knuckles. "Well, how about we just agree we're meant for each other? Now, no more doubting yersel'. You are a ferocious and fiery fucking dragon and I love yer. But now I want to get reacquainted with Welsh Cake."

"I understand. She's hard to contain, Scottie. I've always struggled with my inner Dragon."

"Oh, I can help, darling, and I love all of you, but the unpredictable Dragon inside you scares the shit out of me. Can you promise you'll try to let me get to know Welsh Cake some more, please?"

"Promise!"

"Thank you! Now rest ya head, it's been a long day and even dragons need their sleep."

CHAPTER SEVENTY-TWO

A Celtic Christmas

It was Christmas week and a few months since the death of Blaze. The new business venture in Sunnyville became an instant success, bringing more trade into Sunnyville than it had in previous years. B had fallen in love with her coaching role at the local High school, and Madoc and Rhys seemed to settle in without a hitch. The only thing getting B and her boys down was the heartache they'd experienced, missing their Uskiville family.

B hurried around the kitchen on Christmas Eve, readying everything for her guests arriving the next morning, except for Tiny and Selina, who were due to arrive any minute.

She had just popped some home-made Christmas cookies into a tin when Zander grabbed her around the waist, breaking her concentration from her frantic mind.

"Will you take a minute to relax?" he said, kissing her lips.

"I'm almost finished. I just want to make sure everything is ready for their arrival. I've not seen Selina since I arranged for her move to Uskiville, and I want her to feel at home with everything she's been through."

"She'll be fine. Tiny said she's never been better, and I think he's happy with his VP spot in Uskiville. So, chill," Zander said, turning her away to massage her shoulders.

"Hmmm, that's nice."

"See, me and my magic hands are right. Now how about I fix you a drink and we spend five minutes together before everyone arrives and chaos erupts?"

"It's hardly everyone, sunshine. Selina and Tiny make six of us. I wouldn't call that chaos."

"Yeah, about that!"

B spun around to face him. "What have you done?"

Zander appeared sheepish. "Now, dinnae be mad."

"Spill, Prez, or you'll be sleeping at the club tonight!"

Zander interlinked his fingers with hers. "I've invited Mack, Ari, and the kids!"

"You bloody did what?" she screamed, pulling her hand away.

"Now, come on, darling. I know you're hurting, but he's your best friend. These past months have damn near killed him. I think he's suffered enough."

B shook in temper. "Oh, my fucking days. Are you serious right now? Fuck my life! I could punch you, Scottie."

Zander grabbed her wrists. "Put the fucking Dragon back in her box. You promised me when we arrived home from Uskiville that bitch would remain hidden. You promised, Welsh Cake."

"Yeah, and you promised you'd give me time and space from Mack, but have you?"

"Look. I'm trying to mend bridges between us and Uskiville. This isn't good for club morale," he said as the doorbell rang.

"Well, mend your own fucking bridges. Not mine! And don't dare step one foot into my bedroom. You've ruined Christmas, asshole," she said, slamming the kitchen door on her way out.

It was early evening, and Zander flustered over guests as B remained in her room. She sat cross-legged on her bed, seething at him. She wasn't ready to forgive Mack or Ari. She missed Mack but they'd caused too much pain.

Bloody prick! Ruined Christmas. He can forget about his gift tomorrow. Asshole.

There was a knock at the bedroom door, interrupting her thoughts.

"Not interested, Prez," she seethed.

"Aunt B. It's me. Junior. Can we talk?"

B rushed to open her bedroom door and the gangly teen she'd found on her ridge fifteen months before stood in fear.

"Junior," she whispered. Pulling him into her embrace. "I missed you, sunshine."

"I wasn't sure if you wanted to see me after discovering I lied to you on the ridge that night."

"Oh, Junior. No, mate! I don't hold any ill feeling toward you," she said, pulling him to sit on her bed. "Why would you think that?"

"You've not spoken to my mom or dad for months because of what happened, and I'm part of that lie, Aunt B."

B put her arm around him. "Listen, Junior. I've told you before. You need to stop trying to carry the world on your shoulders. My frustration with your parents has nothing to do with you. A lot's happened since that night."

"Aunt B, I'm worried about my dad. He's drinking all the time, and he looks a mess. I'm not asking you to forgive him, but I'm scared. My mom's a survivor, but dad is broken without you. Please Aunt B. Just look at him, please?"

B's face hardened. Once again, she felt guilted into a situation she didn't want. She wasn't ready to forgive Junior's parents. They'd betrayed her.

"Aunt B. I know I'm being unfair asking this of you. I promise I wouldn't if there was another way to help my dad."

B took an exasperated breath. "I'll come look, but I can't promise I'll talk to him, Junior. Your parents unleashed something on our family I can never forget."

"I understand."

B followed Junior into the sitting room where everyone congregated after settling into their rooms. Nerves, anger, and anxiety threatened B with an imminent attack as she entered her sitting room.

Zander gave her a reassuring smile as she greeted Selina and Tiny. She gave Ari a nod as she embraced Remy and Alex, who, too, rushed to greet her. Casting her eyes around the room, Mack was nowhere to be seen.

"Hey, Dragon," a quiet voice said from behind her.

B turned to see a fragile Mack leaning against the wall with his hands in his pockets. She gasped at his gaunt expression. His clothes hung off him as an emasculated Mack smiled at her.

"Mackie!" she gasped, her hand clasping her mouth.

"I know. I'm as scrawny as the day you met me, right?"

B shook her head in disgust. "What the hell is wrong with you, Mackie? Look at the bloody state of you. I got a good mind to choke you, coming into my house like that. How dare you?"

Mack rubbed the back of his neck. "I-I'm sorry. I've been struggling."

"No shit! Get your ass in that bloody kitchen, now!"

Mack turned on his heels., moving at a snail's pace as B followed him into the kitchen.

"Sit your ass down, sunshine. I'm making you a meal. What the fuck have you been doing to yourself?"

Mack climbed onto the breakfast bar stool as B emptied her fridge and loaded his plate with cold meats, potato salad, and an array of cheese and pickles. She poured him a glass of milk and set it down on the counter. "Well, I'm bloody waiting, good boy. What are you on? Cocaine? Amphetamines? What?"

Mack's sunken eyes didn't make eye contact. He stared into his plate. "Nothing, Dragon. I lost my best friend, and my appetite went with it."

"What? So, this is my bloody fault?" she said, pressing her hands into the countertop.

"No, Dragon, it's mine. I just can't get back to my old self. I can't forgive myself for what I've done to you, and I don't know how to make it right?"

"So, you starved yourself? Junior is worried about you. Look at you? You're a shadow of your former self. Mackie, you're ill!"

Mack's tired face hardened. "Dragon. You think I don't know that? You think I haven't tried? Jeez. You are my fucking world. My best friend and I've struggled without you. When you first left for Sunnyville, we patched things up. We weren't perfect, but we were okay. Three months ago, you refused to talk to me anymore, and no matter how hard I tried, you pushed me away. Three months of not talking to my best friend. You said, 'Best friends never quit!' But you quit on me, Dragon. Tapped out just like Frankie and I've never felt so alone."

B bowed her head. She had no words. She had every right to be angry with Mack, but nothing had prepared her for tonight as her best friend sat fragile, baring his soul. B walked around the countertop and sat on the stool next to him.

"You're right! I quit. It wasn't my intention. Just the only way I knew how to save myself from you. I almost died due to yours and Ari's recklessness. I warned you, Mackie, and you never listened. You broke me, and I've remained broken ever since. I wanted to call you a thousand times, only I feared what might happen if I immersed myself in your life again. I love you Mackie, I just don't want to be in danger any longer."

Mack nodded into his plate. "Hurting you was the last thing I wanted."

B took his hand. "I know and I never wanted to hurt you, so please eat. It's heart-braking seeing you like this."

Mack picked up a slice of ham. His fingers trembled as he raised it to his mouth to take a bite.

B watched in silence as he took slow mouthfuls, washing them down with milk until he couldn't eat any more.

"You alright?" she asked.

"I forgot how good your potato salad was," he said.

B laughed. "Come here!" she said, pulling his forehead to hers. "Say the words and let me go."

"I'm never letting you go again, Dragon, and I'll never stop saying the words. Best friends never quit!"

Christmas morning came, and everyone rushed around the tree to open presents. Rhys and Madoc rushed to give Zander their present from them, handing him a small box.

"Thanks lads," he said, shaking the box. Removing the ribbon, he opened it to discover a key with a note attached.

Will you make us happy and be a permanent part of our family?

Zander's eyes filled. "You want me to move in?"

"Well, my mum misses you through the week and you make her happy," Madoc said with a hopeful smile.

"I'd be honored. Thank you," he said, inviting them in for a warm embrace.

B and Zander both agreed to exchange presents once all the guests had arrived, the excitement overwhelming B the moment the pack entered.

Leading them out to her barn, she opened the door to reveal an array of brand new, personalized motorcycles. One for each of the Sunnyville pack, along with one for Mack, Tiny, and Frankie, who hadn't arrived.

"No fucking way! Darling! I fucking love you!" Zander said as he admired his new set of wheels.

Everyone was ecstatic, unable to conceive B had presented them with such a gift.

Zander approached her, displaying his trademark grin and head shake. "Thank you, darling. Your generosity has blown me away today, and here I thought I was still on your shit list for inviting Mack."

"Oh, don't worry. You can make that up to me tonight, sunshine."

"I'd like to try now," he said, dropping on one knee to present her with a diamond ring.

The barn fell quiet as B froze to the spot.

"Marry me, Welsh Cake. Please?"

B remained mute, the shock proving too much for her.

"Say something. Anything," he begged.

B took a deep breath. Still speechless, she nodded as tears ran down her glowing cheeks.

Zander placed the ring on her finger before scooping her into his embrace as the pack cheered.

"I love you, darling. Merry Christmas!"

"I lo—"

"Congratulations!" a familiar voice interrupted from behind her.

B spun around. Her heart palpated as her eyes met Frankie's.

"I promised, right?" he said.

"Yeah," B said, diving into his open arms.

"Missed you, B."

"I've missed you too, Boyoh! So glad you came! I have your present here," she said, pointing to a sleek, black motorcycle with a red trim.

"Whoa. B. I don't know what to say," he examined the gift as prying eyes followed.

"You like it?"

"It's beautiful. You'll have to keep it a little longer, though, I'm afraid."

B's face shattered in disappointment. "Why?"

"I'm still tying up loose ends. I need to talk to you about it. Can we take a walk through your garden?"

"Sure."

B followed Frankie out of the barn with Zander monitoring his old lady, and as soon as they were out of earshot of the pack, Frankie took her arm.

"I know it's a shit day to do this but you're in danger, B. Jericho somehow got word that you were the one who exposed him to the FBI. Word is, he's coming for you. We've been trying to track him, but he keeps giving us the slip. I'm installing a new security system at the club with links to your house. Cell phone, house locking activation. You name it, it's done."

B stepped into his personal space. "Frankie, I'm not worried. I have a Prez who worships me and a pack of wolves on my side."

"Don't be so naïve. We're good, but he has years of experience on us and he's a sick fuck. There's no telling what he's capable of."

"Are you trying to scare me, Frankie, because it's not working?"

Frankie gave her a gentle shake. "No, I'm trying to pull your head out of your ass. Prez is making you soft, and you might need the dragon to save your life. So, do whatever you need to do to make that fiery bitch come alive again, and be ready for anything."

"I'm not that person anymore. I like who I've become."

Frankie lost his temper, throwing his arms in the air, turning away from her. "What? A fucking pussy? A submissive old lady. Stop lying to yourself. Stop trying to please the Prez. Look, I get it, you love him and you've both had a shit time. I get you're desperate for peace, but the war isn't over yet. There are no white flags here, B. He's coming for you, and I need you to be ready. So, wake the fuck up."

It took B back. Frankie had never spoken to her with such contempt. He appeared scared.

B pursed her lips, choosing her words wisely. "Frankie, Zander's got this. The club has got this. I need to trust them, and so do you. I know how much you want to nail this bastard and we will. You don't need to worry about me any longer, okay?"

Zander shook his head, jamming his hands into his hips. "Just promise me you'll be ready. I'll do my best to protect you, but that bastard will strike when we least expect it."

"And the wolves will take him down and deliver him to you."

"I don't like this B. You're vulnerable and that's dangerous."

"She's no' vulnerable Frankie. I've asked her to trust me to keep her safe, and that's what's she's doing as my old lady," Zander said, approaching from behind.

Frankie shook his head. "No offense, Prez, but you're a fucking idiot. Dragon needs to wake from her slumber if she wants to survive this."

"Dragon is staying put, and I'll remind you to mind your tone in my presence."

Frankie stepped off, putting his hands in the air. "Understood, but if anything happens to her, it's on you. Don't say I didn't warn you," he said, walking away and shaking his head.

Zander turned to B, wrapping his arms around her waist. "You trust me, darling, right?"

"With my life, Prez."

"Good. Now promise me Dragon stays put. Things are great between us. I want nothing to change that."

"It won't, and I have her under control. Just hurry and nail this guy. I have plans for our future."

Zander raised an eyebrow, his dimples on display. "Oh yeah, are you gonna share them with me?"

"Well, now we're engaged. I was thinking about what you said at the cabin before everything unraveled."

Zander's chest heaved. "Oh, Christ! Please tell me you're serious?"

B grinned. "When this is over, yes! I'll get my affairs in order, arrange time off and sort the business."

"Fuck, for real?" Zander clasped his hands together. "You're gonnae let me have this? You're gonnae let me fill you with one of our own?"

B laughed. "Well, we're not getting any younger Scottie, so if we're gonna do this, it has to be sooner rather than later. There's just one thing..."

"What?"

"I need two. We can't just have one, it'll have nobody to play with."

"Christ, darling, I'll give you a pack if that's what you want?"

Zander's elated expression filled B's heart with a warm glow. "Let's aim for two first. Now I'm gonna start preparations at my end and you need to put this Jericho thing to bed, and fast."

"Consider it done, beautiful. I'll hunt the fucker down and kill him with my bare hands."

B shook her head. "No, it has to be Frankie who seals his fate. He won't rest until he does."

Zander's beaming smile lit up the garden. "Welsh Cake wants, Welsh Cake gets."

"Thank you."

"No, darling, thank you. Thank you for trusting me and making me the happiest man on the planet."

B kissed his lips. "Thank you for not giving up on me. I'm so in love with you, handsome. You've made me come alive again, and I can't wait to grow old with you."

"Me too, darling. Me too."

The End.